The Last Honest Seamstress

Gina Robinson

Gina Robinson
SEATTLE, WASHINGTON

Gina Robinson
www.ginarobinson.com

Publisher's Note: This is a work of fiction. Names, characters, places, and incidents are a product of the author's imagination. Locales and public names are sometimes used for atmospheric purposes. Any resemblance to actual people, living or dead, or to businesses, companies, events, institutions, or locales is completely coincidental.

Book Layout ©2013 BookDesignTemplates.com
Front Cover Design by Hot Damn Designs

The Last Honest Seamstress/ Gina Robinson. -- 1st ed.
ISBN 978-0615823539

Seattle

Early Spring 1889

The jail cell smelled of overcrowding. A cacophony of perfumes, applied with too heavy a hand and warmed to extreme effect, escaped through the bars, carrying with it a hint of feminine perspiration and agitation. Fayth Sheridan, already warm and flustered from being packed in and confined with the others, found the odor cloying, nearly nauseating. She tried to appear calm and nonchalant as she smoothed her gray walking skirt and inched closer to the bars. She hoped to separate herself from the rest of the women while she eavesdropped on the two guards in the hall.

Stay calm. Stay calm.

It wouldn't do to panic. Fayth had survived scandal before. She supposed she could weather it here, where the bounds of decorum were decidedly stretched. Seattle wasn't Baltimore, after all. But she needed to get out of this cell and back to business—the real, legitimate business of men's tailoring. And she didn't want to call upon her second cousins for help if at all possible. Elizabeth would be mortified and Fayth didn't think she could stand Sterling's reserved resignation.

The guards' conversation drifted toward her.

"Seamstresses! All of them say they're seamstresses!" The stout, obviously annoyed guard snorted and spat upon the floor. He turned to his colleague, a tall, thin man. "You believe that, Charlie? Seems we got more seamstresses in town than we got whores. Something about that doesn't seem right to me." He shook his head and grinned, showing his yellowed teeth. "Not with how busy the cribs are on a Saturday night." He winked at Charlie.

Fayth disliked him immensely. Not that it was customary to *like* one's jailors. In his case, he was not only homely, but his clothes didn't fit properly; his bearing spoke of an overblown sense of his own importance, opinions, and power. As if that weren't enough, he'd handled her roughly when he'd herded her into the cell with the rest of the "ladies."

"I only ever seen one sewing machine in all the time I been here. And that one was on its way to a widow in Tacoma," he said to Charlie. "Want to lay me odds there's not one of them can so much as thread a needle?" His accompanying chuckle was tinged with innuendo.

That infuriated Fayth more than his words. How dare he label her with the others?

She set her jaw, determined to maintain her equilibrium as she corrected him. "Sir, hand me a needle and thread and I'll make a liar out of you." She spoke deliberately with the broad, elegant vowels of her Eastern upbringing.

The other girls grew silent suddenly, as if she'd really stepped in something now. But Fayth didn't care. If she didn't stick up for herself, who would?

The guard looked surprised and distinctly displeased, as if no woman should dare question his male superiority. He snorted. "Lady, maybe you can, but it don't convince me you aren't a *whore* like the rest of them. And it sure don't change my mind about women who sell their bodies."

"Oh, leave her alone." The slender guard spoke before Fayth could reply, startling her with his defense. "She says she was rounded up by mistake."

"Yeah, don't they all."

Charlie gawked at her, blushing as he gave her a shy smile. "But look at her." He swallowed, Adam's apple bobbing. Clearly, he wasn't used to contradicting his partner. "Her skirt and jacket are gray and plain. And she's not showing any skin, excepting her face. Maybe she *isn't* one of them."

The other guard snorted again. "Of course she's one of them, Charlie. You know any decent lady who would stand in the middle of a group of whores?" He laced his voice with lewd undertones.

Fayth lost her composure. "I am *not* one of them, as anyone with a pair of eyes can see." She smiled at the shy guard. "Thank you, Charlie, for defending me. Now, please, let me out of here."

"You better shut up." The belligerent guard took a step toward the cell and jabbed a finger at her through the bars. "A woman your age should know the rules. You don't mouth off, not to me. I don't like spunky women any better than whores."

Fayth felt a tug at her sleeve and turned to find herself facing one of the youngest prostitutes, a pretty, fine-featured girl with soft strawberry-blond hair. "You won't convince him." On closer look the girl was no older than fifteen. She took Fayth's arm, scolding as she pulled her away from the bars. "Making him angry will only make things worse."

Fayth turned to see the guard chuckling to himself, probably delighted to see her upbraided by a mere girl. Blast him!

"The guards go easier on you if you just keep to yourself." The girl's voice was fresh and delicate, but knowing beyond her years, which pulled at Fayth's heart.

Fayth's new friend sighed with impatience. She raised her voice, obviously for the guards' benefit. "I don't understand it myself. There's obviously been a mistake. Lou pays our monthly fines, never misses a payment. They shouldn't be arresting us, not when we paid. Isn't any law against riding in a carriage on a Saturday afternoon."

The girl cracked a knuckle and lowered her voice so only Fayth could hear. "Lou says carriage rides are good for business. Always brings the men in. They like to see the goods before they come to the house. You know, make their choices ahead of time." She wiped her hand across her skirt.

"Lou says I have to stop cracking," the girl continued. "Gentlemen don't like girls with big knuckles." She stared at her hands, and scrunched up her nose. "Too bad the carriage broke down right by that street corner where you were standing. Sorry we all piled out on you like that."

"Yes, too bad. But thank you. Accidents will happen." Against her better judgment, Fayth was beginning to warm to her young cellmate.

"Don't worry." The girl looked sincere. "Lou will straighten things out. Some official's probably out for publicity again. You know, clean up the streets and all that. Lou'll be here soon enough to bail us out and when she arrives she'll give them the what-for. Lou mad is not a sight anybody'd like to see." She whispered into Fayth's ear with the gleeful tone of a conspirator. "Except maybe us. You'll enjoy the fireworks when she gets here. Lou has friends in high, high places. And she knows how to use them. She'll make those jackass guards pay. She doesn't like business disrupted."

"Nor do I," Fayth said. "I really am a seamstress." She didn't know why she had added that or why it mattered if the girl believed her.

The younger girl smiled knowingly. "Sure you are, like we all are. Let me give you a tip. If you want the police to believe you're not one of us, list your occupation as anything else when they pick you up. In Seattle, seamstress is code for *lady of the night*." She held a tenderly manicured hand out for Fayth to shake. "Name's Coral."

Fayth took her hand. "Fayth Sheridan."

"You shouldn't be working alone, Fayth. You don't want to end up in the cribs. Believe me." She wrinkled her nose in disgust and lowered her voice. "They service dozens of men a night." Coral shuddered.

"You need a nice parlor house, like ours." Coral nodded. "Sometimes we only entertain a single client for the entire night. Gentlemen." Coral winked. "And no matter how much he wants to, one man can only keep going so long before he has to give up and sleep. Come see Lou. I'm sure she'll take you. We've had an empty room since Rose moved out." Coral's gaze flitted over Fayth approvingly. "From the look of you, you'll fit right in. Lou Gramm only hires girls with looks and intelligence. After all, we cater to the elite of the city. Our men like their ladies refined." Her voice held unmistakable pride.

Refined, indeed. Fayth glanced around at her supposed fellow seamstresses to prove how not like them she was. She froze midway as an awful realization occurred to her—the women surrounding her dressed with more flounces and bows, and showed a tad more skin, but she wasn't *dramatically* distinguishable from them. "I'm not a prostitute."

Coral looked crestfallen and turned away. Fayth felt immediately contrite. When would she learn compassion? The girl needed a friend as much as she did.

Fayth reached out and tugged at Coral's arm to keep her from blending back into the crowd of women. "I'm sorry. Thank you for your concern. And your help. The only crime I've committed today is offending you."

What a welcome to Seattle, Fayth thought. Mistakenly herded together with a group of prostitutes as she waited on the street. What next? But maybe Coral could help her. Maybe they could help each other.

Fayth spoke slowly. "Would you help me? Would you tell the guards I'm not one of Miss Gramm's girls; that you don't know me? They'd have to let me out. They have no evidence against me."

"They seldom do." Coral smiled, apparently forgiving her. "Wouldn't do any good—you were in the wrong area of town."

Fayth found this girl both puzzling and fascinating. Coral and her companions were all dressed in stylish, quality clothes. Their hair was fashionably coifed. They looked almost like real ladies. She'd been shocked when the police arrested her with them and she'd realized what they really were. Fayth had never before met a prostitute. In her imagination, she had always pictured them wearing gaudy-colored dresses with short skirts, ankles and far too much skin exposed.

The door at the end of the hall swung open. Someone yelled a command to the guards. Fayth was ushered
with the other girls to an office where a petite, dark-
haired woman paced, led by a bust resembling the prow
of a ship. Coral's savior, Miss Gramm?

As if Coral had read Fayth's mind, she whispered
into her ear. "That's Miss Lou Gramm."

Fayth watched the woman scrutinize the ladies as
they entered the room, voicing their relief. Tiny sighs,
gentle outrushes of breath. The women shuffled past
their madam, whispering their gratitude.

"That's the last time I let someone else drive them.
I'm a busy woman. I haven't got time for this nonsense.
Keep your men in line, Captain. The last thing I need's
some overzealous cop picking on my girls. And on Saturday!"

The girls, Coral included, filed past the older woman. Fayth hung back. She'd suffered enough indignity
for one day. She wasn't going to parade before a madam. The woman's gaze fell on Fayth.

"That one isn't mine." Lou pointed at Fayth.

"You must be mistaken, Lou. She was picked up
with your girls." The policeman's tone was courteous,
but disbelieving.

"I know my girls."

"I'm sure you do." The police captain shrugged and
nodded for one of his men to take Fayth back to the
cell. Before Fayth could react, Lou waved him down.

"Fine, what the hell," Lou said. "Let her go. I can
claim her as easily as not."

The captain called the guard off. The other girls streamed out the door and into a waiting carriage. Fayth nodded a curt thank you to the madam as she walked past. There was courtesy, and then there was courtesy. Lou Gramm made her living selling Coral's young flesh. Despicable. Fayth paused at the door and turned to wave good-bye to Coral. Lou had pulled her aside.

"Who is that woman?" The madam spoke loudly enough for Fayth to hear her from across the room. Probably intentional.

Coral looked down and mumbled something.

"Louder, Coral. So I can hear you."

"I don't know, ma'am. Her name is Fayth. She claims she really is a seamstress." Coral looked embarrassed.

Lou leveled her gaze on Fayth. "Interesting. A seamstress in my pocket. How will I ever call back this favor?"

Fayth turned away from the madam and whispered defiantly. "You won't." Then Fayth walked out the door, past the waiting carriage, and down the street.

CHAPTER ONE

Seattle

May 1889

Fayth Sheridan sat opposite Mr. Sylvester Hoage, regarding him sympathetically as he stammered and struggled to order from a menu written mostly in French. Large of girth, bald, with eyes too small for his sprawling face, he looked like a toad all dressed up in a new suit. His poorly knotted tie sat slightly askew of his collar. Fayth would have straightened it for him, but the gesture seemed too intimate and would have given the poor man false hope of winning her affection.

The Occidental Hotel had a reputation for serving fine cuisine and providing an atmosphere pleasant and respectable enough to impress a lady. Guests of social prominence were given tables with pleasant ambiance where they could see and be seen. The table Fayth occupied in the rear corner of the dining room was just far enough away from the kitchen to avoid being the worst in the house. Mr. Hoage seemed unaware of the slight. He finished ordering. The waiter turned to Fayth.

"What will you have tonight, Miss Sheridan?"

"The salmon."

"Excellent choice." The waiter nodded and disappeared.

"The waiter knows you by name?" Mr. Hoage's voice rang with insecurity.

"I dine here often." Too often. But how could she turn down these lonely men? The handsome, arrogant ones were easy, but men like Mr. Hoage elicited her sympathy. They looked so eager and pleading when they asked, and so dejected when she turned them down. And because she was not attracted to them, they were not a threat to her. One evening was a small sacrifice to make them happy. But only one. She seldom accompanied them twice.

Mr. Hoage didn't appear entirely satisfied with her answer, but dropped the matter and inched his chair closer to hers for the second time since their arrival. "You look lovely tonight, Miss Sheridan."

"Thank you, sir." Fayth forced a smile. She wore a simple gray gown with a small bustle and jet buttons up the front. Her hair was pulled back into a severe chignon with no suggestion of softness or curls. Since the death of her parents and *his* defection, she dressed without regard to pleasing the masculine eye.

"How has the tailoring business been lately?" As Mr. Hoage made a stiff attempt at conversation, he leaned even closer.

"It's been fine, Mr. Hoage."

"Ah." He nodded in what Fayth thought was a vain attempt to look informed and cleared his throat.

Her customers, like Mr. Hoage, were working-class men. Lumberjacks, mill hands, sailors and fishermen, all willing to pay more for her clothes than ready-made ones because of the attention she gave her clients. Taking precise measurements, running her hands over shoulders to ensure a smooth line, snapping pant legs taut during fittings, recommending fabric and styles, and telling her clients how fine they looked in their new attire were all part of her job. Fayth realized they flocked to her shop mostly because she was a single woman in a town with a dire shortage of women, and giving her their business gave them an opportunity to court her.

"I was just thinking, you know, it isn't right for a lady as pretty as you to have to work and worry about business. Wouldn't it be easier if you had a husband?"

She stiffened. Poor, desperate man. Here came the inevitable marriage proposal. She had to cut him off before he could issue it. "I love my work, Mr. Hoage. I have no desire to marry."

He looked abashed, but recovered quickly. "I hear you have a fine hand for drawing and sketching. Maybe you'd let me take you out on a nature walk? I know of a little knoll with a fine view of the mountains and the Sound. It'd make a pretty picture."

He was persistent, she gave him that. Barely half an hour into their evening and he had already nearly attempted a marriage proposal, and once turned away, angled for another social call.

"No, thank you, Mr. Hoage." From his determined look, he wouldn't be dropping the matter easily. Fortunately, she noticed her cousins waiting near the *maître d'* for a table. "Look! There are the Kelleys." She caught their attention and gave them a discreet wave.

A look of disappointment quickly clouded Mr. Hoage's face as her cousins made their way toward them.

"Fayth!" Her cousin Elizabeth was tall and spare, with shiny black hair fashionably styled. Elizabeth, past thirty and unhappily childless, always looked for someone to mother. Her expression warned Fayth to expect one of Elizabeth's motherly lectures.

"Mr. Hoage, do you know the Kelleys, Sterling and Elizabeth?" Fayth always thought Sterling looked exactly like his name. Tonight, wearing a gray suit she'd recently made for him, more than ever. He, like his wife, was lean and long. But his hair was a distinguished silver.

Mr. Hoage reluctantly stood to greet them.

"Won't you join us?" Fayth asked.

"Just until our table's ready," Elizabeth said.

Sterling held a chair out for her.

"Mr. Hoage works at a dry goods store down the street from my shop."

"Really?" Fayth felt rebuke in Elizabeth's tone. "Near Fayth's shop?"

"Oh, yes. Very near." Mr. Hoage fell haplessly into Elizabeth's trap.

"Sterling and I regret her dubious location." Elizabeth's voice dripped disdain. Fayth watched her give him the up and down, saw her expression harden, and knew her cousin had formed a low opinion of the man. "We worry daily about her safety. We'd be so much happier knowing the *right* man was looking out for her."

"Elizabeth doesn't like my shop being so close to Billy the Mug's Saloon."

"And other establishments I won't name," Elizabeth interjected.

"Elizabeth is referring to Lou Gramm's parlor house. I have a friend there." Mr. Hoage didn't give Fayth the disapproving look she expected. Few men approved of a decent woman going near a brothel.

"Fayth!"

"You brought it up, Elizabeth. Mr. Hoage might as well hear it from me so he doesn't get the wrong impression." Fayth looked directly at her dinner companion. "I've made an acquaintance, hoping to steer her away from the immoral, degrading life she currently lives."

"She's actually been inside Lou's house," Elizabeth said in a jovial, scandalized tone. She lowered her voice. "I won't let her describe to me what she's seen."

"As if I would force such debauchery on her!" For the first time all evening Fayth was enjoying herself.

"Many of Elizabeth's close friends have been scheming for months, trying to find a way to get into Miss Gramm's house." She spoke in a confiding tone, addressing her comments to Mr. Hoage. "They want to form a Christian Committee to visit all parlor houses and talk the girls out of the business. I've just beaten them to it."

"If it weren't for Fayth's well-known good intentions, her reputation would be in shreds," Elizabeth said. "Fayth, dear, you've gotten way out of hand, visiting that creature at Miss Gramm's whenever the mood strikes you. The idea was to visit each house once. To expound upon the evils and leave."

"You can't win a person over that way. True redemption only comes through love and friendship. Why should those girls trust someone they don't know? What guarantee will they have of help when they need it? It's not so easy to cast off one's former self, especially when society already pegs you for shame."

"You see what comes of women having too much time on their hands, Mr. Hoage?" Sterling's tone was jovial as he broke his silence. "Last time the good women of our town got this worked up over an issue they shut the parlor houses down. We lost so much revenue from prostitution fines everyone thought Seattle would go bankrupt. We had to repeal the women's right to vote just to keep the city afloat." He chuckled good-naturedly.

Sterling teased mercilessly; otherwise, Fayth would have lit into him about suffrage. "I'm a working girl,

Sterling, and Elizabeth is busy with her charities. Neither one of us has time to get into trouble."

"Oh, look, Miss Siren has just arrived." Elizabeth waved to a matronly woman entering the dining area.

Fayth looked up in time to catch Miss Siren's disapproving look at her escort.

"Come with me, Fayth. We must greet her. Gentlemen, you will excuse us for a moment?"

Sterling stood immediately and pulled his wife's chair out. Mr. Hoage was somewhat slower on Fayth's behalf. Fayth had already wiggled out of the chair before he was fully standing. Elizabeth took her arm and guided her. They were barely out of earshot of the men when Elizabeth leaned in and whispered in her ear. "What in heaven's name are you doing out with that buffoon? And when your good reputation is already in danger? Even the *maître d'* recognizes a lowlife when he sees it. You're seated in a worse location than the last time you dined here escorted. It's positively embarrassing."

"He pestered me for weeks. He looked so pitiful, I finally accepted." Fayth's returning whisper was a frustrated hiss.

"And how is letting him escort you out going to rid you of him? You must be firm with these men. Turn them down cold. You've been seen out too often lately and with such men! Did you see the look Miss Siren gave you?"

Fayth opened her mouth to speak, but Elizabeth cut her off before she could form a word.

"If you turned enough men down, word would get out that you are not courting. Though I must say, you should be courting. You need to forget Drew and move on. But you must see the right sort of gentlemen. And I emphasize, *gentlemen*."

"I've tried Elizabeth. Goodness knows how many offers I turn down a day. But the men in this town are so transient, and the city is growing so fast, that a new crop of men arrives daily. Word does not get out."

Elizabeth frowned. "You must try harder."

Fayth gave her a light smile. "I thought Seattle society was supposed to be tolerant. I came west because you assured me that people here aren't easily scandalized." She gave Elizabeth's arm a little tug. "Thank you for worrying about me."

Elizabeth shook her head and smiled back. Her tone was soft. "What would you do if Sterling and I weren't around to watch out for you? Do you want us to stay long enough to save Mr. Hoage the trouble of seeing you home?"

"I would appreciate it."

Elizabeth gave her a quick hug as they reached Miss Siren. Elizabeth called out an enthusiastic greeting. A pleasant commotion coming from the entrance caught Fayth's attention. Two uniformed ship captains were just arriving, laughing and joking with each other.

Fayth's heart skipped a beat as she recognized the taller of the two as one of her customers, Captain O'Neill. Of good height, with broad shoulders and a narrow waist, he was a tailor's dream. And if she were honest—a woman's. Anything looked good on him. Too

bad she'd written off good-looking men as disloyal, unfaithful, untrustworthy . . .

Well, enough of that. She wouldn't trust a handsome man again, not ever. But she could enjoy the sight
of one. Besides his broad shoulders, the Captain had
snapping hazel eyes and a glorious head of luscious,
thick auburn hair, the kind of hair a woman could run
her fingers through. If she were, of course, the type of
woman who lusted after a man like him. Which Fayth
absolutely wasn't. After Drew, she'd written the male
persuasion off completely. Except for pity dates with
men like Mr. Hoage. Real courting was simply out of
the question.

She watched the *maître d'* seat the Captain and his
friend in a prime location, letting her gaze linger a
moment too long. He looked in her direction, caught
her eye, and smiled. Though he was across the room,
she knew his eyes danced with good humor. They always did. And beneath his auburn beard, dimples
pleated his cheeks. Why was that enigmatic smile of his
etched in her mind?

She looked away guiltily, glad to be standing next to
Elizabeth and Miss Siren, instead of seated with Mr.
Hoage. Suddenly embarrassed about keeping Mr.
Hoage's company, she wondered if a convenient head-
ache would get her home early.

"Elizabeth, I'm suddenly not feeling well."

Her cousin looked at her, followed her line of sight
to the Captain, arched a brow, and took her arm.
"Well, really, darling, then we'll have to get you home,

won't we? I'll get Sterling and have him bring the carriage around."

Weeks later, Fayth kneeled on her skirts at the feet of a tall, strapping man, her mouth full of pins. She measured his inseam with care, paying particular attention to avoid touching the bulge evident between his legs. She hated pinning for the final hem as much as she hated taking the original measurements, but there was no way to avoid either.

"Every man needs a marrying and burying suit, that's what my pa says. Wouldn't you agree, Miss Sheridan?" Her client, a scruffy, bearded lumberjack, bent his knees ever so slightly and dipped discreetly so that her fingers brushed lightly against his bulge. Vulgar man.

"Mmm." As if scorched, she moved her hand away from the man's inseam. With an action designed to hide her automatic disgust, she removed a straight pin from her mouth and secured it in place in the hem. When would these men learn new tricks? Practically every male customer she had tried one move or another to guarantee her intimate touch.

"Brother's getting married next month. Guess I'll look better than the bridegroom, if he decides to invite me to the wedding and doesn't just stop by the courthouse one afternoon as he's been threatening." He leaned down to speak to the top of her head. "I suppose he's a lucky man. There aren't enough women to go around in these parts." He paused. When he spoke he didn't sound particularly envious. "The bride isn't much to look at, but she can cook."

Fayth inserted the final pin and snapped the pant leg down taut over the heel of the logging boot the man wore for the fitting. The hem fell perfectly to the heel's midpoint. She grimaced at the man's reflection in the full-length mirror in front of them. The boots were probably the only pair of shoes he owned, but they looked patently ridiculous with the nearly completed suit he wore. She pushed up on one knee and rose. "All finished."

"So soon?" The man seemed disappointed.

"If I've done my job right, final fittings don't take long." She forced a smile. "You can change now. Just leave the suit on the fitting room chair. It'll be ready Friday. Pick it up anytime in the afternoon." She turned her back to him to log her promise in the appointment book on the counter.

"Miss Sheridan?"

She stopped writing. *Oh please, let this be one man who isn't going to ask to court me.*

"Yes?" She stared at her book. Facing him would only encourage him.

"I know it's only Tuesday, and maybe you don't make plans so far ahead, but I'm hoping that you'll agree to accompany me to Frye's Opera House on Saturday. I hear they're putting on a fine show."

She let out a small, pent up breath. Poor man, had he heard her exhale? Blast! Despite her best efforts, he'd asked her to a play. What should she do now? She turned. The man tugged at his ear and shifted back and forth under her gaze. She would have accepted, more out of pity than anything else, but Elizabeth's warning, issued weeks ago, still stung. Worse still was the memory of encountering Captain O'Neill. Why, she didn't know, but she'd been embarrassed that night. Elizabeth was right, she better either stop courting altogether, or start seeing gentlemen.

"I'm sorry."

His face fell.

She faltered and almost lost her resolve as she tried to soften the rejection. "But . . . I have plans."

Never make excuses, Elizabeth had instructed her. But she felt his loneliness and disappointment. She knew all too well what it was like to want something beyond her reach. *Maybe it's better not to have a taste of it in the first place.* Elizabeth thought so, saying it wasn't kindness to give any unsuitable man false hope. Kindness, it seemed, was a slippery slope that led to unintentional cruelty.

His hopeful look returned. "Some other time then?"

Her assumption had just been verified. "I—Maybe."

Looking relieved and as if he might just have a chance with her after all, he nodded, and boots thumping noisily, went to the dressing room to change. Fayth collapsed in a chair and waited for him to finish.

When he left, she locked the door behind him and watched him walk out of sight down the uneven street, glad the last customer of the day was finally gone. Olive, her tabby cat, bounded out of the office and pawed at her skirts as Fayth turned the lock. Olive's little silver collar bell jingled happily as Fayth reached down and stroked her. "Happy to be free and out of hiding are you?"

Olive hadn't liked men since she was tiny, when she'd been kicked by one so hard she was nearly killed. Fayth swept her up and walked to the small adjoining office, crooning to her.

"No need to worry, kitty. They're all gone today. We won't have to deal with any more men until tomorrow."

A gentle saltwater breeze drifted in through the open window, carrying with it the smell of tide flats and sawdust from the mills at water's edge, ruffling the stack of sketches resting on her well-organized desk. Downtown Seattle was almost always favored with a cooling western breeze off Elliott Bay in Puget Sound. The familiar sounds of horns and steam whistles from ships floated up from the wharves. Seattle, with its shipping and lumber industries, was a man's town. Everything about the city, from the legitimate businesses to the profusion of prostitution cribs, parlor houses, and bars in the ample Tenderloin district, catered to the predominately male citizenry.

Fayth sighed. It wasn't as much fun as she'd thought being a woman in a man's town. Not when nearly every one of them seemed to be chasing her. She'd come to Seattle because she'd heard the town had an independent, free spirit. If anyone had thought to mention that the men themselves weren't independently minded, she would have run the opposite direction.

She walked across the wavy, sloping floor and sat down in her desk chair, settling Olive in her lap. Long evening shadows slanted in through the window. This was her first spring in a Northern city and she wasn't used to such lengthy days. They made her feel slightly off balance. Days and nights should be evenly matched. She scanned the dust that settled on the floor, carried in from the dry streets outside. She should sweep up.

The same sawmills that whined endlessly at wharf's edge were responsible for her nemesis, the uneven floors. Seattle was built on tide flats that had been filled with sawdust and debris from the mills. Unfortunately, the city had already sprung up on the fill when the founding fathers discovered that sawdust decomposed randomly, causing buildings to settle unevenly. Seattle's citizens were forced to put up with the results.

She should buy this building. She had saved almost enough money for the down payment. Renting was just throwing money away, not building equity. She could almost hear her father's scolding voice as she remembered his litany of business and personal advice. Her gaze moved around the room. The water stains up the walls bothered her. The building had flooded last March. Fortunately, all she lost were several bolts of fine wool. Old tide flats died hard. More worrying was whether any damage had been done to the foundation of the building.

Realizing her own inadequate knowledge of construction made her feel two things she detested— helpless and frustrated. How could she tell whether the building was sound, or whether the foundation would wash away during the next rainy season? How expensive would it be to repair the watermarked walls? Could she trust a hired contractor to give her an honest bid

and do conscientious work? The city was full of scoundrels and con artists, men eager and willing to make a
quick dollar off any easy target. And wasn't she the
easiest of marks? Whom could she trust? Her cousin
Sterling was too busy, and knew little more about
buildings than she did. And she had no desire to be dependent on her cousins.

Olive squirmed to get down, already tired of cuddling. Reluctantly, Fayth let her go and turned her attention to the sketches adorning her desk. Designs for
intricate gowns filled the pages. Absently, she reached
for a pen to make minor alterations and additions. She
should be designing for women instead of measuring
men's inseams. Father's voice intruded again. Sewing
for men was good, reliable business. Why had she listened to him?

She looked up and caught her reflection in the new
mirror that leaned against the wall, waiting to be hung
in the fitting room. Yet another task more suited to
male talents. She grimaced and brushed a stray lock of
hair back into place. Only in Seattle, where a plain
woman could draw a line of suitors a block long, could
her face be considered beautiful.

Frustrated, she set her pen down, her creative enthusiasm dulled by her mood. It all came down to men.
She had more suitors than a dozen girls needed, but
she didn't want a single one of them. She wanted to be
left alone to work on her designs, to sew her creations.
What she really needed was . . .

"A husband."

Olive started at hearing Fayth speak. Fayth was nearly as surprised herself. What a crazy notion. She pushed her sketches out of the way. A copy of the latest proposal before the city council sat on the corner of her desk. Mr. Wylie had dropped it by yesterday. They wanted to widen the streets. The extra taxes levied to pay for it, along with the disruption to business, would easily consume several months' worth of her slender profits. The business was her security, her livelihood, the only thing worth fighting for. Anything threatening it was the enemy. And she had no weapons to fight this foe. Only men could vote.

As Sterling had reminded her, two years ago the women of Washington Territory could vote. They lost their enfranchisement when the men decided they didn't like the women's voting record. Why they repealed liquor licenses, and shut down the prostitution cribs—heinous!

Sure, Fayth could speak her concerns at a Council meeting, for all the good it did. Men were openly suspicious of women who involved themselves in politics and business, ascribing to them all manner of do-good notions. With her well-known views on the evils of prostitution she gave them open reason to ignore and scorn her.

Now, if she were only a man, or had the right husband, one who would speak for her . . .

Olive continued to meow her disapproval.

"Whatever you do, Fayth, don't let the business fail. It's your heritage, your life. As long as you have it, you'll be safe," Father had always said. She hadn't believed him. She almost destroyed it. What she had in Seattle was only a fragile, salvaged shadow of what had been in Baltimore.

Everything threatened it. When she'd last gone to see her banker, Mr. Finn, he'd balked at the idea of her buying the shop, claiming she was undercapitalized and had no worthy collateral. Would any reputable bank loan a single woman money for business? Blast! A man could get the money. On second consideration, maybe this wild idea had merit. There were more reasons to marry than love. A marriage of convenience held all the right incentives.

"Oh, poor kitty, I scared you." She reached to pet her, but Olive skittered away. "Olive, we need a husband. Then all those undesirable men will leave us alone. And we'll have someone to hang mirrors, and judge foundations, and cast votes. And how will we ever get a loan without one?"

Olive cocked her head to one side.

"I know what you're thinking. But I think it will work, don't you?"

Olive meowed.

"Yes, I know. Neither one of us trusts men much, or longs to have one around all the time. Still, if we're careful, we can overcome the obstacles. Don't fret, kitty. I'm talking about a business arrangement."

She stood and paced. "Yes, we will find us a husband." She scooped up the cat, cuddling her to her cheek, her mood lighter. She looked Olive in the eye. "Don't worry, darling. I will be very particular. We certainly don't want things worse than they are."

She walked over and closed the window. "Come, Olive. Let's get some dinner."

Three days later, Fayth sat in her office mulling over her list of potential husbands. Half-finished sketches of dresses were pushed aside, ignored. She must settle this matter of finding a husband.

She had compiled her list from customers past and present, shopkeepers, bankers, and men who occupied businesses near hers. Men she had met. Men she knew something about. She would not trust her life and business to a total stranger. As she made the list, she waited for the emotional side of her nature to dissuade her from such cold rationality, from such a businesslike approach to life. But since breaking her engagement with Andrew Hanbrough, she'd done an effective job of subduing her emotions, at least, any tender ones.

Drew. Memories came back unbidden. She should have been his wife for just shy of a year now. Was she happier without him? Or would she have been better off with naive illusions of love and romance, and a philandering, money-seeking mate?

There were times she convinced herself she preferred the latter. To believe love possible, to trust, to rely on another person, to have someone take care of her. Sometimes it sounded like heaven, even if only an illusion. Why let reality ruin it? Was blissful ignorance preferable to truth?

Drew! Blast him! Except for him, she would never have been in such circumstances. Too little money, business so tenuous. Now, sometimes it seemed anger was the only thing keeping her sane.

Thoughts ticked rapidly through her mind. Worries. Fears. Anxieties. She shrugged them all off. She had to narrow the list, find the one.

Her standards were exacting, and why shouldn't they be? Remembering Drew, she crossed off the name of any man too physically attractive. A handsome face could never be trusted. And lust, well, it only interfered with good judgment. She had no desire to be tempted, didn't trust herself to resist a physical pull. And why should she invite other women to admire her husband?

She rejected as unsuitable any man who seemed interested in her, any man who had asked her out, certainly those who had already proposed. Her choice would have to understand that the marriage was purely business. There was no place for physical intimacy in the partnership she envisioned. She was not willing to risk having a baby and giving up her independence. Fulfilling this requirement necessitated crossing off well over half of those she had listed in her first, rough pass.

She ran her pen through the name of anyone with a reputation of frequenting Seattle's whorehouses, or of womanizing. If nothing else, Drew's behavior had instilled a deeply rooted aversion to scandal. Seattle on the whole was a tolerant town, but she didn't care to link herself openly to disgrace again.

The task could almost have been fun, if the list wasn't shrinking alarmingly. Finding a discreet man lost her another half of her remaining list. She excused one man because he didn't seem any handier with a set of tools than she was, and another because he gave incorrect change when she made a purchase at the store where he worked. He was either flustered by her presence, or unintelligent. In either case, she was unimpressed. What she wanted was an uninterested, intelligent, strong, discreet man skilled with a set of tools. And if he owned his own business, all the better.

She wrote the new requirement in the margin and stared at the remaining names. Stumped, unable to narrow the field further, she drew out a separate sheet of paper and made a list of her precise needs, laughing at herself. As if committing them to paper would create the man she wanted!

She shook her head. Her list rapidly dwindled. Her standards were too high, her requirements almost contradictory. Searching for such a man seemed futile. Did he exist in Seattle? If not in a city so full of men, did he exist anywhere? What she really needed was a man who wouldn't interfere in her life. A man with his own pursuits. A man who was gone most of the time—

As the thought hit her, she looked back to her list of men. One name stood out on the page.

Captain Con O'Neill.

She picked up her pen and paused, ready to scratch the name off. How had she missed it? The Captain's name should have gone in the first round of elimination. Too attractive. Even his written name looked bold and handsome on the page. But her pen refused to move. She squinted in thought, bit her lip, and stared at the name.

A ship captain, and not of a local barge or ferry, but a coastal freighter. He owned it, and a small wharf in the south end of town. The captain's ship sailed often, had only been in port twice since she had arrived in Seattle in February. Both times he came to her shop to order a new shirt. She squirmed. He had a fine physique. The pen trembled and hovered, but didn't write.

She took a deep breath. Since the pen wasn't budging, she might as well compare him to the attributes she wanted. Business owner. Well respected. Gone most of the time. Not interested in her romantically. Of all the men on the list, she knew with the most certainty that the Captain was not interested in her. He had never made the slightest move. She continued. No rumors of activity with loose women. The only thing against him was his looks. She set the pen down. He always seemed good-humored, and she couldn't fairly describe him as vain, or in any way aware of his magnetism. But he was dangerous, so dangerous all the same. There had to be something unappealing about him.

"Freckles," she said to Olive. "He has freckles. Although to be fair, they are very faint and not on his face at all. But, we hate freckles, don't we girl? We'll just have to concentrate on them, and our goal. Security."

She picked up the pen and circled his name before reaching down to stroke the cat. "We've found our man. There's only one problem remaining—we know why we need him, but why does he need us?

CHAPTER TWO

It didn't take much research to discover the Captain owned a large warehouse as well as his wharf. He kept no permanent quarters in Seattle, and he had a hired man who managed the business in his absence. Clearly, he needed a competent businesswoman to oversee his operations. Fayth trusted employees very little. He should have someone whose success was tied to his. And she was just that woman.

Every man needed a home, and a wife added respectability to his status in the community. She would keep a finger on the pulse of the growing city and advise him what goods to bring in, what ventures to pursue. How could he keep track of such things during his long absences? With her help he would be at least twice as successful as he was now.

That left only two tasks: perform a final moral background check on the Captain, and find out when he was next scheduled to arrive in town. The latter only required a quick trip to his overseer's office, the former, a visit to Lou Gramm's parlor house to see Coral.

Few of Fayth's acquaintances understood her friendship with the young prostitute, or her sense of responsibility toward her. Despite their skepticism, Fayth was optimistic she could persuade Coral to leave the business, and was willing to suffer scorn herself in the attempt. Someone had to care about the girl.

Lou Gramm's stylish parlor house was located just two blocks up Washington from Fayth's shop, on the corner of Third. From the exterior, it looked quiet and respectable. However, most of the women in the city couldn't walk by it without wincing, while most of the town's leading male citizens found they could not walk past without turning in.

Fayth strode up the front walk, steeled to her mission. Fortunately, Lou's business was slow in the early afternoon. Lou's maid Maddie let her in. Fayth had been inside the house more than once, but she never had overcome the shock of viewing its vulgar interior.

Lou had painted the walls in bright, garish colors. To ward off the dim moral character of the business conducted within, in Fayth's opinion. Nude statues of women sat on pedestals in prominent view wherever space allowed. Photographs of naked women in provocative poses covered the walls. The whole decor was, in a word, lewd.

Rusty, Lou's bouncer, showed Fayth straight to the back of the house, past the parlor reserved exclusively for the male guests, past the bar where men could pass the time with the libation of their choice, to the small, plain dining room off the kitchen. The *lady boarders*, in the delicate vernacular, many of whom had just risen, were in various stages of eating their first meal of the day, an exhaustive affair of eggs, sausage, bacon, toast, hotcakes, juice. and milk that many a lumberjack would be grateful to finish.

As Coral had explained, hers was a strenuous job. It required lithe grace, strength, and a great deal of physical endurance to keep pace with a full night of men. Fayth had halted her partway through her explanation, not wanting to hear more. However, she couldn't help noticing Coral ate more than any woman she had ever known. What must she endure night after night?

Coral sat at the far end of the long dining-room table, wearing a robe that fell open carelessly and revealed an elaborate negligee. She spotted Fayth and called out a warm greeting as she set down her fork and pulled her robe together . The rest of the prostitutes ignored her and continued eating. They were used to her, and as long as she left them alone, willing to tolerate her presence.

"Fayth!" Coral's eyes lit up. "What brings you here today?"

Her pleasure made Fayth's discomfort almost tolerable. She rounded the table and pulled up an empty chair next to Coral. "I came to ask a favor. And to see you, of course."

"Name it. Need a fitting? My opinion of your latest design?" Coral had an eye for fashion. In a town where most women were occupied with the ordinary and taxing affairs of day-to-day living, Coral's interest was refreshing.

"Neither. I haven't been designing lately." If only she were. "I've come for information."

"What *kind* of information?" Coral's tone became suddenly cautious. Because of the clientele the girls kept and the intimate nature of their profession, they knew many secrets and as much about the politics and comings and goings around town as anybody. The girls had a code of confidentiality to which they strictly adhered. Indiscretion would cost them their livelihood in the privileged parlor house and force them to ply their trade in the despised cribs.

Fayth smiled to reassure her. "Nothing that violates your code of ethics, I assure you." She paused, choosing her words with care. "I'd like to know whether a certain man patronizes Lou's. Or, to your knowledge, any of the ladies in the Tenderloin."

Coral cocked her head and studied her as if examining her motives. "Why do you want to know? You aren't spying for a suspicious wife, are you? We aren't allowed to kiss and tell."

Fayth shook her head. "No, of course not. I'd never dream of asking you to betray a confidence. I want the information for myself only." She took a deep breath and plunged on. "I'm thinking of taking a husband."

Coral's eyebrows shot up. She laughed and clapped, delighted. "Oh, Fayth! You've met someone? That's wonderful. It's about time you settled down."

Sweet, romantic Coral *would* believe Fayth had finally met a man to her liking.

Lila, a brash henna-enhanced brunette seated on Coral's right, spoke out. "Hear that, girls? Miss Sheridan is going to take a man and doesn't want to share!"

Several of the women laughed with Lila.

"How will a prude like her satisfy a man's appetite? He'll end up here with us." Lila winked and pretended to stroke a man. "And when he does, I'll be the first to show him a real woman's technique!"

"Shut up, Lila." Coral glared at her.

Fayth ignored Lila. What did she care what Lila thought?

The vile creature laughed and went back to her conversation.

Coral rose from the table and motioned for Fayth to follow her. She led her back to the entryway. "You'll have to excuse Lila. She's mean in the morning. Who's your man?"

"Captain Con O'Neill."

Coral squinted, looking thoughtful.

"Tall, auburn hair, bearded?" Fayth looked at Coral hopefully. Oh, but that description hardly did him justice.

"No," Coral said, "I know who you mean. His bookkeeper comes in once a week. He jokes about the Captain not joining him. I can't be sure the Captain doesn't go elsewhere, but if his bookkeeper comes here, I can't imagine he'd go to a house of lesser stature.

"Thank goodness you've finally picked a decent man, Fayth. I've been worried about you." Coral shook her head. "Rusty would toss out most of the men you've been seen with lately. At last you're moving up to *our* class of man."

Even among prostitutes a hierarchy existed, along with a sense of pride in the establishment where they worked, and the class of clientele they attracted. Fayth bit back a response. She hoped she was picking a class of man who didn't patronize whorehouses *at all*. "You'd let me know if he ever did?"

Coral touched her gently on the arm. "You know I would. In a heartbeat."

For two days, Fayth was too busy to find out when the Captain was due back in town. But she hadn't given up on her plan. She telegraphed her family lawyer, Mr. Benchley in Baltimore, requesting legal advice regarding how to protect her business in the event she married.

Mr. Benchley telegraphed back that he had no expertise in the laws governing Washington Territory, and therefore could be of little help. Further, he advised caution. A young woman of her standing was vulnerable, easy prey for the scoundrels out West.

She crumpled his response without bothering to read the rest of his ridiculous admonitions, dropped it on her desk, and headed for the Captain's offices.

Dust nipped at her heels as she approached the wharves. The city was abnormally dry for the time of year. Small dust devils whirlpooled in the streets, stirring up dirt and debris, only to end their short lives colliding with building corners. She strolled along enjoying the June sunshine, thinking. When she pushed aside thoughts of the Captain's handsome smile and appraising hazel eyes, she didn't feel nervous about approaching him. After all, this was business, not personal. And if the Captain should turn down her offer, his frequent absences would give her time to recover from any embarrassment.

The Captain's office was built on the end of a long, well-maintained pier. She saw his sign immediately: O'Neill's Shipping. It was sturdy and well made, and spoke of a prosperous business. If all went as she hoped, she would be Fayth O'Neill. An odd thought, but another thing in his favor—her name sounded good with his. She headed straight through the office door without pausing to look out over the sparkling waters of the Sound, or notice the ships moored at the wharf. A small bell rang over her head as she opened the door. A man in the front office called out to her without looking up from his books. "What can I do for you?"

"I'm looking for Captain O'Neill."

It was worth the walk to the waterfront to see the expression on his face as he heard her voice and looked up.

"Oh, pardon me, ma'am." He stood awkwardly, as if not used to a lady's presence. He was tall and gangly with angular features too sharp to be pleasing to the eye. A small nameplate on his desk read Silas Tetch. She heard other masculine voices, muffled through a closed door, coming from what she assumed was a back office.

"You're Mr. Tetch? The Captain's bookkeeper?"

"Yes, ma'am."

"Fayth Sheridan." She extended her hand with amicable intent.

He took it uncertainly and shook it limply. "How may I assist you, Miss Sheridan? Are you interested in shipping something?"

"No." She replied slowly, working on a quick lie. Why hadn't she thought up something beforehand?

"I'm a businesswoman here in town. The Captain is one of my clients. I was out making deliveries and checking on some of my other clients. I thought I'd stop by and inquire when the Captain is due back. I have an offer he might be interested in." She smiled to herself. What quick thinking. She hadn't needed to lie after all.

"Of course."

She thought she detected a lewd undertone in his voice.

"I'm a seamstress. I tailor for the Captain. I'm running a special."

"Certainly." Mr. Tetch's thin lips curled at the corners in interested amusement. He obviously didn't believe her story, thought her the same as Coral. "Well, ma'am, if you care to wait a few minutes you can make him your offer today." A smirk.

"Today? He's in port?"

"The *Aurnia* is moored just down the pier from us. She came in last night. The Captain's with a client in the back office, but if you can spare a minute, I'll announce you." Just then the office door swung open and a man stepped out.

"I'm a lousy wharfinger, Jim," she heard a deep voice say from the recesses of the office. "Tetch should have noticed the conflict immediately, and as his boss I should have double-checked the schedule. I can only plead guilt by absence. We'll reimburse you for any spoiled goods."

The other speaker mumbled something unintelligible, but his tone sounded pleasant. She picked up the Captain's voice again.

"I appreciate your willingness to work with us. I'll make good and sure it doesn't happen again." The Captain stepped into view. He looked shaggier than the last time he'd been in the shop. His beard was longer and his hair needed trimming. His eyes lit up in pleasant surprise the moment he saw her.

Her heart hammered in a jagged rhythm, her confidence waning. What was he doing back? She wasn't prepared to meet him *today*.

"Miss Sheridan stopped by on business." The treacherous Mr. Tetch spoke before she could think of a way to escape gracefully.

The Captain looked pleased. When he spoke, his tone was light. "Did I forget to pay for my last order? It seems I've been neglecting my business and personal matters lately."

"No, Captain O'Neill, of course not." For some unaccountable reason she blushed. His smile was too warm, too charming, and she, too flustered by his sudden appearance. "I came to see you about another, unrelated matter. But I didn't expect to find you in."

She glared at Tetch. "I only came by to find out when you would be in port next. I can see that you're busy. May I schedule an appointment with you for another time?" She spoke too rapidly. Her words cascaded one over another. Facing him, her nerve faded quickly and unexpectedly.

"My calendar's clear for the afternoon. The *Aurnia* had a good voyage. We moored her three days ahead of schedule. No one is expecting me. Jim here actually came in to see Mr. Tetch."

"And I'm just leaving, miss." Jim nodded his head toward her, made his goodbyes and walked out the door.

The Captain waited until Jim departed before speaking, "Miss Sheridan, would you mind discussing business over lunch? I haven't eaten yet today." When she hesitated he added, "On me."

"No, it's not that." Why did she stammer? "I came to see you about a confidential matter."

"I know of an intimate cafe. The staff is discreet. I conduct my most secretive business there. Not a word of it has ever leaked out."

Mr. Tetch was watching their exchange and smirking. Maybe it would be best to be out of his hearing. "All right then. I'll entrust my secrets to your taste in restaurants, Captain O'Neill."

"Thank goodness. I thought you were hesitating about being seen with such a scruffy sailor. I haven't had time for a beard trim or a haircut."

For some reason it pleased her that he was embarrassed by his appearance. To be quite honest, she would have dressed up a bit more herself if she'd known she was going to be in a position to propose to him today.

"This way, Miss Sheridan." The Captain guided her gently by the elbow out of the office and into the glare of sunshine outside, his fingers emitting unsettlingly pleasant warmth through the thin cotton of her shirtwaist sleeve.

The Captain led her two blocks up from the wharves to a small, dark cafe run by a Chinese family. They greeted him by name, but otherwise appeared to speak little English. The patrons seated at tables in the dining area were largely Chinese, but no one seemed surprised to see the tall, auburn-haired captain.

They were seated quickly and served bowls of thin egg drop soup and tiny cups of green tea. Their waitress, who Fayth guessed was the wife of the owner, seemed to scold the Captain in a foreign tongue. He merely laughed, then reached inside his pocket and procured a packet of letters and handed them to the waitress. Her face glowed as she received them, nodded her thanks, and started to walk away. The Captain called out to her as she left and she smiled over her shoulder and laughed, nodding again.

When he turned his attention to Fayth, he was clearly amused by her expression. "The owners are friends of mine. They come from my hometown, San Francisco. I carry mail back and forth between them and their family there. They don't trust the US Postal Service, even though I *am* the US Postal Service. The government awarded me a small mail subsidy a number of years back." He smiled broadly. "I'm not as generous as you might think; in return for the favors I do for them, they give me my meals free. Mrs. Wong was teasing me about bringing a guest to dine off their favor."

"I can pay for my own meal."

He reached across the table and covered her hand with his. "She was only teasing."

His hand was too warm, too strong, too virile. His touch made her pulse leap in the most pleasant and disconcerting way. She nearly lost her resolve. The man was confident to touch her and her reaction most dangerous.

Startled by his bold move, she pulled her hand away and hid it in her lap, trying to forget the heat his touch created in her. She cleared her throat and tried to act as if she were not blushing or thinking about how his hands would feel on her cheeks or around her waist. "You speak their language?"

"A little, and they speak a little English, but not enough to compromise our confidentiality." When he smiled, deep dimples hollowed his cheeks and his hazel eyes sparkled.

"Oh." Fayth let an awkward silence follow.

Fortunately, the Captain was an outgoing man. He filled the ensuing silence easily. "I'm glad you came to the wharf today, Miss Sheridan. It was such a pleasant surprise. I was planning to come to your shop later, after I'd cleaned up a bit."

Before today, it had never occurred to her that he would fix up before he came to see her.

"I'm in need of a new suit." He blew on a spoonful of soup.

She sat quietly waiting for her soup to cool, studying the man across from her, wondering whether she could live with him. His hair was coarse and wavy, and long enough to curl up over the back of his collar. Where his shirtsleeve strained back as he held his spoon, a spray of freckles showed beneath the curling hair on his forearm. Her attraction to him was puzzling. She had never cared for any shade of red hair, auburn included. Drew had straight, black hair, and . . .

She didn't want to think about *him*. "Please do stop by." She put a tease and a hint of flirtation in her voice, even though she knew she shouldn't. What had gotten into her? "It's always a pleasure to dress a man who wears his clothes so well."

Had she really just said that aloud? The man muddled her thoughts. He was going to get the wrong idea. What she meant was . . . What had she meant, exactly?

"I mean who's so well proportioned." She felt her blush creep up into her hairline. Wrong thing again. She wasn't getting her thoughts across properly. She didn't want him to think she'd been studying his proportions, or worse, ogling him as she measured him.

He smiled, looking as if he were trying not to laugh at her discomfort. "A good tailor makes any physique look good." His eyes sparkled.

"Um, yes, certainly." What an inane thing to say back to him.

She was all mixed up and flustered. His surprisingly warm tone and the way he was looking at her now, made her suddenly anxious. A small, worrying thought niggled at her. Could she have misread the Captain? Could he be interested in her after all? And worse, was she more physically attracted to him than she'd been previously aware?

For heaven's sake, think freckles, Fayth!

When she replied her tone was stiffer than she intended, "Thank you, I'm glad you like my work."

She expected a compliment in reply. Something along the order of, *Of course I do. You're the prettiest tailor I know.* Something any other single man in Seattle would have said. Instead, his reply was remarkably astute and terribly disappointing.

"You're suddenly very serious, Miss Sheridan."

She bit her lip. "Talking about my work reminded me—I have serious business to discuss with you."

He didn't lose his smile. "Can it wait until after we've finished our meal? I know for a fact that Mrs. Wong is in the kitchen cooking one of her finest meals with a fury. She'll be insulted if we don't appear to enjoy it and ourselves. To be honest, I've never *not* enjoyed something she's made for me. While I'm at sea eating the gruel my cook serves up, I'm always dreaming of Mrs. Wong's egg rolls. Let's not let business spoil them. Have you ever eaten Chinese food?"

She shook her head.

"Then you're in for a treat."

He entertained her with stories through three full courses. Tales of the sea, life in San Francisco, anecdotes from his latest voyage. He asked Fayth questions about herself, which she gracefully evaded. To Fayth's surprise, his manner put her so at ease that she forgot her nervousness. Without analyzing it, she felt as if she had known him forever.

Mrs. Wong arrived and cleared the dishes from the last course, leaving them alone again.

"Okay, Miss Sheridan. Our meal is over, time to discuss serious matters. What is this mysterious business you've come to see me about?"

She found herself suddenly mute.

"You want to ship something?" he said when she didn't answer.

His smile was no longer infectious. Her stomach clenched and her heart raced. She was turning coward on herself.

"Something valuable, perhaps something that no one knows you have? Jewels, bouillon, gold doubloons?" His eyes creased at the corners as he spoke and his tone was teasing. "You may trust my discretion in delicate, confidential matters of shipping."

She hoped she could trust his discretion, period. "I have nothing to ship." She masked her expression, trying to keep her tone even against the hammering of her pulse and the dryness of her mouth, displeased with herself for the disquiet that had overcome her.

"You need warehouse space perhaps?"

She could see from his expression he was genuinely pleased she had sought him out, that he was trying to

keep the mood light. But because of where the conversation was heading, she was uncomfortable, all nerves
now that the moment had arrived. Her thoughts tumbled one over another in a panicked stream. It seemed
there was no easy way to voice her proposal. At a loss,
and needing to speak before she lost all nerve, she took
a deep breath and blurted out, "I need a partner."

The Captain simply stared at her. The first reasonable expression she could attribute to him was pure
confusion. Finally, he leaned back in his chair. "Miss
Sheridan, I know nothing about the tailoring business."

"Oh." She laughed nervously. "I'm not talking about
that kind of partner—I'm talking about a marriage
partner."

His eyes darted over her as if he were trying to de-
termine whether she was actually serious. "You're asking me to marry you?"

"Yes." She admired his composure. Hers had abandoned her. The hands she kept demurely in her lap
were knotted together in a death grip. Too late, she
developed not just pity, but real empathy for all the
men who'd proposed to her. This was torturous business, even when the heart wasn't involved.

He continued staring at her in an unnerving way, as
if he were searching her for something and finding it
lacking. "Why me?"

It wasn't the response she'd expected. In fact, she
was taken aback by his question. She wasn't vain, but
women were in appallingly short supply in Washington
Territory. Any other single man from here to Alaska

would not have questioned his good fortune, but jumped in with an emphatic, *yes*. "Why not?"

His smile vanished. "In a town with a predominantly male population, you must have your share of men proposing to you. Why ask me?" His tone was gentle, and almost hopeful. The Captain appeared unflappable and steady, qualities she desired. He continued to study her.

"Because I'm not interested in any of the men who've proposed to me." Was it her imagination or did his eyes just leap with hope? She didn't want him to get the wrong idea. She continued before she lost the last shred of her nerve. "Those men want more out of marriage than I want to give."

He frowned, looking truly puzzled. "What is it you don't want to give, Miss Sheridan?"

"Myself, my heart."

The light left his eyes. "Then why marry?" His tone turned suddenly stony.

"This is a wild town, Captain, with far too many men. To be quite honest, I'm tired of their advances." That came out wrong again, sounding too selfish. She had to show the advantages to him, explain the arrangement—

"You need a husband to chase them off? Hire a bodyguard. They're a lot less trouble."

Fayth thought his tone unnecessarily harsh, but she had already gone too far to draw back from her plan. "I'm not in any fear for my physical safety. It's just . . ." Why couldn't she frame her thoughts? "You've never shown any interest in me—"

He shook his head and looked stunned. "And you assume that means I'm the kind of man who wouldn't require a wife's love and affection?"

"You've never struck me as a man who's passionate about women."

He cocked a brow. "I hope you're not implying that I prefer men?"

Flustered, she couldn't tell whether he was teasing or not. She felt the heat of embarrassment all the way to her toes. This was going from bad to worse. She couldn't seem to say anything right. "No, of course not. I simply meant that it seems to me that the sea is your first love. A woman would always be secondary. That's why I think the relationship I envision could work so wonderfully. Let me explain."

To her surprise, he didn't make any move to interrupt her. But his calm stare only served to fluster her further and she was rattled enough as it was. She'd made a mess of everything so far. She swallowed hard.

"I'm proposing a business arrangement, of a sort. I need a husband to cast votes favoring my business interests. To advise me on repairs and hire contractors. I need the financial clout of marriage. I don't mean I want my husband's money. I intend to support myself. But the banks won't lend to a single woman. I need a husband to get the loan I need to stay in business."

Spoken aloud, her list sounded manufactured and self-serving. She should have stated the advantages to him first. A man would know how to act with more finesse. How did men do it, convince women to marry them? Turned out, she needed a man just to make the proposal.

"And what would I get out of such an arrangement?" The amusement had left his voice.

"A very competent business manager."

"I have Mr. Tetch."

"You'd be foolish to trust Mr. Tetch, or any employee, implicitly. You need someone whose fortune is vested with yours. Mr. Tetch just about cost you a customer today. Would the man I met in your office earlier have stayed with you if you hadn't been in town to intervene?"

"You don't hold back your opinions, do you?"

She ignored him, concentrating on the carefully rehearsed arguments that came back to her a bit at a time. "You need a home to come home to, homemade meals, stability, the respectable stature that marriage brings to a man in the community."

"Love? Children?"

"I'm talking about a business marriage here, Captain. A marriage of convenience."

"You don't believe you could ever love me?"

What did he want her to say? She didn't believe she could love any man ever again.

"No offense intended, Captain O'Neill. You *are* an attractive man. But I wouldn't want to love my husband, no matter who he was. I don't believe in romantic love anymore. The most I hope for is that I can respect him." She thought she'd said that rather well.

"I've been all over the world, seen more hideous cruelty than you could imagine, Miss Sheridan, and even I am not that jaded." He pushed back from the table as if their interview were over.

She set her jaw and lifted her chin. "You're going to refuse me?" She couldn't believe what she was saying.

He nodded.

She was stunned, shocked. Yes, her proposal was unconventional, but it was eminently logical and mutually advantageous. Surely he could see that?

"I'm sorry, Captain. I mistakenly believed you were a man of reason. If I'd known you were such a romantic, I would have withheld my offer. You're making a mistake, in my opinion. Women are few enough here, at least women worth having as one's life mate. Companionship is priceless compared to love. And I did intend to give you the very best of myself in that regard."

She shook her head in a deliberately chastising fashion, trying to cover her own embarrassment with a judgmental attitude. "I didn't realize men could be so sentimental. We could have made a very equitable arrangement and both prospered because of it. Thank you for the wonderful meal."

She rose to leave. "Stop by the shop. I'd be very happy to make your suit for you at cost. A man deserves something for enduring such embarrassment."

She walked from the table with her chin out and back straight, leaving the Captain before he could reply. She had to escape, get out of the restaurant before she lost her composure completely. As she tried not to cry, she had new respect for all the men she'd turned down. Not one of them had broken down in tears. Wretched, womanly emotions.

Con watched the door close behind her. A woman with less class would have slammed it. He couldn't help leaning toward the window to gawk at her as she retreated. At any other time her regal posture would have caused him to break into an appreciative grin.

Miss Sheridan was unlike any woman he'd ever met—utterly delightful. Who of his acquaintance, even those he counted most brazen, had the confidence to propose to a man? And to support such a brash proposal with logical rationale?

Mrs. Wong rushed over and spoke in hushed Chinese. "The lady no like my food?"

"I believe it's the man she has a distaste for."

"Shame on you." Mrs. Wong shook a finger at him. "You scare off only girl I ever see you with."

He couldn't defend himself, but what choice did he have? Despite what she must think of him and how she must now view him, he wanted Fayth Sheridan in the worst way a man could. He wanted her body. He wanted her love. He wanted to possess her and be her husband in every sense. And he'd settle for nothing less. She'd just offered him up a challenge—he had to make a romantic out of her, too.

CHAPTER THREE

Con walked into Finley's craving a drink like his life depended upon downing a beer. Tobacco smoke fogged the room, giving him a hazy protection from scrutiny. Con was not a man who wore his emotions for all to see, but after his surprising and upsetting meal with Miss Sheridan, he was having a hard time maintaining his usual calm facade.

"It's the Con!" A voice boomed from the bar.

"Bailey!" Con wound his way through the room and slapped the small, dark man on the back as he pulled up a stool and signaled for a beer.

"What's the Con doing back in Seattle so soon?"

Con shook his head. "Having a hell of a time of it."

"The city didn't welcome you home? You need to find yourself a pretty whore. They're always good for a welcome."

Con shook his head. The last thing he needed was a whore. "Seattle's always beautiful to come back to. It's the people who inhabit her that are giving me fits."

Con had known Bailey for more than fifteen years, since they first had crewed together as boys and Con acquired his nickname, the Con, for his ability to steer vessels safely through narrow straits and fog. Con's a nautical term for the station of the person steering a ship and Con was a natural born navigator. Even as a boy, he'd saved Bailey's tail more than once.

"Someone in particular?" Bailey asked.

"Tetch almost lost me a valuable client. Scheduled two ships to wharf at the same time. Left my man with his goods spoiling in the Sound. If I hadn't been in the office because we docked three days early, I'd have lost him."

"So fire Tetch. The man's a slimy bastard."

"I can't. Not over this."

"He's more than likely robbing you blind. Hell, Con, you're never in town to watch him."

Bailey was right, of course. Not that Con would admit it. "You know I don't give a damn about money. I do care about my reputation."

Bailey shrugged. "So do something about it. Speaking of money, you may not care much about it, but some of us do. I'm celebrating tonight. Just got word our mail subsidy's been renewed. Thirty-six thousand a year."

Con whistled. Thirty-six thousand a year was a small fortune. "That deserves a drink." He signaled to the bartender. "One for my friend here, too."

Bailey was the captain of a crotchety old girl, a steamer he sailed between Seattle and Victoria, British Columbia. The bartender set two beers in front of them.

Con raised his glass to Bailey's. "To my good friend's success. One of these days I'm going to give you a run for that route. I might as well extend my subsidy from San Francisco all the way to B.C."

"You're going to have to tune up that old boat of yours, Con. You know the *Eliza* can outpace 'em all now that we swapped out her engine. I went head to head with Bigby last week and left him sitting like a lame duck."

"Watch yourself, Bailey. Someday you're going to tip that boat of yours over, or overstoke her and blow her up. In either case, the government won't be happy. People don't like wet mail."

Bailey laughed. "I never pass up a good race, Con. You ought to know that by now." His eye was caught by something over Con's shoulder. "Smile. Here comes your man Tetch."

Silas Tetch had spotted him and walked toward where he sat talking with Bailey. Con was in no mood for fraternizing with Tetch. But what did he expect when he chose to hang out in a bar on the wharf?

"Boss, what are you doing here?" Tetch said as he approached. "I thought you were out courting a lady over lunch?"

Bailey's ears perked up. He shot Con a look that said, *So that's what's bothering you.* Bailey knew Con wasn't one to share his personal life.

"It was business, Silas," Con said.

"I've never seen you take any of our male customers out for a meal," Tetch said. "And linger so long that you don't come back to the office at all."

"I had errands to run, too." Why was he making excuses to Tetch?

"A lady, Con?" Bailey asked. "Is that what your foul mood is all about? A woman finally penetrated your thick skin?"

"Looks like our captain didn't have much luck with this one," Tetch said. "And it's a pity because she's real pretty, too." Tetch's attention was diverted as a group of his drinking buddies arrived. He slapped Con on the back. "Me and the boys are heading over to Lou's to visit some of the girls. Why don't you come console yourself with us? Lila's always asking to meet my boss. She thinks a rich man like you will leave her a big tip."

Con shook his head. "I never pay for pleasure, Tetch."

"Your loss, Captain. The girls know how to entertain." Tetch winked and walked off.

Bailey leaned over and whispered in Con's ear. "Lila's probably hoping for a bigger pecker."

Con didn't laugh. He chugged down his beer instead and ordered another.

"Hey, what's the matter? Is this really about a woman?" Bailey asked.

Con sighed. "A woman came to me with a very interesting proposal, Bailey. But I couldn't take her up on it. Not today." He took a sip of his second beer. "And as Tetch said, she's a pretty little thing. But, hell, I don't even think she likes me; although, she did imply she *respected* me." He grunted.

Bailey was giving him a quizzical look, but Con didn't care to elaborate. Fayth unsettled him. In one meal she'd upset the careful plan he'd been concocting these past months to woo her. There must have been a reason she selected him. Would a woman propose to a man she felt no affinity for? He raised his glass and downed the rest of his beer.

Fayth sat at her sewing machine, her feet pumping the treadle in time to her stitching. She had sewn with a fury these past two days. Usually the sight of a needle piercing cloth, of perfectly straight seams stretching before her, calmed her and gave her a sense of satisfaction.

She pumped and watched the needle—in and out. In and out.

The motion of the ever-pounding needle, usually so soothing, made her muscles tense and her frustration build. She felt tight and wound up, as if her body longed for something. And she had a pretty good idea what. As if it longed for Con O'Neill.

She watched the needle, pumping furiously as thoughts came to her. She stopped, backed the needle out, flipped the half-finished pair of pants around and backstitched around the fly.

Proposing to Captain O'Neill had been sheer lunacy.

Her feet moved against the treadle with renewed intensity. She burned with embarrassment every time she thought about it. When would the memory fade?

That he had done her a backhanded favor was small comfort. She had come home, had a good cry, and consulted her list of bachelors, looking for another suitable choice. Then, with resignation, she had used her perfectly sharpened sewing scissors to clip the list into pieces too small to reconstruct. No other man on the list was half as suitable as Captain O'Neill. No other choice half as reasonable. The idea was perfect idiocy from the beginning. His refusal merely brought to light her distorted logic. What had caused her temporary lapse of good judgment? Mere desperation? Loneliness?

I should write him a thank-you note. Would he find it as darkly amusing as I do?

She might well have written it, too, but his rebuff had awakened more than her powers of discernment. The physical pull she felt toward him frightened her. He walked into her daydreams unbidden, playing the role of lover. Responses and longings, urges suppressed long ago, flooded back, and with them, memories of Drew, and anger and shame.

Technically, she reminded herself, she was still a virgin. But she had given Drew everything but entry. They were engaged. They had lived in the same house. With such temptation it was miraculous she had kept anything from him at all.

Bare chests. Warm nakedness. Cuddling, stroking, fondling, tingling release. She couldn't congratulate herself on her piety, because what they had done was so very close to sex. Was so very intimate and familiar that even remembering brought a hot flush to her cheeks.

And it wouldn't have mattered if the accident hadn't happened; just a few days more and she would have been his wife. Maybe she should have gone ahead with the marriage as Drew had pressed her to. In retrospect, how she had opened herself up to scandal seemed clear. Maybe because of her indecision, or maybe because Drew was convinced he could change her mind, he hadn't moved out until nearly a week after her parents had died. If they had married, the scandal would have been prevented.

After the funerals, she wanted to be held and comforted, but she just couldn't rekindle her desire for intimacy. Her passion, her lust, had evaporated. The week Drew stayed was completely innocent, but there had been no chaperone to prove it.

Later she had discovered Drew had no problem with lust. Behind her back, he fornicated with the first willing woman he could find who had a promise of an inheritance. When he had snared the woman with a pregnancy, he had walked out on Fayth, leaving her to the howling wolves of gossip. And was he the one to feel the pain? Did the tongues wag about him? His betrayal felt like infidelity, hurt just as badly. But she was just as deeply shamed by her own behavior and too stunned and hurt to defend herself. Instead, she had left Baltimore.

If the Captain had married her, could she have suppressed her attraction, held back her lust? The problem with giving a man her body was that he thought he took only that, but she gave her heart. And having given hers, expected his in return. She wasn't the cold woman she'd presented to the Captain, and that scared her to her core.

It was too easy to believe he would take care of her, like she'd believed Drew would have. She had trusted Drew with the business her father had built, with the one security her father left her. Drew had almost destroyed it. Not because of lack of business skill, but by neglect.

No, it was better for her to take care of herself. Falling in love took away independence. There was always another person to consider. And yielding to physical pleasures led to babies, a certain hazard to her career at the shop. Both only diverted her attention away from the one thing that provided security—the business.

Fayth forced her thoughts in another direction. No use remembering. She didn't know how to describe who and what she had become since Drew had betrayed her. She simply existed.

Then she had come up with the idiotic notion of proposing to the Captain. And, to her great astonishment, his refusal stung. Not just her pride, but something much deeper. The floodgates of her emotions opened, forcing her to admit to her capacity to feel. She cared. She wanted love, but didn't have enough faith to trust a man with her heart again.

With his refusal Captain O'Neill had become almost irresistible. She despised herself for the way her thoughts drifted back to him. Plenty of men would have taken her up on her offer, and then ignored the terms of the agreement. Forced themselves on her. She shuddered as she realized what she had almost opened herself up to. Yes, the Captain had proved himself a man worth having. A man noble enough to trust? The thought frightened her. She hoped she never encountered him again.

Her meal with him left her with too many disturbing questions. What made Captain O'Neill so suitable? Why would no other man do? Why did she remember the way his face dimpled when he smiled? Why did the remembrance of his stories cause her to smile? He was not as arrestingly handsome as Drew, but to her mind, every bit as enigmatic.

She backed her needle out again, snipped the threads free, and tossed the pants into her ironing pile. She hated ironing and refused to heat the iron more than once a day, especially in the warm June weather. She grabbed another pair of pants and inserted it into her machine. Her legs pumped again methodically. Who said honest seamstresses got no exercise?

She engrossed herself in her work and thoughts, trying to think of something other than the Captain. The loud clattering of the machine covered the tinkle of the bell over the door. She didn't realize a customer had come in until she heard a male voice address her.

"Miss Sheridan, good day. You look absorbed. You must love your work. Everyone should be as lucky as you and me."

Her feet froze in the middle of a pump. The machine silenced. She looked up cautiously, trying to calm the fluster his voice stirred in her. "Captain O'Neill?" She could not keep the incredulity out of her voice.

"I have come to order a suit." He offered no further explanation until the pause became awkward. "I never pass up a good bargain." He smiled as he spoke.

She couldn't help admiring his dimples. "Nor should you. Especially not one so well earned."

She hoped he wouldn't notice the tremble in her hands as she spun the wheel and lowered her needle back into the cloth to protect it. She stood and went for her tape measure and the file card with his measurements while avoiding his gaze. "I have the measurements I'll need for the jacket on file, but I will need to measure your inseam for the pants. If you'd stand on the platform . . ."

He stepped up and held out his hands. "All the world's a stage."

She smiled, but inside she was quaking as she approached him. As she kneeled at his feet, she noticed his boots were well polished and covered only lightly with a fine coating of street dust, as if he had just buffed them before coming.

She decided to keep things purely professional, not let any hint of the friendly intimacy they'd had before her ridiculous proposal slip in. If he could forgive and forget, she certainly could. She hoped. "What kind of a

suit do you need, Captain? A summer suit? I would recommend a fine light wool I have in stock."

She set one edge of her tape against the floor and
ran the other up the inside of his strong, muscled leg,
resisting the urge to run her hand up it. What was it
about this man that brought out her lust?

He didn't dip or squirm the way other men did, hoping for an accidental brush of her fingers against their
manly bulges. The one time an accidental touch might
have relieved her tension and he held himself perfectly
still.

"You're very long of limb, Captain." She wrote down
the measurement on the little measurement card. Then
she cocked her head and eyed the fit of the pants he
wore, trying not to look at his crotch as she looked up
at him. "I'll need to measure your thigh as well. Whoever tailored these did a poor job. They strain here."
She gave a little tug at the offending spot. They were
much too tight around his heavily muscled thighs.

"Spread your legs a little farther, if you please." She
pushed up from her kneeling position and ran the tape
around his thigh, conscious of how hard and sculpted
with muscle his leg was. "Pants should have a nice
hang."

"Indeed," he said with a touch of irony.

Too late she realized her unfortunate terminology.
Men liked to consider themselves well hung. She hoped
he didn't think she was making any lewd innuendos.
"Finished."

She wound the tape as she stood. When she looked
at him, she saw no unseemly look in his eyes and was

vaguely disappointed in spite of herself. Another awkward silence ensued.

At last the Captain spoke. "You keep a nice shop, Miss Sheridan. Very prettily decorated."

She wondered whether he was trying to make amends for his refusal of her unconventional marriage proposal. "Thank you. Decorating did present challenges. The floors slope. The rugs always bunch. I'm always half expecting my customers to stumble and trip."

"The building's no worse than most."

"Is it good enough to buy?" She realized her question seemed to come from nowhere, but the issue had been weighing on her for weeks.

"I'm not in the market." His eyes twinkled as he spoke.

She laughed nervously. "You don't trust me now, but let me assure you, I'm not trying to trap you into anything. I meant for me to purchase. Me alone."

She wound the tape in her hand even tighter. "My landlord has given an ultimatum—either I buy or he sells to another. Whether a new owner will evict me or not is anyone's guess."

She paused. It felt good to share her burden. Since she had already reached the epitome of embarrassment with the Captain, it seemed safe to share this worry with him.

"The rent is very reasonable. I don't know whether I could find another suitable location for the same price." She babbled on, afraid of another gap in the conversation. The Captain gave her a slight squint of quick appraisal, then turned to inspect the room with apparent seriousness.

"If I take a loan out, my monthly payments would be about the same, but the down payment would tie up my capital. It makes me uneasy to think of incurring so much debt when I'm only getting started here. And, as I said before, I'm not even certain the banks will lend me the money."

She watched as the Captain walked around the room, looking at the foundation, tapping on the walls. What was it about him that inspired her to spout confidences?

"Surely as a businessman you can understand my worries?"

"I do." He inspected the seam around the window. "The building seems sound enough, but I'm no inspector."

She nodded, disappointed. He wasn't going to give her his opinion. She walked to the counter. "Shall we fill out the order for your suit?"

He followed her to the counter, picked out fabric, answered her questions.

"I'll pay you your regular price for this, Miss Sheridan. I was planning to come in and order one before—"

"No, you won't. A deal is a deal. I'm a woman of my word."

"I can't let you—"

"You'll have to."

"Then let me compensate with a favor. I have a friend who's a builder. Let me send him around to check out your building before you make a decision."

"You're very kind. It's been a worry." She looked down to hide her embarrassment. "I would be grateful."

She finished writing the order and looked up. "You're a remarkable man, Captain O'Neill. I owe you a thank you."

"How so?"

He gave her such an expectant look that she hoped her words wouldn't disappoint him. "Your refusal of my earlier offer made me realize the folly of embarrassing another man with such a ridiculous proposal."

"I see." The expectant look vanished, replaced with an unreadable mask. She had somehow disappointed him.

"I'm sorry for any embarrassment I caused you before," she said. The expectant look didn't return. "I'm glad you came by today." Nothing.

"My pleasure. Well, I must get back to my ship. Good day, Miss Sheridan."

She watched him walk away and close the door gently behind him. He hadn't made one move to court her. She had picked the one man in Seattle who wasn't interested in her. When she sat back down at her machine, instead of pumping madly away at the treadle, she stared out the window tracing his path with her eyes and sighed.

Con exhaled deeply as he stepped out from the shade of the awning into the bright sunlight and headed toward the wharf. He'd been sucked into her shop by a force as strong and irresistible as the magnetic pull on a compass needle. Now the visit, the thought of which had made him as uneasy as sailing through wind-chopped seas, was over and it had been too easy. He had found out exactly what he had wanted to know without having to pry. Or hell, make any attempt at all. She just popped out with it—she wasn't going to propose to anyone else. She actually thanked *him* for that, for bringing her back to her senses.

He couldn't hold down his smile. He must be beaming like an idiot. He had spent two sleepless nights worrying that she'd hook herself up with some scoundrel who'd make her the promises she wanted to hear, then break every one. Maybe he was the only man around fool enough to turn her down, but he'd have her on his own terms or not at all.

He didn't bother to ask himself why he hadn't just accepted and pressed for a long engagement, buying himself time to court her properly. He had been so confounded it hadn't occurred to him until later, and when it had he tossed it out as quickly as it had bounced in. It wasn't in his nature to use trickery or deceit. Mam, and later Captain Will, had impressed him with a sense of honesty and fairness that had become almost innate. He'd never used deceit to achieve his means before, and he wasn't about to start with Miss Sheridan.

She'd caught his attention the day he'd innocently turned into her shop, hoping to find a seamstress capable of producing a decent shirt. He still remembered his first glimpse of her, didn't think he'd ever forget it. She'd been kneeling at the foot of a dressmaker's form, tugging at the hem of a dress, eyeing it to make sure it was even all the way around. The sun shone in on her, illuminating her golden blond hair. In his mind's eye, he remembered her bathed in such brilliance that the background became indistinguishable. There was only her. She turned and looked up at him. Her eyes were a bright, intelligent blue, her face a perfect high-cheeked oval. He had felt like someone kicked the wind right out of him.

Silly as it was, he had never felt that way before and didn't think he would again. He was already thirty-two years old. He didn't suppress his urge to hum as he walked along.

He had been at sea since he was fourteen and had built a fine business. Lately he'd been restless, thinking he might settle down. A wife and family were beginning to sound good. The hell of it was Miss Sheridan was right. He wouldn't give up the sea. Unfortunately there weren't many women who understood its pull, and fewer still that he felt could stand on their own during his absences. Fayth Sheridan could.

His physical reaction to her the first time they'd met stunned him enough to suppress his usually outgoing nature. He'd been quiet, almost unable to speak, forced mostly to listen and observe. To plan. Some man had made her skittish. He determined that fast enough. She proved that again today. One moment she was cool as a northern breeze and the next he caught her looking at him with undeniable interest. She certainly interested him, more with each encounter, but he had to go easy.

She chatted on that first day, making pleasant banter that didn't reveal a thing about her. It wasn't until they were at her desk filling out his order form that another customer had come in. Miss Sheridan had excused herself to wait on the woman, and that's when he discovered what he wanted to know.

They whispered to each other, but he had a keen sense of hearing. The other woman asked her something about her evening out. Miss Sheridan complained about being courted by so many men. About feeling like something on display at the grocer's. They must have realized they were whispering too loudly, because they lowered their voices and he didn't hear anything more.

When the woman had left and Miss Sheridan came back to the desk to complete the order form, she was smiling pleasantly. By that time it was obvious that the only way to court Fayth Sheridan, was not to. Anything else met with immediate failure.

He was a patient man, up to a point. He would keep his head and wait until she spurned so many men she developed a reputation for being cold, until all those other fools stopped coming around. If he could hold back that long. Then he'd court her mercilessly. In the meantime he'd just stop by from time to time. That had been his plan until two days ago. He'd almost had to think up a new strategy, but now he saw that his original plan was salvageable.

He couldn't help wondering what had brought her to Seattle. He wouldn't have selected it for a single woman under his care. Where was her family? He missed his guess if she hadn't run from someone. Some man had hurt her badly. It was the only explanation for her wary attitude.

He wanted to beat the man who'd done this to her. The only thought that caused him to go cold and worry over the success of his plan was the fear that the fellow might show up to reclaim her before he could win her affections.

She wore mourning clothes. Maybe the man was dead. Maybe it was grief that drove her. He wished he knew.

He turned the corner on the last block to the wharf and smiled again as he caught sight of the *Aurnia* in her berth.

Man alive! He couldn't help remembering the way Fayth's hand had felt against his leg as she measured his inseam. Watching her little white hand with its long slender fingers slide up his leg was downright erotic. Then she made that comment about hanging, and he sure as hell wasn't hanging. He was pointing like an Irish setter and hoping against hope that she didn't notice as she surveyed the tight fit of his pants!

He'd been too long without a woman, but he wasn't about to pay for pleasure like Tetch. No, for now he was content to wait. Since Miss Sheridan had decided it wouldn't be necessary to land a husband right away, he had time. He had a plan again. There wasn't anything he couldn't do once he had a plan.

He hummed a little louder as he turned into his office.

CHAPTER FOUR

Fayth sat at her desk with her business ledger spread open in front of her. Even the midafternoon sun shining in on her didn't lessen her ominous, solemn mood. Her landlord was pressing for a decision. Was she going to buy the small two-story frame building she shared with two other tenants, or not? He had a buyer from California ready to purchase it at a moment's notice. Serious one. Rich, too. So the landlord said. No doubt he meant to intimidate and pressure her.

The ledger pages ruffled in a strong northwesterly breeze blowing in off Elliott Bay through her half-open window, the fluttering paper as transitory as her convictions. Business had been brisk and steady since she'd set up shop in February. Given one more good year she could comfortably buy. But using her cash reserves now made her uneasy.

She sighed and stared blankly out at the dusty streets. Next to her ledger sat a list with two columns, one with reasons for buying the building, the other against.

The list for buying was long and punctuated with the words *building sound, no place else to go.* The Captain's man had been in just yesterday and pronounced the building sturdy, fit to occupy, and fairly priced. And she had checked the local papers. There were no notices for other shop space available to rent.

Printed in full capitals under the negative column glared the single damning word—location. She resided on what locals called *The Line.* It ran east to west down Washington Street between Lou Gramm's parlor house at Third and Dexter Horton's bank at Commercial. It was the line of respectability.

Lou Gramm proved her business savvy, positioning her house of ill repute on the very verge of decency and commerce. Just blocks to the south of Fayth's store, near the tide flats, the tough and dangerous Tenderloin District rambled toward the water. Wildly populated with thieves, ruffians, pandering pimps, and whores who did not occupy stylish houses, but serviced men out of rough-hewn cribs, the area deserved its low reputation. Up the street to the east from Fayth, the infamous Billy the Mug's Saloon attracted its share of raucous customers. On Saturday nights, she heard its bawdy rumble from a full block away. The very reasonable rent she paid allowed her to do business, and accounted for her dubious location.

If only she possessed Drew's quick, don't-look-back decisiveness. Or the Captain's. She smiled. The Captain was indeed quick with a decision. Too quick.

She turned to stare at the calendar that hung on the wall. Thursday, June 6. She must make up her mind by tomorrow noon. A clock chimed the quarter hour. Two forty-five. She slammed the ledger shut, at last deciding to lock up and go make a counteroffer on the place.

Fayth had barely turned her sign to Will Return Soon, stepped outside, and locked the shop door when the shrill call of fire whistles sounded. Mr. Wylie, the merchant from next door, stepped out onto the boardwalk with her. In unison, they scanned the horizon in search of flames.

"There. To the north." Wylie pointed as she caught sight of smoke. "Bad day for a fire. The wind's up and everything's dry as kindling."

She nodded and coughed on her first breath of the sickly bitter, smoke-laden air that billowed in. From the direction of the wharves, steam whistles added their deep blasts to the cacophony.

"Smells like a factory going up," Wylie commented.

Fayth watched as shop customers and patrons filled the walks. Volunteer firemen dashed out from businesses lining the road, pulling their coats on as they raced up the street to their posts. The curiosity seekers rushed toward Front Street. Everyone else stood with eyes glued to the billowing smoke churning into the deep-blue sky to the north.

"Well," Fayth said at last. "I have business to attend to."

Mr. Wylie grabbed her arm as she tried to pass by. "I wouldn't leave my shop, Miss Sheridan. The streets are full of rowdies. It isn't safe. And the wind's from the north."

His last statement seemed almost an afterthought, but she heard the apprehension in his voice.

Fayth stared at him, just beginning to feel an uneasy prickle of worry. If Mr. Wylie was concerned, maybe she should be, too. "The fire department will have this fire under control soon. There can't be any need to worry. The fire must be at least five blocks away."

A runner came down the street crying out the news. "Fire started at Front and Madison. The entire block's on fire. When the firemen tried to pull up the sidewalks to stop the fire from spreading, the heat drove 'em back. I seen it."

"Best get back in your shop, Miss Sheridan," Mr. Wylie said. "It isn't safe for a lady to be out and about. Not with the excitement that's building."

She looked at the boisterous mob growing in the street. Yes, Mr. Wylie was right. She'd be safer in the shop. She thanked him for his concern and retreated inside, determined to get back to work. But once inside, she couldn't face the isolation of running the machine in the back room. Instead, she grabbed a stack of pants that needed hemming and sat in the front of the store with the window open so she could hear the news relayed by observers. Hemming always calmed her.

At nearly three-thirty she saw the first tongue of flame leap up and lick a sky no longer deep blue, but smeared black with smoke. The news came in sporadic bursts, as runners from the scene passed her window.

The Denny block is on fire. Just when the firemen thought that they'd controlled it, it would burst forth midblock, blowing out windows and storming through doors with its fury.

Frye's Opera House is burning and feared lost.

The hoses have failed!

The fire seemed unstoppable. The wind carried embers as far south as Columbia. Fayth listened to the reports and continued hemming, but the needle trembled in her hand.

At four, a thunderous blast shook the panes of her windows. She screamed. Mr. Wylie pounded on her door.

"Don't worry, Miss Sheridan! They blew up the San Francisco Store trying to make a fire line. More than six blocks are on fire, including Cherry Street. Me and Willis are going up on the roof with wet blankets to stave off any sparks. You'd be advised to haul down anything from the second floor that you might be wanting to save, just in case we have to pull our goods out into the streets." He didn't sound optimistic. "And hang as many wet blankets as you can out the windows."

"Mr. Wylie, are we *really* in danger?" She was hoping for a denial.

"Miss Sheridan, without water the firefighters are hamstrung. The few hoses still trickling are melting in

the heat and everything's as dry as summer grass. Just
the sheer heat is causing adjacent buildings to burst
into flame." He must have seen her worry. His next
words were softer. "We've got reason to be concerned."

"Do you have enough blankets, Mr. Wylie?"

"You just hang what you got out the windows," he
said and disappeared, off to try to save the roof.

Con stood at the end of his pier watching the fire
approach. When word came that the hoses had failed,
he called for Sweeney, his first mate.

"Prepare the *Aurnia* to sail. I want every crewman
that's not essential for launch at the warehouse. Tell
them to load everything they can onto the *Aurnia*.
Start with the most valuable, easily moveable things.
Tell them to hurry. We haven't got much time."

He yelled for his cabin boy Billy and made his way to
the office with the fourteen-year-old tagging after him.
"Tetch, load all our records onto the *Aurnia*. Don't forget the cash box. I hope to hell we have a pile of cash on
hand. Who knows whether the banks will burn or not.
Then get out in the street and recruit any men you can
find to help us load the warehouse stock onto our girl.
Pay them whatever you have to."

"Yes, sir." Tetch was already busy grabbing ledgers
as Con spun around and almost ran into the boy.

"Billy, come with me." Con paused a minute on the
pier outside the office to gaze up into the city. His face
was set. People were pouring down to the waterfront.
It wouldn't be long before the smoke and the sheer vol-
ume of people would make the streets impassable.

Fayth was up there somewhere. Alone? Without help? He mindlessly punched one fisted hand into the other. How was a lone woman going to save herself? Or anything of value from her shop?

"Billy, I want you to find me a horse and wagon."

The boy turned to him with eyes wide with fear and confusion. "What do you need a horse for?"

"I've got an errand in the city."

"We're going into the city?" The look on Billy's face said he thought Con was crazy, but the boy was smart enough not to voice his opinion. "There's no way I'm going to be able to find a horse and cart that's free, Captain. Looks to me like every one in the city's being used. Half of 'em at least are heading toward us."

Con surveyed the sight in front of him. The boy was right, but he wasn't deterred. He couldn't leave Fayth alone to fate in the hell fury of flames terrorizing the city.

"We're going to get us a horse and cart if we have to steal them. Come on." Con turned on his heel in time to see Tetch headed up the pier with the cash box under his arm. Con felt in his pockets. He hoped he had enough cash to get what he wanted.

"Tetch!" he yelled. "Tell Sweeney to sail if the pier's threatened, whether I'm back or not. Captain's orders."

Fayth soaked an old blanket, and struggled to hang it. Wet, it was heavy and awkward to handle. Frustrated, she tossed it down and tried hanging out a dry one, pouring water over it with a pitcher, hoping that it would wick down.

A volley of gunfire sounded. She screamed and pulled back from the window, certain the crowd of desperate people had gone mad and violence had erupted.

Someone yelled from the street that the ammunition store had gone up. It was just possible to hear him over the continuing gunfire. Fayth dropped the blanket she held. It was no use. She didn't care about the building.

She gathered her most treasured possessions together, threw some of her clothes in a suitcase, and carted them downstairs, dragging an empty suitcase with her to the sewing room. Her fingers trembled as she began undressing the dress forms that held her precious half-finished gowns, throwing them into the suitcase as she went.

Con bribed the owner of an empty cart with all the cash he had in his pocket. "I'll bring her back to the wharf. I promise."

"Don't bother. Give it to the next guy who needs it. I stole it myself." The man jammed the money into his jeans and disappeared into the crowd.

Billy scrambled up into the passenger seat next to Con as he clucked to the horse. "I hope you're not planning on hauling much, Captain. If you are, you wasted your money. This old nag hardly looks like she can pull us."

"She'll do. See how calm she is in all this commotion? She'll keep her head and get us through, that's the main thing." Con slapped the reins. They pulled out into the thickening throng, headed for the smoke and flames up the hill.

Bedlam reigned in the dust-covered streets outside as merchants dragged their goods into the middle of the uneven madness. The fire burned less than a block away. The smoke sat in the air thick and heavy. It was as if night had fallen. Those lucky enough to own carts and horses were loading their goods to carry them up the steep grade to the top of the hill over Seattle, out of danger.

Fayth looked wildly around her shop. She scooped Olive up and put her in her basket, setting it carefully by the door. "Stay," she commanded. "I've got to save our machine. I'll be right back."

She flung open the doors that blocked off the sewing room and the doors from the shop to the street to clear her path. In a flash of inspiration she spied a bucket of water she'd drawn, grabbed it and doused all the fabric and partially finished garments she could reach, then ran to her machine.

It had taken two strong men to move it in. She couldn't lift it alone. She tugged at it with all her might. The machine didn't budge.

Oh, to be a big, well-muscled man!

She ran around to the back of it and braced her shoulder against it, trying to use the strength of her legs to move the thing. The machine slid bare inches across the floor.

"The block's on fire, Captain! We'll never make it before it all goes up! She'd be crazy not to have left already," Billy said.

"We'll find that out soon enough. We aren't turning back 'til we're sure."

The horse came to a stop, unable to find its way around the debris in the street through the dense smoke. Con handed the reins to Billy and jumped down. "I'm going to guide her, you drive."

The shop was filling with smoke. Fayth's eyes and throat stung. Her lungs filled with the biting air. She couldn't stop coughing. The heat of the advancing fire heralded the flames' arrival. Perspiration trickled down her back and beaded on her forehead. The heat of the June day offered no relief. She looked up and out the door to see flames engulf the buildings across the street. She pushed until the backs of her legs ached with exertion. She tried another position and pushed again, head down in determination. The roar of the flames across the street was like the incessant battle cry of a great hoary beast. She shuddered. Wylie and Willis came scrambling down off the roof yelling.

"Get out, Miss Sheridan! Save yourself. The roof's caught fire!"

Fayth knew she had only minutes before the entire building would be consumed. She'd heard that fear gave people unnatural strength, but no such energy came to her, only wild panic.

Raging desperation overtook her. If she made it to the street where would she go? Would the machine stand up to the blast furnace fury of the fire?

The roof cackled overhead as the second story was overtaken. She was going to die in the licentious, laughing fire. She gave one final vehement push with quivering forearms. Suddenly the machine moved across the uneven floor and slid toward the doorway.

She looked up through the smoke to see the silhouette of a man at the other end of her machine. She'd neither seen, nor heard him approach, but she thanked God for him now. She ducked her head down and resumed pushing, praying he wouldn't desert her before they reached the street. At the boardwalk the machine came to an abrupt halt as the man stopped.

"Please! It must go to the middle of the street!" She hardly recognized her own high-pitched, hoarse, pleading voice. Sparking embers fell around her, lighting on her skirt, burning tiny holes. She swatted at them as if they were bloodthirsty mosquitoes. She heard the roar of the fire overhead and glanced up to see flames dance across the roof over her apartment. Across the street a building imploded and collapsed, devastated by flame. "Please!"

"But, darling, I have a cart." The voice was calm, strong, and unequivocally unafraid.

"Captain O'Neill!" Fayth wondered if he heard the rapture in her voice.

He spoke the truth. The thick smoke made it nearly impossible to see more than a few feet away, but she saw the outline of a cart, and a horse whose reins were held by a tall, slight figure, perhaps a boy.

The Captain shouted to the boy who immediately jumped down and helped load the machine. She remembered Olive and the things she'd brought from upstairs—the picture of Mother and Father, the photo of Drew, her jewelry and clothes. She turned on her heel and headed back for them. But the Captain was quick. He grabbed her arm before she could enter the building again.

"You can't go back in there!"

"Olive's in the basket just inside the door, please!"

She caught the Captain's arm as he stepped back toward the doorway. "And my pictures! Please, they're all I have left to remember my family."

"Where?"

"The box next to the window by the door."

"What else?" He shouted over the thundering rage of fire that consumed the block.

"The suitcases next to it."

She released him. He lunged into the doorway, stepping out seconds later with Olive. He gave her the cat, then handed Fayth to the boy with instructions to help her into the wagon, and make sure she stayed put. Then he disappeared into the black, smoke-laden recess of her shop. Time ticked by audibly as they waited for the Captain's return. Fayth heard every hammer of her heart, grew more nervous with each beat, fearing that she had sent a man to his death for a few trinkets. She stroked Olive mindlessly.

Suddenly he reappeared through the dense smoke carrying several bolts of cloth; her photo box was tucked under one arm, her suitcases under the other. The boy wasted no time helping him load the bolts of fabric. With surprising gentleness, he set the photo box in her lap and the suitcases at her feet. Before he could mount the wagon, the second-story window exploded above them, showering them with tiny shards of glass and glowing embers. The Captain shoved her down, batting at her and patting her down. She struggled without understanding.

"Stop struggling, you're on fire." His voice was commanding, sure and authoritative. She obeyed without thinking. He turned, took a few steps to the first-floor window and pulled the wet blanket from it, smothering the fire before she could be certain what part of her had been burning. The heat from the summer day and the fire around them was so intense that every inch of her skin stung. In the panic, she let go of Olive who scrambled to the edge of the wagon. The Captain unwrapped her in time for her to see the boy lunge for the cat.

"No! Don't touch her!" She screamed too late.

Olive, already terrified by the fire, and always skittish where men were concerned, bolted over the wagon edge and disappeared into the smoky street.

"Olive!" Fayth tried to scramble out of the wagon after the cat. The Captain's hard grip restrained her.

"We couldn't possibly find her in this melee. We can't risk our lives going after her. Get back in the wagon."

She complied, too stunned by Olive's defection to fight him. The Captain covered her and the boy with the wet blanket, swung up into the wagon and clucked at the horse.

The wagon shuddered, shook, and swayed as it careened around corners, people, and obstructions. When Fayth got up the nerve to peek out, she could barely make out the buildings that lined the street. The smoke was a fog so dense the only images bright enough to penetrate were the leaping, twisting contortion of flames on either side of them.

The Captain drove the horse on, his profile hard and fearless silhouetted against the glare of flames. She couldn't tear her gaze away from him. Only in the steely set of his face was there any comfort. He stood between her and the terror that surrounded them.

Explosions shook the streets from every side as firefighters demolished buildings, trying to create an ever southward-moving fire line. Volleys of shots rang out as another ammunition store caught fire.

In the heat of the lashing fire, Fayth was cold to the core. Her teeth chattered, her hands trembled even as she gripped the wagon side. The cart tipped like a sailboat yawing in a stiff breeze as they ran over an unknown obstruction. Fayth screamed as the boy fell into her. They were in hell. Doomed to crash and be sent flying, broken and beaten, into the streets to be consumed by the unholy wrath of the raging inferno.

The wagon righted. They jounced through the thick smoke over the uneven streets of Seattle.

The boy smiled at her fear and reassured her, "They don't call the Captain *the Con* for nothing. He's found his way through fog and storms worse than this."

She didn't understand his cryptic message, but his words brought her back to her senses. She recognized the intersection they were crossing. They had just turned left on Yesler from Commercial.

She lifted the blanket and tugged on the Captain's sleeve. When he looked at her, his hazel eyes burned like the fire they reflected. "We're going the wrong way!" she shouted, pointing at the same time. "We're heading west. We must go east, up hill behind us."

The boy pulled her back down before the Captain could speak, looking at her as if she were crazy. His expression told her that no one questioned the Captain. "We aren't going up the hill. Yesler's a forty percent grade. No one's going to make it up that hill with a loaded cart. And we sure aren't going to make it with the old nag we got."

Panic blocked her reasoning; she didn't understand. "Then where are we going? We'll be burned up."

The boy must have thought her stupid. It took a second for him to answer. "To the wharf, of course. If we can make it. Washington was almost blocked when we came through. Looks like the Captain is going around the block, hoping to avoid the crowd. He gave orders to hold the ship for us, but not if the wharf caught fire."

Oh God Almighty, she thought. It was less a prayer than a desperate appeal. Please don't let us die. Please let the wharf be intact. In her next thought, she realized the Captain had come purposefully for her. Astounding. She pulled back beneath the blanket, suddenly trusting him to deliver her to safety. *Why did he come for me?*

Sometime later, Fayth could not decide whether an eternity had passed, or only minutes, the Captain reined to an abrupt stop at the edge of the pier. They were out of the height of the fury, but the roar of the encroaching flames pressed hard at their backs. He had jumped down and begun shouting orders before she realized they'd completed their journey. The boy scrambled out.

Fayth rose slowly from beneath the blanket to view the scene in front of her. The wave of humanity that coursed over the wood plank wharves was astonishing. As she looked back through the smoky air, less dense at the wharf's edge, to the path they had traveled, she realized the miracle of their safe arrival.

The streets were crammed with carts and people barely moving in the stifling traffic. All fled to the Sound, hoping to move their goods by ship into the safety of Elliott Bay. It was not lost on Fayth, or anyone else from the comments she overheard, the irony of the city burning for lack of water when it rested on such a superb, sparkling blue bay. Man's shortcomings had doomed them.

Hands reached up over the wagon sides, removing her belongings, pulling at the cart. People fought to overtake it. She looked around in desperation, ready to swat at the greedy, clawing people that swarmed. The Captain held out his arms to her from the ground.

"Miss Sheridan, my ship's waiting." His voice was as calm and unflappable as it was the day she proposed to him in the Chinese cafe.

"My things—"

"My men." He nodded toward the two toughs who worked at removing her machine. "They've got orders to load them on the *Aurnia*. Others need the wagon."

"I'm sorry. I didn't realize . . ." She clutched her photo box to her chest.

The Captain reached up and swung her by the waist to the ground. Her knees buckled as her feet touched down. He swung her into his arms—strong, broad, reassuring arms—and carried her up the ramp.

Over his shoulder, she watched the cart they'd left behind. A pair of hands grabbed for the horse's reins. As soon as the two sailors finished unloading her goods, a new driver mounted and drove it slowly into the crowd, back into the smoke and the burning city behind them.

"Your horse!"

The Captain smiled. "I rented it." He must have recognized her alarmed expression because he added, "Don't worry. They'll take care of it. It'll get back to its owner somehow."

She was surprised that he should be so trusting. She had no such regard for people.

Moments later, Fayth stood on the deck of the *Aurnia* next to her pitiful pile of belongings, a solitary, still figure amid the fury. Sailors scrambled around her securing loads. On the docks below a bucket brigade soaked the pier, trying to save it. She watched the city burn, watched the remains of her life drift away, ashes on the wind. Where would she go now?

Con kept his ship at dock, trying desperately to save the stores of his warehouse. The *Aurnia* was a converted schooner still rigged with sails, a coastal vessel with a flat, open deck used mainly for hauling lumber south to California. Below was a large cargo hold he used for transporting mail and miscellaneous cargo people paid him to ship.

Con had the single screw steam engine installed furthest aft shortly after he bought her. She had no bridge, only one long poop and a forecastle above deck. The wheelhouse and captain's quarters were aft, the crew's fore. In Con's eyes she was a beauty. By day's end, she might be all he had left.

The *Aurnia's* deck was littered with indiscriminately placed goods. Fayth stood amid the mess, watching the crowd disperse and head southward with the advancing fire at their backs. Others grappled with the Captain's men as they fought to keep a path to the ship clear, and prevent stowaways. The boy from the cart appeared from the scurrying mass and made for her side.

"Name's Billy. The Captain sent me to watch out for you." He bounced on the balls of his feet and rocked back and forth as if agitated at being banished from the action. She was eager to set him free and be left alone.

"That's very kind, but I'd like to be by myself."

"Sorry. Can't leave you. Not until Captain Con tells me I can."

Fayth brushed a stream of dampness from her cheeks with the back of her hand. Her eyes stung, but didn't account for all the tears that filled them. She didn't think Billy believed it did either. He looked away from her self-consciously.

"Where is the Captain?"

"At the warehouse. Sent me on ahead. We're going to put out. They can't save the wharf."

He needlessly gave voice to the obvious. The block of buildings lining the wharf was on fire. The vicious flames advanced west and south, stopped only by the gentle, lapping waves of the Sound. The wooden piers, though poised above the water, were not immune. Sailors and dockworkers continued the bucket brigade to douse the piers and warehouses at water's edge. Others beat out embers that lit on the docks. But the fire had more energy than any number of men. The breeze was still stiff. It arced flames from across the street to warehouse roofs. The dragon breath heat drove the men back, forcing them to the safety of the water. Anyone could see it was a losing battle.

Billy barely finished speaking when the Captain boarded the ship. "Load anyone onboard who wants to sail," she heard him shout. He followed with a string of commands in sailing jargon she didn't understand, but the confidence in his tone was enough. For the first time in hours some of her apprehension slipped away.

"Billy! To your post. We're putting out—now!"

Released from the tedium of watching her, Billy's movements became smooth. Moments later the anchor was raised. As they pulled out into Elliott Bay, the Captain's pier burst into flame.

CHAPTER FIVE

They anchored in Elliott Bay to the north and west of the wharves, far from the reach of the angry flames. The Captain emerged from the wheelhouse onto the main deck and walked to where Fayth huddled against her belongings. She sat with her arms clasped around gathered knees, eyes filled with tears. The shop, her security, was gone. Olive was gone. She shuddered, couldn't force herself to imagine what fate Olive had met. Every direction her thoughts turned ended in tragedy. The smell of smoke enveloped her, clung to her clothes, tinged the very air. Seattle smoldered in the distance. When would the angry flames be appeased? How much destruction would be enough?

Out on the water, the destructive breeze felt refreshing and cool as it kissed the deck and played with the sails overhead. To the west, the Olympic Mountains stood before the setting sun.

"I told Billy to look after you." The Captain stood over her with a hand outstretched.

Instinctively, she reached for it. He pulled her to her feet. With reluctance, she released the lifeline of his grip, wiped her eyes with the back of her hand and looked helplessly at him. His gaze was elsewhere, focused on the shorefront. He moved to the railing. She followed him, matching his line of sight.

The wharves were fully engulfed in flame now. His warehouse a memory. His pier a fiery bridge collapsing into the water. His stoic expression never wavered, piercing her heart. She rested her hand on his arm, feeling his pain, knowing his loss.

"Gone." His tone was flat. He turned to her. "Material things, unlike people, are repairable, replaceable."

"You believe that?" The breeze blew a scorched lock of hair across Fayth's face. She made no move to brush it away.

The Captain reached over and carefully tucked it back into place.

"Yes, of course." But his tone held little conviction.

Fayth realized he was stung by his losses. He had to be. Just as she was.

"Don't you?" he asked.

"Material things are all I have left. Had left." She paused, thinking of everything the fire had destroyed before her eyes. None of them important simply as things, but they held her past, reminded her of who she was, of people she loved.

She thought of her parent's four-poster cherrywood bed. She had moved it from Baltimore at great expense, leaving her own much smaller bed behind, because her parents' was where she'd been born. She loved sleeping in it, remembering cuddling with her parents as a small girl. Things, at this moment, did seem important.

"Things connect us to who we are," she said aloud. "They represent the sum of what we've worked for. They stand as trophies to our successes. It's all right to be sorry they're gone, to mourn them." Her words seemed inadequate, the comfort she tried to offer so very meager, but she had never been more sincere. She was desperate to relieve his suffering, if only minutely. Somehow, she felt it would help ease hers. A bond was forming between them, a bond she could not stop. And it frightened her. She owed this man who'd refused her, her life.

Mercifully, he turned back to stare out across the water to the pier. "You have no people?" he asked, at last.

"I am an only child. My parents were killed in a carriage accident last year."

He did not offer a hollow condolence, but listened with an intense and compassionate expression.

"I let our business flounder. I let Drew . . ."

She clutched the deck rail. "It doesn't matter. They died and I had to sell the business. Everything good died with them. I couldn't stand the wagging tongues in Baltimore anymore, so I came to Seattle." She stopped abruptly. She'd said too much.

He turned to look at her, studying her intently. She saw the question in his eyes, but to her relief he didn't probe about the gossip that had driven her from her hometown.

"There's nothing stopping you from loving, from making someone else matter in your life." He spoke softly, seductively, with a passion she hadn't expected. As if it seemed important to him that she did find someone else.

Was he talking about himself? Could he mean . . .

She swallowed hard, confused by his tone and not wanting to hope, not when she felt so desolate again. "Isn't there? A dead heart doesn't count?"

At the look he gave her, she felt a stirring of some wonderful, frightening, ethereal emotion. She spoke quickly to suppress it. "And now look at Seattle; she's dead, too."

"Don't worry about Seattle. She won't die. People here don't give up. Like you, Miss Sheridan, they'll find the courage to survive tragedy. Seattle will rise from the ashes like the phoenix, more beautiful than before."

Yes, Fayth had survived one tragedy, but at what cost? How had he missed seeing her for the fake she was? She was not surviving. She merely existed and she wondered whether she had the strength to continue now. Not wanting him to see her expression, she turned from him to look out over the waters.

He muttered something.

"Your shoulder's burned! I should have seen to it earlier." He yelled for Billy. "Fetch the medical supplies and meet me in my quarters."

Despite her protests, the Captain led Fayth aft through the wheelhouse to the shipmaster's cabin. She barely had time to take in the surprising opulence—the deep wood paneling, marble fireplace, and fine quality furnishings—when Billy burst in with medical supplies in hand.

The Captain took them from him. "Fetch Miss Sheridan's bags and leave them by the door."

As Billy disappeared to obey the order, the Captain led Fayth by the arm to a wooden dining chair next to a fine, matching table. "Sit." He guided her onto the chair and set his kit on the table, pulled up his own chair behind hers, and sat facing her back. She heard him open the kit. "Pull your dress down, if you will."

"Captain O'Neill, I thought that you had more finesse! A gentleman never tells a woman to drop her dress."

She had been around Coral too much lately. A year ago, she would never have said such a thing. A decent woman should never intimate anything unseemly, let alone say it directly.

The Captain didn't seem offended. In fact, he laughed. "A gentleman probably doesn't cut it off, either, but that may be the ultimate solution. You'll have to forgive me my roughness. I'm not used to treating a lady."

"Then we should find a woman to look at my shoulder. You're much too busy to bother about me—"

"You're the only woman onboard."

The thought stopped her cold. She hadn't noticed. She'd been too distraught to think of others and pay attention to the mix of people who were part of the chaos on deck. She was the only woman he'd rescued? Given his refusal of her marriage proposal, she was dumfounded. Why her?

"Your sailors couldn't think of any other damsels to play hero to?" She turned to look back over her shoulder at him, catching him off guard and getting a fleeting glimpse of raw hunger so powerful a surge of heat encompassed her. As if she weren't burning already.

"Apparently not." His tone was dry. "Will you settle for a man with some knowledge of medicine?"

"Do I have any choice?" Shaken, she turned around. "You'll have to unbutton me."

Maybe it was only her imagination, but he seemed to fumble at the buttons. Was the calm, unflappable Captain actually nervous? Was he fighting the pull of attraction, too? She looked straight ahead, trying not to smile at the thought, trying to ignore the fact that a handsome man was disrobing her, touching her neck, exposing her back—

"It's no use, Miss Sheridan—

"Fayth."

"Fayth." He rested his hand at the base of her neck where it burned her skin nearly as much as the embers had. He whispered into her ear, "As I feared, I'm going to have to cut it away. The fabric's scorched and stuck to your skin. The dress is a loss."

She glanced down at her shoulder and winced at the sight of her blistered skin. He was right—it would have to be cut off. "What isn't?" She looked straight ahead again and braced herself. "Cut away, Captain."

"Let me get the scissors from my desk."

He removed his hand and walked across the room to the desk. She felt the absence of his touch immediately, and the lack of his body heat behind her. After the brutal temperature of the fire, she should have relished any form of coolness. So why did she will him to come back and rest his hand where it had been? Imagine him unpinning her hair and nibbling her neck?

What had gotten into her? Those were dangerous thoughts. The same treacherous feelings had led to her dropping her guard and letting Drew go too far with her. Far too far.

The Captain returned with a washcloth, scissors, and a basin of water. She didn't look at him. She couldn't for fear of giving herself away and encouraging him. Or making a fool of herself again. He tugged at the shoulder of her dress. She winced.

"I'm sorry. I didn't mean to hurt you. I'm going to have to soak it loose."

She turned her head to the side and watched as he dipped the cloth in the basin. "Captain, your hands!" Was there no end to her selfishness? Where were her womanly instincts? Why hadn't she noticed he was hurt, too?

The fading sunlight glinted off minute shards of glass buried in the skin of his square, masculine, but scraped and bruised hands. Even the hair on the back of them was scorched. She turned sideways in her chair and grabbed his wet fingers in hers. "You must take care of these."

Their eyes met and her breath caught. He was looking at her exactly as a man in love looks at a woman. But that made no sense. None at all.

He gently pulled his hand free and looked away. "Your shoulder first."

"Certainly not. I must insist that I take care of *you* first."

He shook his head and laughed. "Fayth, you don't want to be dangling half undressed before a sailor a minute longer than you must. We only have so much willpower."

Her eyes went wide. She stared at him. He was joking, teasing her. Surely he must be.

She couldn't help herself; she smiled back at him and laughed at her own foolishness. "Good point. Think of the scandal if word of my wanton behavior should get out. My cousin might make you marry me. And we wouldn't want that."

Her tone was light and airy. She was teasing him; of course she was. Jibing at him just a little. Or was she flirting with him? She couldn't be certain. All she knew for sure was that the air in the cabin suddenly felt quite close.

He cleared his throat. "No, certainly not." He didn't sound completely convincing.

Bewildered, she turned around and faced straight ahead again just as a loud thump announced that Billy had dropped off her bags. The Captain applied the cloth to her blistered skin with a startlingly gentle pressure. His touch was soothing and tender as he soaked the fabric free from her blistered shoulder, then carefully covered the burn with ointment and bandaged it. His mere attentions healed. Fayth's worries and fears slipped away. When he was finished, he got up and retrieved her bags from where Billy had unceremoniously dumped them.

"You must have a blouse in one of these?" he said.

"That one." She pointed to the bag she wanted.

He brought it to her. She opened it and got out a clean shirtwaist.

He took it from her and slid it gently around her shoulders. "There. Now you're decent."

"Good. Now I can take care of you." She turned her chair around to face his and held her hand out, indicating he should sit.

He smiled and took his seat. They sat disturbingly close, skirt to pant leg, knee to knee.

She took his hand, placed it between hers, and grabbed a pair of tweezers from his medical kit. His hand was rough and calloused. He obviously was a captain who pitched in and did the dirty work of physical labor when necessary. But it was also well groomed, or had been before the fire had gotten hold of it. And it was so nice and reassuring to hold.

She smiled up at him and got to work, head bent over his hand, deftly pulling out every shard she could find, squinting to make sure she didn't miss any. She worked in silence, as he had, marveling at the strong character of his hands. She felt him watching her as she bent over his hand.

"You're very serious when you work," he said.

"This is serious business. A man needs his hands in working order." She looked up into his eyes. "I'm just glad I haven't had to use a needle to dig one out yet. Although, I am exceptionally good with one." She stopped short.

He was staring at her as if she were the most beautiful thing he'd ever seen. Yes, she recognized a look of admiration when she saw one. And this one confused her. "I'm not hurting you, am I?"

"Definitely not. Not at all." He sounded almost as if he were enjoying her attentions.

She nodded and dropped her gaze, getting back to work though her pulse raced. Finally, she didn't see any more glass. She ran her hand lightly over his, feeling for remaining shards of glass. Satisfied, she stared at his baby finger. It was bent, the knuckle permanently swollen. "This?"

"Dislocated it years ago rigging a ship. Fixed it myself."

"And I trusted my shoulder to you, with this amazing medical skill?"

He smiled and winked.

She shook her head, dipped a cloth into the basin and wrung it out, intending to bathe his hand. But when she looked up, it was his face that caught her attention.

It was streaked with soot and perspiration, his beard singed in places. She was overwhelmed with the gentlest emotion she'd felt in over a year. Without thinking she reached up to wipe it with the cool cloth. "Look at you."

"Look at us," he said and reached for her wrist. Their eyes met and held. She pressed the cloth to his cheek. He encircled her wrist with his grip.

Her face must have been streaked, her hair disheveled. How did she look to him? Did he see by the rapid heaving of her chest that his touch aroused? Her world was reflected in his eyes. She was more frightened than she'd ever been.

He cupped her cheek and leaned toward her. She tilted her face toward his. He smelled of smoke and heat and maleness. She parted her lips.

"Captain." The male voice startled them both.

She sat back, feeling herself blush, and probably looking completely guilty even though absolutely nothing had happened.

The Captain swung around. "Sweeney?"

"Sorry to interrupt, sir. We've got trouble below. With the engine."

The Captain glanced at Fayth with a look of apology, and back at Sweeney. "I'll be right there."

Sweeney departed. The Captain pushed his chair back. The moment was lost.

"You'll be wanting to get cleaned up. Billy dropped your bags by the door. The sleeping quarters are back down that hall. The head's on the way." He pointed. "Shall I move your bags back there for you?"

"No, thank you. The what?"

He laughed. "The head, the bathroom. It has a big tub. Just keep your shoulder dry."

"A bath sounds heavenly."

"I'll have Cook bring you something to eat and leave it on the table for you. Then you should get some rest. Make yourself at home in my quarters. Sleep as long as you like."

She wasn't sure how he meant for the arrangements to work, but she couldn't stay alone with him. "I can't stay here. These are your quarters. Where will you stay?"

He smiled as if he took her meaning. "Across the deck with the crew. They'll be happy to have me." She recognized the tease in his voice. "And if they're not, they'll fake it."

"But you can't. You must stay here." Her words came out wrong. "I mean—"

"I'm sorry, Fayth, but I can't let *you* sleep with the crew. They don't always restrain themselves around the ladies." He winked and turned toward the door.

She took a long, cool soak in the claw-foot tub. Had she really almost kissed the Captain? Electric lights illuminated the small bathroom with a warm yellow glow as the sunlight faded. Sitting naked in the Captain's tub, she felt an odd, titillating intimacy with him. Worse yet, she let herself enjoy it. What did she have to lose now?

She stepped out of the tub onto a soft mat and turned to the sink to examine herself critically in the mirror. She looked better cleaned up, but for the first time in ages she wished she were prettier. She wound her damp hair up, pinned it back, and studied her reflection. Too severe. She hooked a finger through the hair on either side of her head, pulling a few tendrils loose to soften the look. The loss of austerity made an astounding difference. She looked more like the Fayth she remembered. A year was up. Maybe she should come out of mourning now, both for her parents and Drew.

Her gaze was caught by a shaving mug perched at sink's edge and the leather strapped razor that hung on a peg above it. It never occurred to her that bearded men still shaved parts of their face and neck. There was so much she didn't know about men. What she did, she had learned from Drew, and she was beginning to feel her information was desperately inadequate.

She ran her finger around the rim of the mug, picking up stray beard hairs. They were coarse and wiry and as thick as three or four of her hairs put together, entirely masculine. Mysterious. Enticing. She shuddered and washed the hairs down the sink. She must suppress such thoughts.

Later, relaxed from her bath, Fayth studied the shipmaster's quarters as she ate. The cabin was paneled with rich mahogany. Bookcases lined one wall, filled with leather-bound volumes of classic works and books on sailing, shipping, and navigation. A heavily gilded gold mirror hung above the fireplace. The ceiling was inlaid with panels lined with three different moldings. But the most beautiful feature of the room was the rounded wall corners, each hand carved, all similar but unique.

The cabin was appointed with finely made wood furniture. The main room held an upholstered chair, the table and chairs where she sat, and a roll-top desk, now closed. The Captain was meticulously neat. Not one item was out of place. The same with his life, she presumed, shaking her head in irony. She could not have picked a person less in need of a business marriage to clutter his life. She finished her meal and walked back to the bedroom.

The Captain's bed nearly filled the small room at the rear of his quarters. It was surrounded by built-in cupboards of the same rich mahogany as the main room. The Captain's sense of elegance and quality evidently wasn't only for show. His private room was every bit as beautiful as the main one. She undressed and climbed into his bed.

Fayth snuggled down into the deep featherbed and inhaled deeply. The Captain's sheets smelled of him, tinged with a hint of cologne. She liked it. She liked him. Lulled by the pleasant sensation of security and the gentle rocking of the ship in the waters of the Sound, she fell asleep.

She was surrounded by black water, barely afloat. Her scorched skirt bobbed up around her waist. As she watched, it became saturated. Slowly, its folds sank before her eyes. The heavy weight of the water-laden cloth pulled her down. She screamed, but the darkness swallowed all sound. Her arms windmilled the air furi-

ously, searching for a stronghold, anything solid to hang on to. She couldn't see. There was no light, only all-engulfing dark water. She was being sucked under—

Fayth woke with a start, her heart hammering in her ears. She sat up, trying to calm herself by rocking gently like a child. The ship was still. The wind had ceased and the waters calmed. Through the open window, she heard only the gentle lapping of water against the *Aurnia's* hull.

Another dream, another nightmare. They had been common this past year, but never as terrifying as this one. She shuddered as she fought to release her terror and return to reality. The nightmare left her feeling impotent, powerless. She had to take control, get rid of that dress.

She slipped out of bed and pulled a plain shift from her bag. She dressed quickly, burst out of the bedroom, and scooped up the ragged remains of the dress still slumped in the hall by the bathroom door. She stared at the drab mourning garment for a moment. Blast! Her parents' death had nearly defeated her, and now this. She'd survived one tragedy. She would survive this one. No weakness. This time she would take control of her destiny.

An idea formed as she held the dress out in front of her. She couldn't hide behind grief. The only way to succeed was to meet this challenge directly, to be the opposite of the drab woman she had hidden behind this past year. She smiled. To be as colorful as Lou Gramm, only on the right side of virtue. She balled the dress up and headed for the deck.

The deck was quiet and deserted. The sailors had the good sense to rest while they could. Serene moonlight lit the water. With her anchor dropped, the *Aurnia* bobbed like a gently rocking cradle. Fayth walked to the rail and threw the dress triumphantly into the lapping waters below.

"Death to the old. Life to the new." It was a victorious, audible whisper.

She climbed up on the railing to see over the edge and face the substance of the nightmare. Her dress floated eerily for a moment, billowing out and riding the waves in the dark, bottomless water. She watched until it sank into the blackness.

"To new life," she said to herself.

"Not planning to jump?" The Captain stepped from the shadows. Strong arms encircled her before she could lose her footing and fall back to the deck on her own. Her heart hammered at the touch, less from the surprise than from the firm masculine presence.

"Drowning the old." Her voice was giddy.

The Captain looked confused, and worried.

"Getting rid of garbage." Her explanation didn't seem to satisfy him. He didn't release her. She laughed when she realized what he must have been thinking. "Don't worry, Captain. I didn't mean me. I had no intention of tossing myself overboard. I'm a survivor, remember? Earlier, you told me so yourself. You don't doubt your own judgment, do you?"

She loosened his grip enough so she could spin around to face him. He kept his arms looped loosely around her waist. Did he still think she would jump?

"You threw something over?"

"The dress I wore today. What's the use of saving it? It's full of ember holes, totally ruined. But if I had all my drab old clothes with me, I'd toss them all into the Sound. It's time."

He must have thought she was crazy. By now he had reason to think her insane.

"As it is, the fire's done me the favor of ridding me of them. It's time I became colorful again." Without further explanation, she looked toward shore where Seattle glowed in the darkness. "Seattle still burns."

"The fire's almost spent herself. She'll be nothing but embers by morning."

"You're so certain?"

"Fires have to burn out eventually."

"All fires, Captain O'Neill? You're not the romantic I thought you were." She turned to look up into his eyes. Every emotion she felt was at odds with what she should be feeling. Maybe it was shock. Maybe tomorrow the horrendous circumstances of the day would crash down with awful reality on her again, but for this moment she felt light, and free, and flirtatious. She smiled openly at him.

His grip tightened around her waist as he drew her to him. As his lips came down on hers, she was lost in a maelstrom of emotion. He tasted wild and wonderful, salty and sweet. She was un-corseted and consequently, unable to fasten the middle back buttons of her dress.

The warmth of his hand leaped through the gap the open buttons created, through the thin cotton of her chemise. She leaned into him, opened her mouth and for one beautiful moment, savored the sweetness.

Their tongues danced together, igniting desires long forgotten. She pressed herself against him, wanton and free before she let reason carry her back to reality. She wanted independence now, a purpose that he could only interfere with. His mouth on hers was too good, too wild, too wonderful to be trusted. Why did a handsome face always distract her? She couldn't let it this time. Any diversion, especially a man, could be disastrous. Cold, wet fear brought back her sense of propriety. Distrust. Denial. Fear of another betrayal. All careened through her. She pulled away abruptly.

He looked confused, hurt, surprised? She couldn't tell. Not wanting to know, to see, she dropped her gaze. He released her.

"Fayth—"

She shook her head to silence him. "Don't apologize, Captain." She turned and walked away from him. Took a few uncertain steps, paused, and turned back. He was staring silently out over the water. She wished she knew his thoughts. Was he regretting the kiss? She fervently hoped not. She didn't.

In that instant, she knew she would never forget that beautiful, romantic image of him—a tall, strong figure silhouetted against the smoldering city. A bulwark, salvation. "I haven't thanked you for rescuing me."

He turned to look at her.

"Thank you, Captain O'Neill. I needed a hero—more than you'll ever know. Goodnight." At that she spun around and ran back to the cabin.

Her heart pounded furiously as she slipped under the covers in the Captain's bed, holding her photograph of Drew, staring at it, trying to push away alluring thoughts of the Captain. Anger, hate. That's all she felt now when she stared at the handsome face smiling back at her.

Originally, she'd kept it because she couldn't throw it out. Drew had been too much a part of who she was. Now she used it like a talisman to ward off the feelings the Captain stirred. To remind herself that she was easily distracted by a handsome face, to remember what treachery felt like.

And now her own body was the traitor, reacting with treasonous passion toward the Captain. Suddenly she couldn't see the freckles, only the firm set of his jaw, and the sparkle of his hazel eyes. She was frightened beyond reason.

"Damn you, Drew! Damn you straight to hell!" She whispered into the dark night air, swearing aloud as only thoughts of Drew made her do.

She tossed Drew's picture onto the bed beside her, covered it with the sheet so she did not have to face his mocking, lying eyes. She wiped at the tears on her wet cheeks, fearing the sensations the Captain had awakened, knowing she had to distance herself from him. She had to get back to the city. As soon as they docked, she would forget the Captain and begin to rebuild.

It had been one long, nightmarish day. Exhausted, she fell back onto the pillow that smelled like the Captain. Tucked his sheets around her. Inhaled deeply. Pictured him on the deck. Just this night she would sleep in his bed, revel in the warm scent of him, draw strength from him. Tomorrow, she would leave.

Fayth woke to the sounds of loud male voices, confused. Instinctively, she reached for Olive. Where had she run off to? It took a minute in her foggy fight to wakefulness to remember where she was, and another to remember how she got there. Memories of the previous day cascaded over her. The fire. Olive disappearing into the smoke. The Captain rescuing her. Her neat, orderly existence was gone, swept away by a rush of flames. The night had provided a dark, surreal buffer between terror and ruin. How could she face life in the harsh reality of day?

Two men shouted to each other somewhere outside her cabin. Light filtered in through the curtained porthole. The Captain's clock read six-thirty. She breathed in the warm, manly scents that clung to Captain O'Neill's bed linens, and, for a moment, savored the pleasurable tremor they evoked. She pushed herself stiffly into a sitting position. Her shoulder throbbed in rebellion at the movement. A glance at it confirmed that the moist dressing needed changing. She remembered the Captain's gentle tending of her wound, the concern in his eyes, and his kiss on her lips. She closed her eyes and breathed deeply.

Regrettably, she must forget. Once, she had trusted a man to be her salvation. She would not repeat that mistake. Not with the stakes so high. When Drew had abandoned her, she still had the sum from the sale of her father's business to sustain her. This time she had nothing but the slimmest of cash reserves.

She needed to direct all her energy to survival. Somehow she had to rebuild. How could she accomplish this while distracted by a flirtation? Dared she even think of it as a courtship? Maybe what happened last night was only a mirage, a reaction to tragic circumstances. How else could she explain the Captain's sudden interest in her? Whether it was real or not, it could only complicate her life. Reason told her she must face this particular tragedy alone, but it could not prevent melancholy from sweeping over her.

She pushed the sheet down around her, wincing again at the pain in her shoulder before sliding out of bed to the open porthole. The first unpleasant task she would learn to do for herself was tend her injury.

She cocked her head toward the porthole. One of the voices drifting in belonged to the Captain. She could not see him from where she peeked through the curtain, but the way her heart fluttered at the voice confirmed his identity. Another vessel had pulled up alongside them. She could just make out the name, the *Eliza,* and a man, clearly the captain of the other vessel, leaning over the rail, yelling to Captain O'Neill.

"There are at least four wharves still intact and operational, Con," he yelled. "Schwabacher's, Almond and Phillip's, Manning's, and Gilmore's. You can put in at one of them or sail to Tacoma and have your goods shipped up by rail."

"Aye, we'll dock in Seattle. Appreciate the information, Bailey," the Captain said.

She let the curtain drop. They were going to port. Probably today. As much as she feared facing the destruction that awaited her on the shore, after the events of last night, she feared confinement with the Captain more. She fell gingerly back onto the bed. She had better get moving if she was going to be ready. It wouldn't take long to reach shore.

Half an hour later, the *Eliza* gave a fierce blast of her steam whistle as it pulled away, startling Fayth as she bent over her sewing machine on the main deck. There didn't seem to be any damage. Fayth was absorbed with thinking of a way to get it moved off the ship and back to shore. But where was she going to take it? Her inspection was interrupted by the Captain's approach.

"You're up and about early this morning, Miss Sheridan. I trust you had a pleasant night's rest? How is your shoulder?"

She had hoped to avoid speaking to him. "My shoulder is better, thank you."

His eyes traced it.

She remembered his gentle, caring touch. The way he leaned in to kiss her. Was her flustered state as evident as she thought it must be?

"And my night was as pleasant as could be expected, given the circumstances. Your quarters are very comfortable, Captain." Her tone was cooler, and shakier, than she intended. "We're going to dock in Seattle today?"

There was nothing intimate in his posture, expression, or tone. Not like last night, but the deck was filled with sailors this morning.

"Yes. The wharves to the north of the city are intact. We're carrying goods and food the city desperately needs now."

"It's still on fire." Fayth looked to the thick black smoke rising above the southern area of the city.

"Coal bunkers. It'll be days before they burn themselves out, but they're not a danger. They're contained."

Seattle looked ghostly and colorless and strangely at odds with the bright-blue summer day as her charred silhouette stretched skyward. Neither said a word as they both stared at the remains of the city. Con's sailors raised anchor. The steam engine roared to life.

"I'm almost afraid to face it. What do you think we'll find?"

"I wish I knew. And even more, I wish I could assure you that in some small way it would be pleasant," he said.

"Pleasant would be finding Olive. *Alive.*"

"Yes." It wasn't convincing. He cleared his throat. "The militia has been in charge of the city since just after the fire started. They'll be guarding the burned-out area against looters. Captain Bailey told me it'll be a while before they let anyone in, even those with legitimate need."

She stared at him openly now, not believing her ears. "But they have to let us in. Where else will we go?"

"You can stay on the *Aurnia* for as long as you need. Or, I can take you to Tacoma, somewhere safe, until the city's reopened. Looters and hellions of all kinds are already descending and the smoke hasn't even cleared. It isn't a safe place for a lady."

"It never has been, Captain."

He took her arm. "Promise me you'll stay, Miss Sheridan." His eyes pleaded with her.

How could she lie to him? "I—"

One of his men called to him, saving her the trouble.

When he returned his attention to Fayth, he was back in his role as captain. "I must assume command now. Billy has orders to attend to your needs."

"Thank you, Captain." She had absolutely no intention of staying. And Billy just might be her means of escaping.

CHAPTER SIX

The *Aurnia's* whistle sounded, announcing their arrival at the pier.

Docking, already? Fayth hastily signed the letter she'd been writing to the Captain and secured it to the table with a paperweight. Call her cowardly and she wouldn't deny it. A note wasn't the most personal way to thank him for the great service he'd done for her—she owed him everything—but it was surely the kindest way to let him down with the least embarrassment to either of them.

She flew around the cabin collecting her things and reached the deck just as the *Aurnia's* crew lowered the gangplank. Almost instantly, the deck swarmed with people coming to reclaim their rescued possessions and unload supplies. She picked her way through the throngs to her machine and set her suitcases down. She was still wondering how she was going to get her possessions off the ship when she spotted Billy.

"Billy!" She waved to get his attention. She had to shout his name three times, but at last he made his way reluctantly toward her. "I need to unload my machine."

He hesitated. "I don't know, miss."

"The Captain gave you orders to assist me, did he not? I need help moving my sewing machine ashore."

Billy eyed her warily. It was a fine thing when a ragamuffin like Billy didn't trust her.

"He didn't say anything about you leaving the ship."

The last thing she needed was Billy fighting her, too. She knew full well the boy didn't like her. She hoped at least he'd listen to reason. "He didn't say anything about me being a captive here, either." She put her hands on her hips and stared him down. "Are you going to help me, or disobey captain's orders?"

He stared at her with steely eyes and finally shrugged. "I'll help you get it off the ship and onto the dock, then my duty's done."

She gave him a curt nod. "Fair enough."

They pushed the machine down the gangplank. By the time they got it onto the dock, Fayth had broken into a sweat, from anxiety as much as exertion. Did she even still have a shop to go home to? And how was she going to get there if she did? She didn't possess the Captain's ability to acquire carts out of nowhere.

As Billy made a trip back to the ship for the rest of her belongings, she surveyed the melee around her. The Captain had been right. Militiamen were everywhere she looked, even though the fire had not reached this far north.

One saw her looking lost and approached her. "May I help you, ma'am?"

"I need transportation to take my sewing machine and bags back to my shop."

"I can help you secure a cart, ma'am. But if you're looking to get back into the area the fire destroyed, you'll be disappointed. The area is closed, by order of the mayor."

Billy appeared at her elbow and unceremoniously dropped her bags at her feet.

The officer flagged down a fellow militiaman who was mounted on a sturdy wagon. "Mr. Boggs will take you wherever you want to go, outside of the fire area. Just give him directions."

Billy, who'd been standing by impatiently, tossed her things into the wagon, not waiting to help load her machine before he ran off toward the ship.

The militiaman gave Fayth a hand up into the wagon. "Where to, ma'am?"

She gave him directions to her cousins' home. What else could she do?

Con had been too busy taking charge of unloading the ship to notice Fayth had left the *Aurnia* until too late. He first spotted the empty deck space where her machine had been and was about to call out to Billy when a blonde woman in the sea of men on the docks below caught his eye. He shielded his eyes with his hand. Sure enough, Fayth was being helped into a wagon by a uniformed member of the militia as another loaded her sewing machine. Moments later the militia-man clucked to the horse and they disappeared into the throng.

Con cursed under his breath as he strode back to his quarters. Her letter on the table caught his attention. He picked it up and studied the perfectly formed, flow-ing feminine hand.

Dear Captain O'Neill,

There aren't words of gratitude enough to thank you for rescuing me yesterday. Your hospitality and generosity are overwhelming. I thank you for your kind offer of transporting me to Tacoma, but I believe it is best for me to return to Seattle. I cannot continue to impose on your gracious nature.

With sincere gratitude,

Fayth Sheridan

Cold, formal, impersonal. He carefully folded the letter and slipped it into his desk drawer. He never should have kissed her. It had been damn reckless of him. Because of his loss of control, Fayth was alone out there in the ravaged city. A city full of vagabonds and looters. Abounding with shysters ready to take ad-vantage of a woman's vulnerability.

He strode back to the bedroom. A lump in the hasti-ly made bed caught his attention. He threw back the covers to find an overturned picture frame. He reached for it and turned the gilded frame over slowly. A hand-some, dark-haired man smiled back at him. His eyes narrowed as he stared at it, then looked out the port-hole into the startlingly blue sky.

He rose and strode back to the main room where he tossed the frame onto the desk with what he hoped was enough rancor to crack the glass. Whoever the man was, he obviously meant a great deal to Fayth. Why else would she take the man's picture to bed?

The bastard!

God alone knew how much more desperate Fayth would be to find a husband now. She claimed she'd given up the notion, but that was before the fire. He slammed his fist into the desktop. Was she loose in the city with another candidate already in mind?

He had to find her.

Late the first evening of Fayth's stay, Sterling Kelley related the good will and can-do spirit of Seattleites to his wife and Fayth as they sat in the parlor enjoying their after-dinner coffee. In Fayth's opinion, Sterling could afford to be gracious and rather jovial about the disaster. His home sat well out of range of the fire's ultimate reach. And as a manager for Mr. Hill's Minneapolis and St. Cloud Railway, which had yet to reach Seattle, his job and business were in no jeopardy. Even his leased railway office which sat just south of the fire line hadn't been harmed by more than a little smoke. Yes, he was very lucky. And good luck made it easy to be magnanimous.

"You would have been proud, Elizabeth. I've never seen such Christian spirit. When George Adair called for a vote to decide whether we should still send the funds Seattle collected for the victims of the Johnstown flood before the fire, the cry was a resounding. *Send it away! They need it!*

"I've never seen such unselfishness."

"That's wonderful, Sterling." Elizabeth held her coffee delicately in front of her as she sat ramrod straight on the edge of her chair. She glanced nervously at Fayth. "Of course, Johnstown *did* lose nearly two thousand lives. As far as we know, there hasn't been a single confirmed death from our fire. What else did you hear in town?"

Poor Elizabeth! She was trying so desperately to be optimistic and steer Sterling away from thoughtlessly throwing Fayth's reduced circumstances in her face.

But Sterling was having none of it. "There may not have been a loss of life, dear, but our people are just as homeless and destitute as Johnstown's survivors." He seemed determined to wear other people's tragedies as if they were his personal stripes of honor.

"Sterling." Elizabeth shook her head subtly at her husband, reproving him for his lack of tact, nodding toward Fayth.

"It's fine, Elizabeth. Sterling is right to be proud of Seattle. How much did we collect?" Fayth was only half engaged in the conversation. The full force of her mind wrestled with weightier issues, namely self-preservation.

She was still reeling from the devastating afternoon blow of discovering the bolts of cloth the Captain had saved from the fire were not the wools and broadcloths she needed to sew for her male clientele and rebuild the business. No, he'd rescued the bolts of pink and yellow figured silk, and the light, watery blue plain silk from her office, the costly material to bring her sketches to life. Costly, but basically worthless to her here in Seattle. Even those smelled of smoke, but then, what in the city didn't? She could air them out, for all the good they'd do her.

The Captain had risked his life for nothing. She couldn't blame him. The smoke had been blinding. He'd grabbed what he could. Now she'd have to rely on her slim savings to get started again and hope she could get a shipment of cloth in time to get back in business soon.

"Doesn't everyone know the amount? It's been in all the papers since the day before the fire," Sterling said. "Five hundred and fifty-eight dollars, and every penny of it could just as easily be used here in Seattle." Sterling sobered and lowered his voice, "That is, if the bank vaults weren't destroyed by the fire."

"What?" Fayth nearly sloshed coffee all over herself. With one simple statement Sterling had captured her full attention. She hadn't considered that the vaults *could* melt. The money in the bank was her last line of salvation. If all her money had been lost as well . . .

"You don't think they were?"

Sterling looked at her sympathetically. "I hope not, Fayth. I sincerely do. But no one knows yet. At best they're all buried under layers of rubble. The mayor has asked the militia to help with the excavation. It's hoped the vaults will be recovered within the week. We'll just have to wait and see."

"Thank goodness the bulk of our assets are still back East," Elizabeth added, evidently operating under the misapprehension Fayth hadn't moved her money west, either.

Unfortunately, Fayth *had* trusted the local banks and had put all of her money in them when she'd severed her ties with Baltimore.

Sterling cleared his throat. "Well, not to worry now. I have more news to report—the powers that be are talking about raising Front Street and replatting the city. Imagine! Roads that lie on a grid and actually make some kind of sense on a map!"

By changing topics, Sterling surely meant to be kind and distract, Fayth. Unfortunately, he was failing miserably.

"How much higher of a regrade are they talking about?" Just another worry. How would the replatting affect her ability to secure another location for her shop downtown? And what would the cost be to local merchants?

"Nothing's been decided yet. Though the mayor was reported to say, when the question was brought up, *High enough so we don't have to put our bathrooms on the third floor or suffer the indignity of our crapper devices spouting geysers at high tide!*" Sterling chuckled.

Elizabeth silenced Sterling with a reproving look.

Everyone complained about the inadequate sewer system. The sewer pipes laid into Elliott Bay to flush sewage out into the Sound were not extended far enough, or laid high enough above the incoming tide.

Every day the outgoing tide washed Seattle's waste out to sea and every day the incoming tide washed Tacoma's waste right into Seattle, backing up the sewer pipes and erupting out of Seattle's toilets.

"Of course the water system must be improved," Sterling said. "If we'd had proper water pressure, we wouldn't have lost the city."

Fayth's mind was already at work on how to get back into business.

Elizabeth misread her faraway look. "Sterling, you're upsetting Fayth."

"Sorry. Didn't mean to be inconsiderate. But everyone's saying that Seattle will rise like a phoenix from the ashes. And so shall you, I say."

"Who, specifically, is saying that, Sterling?" Fayth asked.

"The entire city, I should imagine. I first heard Captain O'Neill give voice to it."

Fayth's heart beat in an odd rhythm. *Captain O'Neill.* Why did everything come back to him? Especially when she was trying to forget him.

"Sterling, I believe you're right. We will be like the phoenix. And I intend to start the transformation." Fayth set her cup down. All that pretty fabric might be of some use after all. She had vowed to come out of mourning and get rid of her drab clothes. If she was going to be destitute, she may as well do it with style.

Elizabeth smiled at her. "Good! You'll brighten everyone's spirits when we begin helping out at the relief tents tomorrow."

Fayth worked less than a full morning beside Elizabeth before being dispatched from the Armory to help the people from Tacoma in their relief tent at the corner of Third and University. All morning she served endless loaves of bread and plates of donated foods to hungry, flirtatious men under the watchful eye of the former Occidental Hotel steward, Thomas Moore, who, she was certain, intended to operate the tent like the fancy restaurant she had frequented so often. She worked in the stifling heat until the underarms of her gray work shift were ringed with perspiration and her arms leaden.

She wondered briefly about Coral. Lou Gramm's parlor house had burned to the ground, too, but she doubted Lou would let that stop business for long. Seattle's men may have lost their homes, sources of income, and places of occupation, but they had not lost their appetite for women. There were rumors that tents of prostitution were already being set up in the Tenderloin to service the restless men. And she worried about Olive, asking after her of any man that had been in the area of the fire that day. No one had seen a stray cat.

The Tacomans were cheerful and neighborly in their generosity toward their rival, now disaster-plagued, city. Despite their charity and good-natured attitude, Fayth didn't feel completely comfortable among the badged volunteers. She wondered to herself all day at how they had managed so quickly to secure the large white badges they wore that read "Tacoma Relief." She would have preferred to continue on at the

Armory, surrounded by her sisters in disaster and empathy, but at the end of the day, when Sterling came to pick her up, they pleaded with her to come back the next, early in the morning to help take down cots and set up tables for breakfast. Fayth demurred, giving them a noncommittal answer as Sterling escorted her to the door.

"You'll have to go back tomorrow. I'm afraid Elizabeth won't let you get by with less."

"Not if I'm needed at the Armory." As Sterling helped her up into the buggy seat, her attention was caught by a small girl. The tiny thing, who couldn't have been more than two, played in the shade of the tent next to her mother. She wore a smock stained with ashes and smoke, ripped at the hem. Her mother looked tired, defeated. Fayth's heart went out to them. They must have been left homeless, too. But they had nowhere to turn, save the tent that the Tacomans were erecting to house homeless women. Last night they hadn't even had that.

While there had been a flurry to erect shelter for the men, somehow the women had been forgotten. Fayth shuddered in the heat. At least she had only herself to provide for; what must it be like for that mother? A woman who must be close to Fayth's age? Sterling urged the horses on. The little girl disappeared from view.

Fayth stared straight ahead. Seattle was nothing more than a black and white photograph, she thought. Except for the taunting blue sky overhead, the city was colorless. Fayth squinted against the sun. "Not when I'm through," she whispered.

Con sat at his desk and watched Tetch leave his office. The poor son of a bitch was convincingly shaken. Con should have fired him, but he owed Tetch's father too great a debt. However, it didn't excuse Tetch's lack of responsibility, or lessen Con's losses. Con had put him in charge of the cash box. Stolen!

Con thumped back in his chair remembering their conversation.

"Stolen?" he'd asked.

"Evidently someone took it in the mayhem when we docked, sir. There were people everywhere; security was nonexistent," Tetch replied unevenly. "I've already notified the police."

Con's expression narrowed. "Lot of help they'll be. They're up to their asses in looters."

"Yes, sir."

"You scoured the hold?"

"Yes, sir. Not one coin left behind."

"No one saw anything?"

"No, sir."

"How much did we lose, best guess?" Con was so angry he could barely speak.

"May's receipts."

"A month's worth of receipts!"

"We never bank until the tenth."

The urge to physically punish Tetch for his stupidity was almost insuppressible. Why hadn't the fool secured the cash in the safe in Con's quarters rather than stowing the box in the hold?

"Keep me apprised of any news." Con dismissed him before he gave in to temptation and threw him out of the office bodily. Part of this was his own fault for trusting Tetch and his sticky fingers. But even Con couldn't imagine Tetch would boldly steal an entire month of receipts and expect to get away with it.

Con came back to the present. What was he going to do now?

Fayth walked into the dining room the next morning dressed in a deceptively simple, pink silk gown, so new the seams had barely cooled from the touch of the iron. Her hair was brushed up and back in a regal pompadour with soft wisps curling around her face. She carried a small twine wrapped package under her arm. Mrs. Beard, Elizabeth's housekeeper, did a double take when she saw her.

Miss Sheridan, you look a vision. Your gown, it's . . . wonderful."

"Thank you. I designed it years ago, but just finished it last night. Elizabeth's left for the Armory?"

"Half an hour ago. May I fix you some breakfast?"

"No, thank you. I'm in a hurry. I'm afraid I fell asleep early this morning. I hadn't meant to. I must be getting older. I used to stay up sewing all night and not feel the worse for wear the next day."

"It's the recent strain, Miss Sheridan. Go easy on yourself."

"Is Sterling here? I need to get to the relief tent."

"Mr. Kelley is upstairs. He should be down directly. Shall I let him know that you need a ride?"

"Yes. Thank you, Mrs. Beard. You're a gem."

By the time Fayth arrived at the tent, all the cots had been collected and tables installed in their places. Her heart raced as she scanned the eating masses until she found the little face she sought. She approached the toddler and her mother cautiously, with a friendly smile.

"I have something for your little girl. May I give it to her?" Fayth asked the mother.

"We don't accept charity." Though Fayth did not lift an eyebrow at her ridiculous statement, the mother blushed. "I mean, any further than we have to. I have to feed my child."

"I'm not condemning you. What hypocrisy that would be! I'm living off the charity of relatives right now myself."

The woman eyed her new dress suspiciously.

"I lost everything in the fire, the same as you, I suppose."

The woman didn't reply.

"I'm a seamstress."

"Huh, that I can see." The woman pulled her child to her.

Fayth ignored the insult. "I've made something for your little girl."

She leaned down close to the woman and the girl. "A friend of mine told me, just after the fire, as the city still smoldered, that Seattle would rise like a phoenix from the ashes. I believe him. I believe we will. But in the meantime, it struck me, there's no color in this city. So I made a vow. I would create some. Wouldn't you like your daughter to be part of that, part of the revival?" She held the package out to the woman who took it cautiously.

Moments later the twine lay on the floor and the little girl was dressed in a bright yellow smock, preening before her mother. The women around them showered the girl with attention. Fayth pulled from her pocket a handful of colored fabric scraps looped with pins and began passing them out.

"Wear your badge with pride, ladies!" she shouted. "We shall start the revival here! Today!"

A cheer resounded.

"We will restore Seattle to a greatness beyond her former glory. When historians of the future look back on this time, they will say, *Seattle would certainly have died without the colorful spirit of its women!*"

The mood became optimistic. Fayth was surrounded by hands reaching for pins, so occupied she barely caught sight of the slight form of an adolescent boy studying her with intensity from the door of the men's tent. Billy? Her attention was momentarily diverted. When she looked back, he was gone. It must have been someone else.

Had it been folly to use the precious material for something so frivolous when she might have found a rich woman willing to pay to have a dress made? What if the vault of Jacob Finn's bank had melted and all her remaining assets were destroyed? If it had been folly at all, it was a kind of folly that could not be measured against dollars, only against hope.

Billy burst into the shipmaster's quarters, chest heaving and breathless. "I found her, Captain!"

Con finished the entry he was writing in the captain's log before looking up at Billy, even though his heart pounded with excitement. "You're sure?"

Billy gulped for air twice, nodding.

"Where is she?"

"The relief tent them Tacoma folks set up, just like you heard. I almost gave up, had to wait around all morning. She was late showing. Missed the breakfast rush."

"She's not staying there?" If she was living in that forsaken tent, he was going to swoop in and rescue her, against her will if necessary.

"No." Billy hedged, acting as if there was something he didn't want to say.

Damn. Whatever it is isn't going to make me happy.

"No?" Con hoped he could draw it out of Billy without having to command him to tell everything he knew. "You're sure?"

Billy shrugged. "She showed up in a fancy carriage driven by some stuffy looking dandy dudded up in banker's clothes. He helped her down like a gentleman, looking real possessive and protective of her."

Not her banker then, Con thought.

Billy looked too pleased as he relayed the bit about the man. Then again, he would. Billy didn't like Fayth for the simple reason he felt Con deserved a better woman—specifically, the sea. Billy didn't see any reason a man needed more.

A gentleman? Con gripped the pen he was holding so tightly his knuckles turned white. He made a note to find out who the *gentleman* was. He hoped to hell whoever he was, he was a gentleman and not a scoundrel. Or worse, her new husband. She couldn't have gotten married in just two days, could she? "And?"

"She was all dressed up in a fancy new dress." He paused as if for dramatic effect.

Con waited.

"I could tell it was new. Everyone could. It was this light pink color. Fancy cut, looked society, like it come straight from New York. And her hair was all floofed up."

"Floofed?"

"You know, combed up big and fancy. I don't know what they call it. She walked into the main entrance and straight through the men's tent like a queen. Head high, kind of determined like." Billy shrugged, obviously warming to his role as informant. "You ought to see her now. Every eye in the tent followed her as she walked along. Got her share of catcalls, I tell you. And propositions, too. Dressed up like that she's kind of pretty."

That was some admission coming from Billy, who clearly was threatened by Con's attention to her.

"And how did she respond to all the attention?"

"Ignored it, like a lady should." Billy paused again. "'Course, maybe it was the gentleman she had on her mind."

"Is that all?"

"No. I stayed to see what she was up to, like you said."

"And?"

"She marched into the women's tent and gave a present to a little girl. Then she started making speeches to the women and handing out these bright ribbons, or something. She was talking about revival and Seattle. Something about phoenixes and bright colors."

Con allowed himself a sliver of hope. Fayth was becoming a phoenix, was she? At his suggestion? He opened his mouth to give Billy his next orders.

Billy anticipated him, cutting him off. "Damn, damn, damn! Why do I have to be out spying on girls when I should be here learning how to be a sailor?"

"Because your captain gave you an order."

Billy scanned the open logbook. "You're going back out onto the Sound to conduct another sightseeing trip, aren't you? And I'm going to be landlocked!"

"Yes."

"Hell, when you were my age you weren't stuck on land; you were out getting a reputation as the Con."

Con stood and put his arm around the boy. He wouldn't stand for insubordination from his men, but Billy was still in training. "Look, Bill, after I take this last group of Tacomans on a sightseeing tour, we'll get back to business as usual. I promise to stop neglecting your education."

Billy nodded. "You donating the money from this tour to the relief fund, too?"

The Captain nodded. "Wouldn't be right to profit from another's tragedy. We're called to help those in need."

"Seems like you had tragedy, too. Others are already starting to rebuild their wharves. Heard that Yesler's will be reopening shortly."

"Don't worry, Billy. I'll be going to see Finn about financing right after this last tour."

And I'll be taking care of Miss Sheridan, too, he thought.

Con pulled a silver dollar from his pocket and pressed it into Billy's hand. "For a job well done. Now get out there and back to it."

Men don't realize a woman dresses as much for herself as she does for them.

Fayth struggled to make a perfect bow of the sash on her latest creation and prepared for her third day at the relief tent. She dressed to enhance her new, colorful image. Wearing the bright clothes made her feel alive and vibrant, and was already creating the stir she wanted. A beautiful dress made her feel confident. She needed confidence more today than ever. Yesterday, she had heard rumors that they had uncovered most of the bank vaults and some of the vaults of the larger stores in town. The militia had guarded them all night and was most likely eager to be relieved of that duty. The citizens were all anxiously awaiting their opening. For many, like Fayth, the money they placed in the bank was all they had left. If the banks went under and didn't honor their deposits . . .

Fayth didn't want to think about it. The vault at Jacob Finn's bank had to have held. When they opened it all her money would be there, along with everyone else's. *It just had to be.*

Her thoughts whirled around the idea of getting her money. Once she was sure she had some capital left she would purchase or rent a tent. The city government had already passed an ordinance allowing businesses to erect temporary tents to conduct business until permanent buildings could be built. As soon as the militia pulled out, Seattle was set to be a regular tent city. She heard that the lines were already long to get the permit.

She could operate out of a tent, if Elizabeth would allow her to do the actual machine sewing at her house. As soon as things settled down she would make an offer on the piece of property where her shop had been. The owners had been anxious to sell before, she was certain they'd be doubly eager now. Then she would see Jacob Finn about a building loan. That was, if the vault had held and he had any money to loan. Otherwise, she would be forced to accept one of her many marriage proposals. She imagined herself pressured to marry some respectable man Elizabeth turned up.

Her thoughts roamed to strong arms. A kiss. Lapping waters.

With a start she came back to reality, jolted by the realization that it had not been Drew she'd been thinking of. She pulled the sash taut and strode from the room.

CHAPTER SEVEN

No one was allowed into Seattle's ruins without a permit. Consequently, the eager crowd that gathered to await news from the bank vault openings congregated on the perimeter. Nervous anticipation rippled through the masses. Fayth felt it the moment she stepped forward into the mostly male crowd, hoping to be invisibly lost in the confluence. But the men were all too gentlemanly. They shuffled her to the front, to the edge of the ashes, whispering to her to be their luck.

Con spotted Fayth as she was pushed forward to the stakes and rope that cordoned the crowd back from the burned city. He watched from another street perpendicular to where she stood on the front line. She wore a cornflower blue gown that matched his memory of the color of her eyes, tied with a deep-blue sash swooped up over a bustled back, cut close, showing every curve she owned. She looked like sand struck by lightning. The woman, who a week ago had no luster, now shone like polished glass. Billy had not exaggerated--she was beautiful.

As Coral stood next to her madam Lou Gramm, she spotted Fayth in the crowd. "Look, there's Fayth! Thank goodness! Look, Olive." The cat purred in her arms. "See, there's your mistress. Doesn't she look beautiful? I told you she'd come through just fine. Fayth has as many lives as you do." She snuggled the cat up against her cheek and turned to look at Lou. "Do you think the bank vaults held?"

Lou was studying her ragtag group of girls. Most of them were still dressed in the gowns they escaped in, bedraggled despite faithful laundering. There wasn't a gown among them that would catch the eye of a single one of their high-class clients. What a damn waste! Their entire wardrobe up in flames! Her regular seam-stress, Mrs. Green, had lost her sewing machine in the fire and left Seattle in despair to live with her sister in Chicago. Which left Lou in a bit of a predicament. There were few enough women around who had the skill to design and sew for her girls. And even fewer, perhaps not one, who would agree to.

Lou turned her gaze across the crowd to Fayth. "Where did she get that gown, do you suppose?"

Coral answered enthusiastically. "She made it herself. Fayth sews like a whirlwind. I saw the sketch of that very dress on her drawing board just days before the fire."

"That's her design? Very nice. She has talent." Fayth just might be the solution to Lou's problem. She had to act quickly to maintain her status as Seattle's premier madam. Everyone expected better of her than shabbily clad girls. Most of her clients had lost something to the fire—a business, an investment. They wanted entertainment. They wanted to forget their misery. She needed Fayth's designs to create the proper lighthearted illusion that all was well.

"That's not even one of her best, but I'm guessing it was one she could make up fast." Coral's words interrupted Lou's thoughts. "She has sketchbooks full, or did."

A slow smile spread across Lou's face. "Time to call in a favor," she said lightly. Her eyes did not leave Fayth.

Word came by way of a reporter let in to cover the excavation. The Finn vault held! Fayth jumped up and down, screaming at the news. The logger next to her grabbed her in a bear hug. Men slapped each other on the back and pumped each other's hands. The banks were solvent. There would be money for loans. Savings were safe! The masses went wild with euphoria. She had a chance to recover now. A slim chance, but it was better than nothing.

Con watched Fayth as she was swallowed up by the crowd, half relieved by the news, half upset. Fayth would never have him now. He met Bailey on the *Eliza* and joined him for a celebration drink. The mayor of Seattle had pulled all liquor licenses the day after the fire; Seattle was dry. That didn't stop them. No one but them commanded the waters of the Sound. Bailey showed him to the captain's quarters and offered him a tankard of the beer he'd hauled up from Tacoma A couple of beers in, Con unburdened himself to his old friend.

"You turned her down?" Bailey's tone was incredulous.

"I've told you I did at least a dozen times." Con was losing his patience.

"Yes, but go over your reasons again, Con. They're so damned amusing."

Con scowled at him and slammed his beer mug onto the table.

"Let me see if I have this right. You turned down Miss Sheridan's marriage proposal, damned amusing in itself, now if some gal proposed to me—"

"Not a chance in hell, Bail," Con interrupted.

"Now you want this woman," Bailey continued smoothly, "always did, but you had a brilliant, highly logical plan for courting her, which is, not to court her. Forgive me if I miss your logic."

"Careful, Bail. I'd dump this brew on you if it weren't so hard to come by." Instead he lifted it to his lips and chugged half the glass in a single gulp. "I told you,

I didn't want some business arrangement. I wanted her."

"Never knew you were such a romantic, Con."

"I'm not sure it's romance, Bail. Maybe it's simple lust."

"You are a romantic, Con."

Con shrugged and shoved the copy of the *Seattle Post Intelligencer* toward Bailey, tapping on an article. "Read this."

"So?" Bailey said when he finished reading the *PI's* account of the beautiful and stylish Miss Sheridan who worked at the relief tents. The article stated she handed out colorful ribbons, and clothes for children. A brief quote said that her mission, in her own small way, was to bring color and life back to Seattle. Bailey had seen a few of those ribbons himself. The article ended with a quip about Miss Sheridan being a beautiful spot of color herself.

"It's her," Con said. "She's going around all dolled up. You figure out what it means."

"Why don't you tell me what you think it means?" Bailey said.

"Why do women usually get fixed up?"

"I assume that's a rhetorical question."

"To catch men," Con said. "Before the fire, she dressed in mourning clothes." Con leaned back in his chair. "She's wearing her hair up in some fancy knot, with bunches of curls around her face. Curls!"

Bailey laughed again. "Spare me the fashion details. What's to say she hasn't just decided to change her look? Women do, you know. My sisters—"

Con waved him into silence. "No."

"Well, why not? She was trying to lure you into wedlock and she wasn't dressing up then."

"Nice of you to point that out, old friend." Con shoved his mug across to Bailey. "Pour me another. You're by the keg."

Bailey talked as he held Con's glass beneath the spigot. "You told me she changed her mind about marrying. What's changed?"

"Before she only *thought* she was desperate. Now, she's got to be panicked for real, wild for money. Everyone is." Con took his glass from Bailey and stared at the white foam on top for a minute. "The whole city reeks with the odor of a wild, desperate euphoria. Ordinarily decent folks looting. Scams everywhere. What crazy thing is she going to try now?"

"So? Save her the trouble. Propose to her yourself, Con." Bailey's tone was only half serious.

"I can't, she wouldn't have me. I kissed her the night of the fire. Right there on the deck of the *Aurnia*. My men would be sucking bilge water, or looking for another job if I ever caught them courting onboard. I'm not any happier with my own conduct. For more than one reason. It scared her off. The next morning she left without a good-bye."

"Then I'd say you need some practice kissing, my boy. You better stop by Lou's for a little drill in the intimate arts before you pursue this matter further. Maybe there's a reason a kiss is all you got for your trouble." The teasing light was back in Bailey's eyes.

He was no help at all. "I'd have expected a greater show of appreciation."

Con's glower silenced him.

"I see. This must be something serious if you're protecting her reputation." Bailey was silent for a moment. "Lend her the money yourself."

"Haven't got it."

"Use your connections to throw some her way."

"How? Who do I know who needs a seamstress?"

Bailey shrugged. "As a last resort, you could try courting her, for real."

"I don't have time. I've whiled away all I can making these peanut runs between Seattle and Tacoma. As soon as I get Jacob to lend me the money to rebuild the wharf, I'm going to have to take on the longer runs out of town. No one in Seattle is shipping timber now. I need money myself. Seattle's crying for goods. There's a pile of money to be made long hauling—something you mailmen don't have to worry about."

Bailey laughed. "True. The government keeps paying me despite the fire."

"Yeah, lucky you. Unfortunately, my mail subsidy is too small to bail me out and if I don't make my next run to San Francisco I lose that, too." He drummed his fingers on the table. "I can't chance her being scammed or accepting some fool's proposal while I'm gone. If she hasn't already. I told you about that fancy gentleman Billy saw?"

"You did."

"I don't think she'll embarrass herself by proposing to me again." Con didn't like the dark turn his thoughts kept taking. "But there are enough rutting bucks around, she'll be able to snare one quick enough. Somehow, I have to link her to me."

Bailey was silent for a moment, thinking. When he finally spoke, his words hit Con with a strange profoundness. "Then you'll just have to force her into marrying you. Quickly."

From the parlor, Fayth saw Mrs. Beard in the entry, surreptitiously pulling back the curtains that shielded the narrow window flanking the door. Curious, Fayth looked out her own window and spied a fancy carriage as it came down the block.

A plain young woman, no more than sixteen and dressed in worn clothing, alighted from the carriage. Fayth turned away from the window and came around to the parlor entrance where she could see the guest over Mrs. Beard's shoulder. The girl at the door held a cat with a tiny tinkling bell on its collar.

"I've been told Miss Fayth Sheridan is a guest here. I believe I've found her cat and have come to return her—"

"Coral!" Fayth rushed past Mrs. Beard. "I barely recognized you." She addressed the cat. "Olive! You're alive." She hugged them both before taking Olive into her arms. "Oh, you naughty girl! You gave me such a fright!" She caught Mrs. Beard's disapproving look.

"It's all right, Mrs. Beard. Coral is a friend of mine."

Mrs. Beard stood in the entry like a scowling sentry, apparently intent on blocking Coral's entrance into the

Kelleys' home. "You ought to choose your friends with more discrimination," she muttered under her breath.

Fayth took the hint and stepped out onto the stoop to talk to Coral.

"Fayth, you look stunning. What convinced you to trade away mourning clothes?"

Fayth laughed. "I've decided to be more colorful. Look at you! Looks like we've traded places."

"I left the face paint off when I realized I had to come here to find you." Coral's voice lost some of its gaiety. "Our whole wardrobe was destroyed in the fire."

"Oh, poor baby." Fayth held the purring cat to her cheek. "Both of you! Where did you find her?"

"She was wandering in the street when we evacuated."

Fayth looked up to the carriage at the end of the drive. Lou Gramm waited inside for Coral, watching their conversation with interest. "What's *she* doing here?"

"Lou wants to talk to you."

"Another time." Fayth nodded toward the matron in the window.

Coral shook her head. "Either you come out to the carriage, or Lou marches up here to their door. Sorry, but those are your options."

Fayth set Olive inside the door, called to Mrs. Beard to look after her, and turned toward the drive.

At the carriage, Lou greeted her with a measured smile. "Miss Sheridan, how nice of you to join me." She offered her a hand up. "Please come up and sit with me. I insist."

It was futile to defy Lou. Fayth ignored her hand and climbed up unassisted. Coral climbed in behind her.

"Thank you for allowing Coral to look after my cat."

Lou opened her hands in a magnanimous gesture. "You're most welcome." Her gaze flitted over Fayth.

"Why did you want to see me?"

"My! How you cut to the quick of the matter, Fayth." The madam gave her a generous smile. "I've come to make you a business proposal. Your beautiful gown caught my eye when we were out the other day. You're the only woman in Seattle dressed in anything even reasonably fashionable. I wondered to myself where a woman of your simple means would get such fine gowns."

"I'm a seamstress." Fayth resisted the urge to snort. "I designed and made them myself."

"So Coral informed me. You have talent, Fayth."

Fayth let the compliment pass. A compliment from a madam was no compliment at all.

"All our finery, our beautiful wardrobe," Lou sighed, "lost in the fire. And now my regular seamstress has run off to Chicago. Our men have a sophisticated eye, and prefer to see their lady friends dressed in the height of fashion. We'll lose their business if we mope around in these scorched rags. The girls in the cribs are dressed as well as we are." She shook her head in disgust. "I will pay you handsomely to design and sew your gowns for us."

"I don't sew for women in your profession." Fayth tried to hop down, but Lou's grip on her arm stopped her.

"I'm asking for the return of a favor."

Fayth shook Lou's arm off. "What favor? I was innocent! I didn't need you bailing me out."

"But I did just the same. Don't you feel any debt of honor?"

Fayth set her jaw.

Lou laughed. "Even if you don't, I know you're pinched in the pocketbook. That's where I can help. I have cash, plenty of it. Can you afford to turn it down?"

"Yes."

Lou laughed, loud and cynically. "You're a naive girl, Fayth. That little shop of yours burned to the ground, just the same as my poor house. You'll need to get a loan to rebuild the business, to survive, my dear."

"Fortunately, there are bankers."

"But that's the point, isn't it? There are so few bankers, and so many people needing loans. As I see it, the bankers have the upper hand. They can be very discriminating in handing out their money. What do you have to recommend you, Fayth? You're a woman in a man's venue. A proprietor of a small shop." Her smile spread nastily across her face, lighting her eyes with a malicious glimmer. "I have influence in the banking arena. I could throw it in your favor." She paused and delicately shrugged her shoulders. "Or not."

A cold wave of fear ran down Fayth's back. She sat up straight, trying to ward it off. She wouldn't cower before the madam. She needed a loan to start again.

The only item of real value she had salvaged was her machine. In a bold move calculated to help her secure the money she needed, just yesterday she used her savings to buy the lot where her leased shop space had stood. She needed the land as collateral against a building loan. She got it for a steal, but the purchase left her cash poor.

Lou was rumored to be extremely powerful in Seattle. The madam had many influential clients, and obvious influence over them. Coral had told Fayth stories without mentioning names. They came flooding back with crushing clarity. Lou had the power to make good on her threat. "You wouldn't."

"Try me."

Fayth stared ahead, her mind racing at a frantic pace, trying to come up with a way to extricate herself from the situation. "I don't sew lingerie. Find someone else."

"Oh, dear." Lou was laughing. "I didn't come to you for lingerie. I need elegant gowns to wear out, to bring in the crowd. Lingerie is the last thing we'll be needing to replace. Unveiled, my girls' natural assets don't need any embellishing."

Fayth's thinly disguised discomfort only seemed to heighten Lou's amusement. Blast the woman!

"I'll tell you what. I am a fair-minded woman. I'll give you a day to think about it and send a driver over for your answer day after tomorrow. I'll need a day or two to see what material I can scrounge up, anyway. Someone in Tacoma should have something suitable."

She handed Fayth a slip of paper. "If you make up your mind early, you can reach me at this address."

"She hasn't come to see you yet, Jake?"

"You know I can't divulge client information, Con. But if I recall correctly, the last time I saw Miss Sheridan was just before the fire. She was interested in buying the building she was renting. Of course, that deal is surely sour now, assuming she hadn't already put her money down. And she would have had to do that the day of the fire, before it struck."

"She'll be coming to see you soon. For all I know, she's in line right now." They sat in Jacob Finn's temporary quarters where he, as one of the financiers of the rebuilding, held court. The line to see him was a spectacle in itself, but Con was an old friend.

"What is your interest in the woman, Con?" Jacob looked over the stack of papers before him. "I can lend you enough to repair your wharf. But let me warn you, you hook up with her, I can't lend you enough to repair both businesses."

Con didn't shift in his chair. "I won't take the loan out today, Jake. Put a hold on enough cash for the wharf, will you? I'll be back tomorrow, if not, the next day."

"Certainly, Con. And if she comes to me in the meantime?"

"You have reasonable grounds to deny her."

"You're not asking me to doing anything unethical, are you?"

"You know me better than that." Con took a deep breath and leveled his gaze on the banker. "I'm asking you not to use extraordinary means to get her the money."

After a grueling wait in line, Fayth sat facing Jacob Finn in his office. "What do you mean, Mr. Finn, that I can't have a loan unless I have a man to oversee the rebuilding? Surely I can hire a contractor for that, and my cousin, Sterling Kelley, has offered to assist me. You insult me by insinuating that I can't run my own business, when you know very well that I can. In the months that I've been here my business has grown very nicely and your bank has seen the results in the increase of my deposits."

"I mean no insult, Miss Sheridan. I'm only following orders from the bank's board of directors. As you well know, we've had a run on loans. We only have so much capital. We must lend it discriminately.

"I've seen what a capable businesswoman you are, but that does not assure me you can manage a construction project. There will be dozens of con artists flocking to Seattle and they will be targeting the most vulnerable people as victims. Please illuminate me on any experience you have, and I'll be happy to reconsider."

He'd trapped her on purpose. He knew very well she had none.

"I don't have any. But I learn quickly. And I'll hire a reputable contractor at your recommendation."

Finn shook his head. "That's only the first strike against you, Miss Sheridan. Your cash assets are small. Speaking plainly, you're undercapitalized."

"Isn't everybody, Mr. Finn?" Her voice involuntarily pitched an octave higher in frustration, making her sound weak. It was times like this when she longed for a nice, deep voice.

Jacob Finn smiled. "Not all. What you need, Miss Sheridan, is a private investor, a backer, or a partner with assets. Come see me again when you've worked something out." He dismissed her.

Fayth stormed out of his office and down the street, muttering to herself. *Lou's show of power.*

Two hours and two more failed loan attempts later, she arrived at Lou's temporary parlor house, a house Lou was renting while she rebuilt. What could Faythe do? Unless she wanted to live off of Sterling and Elizabeth's charity for the foreseeable future, she was out of options.

"Call off your dogs, Lou," Fayth said as she stepped into Lou's office. "I'll sew your dresses."

Lou looked momentarily surprised at such a sudden capitulation. But she recovered quickly and smiled in gracious victory. "I'll pay you handsomely for your work."

"I want more than good pay. Your friend Mr. Finn has denied my application for a loan. Use your influence, as I'm sure you did to set him against me, to change his mind."

Lou looked genuinely bewildered. "I have no influence over Jacob Finn. I merely bank at his establishment. I *can* promise you no additional problems from my sphere of influence."

Fayth waited until Sterling was out and she and Elizabeth were enjoying afternoon refreshments in the parlor before she spilled her news to her cousin.

"Fayth! You can't work in that *whorehouse*." Elizabeth's last word was a barely audible whisper.

"What choice do I have? It's not as if I'm entering their business. I've been to three different banks, and even though I own the land, none of them will lend me the money. Miss Gramm is going to pay me well for my dresses. I can't afford to be finicky."

"But you can't! Let us lend you the money."

Fayth shook her head. The fire had hit everyone in the pocketbook. She doubted whether her cousins had enough capital to lend her, even if they wanted to. "I can't let you put your own security at risk. And I won't be dependent on your good graces. You've done so much for me already."

"But, Fayth, it was one thing for you to pay a call to that Coral person, but to be under the Madam's employ!" Elizabeth shuddered. "This will devastate your reputation!"

"You think so? I don't. And anyway, I'm past caring. Who knows, maybe the publicity will bring clients in?" Fayth set her teacup down. "As soon as I've been paid for the first dress, I should be able to afford to put up a tent on my property. Then I'll be back in business. I'll drop the Madam's business as soon as I start making money again."

"Fayth, I can't believe you bought that property sight unseen."

"Unseen? I lived there, remember? Besides, I got it for a steal and I thought it would guarantee me a loan."

"But who knows what kind of shape it's in?"

"I'm going to see it tomorrow, when the militia pulls out. But I'm fairly well convinced that the fire cleared it for me."

"Please, let Sterling send one of his men out for you. It's going to be dangerous. And I beg you; give up this notion of sewing for that woman."

"Elizabeth, you can throw me out if you want, but I'm not going to change my mind."

Her steely look must have convinced Elizabeth. She put a hand on Fayth's shoulder. "I'd never turn you out."

"Elizabeth, remember the Christian Committee you and your friends have been talking about starting to save the fallen women of the community? Consider me the first member on active duty. Maybe this will give me the opportunity to save Coral."

"Oh, Fayth! We're all married women! But, you— you just shouldn't be in such a place!"

"No one should be," Fayth said calmly. "Married or otherwise."

Fayth didn't report to the relief tent for work the next morning. Instead she worked her way into the crowd of humanity waiting at the perimeter of the fire. The militia was scheduled to withdraw at seven when the restriction for going into the fire district without a pass would be dropped. The mayor was confident civil police and authorities could now take over the task of maintaining order.

Fayth studied the militia as they passed her. For five days now they had taken four-hour shifts of duty, spelled by four hours off to sleep. They were as weary and worn out as the citizens. Almost as soon as the last man trudged across the border of the burned district, pandemonium broke out. The crowd charged headlong into the charred remains of Seattle. More than five thousand looters were on the loose. Fayth was jostled and bumped, propelled forward by the force of the crowd. About midblock the crowd broke into different directions, allowing Fayth enough room to escape its clutches and head for her land.

Her pulse roared in her ears as she rounded the corner and surveyed the block. Though she had been warned about the destruction the fire had caused, she was not prepared for the damage to human decency. The reckless irreverence of the people who crowded the streets horrified her. They combed through wreckage not theirs, scavenging and looting before the eyes of the rightful owners of the scorched remains. The few legitimate merchants and shopkeepers she recognized had varying attitudes toward the heinous, hoarding throngs. Some charged at them like angry bulls. Lone figures trying to chase off buzzards. Mr. Pare waved at the looters on his property, trying to scare them away. Others stood at the edge of their property, pleading to deaf ears. All were desperate, all ineffective.

The lone policeman she saw had evidently given up making any attempt to stop the thieving. When she reached her property, it was covered with men picking through the ruins.

Raw fury welled up inside her. She yelled without thinking, barely suppressing an epithet. "Get out! The whole thieving lot of you!"

One man, of the dozens, paused to look up at her. And he with only mild curiosity, as if to gauge whether she had a weapon, then he calmly continued with his business.

"They won't find anything of value."

The calm, strong voice from behind stopped her cold. She turned around slowly, hoping he hadn't seen her outburst.

"Captain O'Neill," She nodded. "What makes you so certain? I may hope the fire has left me something."

He stepped down from a runabout led by a horse the same raw chestnut color as his hair. He looked the perfect picture of honor and inscrutability. With the sun at his back, he cast a tall shadow that emphasized his broad shoulders and lean, hard build.

"I was hoping to find you here. I've brought you something." He reached into his saddlebag and handed her a small parcel. "All that was found in the remains of your shop."

"Thank you." She stared at him, stunned and nearly speechless. "But how?"

"My men combed through it yesterday. I knew the mayor was dead wrong to let the militia go. The civil authorities wouldn't be able to stop looters. What few

police Seattle has have been posted near the remains of
the jewelry stores. It was like a treasure hunt when I
rode by just now. People grabbing melted hunks of
gold, anything they could find. I saw a policeman chase
after one man, but he never did catch him.

"Mark my words, Miss Sheridan, the mayor will
have to call the militia back in. He'll have no choice."

She noticed the formal way he addressed her. With
the immediacy of the tragedy behind them, they were
reduced to strangers. Or did he wish, as she did, to distance himself from the undeniable attraction growing
between them?

"Thank you for your consideration, Captain." She
marveled at his clear thinking and decisive nature. Not
to mention his connections that allowed him access before the general public.

He watched her closely. "You shouldn't be out here
alone. Is there no one you may ask to escort you?"

"Oh, my cousin Sterling would have come, but he
had business of his own to attend today. I'm staying
with him and his wife Elizabeth."

"Next time, you must insist." At the mention of her
cousins, he sounded relieved, almost happy.

Embarrassed by his admonishment, she concentrat-
ed on the men sifting through the ashes of her property. "Why would they bother with my poor shop?" She
turned to look back at him. "How did you get a pass?
They were impossible to come by."

"I have connections." He looked devastating when he
smiled.

"Captain O'Neill, I hope you are right, that the mayor won't delay in calling the militia back. But those poor, exhausted men need rest. Did you see them march out?" She paused, then decided to confide in him. "I own this land now."

"Do you?"

"Bought it a few days ago." Her eyes narrowed as she thought of rebuilding. She almost told him about her troubles with the banks. She changed the subject instead. "You were right about Seattle rising from the ashes. Everyone all over town is quoting you."

"You, Miss Sheridan, personify my theory. You look like a beautiful phoenix today yourself. You're the only spot of color in the place."

His compliment quickened her pulse. She pushed away thoughts of his strong embrace and warm kisses—thoughts too pleasurable, too dangerous and out of place against the stark reality before her. Instead, she focused on his amazing perception. How did he read her intentions so clearly?

A warm breeze blew off the water, ruffling her skirt. She must speak. "Thank you." Her voice caught. She turned the small package over in her hand, contemplating whether to open it or not. This was all that was left of her life? Nothing more?

"A few buttons and bobbins," he said, as if he'd read her mind again.

She blinked to draw in tears that suddenly threatened. Was she, after all, destined to be Sterling and Elizabeth's poor live-in relation? How could she ever recover and rebuild?

"This can't be all." Impulsively, she ran from the street into the midst of the ash and ruins, desperately seeking something more. She was ankle deep in soot by the time she stopped in the area that should have been the storeroom. Two stories of building and life reduced to inches of ash. She heard footsteps behind her, but paid no attention. She was too busy scanning the debris for signs of something recognizable. But there was nothing but burned, flaking timber. Thin, black-edged flakes of charred wood no thicker than paper dislodged with each gust of gentle breeze and blew about like desolate, falling snow.

"There must be more." It was her voice, but so agonizingly high-pitched she barely recognized it herself.

He was close behind her, so close she practically felt him. One tiny step back and she knew she would butt up against a hard chest and firm thighs. Trembling, she took a step forward.

"Let me assure you; my men were thorough." His sympathetic voice tore at her. When was the last time a man had addressed her with such tenderness?

"But I poured water over everything; how could it burn?" She knew her statement was absurd the moment she uttered it. There was nothing that inferno wasn't capable of consuming, wet or otherwise.

He gave her no answer, evidently assuming a rhetorical nature to her question. She turned to face him. His shoulders were covered with scales of falling ash. They alit in his hair as they danced about him. And his immaculately polished boots were gray with soot. He held his hand out to her. "Please, Miss Sheridan, let me escort you home. There's nothing more you can do here today and it's not safe for a woman to be out alone."

"Home? Isn't this it?" Her voice was softly ironic.

"To where you're staying then."

She put her hand gently in his, fighting to steady her voice as she spoke. "Thank you, Captain."

He handed her into the runabout before jumping up beside her and settling so close to her in the narrow two-person seat that their thighs brushed—his, hard and powerful, hers, outlined by skirt. She looked straight ahead as they rode, thinking how safe she felt riding with a large, powerful man, chiding herself in the next moment for her traitorous thoughts. Security came only from independence, certainly not from a handsome man.

He negotiated through the crowds and out of the city. The air lost its acrid burnt smell as they left the business district behind and headed for the surviving residential area. She breathed in deeply, inhaling disturbingly fresh smells of leather, horse, and bay rum.

She rode straight-backed, trying to distance herself from her own physical response to him, vowing that once home she would forget him. When they arrived, Mrs. Beard stood posted at the window, wearing her usual disagreeable look. It seemed nothing about Fayth's conduct pleased the aging servant.

The Captain helped Fayth down from the runabout. "May I be so forthright, Miss Sheridan, as to ask you to dine with me tonight?" Her face must have given away her intent to refuse; he continued before she could speak. "Please don't deny me an evening of distraction from the present grim atmosphere."

She accepted before better sense took over. But given such an eloquent plea, how could she deny him?

Il Pesce was one of many restaurants temporarily located in tents on sites of what were formerly full-fledged buildings. Fayth had never been to the restaurant before the fire. From the linen tablecloths and napkins, she realized that it had been a step above the Occidental in class and elegance. The staff deserved credit. Despite being housed in a tent, a pleasant, intimate atmosphere pervaded. The Captain seemed at ease in such surroundings. He dressed for the occasion in a white uniform with captain's braid at the sleeves.

Freckles. Freckles. Freckles.

She mentally repeated the word like a prayer to ward off the flutter of her heart, the trembling of her hands, and the floating, lighthearted feelings he brought out. She allowed herself to remember another man who once had the same effect on her—the darkly handsome, treacherous Drew. A good-looking man could again be her downfall. She must remember that.

Thoughts of Drew set her heart pattering nervously. She had gone through her things over and over again, but couldn't find Drew's photograph. She last had it in the Captain's bed and feared that's where she had left it. The Captain hadn't returned it in the parcel. In all probability he knew nothing of the photograph, for surely he would have returned it. Despite herself, she worried that he would find the thing and get the wrong impression. She could live without the photograph, if only he never found it. How to recover it without him knowing? How to approach him without giving away what she was looking for?

"I've been meaning to ask you, Captain—I didn't happen to leave something behind in your, er, bedroom, did I?" She sounded like a nervous fool.

He cocked an eyebrow. "Such as what?"

She bit her lip, a bad habit she must break. It gave away her nervousness too easily. "A photograph."

A look of consternation crossed his face. "No, not that I know of. I had the crew clean my cabin the day we docked. They didn't mention anything. But I can check with them for you. What was it a photograph of?"

She blew out a relieved breath. "Nothing important," she assured him too quickly. "I can live without it."

His gaze darted over her face searching for something, but she couldn't imagine what. Whatever it was, he must have found it, because he smiled, obviously pleased.

The waiter arrived with their first course. Fayth spoke as soon as he departed, trying to steer the conversation onto safe ground. "I have to say you were right about the militia, Captain O'Neill. I'm glad the mayor called them back in."

"He was a fool to dismiss them so quickly in the first place. Seattle lasted, what, all of three hours before the mayor begged them back into service?"

Fayth smiled. "Will you be sailing again soon? I'd heard that you made several excursions taking sight-seers to view the ruins and donating the profits to help those left homeless. That was very noble of you."

"You think so? Billy thought I was an idiot. As you can imagine, we need money ourselves. But my charity work is done now. I have to oversee the rebuilding of my wharf and warehouse. Many of the other wharfin-gers have gotten the jump on us already.

"But I must tell you, Miss Sheridan, how very pleas-ant it is for me to think of you keeping abreast of my activities. It makes me feel vindicated for my interest in yours." His dimples showed through his beard when he smiled.

"It was in all the newspapers." She felt her own blush. And then a confused question occurred to her. "Interest in my activities?"

"You were in the newspapers, too."

"Oh, yes." Why was her laugh such a nervous titter? "It seems we're both celebrities."

In truth she was disappointed in his response. And maybe she was only imagining, but it seemed he bit back what he really meant to say. They spent an awk-ward moment staring at each other until Fayth was compelled to speak, "Captain O'Neill, after all we've been through together, I hate to see us acting like nervous strangers."

She thought she saw a spark of hope light his eyes. She leaned across the table toward him as if to whisper a secret. "Can we forget what happened on your ship? Chalk it up to emotions heightened by tragedy. In the balance of a scale, it can't outweigh the embarrassment of my proposal, and we survived that. Can we be at ease with each other now?"

"We can, if you allow me the honor of one further embarrassment." His tone was almost mischievous.

"And what would that be?" With the tension lifted, she found herself smiling.

"I have a favor to ask of you."

"You don't need to feel any embarrassment, Captain. I owe you a great debt. Ask away," she said lightly.

"I'd like you to marry me, Miss Sheridan." His tone held no teasing now.

CHAPTER EIGHT

"What?" Fayth spoke a little too loudly. The group at the next table turned to gawk at them. She ignored them and leaned across the table to whisper above the patter of her heart. "Why?"

"Why not? It's a wild and reckless time. The fire blasted everything out of kilter. If ever there's a time in our lives to do something just because, this is it. Will fate ever provide us the opportunity to be so free from convention again?"

Her mouth was so dry she couldn't respond. What was he talking about? Free from convention? Wild times? Marriage?

She knocked her nearly empty water goblet over as she reached for it. Not one of the dozens of marriage proposals she had received since arriving had set her at such a tilt.

He righted the goblet before she could reach it. She avoided looking at him, swiping her napkin at the dribbles on her dress.

"You look a vision tonight. Blue becomes you. I thought so this morning. You are like a mirage in a desperately dry city."

She laughed nervously and continued to dab at her dress. "Look at me now—what a mess I am." But her dress was not nearly as messy as the emotional maelstrom inside her.

"You look wonderful." He reached across the table and grabbed the hand that held the napkin. "Are you going to give me an answer, or string me along indefinitely?"

"Are you going to explain to me why you're proposing now, when you turned me down less than two weeks ago?"

He released her and settled back in his chair.

She set her napkin on the table. Would she ever understand this man, or herself? Why didn't she refuse him outright like she should?

"I'm old-fashioned. The man should do the proposing." His tone was light again.

She couldn't pin any specific emotion, or motivation, on him.

"You, of anybody, ought to know better than to propose a real marriage to me. One little kiss hasn't changed my mind about what I want. I will only marry for business reasons."

He held his hands up in defense. "I wouldn't presume."

"Then what changed your mind? What happened to the romantic? I want the truth, not pretty lies about how you've suddenly decided you're a lonely man, and I'm the only woman who will suit you. I've heard those lines too many times to ever believe them. If you're going to convince me to say yes, you must have some immediate, horrendous need. Something dire enough to convince me of this change of heart. Something that plays on my sympathies." She folded her arms.

"The bank's balking at giving me a loan." He was serious now and it caught her off guard.

"What? How can they? You still have your ship. That has to be worth enough to back any loan you could want."

"They don't believe a single man is a good risk."

Fayth unfolded her arms and leaned toward him. Indignation welled in her. She felt her cheeks flame with it. "That's absurd! How can they make such a claim?"

"The bankers are in a position to be extremely selective. They seem to think I'll default and go sailing away into the sunset with my collateral, leaving them holding the debt. I have no family to anchor me here, to keep me working hard."

"Then show them; get a loan in San Francisco." She couldn't keep her voice from shaking. Father always warned that it wasn't becoming for a lady to lose her composure, but when faced with unjust circumstances, Fayth couldn't contain herself.

He shook his head. "Tried that. They're only lending to the biggest players. My best bet is to sell my waterfront property. Sell out to the big wharfingers, take the profit, pay off my debts, and invest the rest in the shipping business. Do you know anything about how the shipping industry works?"

She shook her head.

"All ships pay a docking fee to the wharf owners. I've always tried to run an honest business and keep my fees low. If I sell my wharf property, I'll be at the whim of other wharfingers, who are sometimes only greedy, at others, downright criminal. The wharfingers hold the power in this business. They dictate who docks and when. If they decide you're not worth their trouble, you sit out in the Sound with your goods spoiling. The big wharves always cater to the major lines and large ships. Small guys like me get squeezed out. Waterfront is already at a premium. If I sell, I'll never get it back and I'll lose my autonomy."

"No! That's insufferable! We can't let that happen." She realized too late that she'd linked herself with him. Were the bankers out to ruin every respectable business in town?

"Exactly."

"I must confess, Captain, I sympathize with your situation. Every bank in town has denied me a loan as well." Her voice shook. "Nobody believes a woman alone can make a go of it. The only woman who seems to be above it all is Miss Gramm. No one minds a madam making money.

"But I can't get a loan because I'm undercapitalized, *so they say.* If we married, the bankers would expect your business to be used as collateral against any money I borrow. And I would borrow. Are you willing to risk that?"

"I've already considered it. The benefit to me outweighs the risk. You have faith in your abilities as a businesswoman?"

"Certainly."

"You think you can make it on your own?"

"Yes."

"That's good enough for me. My assets aren't holding me back from the loan, and I've reason to believe they'll sway the banks in your favor. We'll make a gentleman's agreement not to mix our business funds. Let the banks think what they will."

He seemed sincere about the marriage being business only, but why this sudden turnabout in philosophies? She wasn't quite convinced.

"A marriage would complicate your personal life. I have no family to worry about. How about you, Captain?"

"You've thought this out since the last time we discussed it." He smiled, unruffled. "Grandam and Mam have long been pressuring me to marry."

"Not under these circumstances, I imagine. What would you tell them when no grandchildren came? What would I say if they pressed me?"

"That you were barren."

His response was so deadpan, she laughed. "No one gets the better of you, do they?"

"Not if I can help it."

"How would you feel about that? Not ever having children?" She shouldn't ask such a personal question, but since she was considering marrying the man . . .

"It was you, I believe, who stated I was married to the sea. With such a mistress I have no time to be a good father. You?"

"I'm not used to children, or family. I can live without them." Her tone was sharper than she intended.

"Then you accept?"

"Not so fast. I have a further concern. You mentioned mistress in jest, but I've had enough scandal to last me a lifetime. I don't want to be disgraced, in that way, here in Seattle. You must agree to take your pleasures elsewhere and be discreet about it." She couldn't tell if she shocked him.

He nodded his assent too quickly. "I have no intention of disgracing you."

"So you say now."

"I'm a man of my word."

Did she look as skeptical as she felt?

"Accept my offer, Fayth. You aren't going to get a better one. Accept and we both get what we want."

"What is it you want, Captain?" Her heart pounded in her ears. Could she really be considering accepting?

"A loan, the survival of my business."

His answer was both pleasing, and disappointing. But wasn't this what she wanted, too? How could she say no?

"You are a man after my heart, Captain. I accept your offer and pledge what you have offered me. I promise you my fidelity, and give you my word that I will do my best to bring honor to our name."

A strange, almost triumphant light shone in his eyes. "Excellent. I'll rent us a house. I have my eye on one already. A small, yellow clapboard with a view of the Sound."

"Separate bedrooms?" She wavered. Could she do this?

"Of course."

"I must say, Captain O'Neill, I am disappointed, although not surprised, in the death of another romantic."

He swept out of his chair and was on one knee before her before she realized what he planned to do. He pulled her hand from her lap and enclosed it between his. "Miss Fayth Sheridan, I'm deeply, ardently in love with you. Please end my suffering and consent to be my wife." He winked at her and mouthed, "The romantic lives."

She laughed.

The room grew still. All the restaurant's patrons watched them as she quietly whispered back.

"Just so you know that I have not lost my jaded view of the world, I must tell you that under no circumstance other than one this desperate would I marry you. But as it is, I give my consent." She winked back. "A cynic never dies."

He started to pull her hand to his lips, but she did him one better and bent to brush his lips lightly with hers. She shouldn't have done it. The jolt of attraction that leaped between them almost caused her to reconsider marrying him.

A loud cheer erupted from the tables around them.

She straightened jerkily, shaken, realizing they were the center of attention.

He shouted to the watching crowd. "Miss Sheridan has agreed to become my bride."

Congratulations echoed from all corners. Someone called for a celebration drink. As liquor licenses were still suspended, water had to suffice. Amid it all the Captain's eyes never left hers.

"Day after tomorrow," he said. "Marry me day after tomorrow."

"Yes." She couldn't help feeling that she'd been somehow bamboozled, but how could that be? She was getting what she wanted.

Fayth could only describe the Captain as beaming when he lifted his water goblet and toasted. "To us."

Pastor Wilson's office was a tight, tidy cubbyhole at the back of the church. Neatly lined bookshelves filled with leather-bound volumes of sermons shadowed the walls. In the heat they emitted a warm scent of leather and dust, creating a pleasing aura of piety, hominess, and solemnity.

Con stood with Bailey, waiting for Fayth's arrival. The sun glinted in from a small window behind him, adding to the stifling heat in the room.

"Hang in there, old man," Bailey said, and slapped him on the back. Did he look that nervous?

Fayth stepped over the doorsill, accompanied by the swishing of skirts. Following her was a distinguished looking couple who must have been her cousins. Con recognized Sterling Kelley as a representative of the Minneapolis and St. Cloud Railway who was active in city affairs, and nodded to acknowledge him and his wife, but in truth, barely noticed them. Man alive! He restrained himself from punching the air in victory. She had shown up.

Fayth looked beautiful, like a pale pink rose in the dress she wore. She had fixed her hair in a light, airy style and her cheeks were nicely flushed, a good sign. She looked nervous, but why shouldn't she be? This was her wedding day.

He was nervous, too. But not, he presumed, for the same reasons. He had no doubt he wanted this. He only hoped he wasn't wrong for marrying her, believing he could make her love him, lying to her about his motives. He had no intention of remaining a celibate business partner.

Bailey crowded the wall to make room as the bridal party filed in. The room was just wide enough to accommodate them all.

Pastor Wilson stood across his desk from the group. "Shall we begin? The bride and groom will face each other."

Con turned, and impulsively took her hand in his. Slender and small, it trembled in his grasp, but she didn't pull it away. He gave it a little squeeze of encouragement. He would have winked at her if she would have looked up. What was she afraid of? She believed this was just business. He meant to prove her wrong.

"We are gathered here today to join this man and this woman . . ."

Lost in thought, trying to appear calm, he didn't hear another word until Fayth's tremulous voice echoed the pastor's, reciting promises to love, honor, and obey him. Did she lie so easily? It would have been a complete mockery if he didn't believe she could love him someday. Then he spoke his vows with a clear conscience. He would protect and honor her. He loved her. Someday he'd show her how much.

She looked surprised when Bailey handed him a ring and he slipped it on her finger. Her hand shook as she held it out to him.

"If anyone has a reason why this couple should not be married, let him speak now, or forever hold his peace."

She stood rigid. For one crazy, interminable instant, Con imagined her voice raised in objection. The moment passed. No one spoke.

"By the powers vested in me, I now pronounce you, man and wife."

Fayth exhaled a small, nervous breath.

"Well, what are you waiting for Captain? Kiss your bride." The pastor smiled.

Con seized the moment and pulled her into his arms. With one arm he encircled her waist in a firm grip, and with the other hand caressed her cheek before cupping the back of her head, tilting it to his. His mouth came down on her soft, trembling lips. The scent of rose water filled his senses. In his arms, she flushed and yielded against him. There was hope; there was hope yet. He released her to cheers and congratulations.

Mrs. Kelley's smile reached ear to ear. Bailey said something about him being an old dog and shook his hand.

Pastor Wilson laid out a license for them to sign. "Ladies first."

Fayth signed quickly, with a flourish, and turned away without watching him sign. Mrs. Kelley tugged at her and pulled her back a few steps from the desk to whisper in her ear. He wasn't supposed to, but he heard her words as he signed his own name to the license.

"Fayth! That was the kiss of a man in love if ever I saw one. It was almost scandalous."

At least one woman recognized him for what he was. When would Fayth? Later, alone in the carriage as they pulled away from the church, he stared at her, couldn't pull his gaze away from her. He knew he grinned like a fat frog, ear to ear, but he couldn't suppress that either. "Well, Mrs. O'Neill—"

"Mrs. O'Neill." She tittered. "I just can't believe that I *am* Mrs. O'Neill."

"Take your time getting used to it. You have a lifetime."

"Yes." She sounded thoughtful.

"Any regrets?" Why did he ask such a foolish question? Odd as it was, he wanted to hear her reassurances, even if she manufactured them.

"No, of course not. You?" Her hands were tightly knotted in her lap.

"I'm happy."

"Good. We made a fair deal."

Only a fair deal?

She held her left hand out in front of her, as only women do, examining the garnet ring on her finger. "You shouldn't have. I mean, you didn't have to."

"I didn't?" He had spent the better part of yesterday afternoon hunting for just the right one, before settling on the oval garnet set in gold filigree. The best jewelry stores had burned down in the fire. Their stock was melted, destroyed, or later, looted. He'd been lucky to find one at all, let alone one so fine. "And let people think that I don't love my wife?"

She laughed. He loved the sound, and the way her face lighted up.

"Well, you don't. But thank you. It's beautiful."

Couldn't she see? Didn't his elated expression give him away? He should be happy he hadn't lost his poker face yet.

Fayth fell in love with the small one-story clapboard cottage the moment the carriage rounded the corner and the cottage came into view. Yellow with white trim, it was as quaint a residence as she could have imagined. Elizabeth, Sterling, and Captain Bailey followed in their own carriages a short distance behind them. Fayth insisted on seeing her new home before going to dinner, and no one was about to deny the bride her wish.

"It's beautiful, Captain," she said as he helped her down from the rented carriage.

"Quaint at least."

"Beautifully quaint." She stood in the drive admiring it.

Twin hedges of azaleas in their last bloom lined the walk. Two immense rhododendrons by the house capped off the hedge, their spent blossoms like brown sticky spiders over the bush. A lavender clematis trailed over a trellis that leaned away from the wall.

Captain O'Neill strode up the walk and unlocked the door, pausing to snap a sticky dead blossom from the rhododendron next to the door. "It needs a bit of work. These will all have to be picked or we'll get no blooms next year. After you, madam."

He stepped out of the way and held the door for her. It all seemed so homey, so familiar. This is what life should be like, talking of mundane things such as whether there will be flowers next year, living with a strong, stable man.

"No matter, it's lovely." She stepped past him. The interior was simple. A large bow window at the back of the main living room caught her attention. She walked to it and took in the view. Puget Sound sparkled in the distance below and farther out the white-capped Olympic Mountains rose tall.

"A captain's home should have a view of the water. Look." He stepped close behind her and pointed.

She felt his warmth against her back, and resisted the urge to step back against it, to dream about his arms encircling her.

"You can see the wharf. If I get you a spyglass, you'll be able to see me coming home."

"Or leaving," she said. The thought brought an odd despondency.

"Coming home," he corrected.

His presence behind her was too compelling. She forced herself away, walking the length of the window before turning to face him. "I suppose you're right, Captain O'Neill."

"Are you going to call me *Captain O'Neill* for the rest of our lives? We're partners now."

She was taken aback for a moment by the sudden intimacy of the relationship they had entered into with so little thought to small details. "What should I call you? Dutiful husband?"

He laughed. "Sure, and I'll call you something respectful like, *my old lady*."

"You will not! You'll call me Fayth, like the night of the fire." She liked that thought.

"And you'll call me by my given name."

She realized she didn't even know the name of the man she had married. Blast! She had to guess. "Connor?"

He looked puzzled for a moment, then broke out laughing.

"What's the matter?" She was making a fool of herself.

"Why would you call me Connor?"

"Isn't that your name?"

"Not even close. My name's Con."

"Not your given name. What is it? Conrad?"

"You married me and you don't even know my name. You would have, if you'd watched me sign the license."

He patted the document in his pocket. "It's all right here."

"Let's not play Rumpelstiltskin. Or maybe your name is Rumpelstiltskin. It must be something hideous for you to keep it secret." She let her voice slide lower, teasing. "Tell me your name, Captain, or I'll be forced to write your mother."

"Promise me your firstborn."

He looked devilish. She laughed. "Since there aren't supposed to be any, I think I'm pretty safe in promising."

"All right, I'll come clean and share one of my darkest secrets with you; my mother named me Sheary, but my name is Con."

"Sherry? Delightful! A woman's name!" She laughed, but it didn't seem to disturb his good humor. He looked amused and as dashing as ever. A man who bore such a name with good grace couldn't be other than diplomatic and easygoing. There wasn't a thing to dislike about him, not one thing to focus on, to keep her from falling hopelessly.

"Yeah, well, how do you like it, Mrs. Sheary O'Neill?" He spelled it. "It's not a woman's name. It's a good old Irish name. Irish for Jeffrey, means *peace of God.*"

"I can see why you took a nickname. Where does Con come from? What does it mean?"

"A con is a navigator on a ship. I'm the best one around."

"Oh?" she said. Her laughter died away. So that's what Billy had been trying to explain about the Con. She smiled. "I think I'll just call you Captain."

"Call me whatever you like." His tone was still easy, but she thought she detected an edge of disappointment. What had she said wrong?

"Would you like to see your room?" He offered his arm.

She took it as she heard gravel crunch in the driveway. The others had arrived.

Later, Fayth sat on the edge of her bed brushing her hair, alone on her wedding night in the cozy room that was now hers. Next to her on the nightstand stood a bowl of fragrant, freshly cut old-fashioned roses. Yellow—the color of friendship. Did he really mean to be her friend? Whatever he meant, he touched a deep chord of tenderness in her.

Friend or no, the Captain had given her the wedding day every bride deserved. He'd taken the wedding party to dinner, been properly reticent and embarrassed when Captain Bailey toasted their nuptials, and had engaged in pleasant, amusing conversation with Sterling and Elizabeth well into the evening. When he noticed she was tiring, he made the proper excuses to allow them their departure and even endured the knowing, sly, though misplaced, looks given to any newly married couple on their wedding day.

When they had arrived back at the cottage, he was a perfect gentleman. He pleaded his own fatigue, escorted her to her room, and then retired to his own to look over plans for his new warehouse.

She set the brush down and lay back waiting for the sweet breeze from the open window to lull her to sleep. She had married a good man. Tonight her dreams would be peaceful.

Con propped himself up against his pillows as he sat in bed with plans for his warehouse strewn around him, clever decoys for his real thoughts. His shirt was open, his tie loose, and his boots toppled on the floor. Across the hall and two doors down was a woman as lush and beautiful as any he'd encountered. And she was his. And not his at all.

Hell! He squirmed and tugged at his pants, rearranging himself as he grew hard. He had to stop this line of thought. It was blasted uncomfortable and unproductive. Of course, most men relieved themselves differently on their wedding night. Man alive! He was no steer; what in heaven was he doing? Somehow, he never pictured himself sleeping alone.

He sighed. He'd give her these two days until he sailed, and then the length of the voyage. He had to wait until she trusted him. Once she had her loan and her anxieties about her business quieted, he would seduce her. How could he resist?

What a liar she'd made of him! He never told so many in his life. *Yes, Fayth, we will live like brother and sister, like strict business partners for the rest of our lives.* She was too naive. Good thing he'd gotten her before some other liar had. Liar—he hated the word, hated the meaning. His own dishonesty was the only thing that egged his conscience in this affair. No use dwelling on it. It had been necessary. She was the woman for him. He wouldn't lose her.

He turned back to the drawings, trying to divert his thoughts. He sure wasn't sleeping tonight.

Fayth was up early the next morning and puttered around the kitchen, trying to make some kind of breakfast. The kitchen was well stocked and she wondered again how the Captain had been able to accomplish so much in only two days. Had he set his whole crew to the task? The thought gave her a smile. She heard footsteps in the hall and turned to find the Captain standing in the doorway.

"You're up early," he said.

"I woke with the sun. Until then my slumber was perfect. Yours?"

"Reasonable." His tone led her to believe otherwise. There was a wry twinkle in his eyes and undeniable happiness in his countenance; she thought she saw anticipation there and something she couldn't quite name, but it sent her heart flip-flopping just the same.

"Are you ready to face the bankers?"

"I am." He grinned.

"Won't Mr. Finn be surprised to see us show up in his office this morning with all of his objections put to rest? He can't deny us now!"

His smile was infectious. "He might still deny you. There isn't a woman in town who looks less like she needs a loan. Look at that new gown! You're beautiful this morning."

She glanced down at her bright-yellow dress. "I have you to thank for that."

He tensed suddenly, if nearly imperceptibly, and a serious glint overtook the humor in his eyes. She felt the change and wondered at the cause.

"You saved this material from the fire."

He relaxed, and even though he hadn't lost his smile, she sensed his disappointment. She'd said something wrong again.

"I have good taste." His light humor seemed restored.

She smiled. "What would you like for breakfast?"

"Let's stop for something and celebrate after we've gotten our loans. If we hurry we can get a good spot in line. Every man in town, and at least one woman I know, wants Finn to loan them money. Let's be the first to get some today."

She took his arm. "You're a man after my own heart, husband."

Fayth barely contained her happiness as she waited for the Captain outside Jacob Finn's office. Captain O'Neill insisted each of them conduct their business interviews separately. They had married to improve their business success, not lose their autonomy. He was gentlemanly enough to allow her to go first. So now she waited with bank draft in hand, dreaming of buying a tent to conduct business in until her building was completed. Dreaming of architects and contractors. Imagining sharing her triumph with her partner, Con O'Neill.

Mr. Finn made only one stipulation; that she continue sewing for Miss Gramm. He claimed the Board would frown on her turning down paying customers, no matter who they were. Lou certainly knew how to wield power in this town. Fayth had an appointment with her later in the morning and had been hoping to tell her that she would no longer sew for her. As far as Fayth knew, the Captain knew nothing of her association with Lou or Coral. She would have to confess about Coral sooner or later. Originally she hoped to avoid telling him that she worked for a madam. She couldn't imagine he would be anything but unhappy about it. Now she *had* to tell him. Later. She ran her fingers over the edge of her draft again, wanting nothing to dim the happiness of the moment.

"I told you I couldn't loan you the money you'd need if you hooked up with her, Con. The Board would have my head. My full congratulations, by the way. She's quite an impressive little woman."

Con ignored his well wishes. Business was forefront on his mind. "I'm not asking for the full amount. I've refigured my finances. I can get by with three-quarters of what I was asking for before. Surely my wife's debt is no more than a quarter of mine. The total has to be the same."

Jacob shook his head. "Miss Sheridan, I mean, Mrs. O'Neill's business is a much riskier venture than yours, Con. I have faith that you'll succeed, and personally I'd lay odds on her as well. She certainly has pluck, but the Board won't see it that way. If it weren't that I can use the *Aurnia* to secure her debt, I'd have to answer to them for loaning to her at all."

"Come on, Jacob, how can you use my assets to back her loan? She's got her land to secure her debt. I know she offered it up as security. She'd never presume to offer mine."

"She didn't. I did. Her land is too near The Line. Not worth half what I lent her."

Con drummed his fingers on the desk in front of him. "Then lend me whatever you can."

Jacob shook his head firmly and reached for his pen and a piece of paper.

"Nothing? You can't lend me anything?"

"I warned you, Con."

"Jake, we've been friends for too long. Don't tell me you're in cahoots with the big shipping conglomerates? Surely you're not going to tell me to sell my waterfront property."

Jacob was scribbling furiously on the paper in front of him. "Con, I thought you understood. I gave you my tacit pledge that I'd take care of you. The bank can't give you a loan, but my endorsement on this piece of paper to a business associate of mine is all you need to get the money." He turned the paper around so Con could read it.

"Lou Gramm?"

"I'm afraid you have no alternative, my friend. But, believe me, she is a fair-minded businesswoman. She'll deal with you honestly. And, at my urging, give you a fair rate."

Fayth chattered giddily as she and the Captain walked out of the bank's temporary headquarters and down the street. She ignored the serious glint in his eyes and his cool, thoughtful silence, not wanting anything to lessen her joy. She convinced herself that it was his way of showing excitement. She hadn't seen his composure crack under strain and pressure, why should it break with excitement?

"And I'm going to buy a tent, or at least rent one, and put it on my property right away. What do you think? Will you help me erect it?"

The corner of his mouth curled up slightly. "I should think I'd have to help you. Have you seen the size of those things? In fact, I'll need the help of a few of my men."

"Billy?"

"I said, my men."

She laughed.

"I suppose you'll want your machine moved there?"

"Oh, no." She shook her head. "The dust will ruin it. I'm going to take orders, do fittings, and take measurements in the tent. Hand sew what I need to there. I'll use the machine at home. But for the most part, I need the tent so the men can find me."

He cocked a brow. "Men? I was hoping you'd give up measuring crotches once we married and start sewing for the fairer sex. The ladies need your talent more than ever now. Have you noticed the drab clothes they've been wearing lately? Most of their dresses went through the fire and look it."

She laughed again and decided to tease him, just a bit. And string him along before it was necessary to reveal that she was already sewing for women. "I *have* noticed them. But you shouldn't. You're married now."

He shrugged. "I made my observations yesterday, before the ceremony." And then he winked at her.

She shook her head again. "You think quickly. Too quickly sometimes. Will I ever get the best of you?"

"I hope not." He sounded serious.

She studied him. She hated to remind him, but she had to make sure he knew his place. "You're not thinking you can dictate what I do with my business now, are you?"

"No. Absolutely not." He sounded sincere, but his eyes twinkled. "That was the agreement, wasn't it? I'm merely suggesting a profitable line of business to you."

"And I appreciate your advice." She paused. "I just realized. I didn't see you come out of Mr. Finn's office with a draft. Did you get your money?" She kept her tone light and teasing. She would have liked a look at his note, just to see how much Mr. Finn loaned him.

"I did." But he didn't offer to show it to her.

"Good." She took up his arm. "Would you like that breakfast now? It took so long at the bank that it'll have to be quick. I have an appointment at eleven."

"Let's celebrate later. When we have time to linger and enjoy it. I have an errand to run myself. Where are you off to? Do you need the carriage?"

She paused, debating whether to tell him about Lou. No, not now. Why ruin the happy mood? That revelation could wait until another day. Instead, she threw him off by camouflaging her true business in a way that should make him happy. She grinned at him. "I'm fitting a woman for a gown up in the north of town."

"Why, Fayth! Sewing for women, why didn't you say so in the first place?" His eyes lit up. He was undeniably pleased.

She shrugged. "Just on a case by case basis for now." She didn't want to lead him on *too* far. "To see how it goes." She hesitated. She wanted a ride to Lou's. It was too far to walk. But she didn't want to rob the Captain of his transportation. And then she hit upon a solution. She'd have him drop her off at a house near the madam's and pretend it was her client's. "If you give me a lift to my client's house, I'll have her driver drop me home and you can have the carriage."

"My pleasure," he said as they walked to the carriage. "What's the address?"

"The address?" She took a deep breath. "No idea. But I know how to get there."

"There! That's the house. I knew I'd recognize it once I saw it." Fayth had given the Captain instructions to the street, but gotten all turned around in the process. She panicked when she realized they were getting too close to Lou's and pointed at the first respectable house she could find. She forced a smile, hoping she looked calm.

The Captain reined the horses to a stop. "I'll walk you in." He climbed out and helped her down.

She would have bounded out unaided if it hadn't been for the dress she wore. Fashion was not made for jumping out of carriages. "No, no need."

"It's no trouble." He took her arm as she glanced wildly over her shoulder at the house.

"No! You'll scare old Mrs. Brown. She's very private and shy."

He hesitated and frowned.

"Please. She's an excellent client. I can't afford to lose her." Her begging tone must have convinced him.

"I'll see you at home later, then." He gave her a suspicious look and climbed back up into the carriage.

"Yes, later. And we'll celebrate." She waved at him as he rode off, slumping in relief when he was finally out of sight. Her relief lasted exactly two seconds. Then she realized her mistake. She'd panicked too early. She was farther away from Lou's than she'd originally thought. Curses! Why didn't she have a better sense of direction?

Walking at a brisk pace, it took her nearly twenty minutes to reach Lou's temporary home. By that time, her feet hurt and some of her earlier good mood had dissipated. She spotted Lou's house from half a block away, just in time to see a jaunty male figure bounce down the steps. The sun lit his hair. Red highlights shone bright. *The Captain.*

She froze and watched him walk in the opposite direction, away from her, with an obviously happy spring to his walk. For one awful moment the sight before her made her feel as if she had had the wind knocked out of her. She simply couldn't get her breath. Why would the Captain be leaving Lou's? *Other than the obvious.*

CHAPTER NINE

Fayth froze, finally willing herself to breathe deeply. By the time the Captain disappeared from sight, she convinced herself it couldn't have been him. There had to be hundreds of tall men with red highlights in their hair. From the distance, she couldn't make out any other detail. She couldn't even remember if the man had a beard. Drew had made her skittish and distrustful. She hated him for it.

But the awful image lingered with her through the fittings. Through Coral's surprise and delight at her marriage. Through the teasing the other girls gave her. She lost her patience and threatened to design dresses so hideous the girls would be laughed out of Seattle. It lasted through the silent ride home in the carriage with Lou's driver. It persisted still as she paced the kitchen.

She must have more faith in him. She couldn't let Drew's actions color her opinions of every man, least of all the Captain.

He was very late coming home. It was nearly dark. She came back from Lou's expecting a celebration and ended up dining alone. Where could he be? She took another deep breath to calm herself. Since the death of her parents she couldn't tolerate lateness, always fearing the worst. Everything had been normal that last evening she waited for them to come home from the shop. But they never had.

Drew later accused her of being obsessed with promptness. Said it was stifling him. He shouldn't have to account for every minute away from her. But he should have, the unfaithful bastard. She never said the word aloud, but she didn't feel guilty thinking it. There was no other way to describe Drew. And she preferred anger to the weepy guilt that had consumed her after he left. She still saw the steely set of his jaw as he accused her of driving him away. Only recently she realized he had chosen to leave. But the Captain was not Drew, and he owed her no explanations.

The front door, swollen in its frame from the heat of the day, shuddered open. Fayth jumped and raced into the entry. The Captain's smile melted her fear and anger away at first glance.

"I'm sorry I'm so late." His eyes were full of devilment and delight. "I had to spend all day doing it and scour the city in the process, but I got us a contractor, and you a tent."

"What?" Could he be serious? The wonderful man! She nearly hugged him.

"I know you talked about getting the tent yourself, but I wanted to surprise you. They're going to put it up for you first thing tomorrow morning. We're back in business!" He had a box of candy tucked under one arm and a newspaper under the other. He held the chocolates out to her. "To us and sweet success."

"That's wonderful. Yes! To us!" She clapped, delighted.

He set the paper down, picked her up and twirled her around as they both laughed. His arms felt good around her.

"You, sir, are amazing!" Her eyes swept over him. How could she even think that this man had been at Lou's? What an idiot she was! She let her relief out.

"Hey, you were worried?" He set her down too soon.

"Just thought you might have decided to stay on the *Aurnia.*"

"What? Desert my bride? Not a chance." His words were light, his tone serious. "I've got a reputation to maintain. What do you think my crew would think? That I can't, you know. Or that we've had our first spat. Not on your life. You're stuck with me, lady."

She couldn't have imagined his words would make her heart dance as it did.

She followed him as he walked into the kitchen and spread the newspaper open to point out an article.

"Love ignites in the ashes," she read aloud. "Yesterday afternoon Captain Con O'Neill and Miss Fayth

Sheridan were joined in matrimony before the Rever-
end Wilson—"

"Thought you might want it for your scrapbook."

"Elizabeth! It has to be her!"

"Now you see the need for pretenses. The lonely fel-
lows of our fine city will be keeping an eye out to see if
this thing sticks." He lifted the lid off the chocolates.
"Shall we?"

She woke with a start, her heart hammering in her
ears. She sat up and tried to calm herself. Olive usually
comforted her when she woke from a nightmare, but
she was still at Elizabeth's.

Fayth shuddered. Why did this dream frighten her
so deeply? She didn't understand where it came from,
or why. Like most dreams, it wasn't the content as
much as the ethereal emotions she experienced in its
grip that scared her. Though she couldn't describe
them in words, they were terrifying. She needed a
calming drink of cool water or she'd never get back to
sleep.

She stood in the kitchen with a glass of water; the
Captain's voice from behind her made her start.

"Are you all right?"

"Fine." Her voice sounded squeaky. "Had a bad
dream. Didn't mean to wake you. A glass of water always calms me."

He drew up a chair at the table and motioned her into a seat across from him. "Very wise. Mam always
brought me one when I was a child with a nightmare.

Too bad we have to grow up and get our own." He studied her as she sipped. "Want to tell me about it?"

She ran her finger around the rim of her glass, trying to hide her embarrassment. "It's so silly. Since the night of the fire, I've had this nightmare that I'm drowning. I thought I had it figured out. That it would go away. But I haven't been able to shake it yet."

"You'll never drown as long as I'm here." He grinned at her. "I have a big boat."

She couldn't stop the smile that tugged at the corners of her mouth, but she didn't speak. Instead, she watched him stare at her.

A serious expression overtook his face. "I suspect you're feeling overwhelmed by all that's happened in the last week. I'm here to help you now. The burden isn't yours alone."

She nodded. He hummed some nonsensical little syllables. Words she couldn't recognize.

"What are you trying to sing?" The effects of her nightmare drifted off into the nebulous night, chased away by Con O'Neill's reassuring presence.

"Trying? Are you saying I can't carry a tune?" He laughed. "It's a little child's ditty about a yellow seaweed in Ireland. It's always been very comforting to me."

"But you're not making any sense."

"Sure, I am. You don't understand Gaelic is all."

"And where did you learn it? On your travels?" She sipped her water.

"With a name like Sheary O'Neill, are you kidding? At home, darling. At home. My mother used to sing it to me." She hadn't noticed his slight brogue before. Did he put in on just for her?

"You don't have to sing to make me feel better. Just promise to take me to see my tent go up tomorrow."

Con stopped singing and shook his head, giving off a little snorting laugh as he did. "That's my girl. You are feeling better. Your mind's back on business again."

He reached across and patted her hand. "I give you my promise. Now off to bed with you. And me. We'll have to be up early to meet the crew, such as it is." He pushed back his chair and rose to leave.

Fayth was slow to her feet. She watched him a moment before rising. "Thank you."

He nodded. "Goodnight, Fayth."

He walked out of the room down the dark hallway. She listened to his comforting footfalls until they receded, wondering about the man she married. Wondering that he so easily chased the dream away. Then she made her own way down the hall to bed humming a little tune about yellow seaweed.

The next afternoon the house was quiet as Fayth swept in the front door, harried and late. She had stayed too long at Lou's. Tentatively, she called the Captain's name.

"On the back porch, Fayth." His response startled her. She hurried to him.

The picture he made on the porch as she came through the door returned her sense of serenity and well-being. He sprawled lazily in a chair, the very picture of handsome nonchalance. Olive curled in his lap. A package sat on the floor beside him.

"Sorry I'm late. Mrs. Brown kept me longer than I intended."

"Did she?"

"Don't the two of you look comfortable?" She walked over and scratched Olive behind the ears. The cat climbed up the Captain's chest and dug her claws into his shirt as if to tell her not to think of extracting her. "Traitor!"

"Me, or the cat?"

"Both of you!" To Fayth's amazement, Olive and the Captain had made friends bare seconds after she had retrieved the cat from Elizabeth's.

This after Fayth spent the better part of the morning before she brought Olive home warning the Captain to keep his distance. Olive distrusted men. She'd barely set Olive down when the Captain clucked to the cat. Olive ran to him as he knelt, curling herself around his legs and purring until he picked her up.

"You have to know which men to trust. Can't let one man's mistreatment influence you against the whole lot." He held the cat up to lick his face.

Fayth couldn't help feeling he was speaking to her, not Olive. That night, Olive abandoned Fayth's bed for the Captain's. Fayth still felt the sting of it.

"If I didn't know where Mrs. Brown lived, I'd almost think she lost her entire wardrobe in the fire. She must be quite fashionable. She's been keeping you so busy it's like you're sewing for half a dozen ladies." His tone was too casual. He suspected something.

Fayth dropped into a wicker chair opposite him. "You believe in honesty, don't you?"

He tensed, and gave her an odd, expectant look. She didn't know exactly how to describe it. Guarded? Hopeful? When he looked at her that way, his hazel eyes appeared more green than brown and burned with an almost frightening inner intensity.

When he didn't answer immediately, she spoke. "I do. What is a marriage without it?" She took a deep breath. "I have a confession to make."

He looked poised for the worst.

She plunged ahead before she lost her confidence. "There isn't any Mrs. Brown. I made her up. I've been sewing for the *lady boarders* at Miss Gramm's."

He didn't waver under her expectant gaze.

She clenched her hands in her lap and waited to be upbraided.

"Don't look like you're bracing for a fight, Fayth. What are you expecting from me? Recrimination?" His tone was kind, almost amused.

"I haven't known a man yet who would be happy to discover his wife works for a madam." As she spoke the corners of his mouth twitched, fighting laughter.

"Depends on what she's doing for the madam. I admit, I have more cause than most husbands to be concerned. After all, my wife claims to be a seamstress, and we know what that usually means in this town. But I have the satisfaction of having seen you sew."

Fayth was struck by the irony of his words, and not altogether certain he hadn't intended it. The Captain had seen her sew, but not *sew*, not in the manner of the prostitutes. Not like was a husband's right. She laughed nervously. "I, sir, am an honest seamstress. I promise."

"Just so it stays that way." His laugh held a deep, baritone timbre. In the next moment he became nearly serious. "These *lady boarders* pay well, I assume?"

"Yes, but that's not why I sew for them. I was co-erced into it." She noted his confused expression, and the odd impression struck her that he looked almost guilty. "It's too long a story to tell now. Suffice it to say that I owe Miss Gramm a favor, as does half the town, I expect. As soon as it's repaid, I'm quitting."

"Because of what, public opinion? Seems to me that designing their fancy dresses would be challenging and fun for someone with your talent. Don't quit, and don't apologize, Fayth. And don't think I'll stop you from doing what you love."

"Thank you." She unclenched her hands, resting them lightly in her lap. "You are an amazing, percep-tive, liberal-minded man. And I appreciate it. But it's not the opinion of others that matters to me, or stops me. It's that by her trade Miss Gramm encourages women to be victims. I can't condone the behavior of anyone who makes money through immoral means, es-pecially flesh-peddling. I'm half ashamed that I have anything to do with her, but I have another interest there. A girl I've befriended. She may still be young enough to save."

If she wasn't mistaken, he looked proud of her. "I hope you can. That's what I love about you, Fayth. You

stand on your principles. You care about others. Is
there anything I can do to help?"

Love about you? Silly, she knew his words were light
and careless, but her heart fluttered all the same. She
smiled. "Not presently."

His expression changed. He looked amused again,
and slightly contrite as he changed the subject. "I have
to admit to something myself. I knew there was no Mrs.
Brown. Yesterday afternoon I stopped by the house you
pointed out as hers, thinking to save her driver a trip
taking you home. You should have seen the look I got
from the owner when I asked for you."

"No! I never thought you would stop there!"

They laughed together.

"I'll have to use more care next time I concoct a deception."

"Don't let there be a next time, Fayth," he teased.

She blushed. "Of course not. What's in the package?" She pointed next to the chair.

"A present for you." An eager anticipation filled his
voice as he handed it to her and watched her open it. "A
spyglass. Every sailor's wife should have one."

She cradled it gently in her hands, staring at it, not
knowing what to say. "Thank you. It's beautiful."

He laughed. "Practical, at least. You'll be able to
watch for me when I'm due home. Look for me there."
He pointed through an opening in the evergreens and
firs framing the view of Puget Sound in the distance.
"I'll be sailing in from the north. You'll be able to recognize the *Aurnia* by the green and gold flag flying on
the mast."

He stood and pulled her to her feet, leading her to the rail of the cantilevered deck. "Give it a try."

He stood behind her. Encircling her with his arms, he guided the glass to her eye. She felt oddly tremulous in the secure round of his embrace. His bearded chin rested just on top of her head as he held the glass in front for her. Taut biceps brushed against the outside of her arms. A firm chest braced her from behind. Flustered, she bobbled the spyglass, catching wild, fleeting glimpses of sky, trees, dirt, and blackberry bushes before he balanced it and directed it toward the water. Embarrassed, she let him hold it so he wouldn't see the trembling of her hands. A tiny speck became a paddle-wheel ferry, so clear she could nearly read the name lettered on the side.

"Amazing," she said.

He brought his head around next to hers so that his cheek grazed hers. "What do you see?"

"Everything. A ferry. Whitecaps on the water. Seagulls flying."

"Excellent." He lowered the glass from her eye and handed it back to her before stepping back.

Her emotions and thoughts were as jumbled as the blackberry bushes that cascaded and tumbled down the hillside beneath them, so entwined she couldn't separate them. One minute the Captain seemed to be courting, giving her presents, finding excuses to hold her. The next, he stepped back, gentlemanly and uninterested.

Her own emotions were even more tangled and dangerous. She didn't want to fall in love with this man.

Where could it possibly lead? Her body might betray her, but her mind knew better—she was best off with him as her friend and partner. Loving him would inevitably hurt her.

She turned to face him, forcing a trembling smile. "How long will you be gone?"

"Two weeks, maybe three. It's hard to predict an exact schedule. Everything depends on the weather and number of stops we make."

She looked at the spyglass in her hand and back to him. She had known, even counted on him being gone often. But his leaving had crept up on her. She just wasn't ready for it. Only because she would miss his advice and help, she tried to convince herself. But she knew better. "Promise me you'll be careful?" Her eyes misted. She dropped her gaze.

"Naturally."

She clasped the glass to her chest, thinking it was the best present she had ever received, and trembling with irrational fear. People she loved just didn't stay. They were either taken from her, or they ran off with someone else. If she let herself love him, which category would the Captain fit into?

Fayth stood on the waterfront, which teemed with people and activity. The Captain's pier was still just reconstructed pilings with a framework as open and delicate looking as a spider's web stretching out over open water. He'd have to dock to the north. Fayth bet on Schwabacher's and headed directly there. If she was wrong, she'd find him. All the remaining wharves were in sight of each other.

The undamaged wharves were doing two to three times the business they were designed to handle. Goods and rebuilding supplies streamed into the city. Fayth wove through the throng of people, mostly men loading and unloading cargo, arriving at the pier just in time to see the *Aurnia* pull in.

Before leaving the house, Fayth had changed into her newest walking gown. The bodice was cut low in a square outline, the sleeves short and puffed. She wore no jacket; the day was too warm, which suited her. The dress was more becoming without one and she wanted to look pretty for the Captain.

The *Aurnia's* crew lowered the gangplank. Fayth breathed deeply and watched the deck. She couldn't see the Captain. Patience. He'd be out soon enough. There was a commotion on deck. The wheelhouse door flew open. Fayth swept her arm up to wave to him. He wasn't expecting her; she wanted him to spot her in the activity onshore. Fayth froze. The Captain didn't emerge from his quarters behind the wheelhouse; a woman carrying a duffel did.

Fayth's stomach fell. Her heart thudded hard in her ears. She dropped her arm. The woman, immaculately dressed and coifed, looked cultured, if a bit hard. She turned back to yell something into the cabin. When she faced the pier, she was smiling and laughing.

Fool, Fayth chided herself. How could she have been so naive! Fayth felt flushed, ashamed. With one hand, she clutched her stomach. Her stays felt suddenly too tight. With the other she pulled at the neckline of her bodice, absently trying to draw the sides together to cover her bosom, or her naked emotion. She didn't know which felt more exposed. She took a deep breath and turned away, hung her head. Tears stung. She blinked them back.

Shocked, her mind worked in short, indifferent bursts. What had she thought? That he would be any different than any other handsome man? Blast! Anger, familiar and harsh, welled up inside her. She had warned him to be discreet. When she turned back to look, the woman descended the gangplank and merged with the crowd on the pier. Fayth half turned to leave, then stopped. She wouldn't go. No running, not this time. She'd come to greet him and show him the new construction, and she would.

"Ma'am, ma'am." It took Fayth a second to realize someone, *the woman,* spoke to her.

Fayth turned to face her. Up close the woman looked young, and heavily highlighted with rouge. "Yes?"

"You look like a friendly face." The woman's sweet voice grated on Fayth. "We arrived early and my ride isn't here to meet me. Is it possible to hire a cab from here?"

"There. That way." Fayth pointed, stubbornly refusing to speak one unnecessary word to the creature. Wanted to claw her. "You can catch one on the street."

"Thank you. I knew you could tell me." The woman winked.

Sudden curiosity overwhelmed Fayth. She ignored the woman's innuendo. She had to know her destination. "Wait. Where are you headed? I might be able to give you directions. You may be able to walk there."

The woman laughed huskily. "With the trunks I brought? Oh, honey, I don't think so. Miss Gramm's is certainly too far away."

A whore. Fayth had thought, a mistress maybe, but a whore!

And then she hoped . . .

Well, she was a fool. Was this the Captain's idea of discretion, a whore at sea? She took another deep breath. He had hurriedly scuttled the woman off the ship first. No one they knew had seen her, no one but Fayth. It was his business. Now she would attend to hers. As she waited for him, she forced a smile, which felt as painted as the ones on the porcelain dolls of her childhood.

Con finished the log, grabbed the packages he'd brought back for Fayth, and headed for the deck. He was halfway down the gangplank when he spotted her coming toward him. She'd come to meet him. Was he grinning like a monkey?

"Fayth! How did you know to meet me?" He wanted to kiss her, but she held herself back from him. For now he'd have to content himself with the sight of her.

"Oh, I don't know." She smiled coyly. "My husband gave me a spyglass. I was just admiring the Sound."

"No!" She had watched for him? He barely allowed himself to imagine it possible.

She shrugged and laughed, perhaps a bit too brightly. "What are the odds I'd be watching as you sailed in? I was about to leave for town when I saw the green and gold. So I came to meet you, thinking you might like to see the progress that's been made since you left."

"And I'm glad you did."

"The carriage is parked up the street. Can you leave now, or should I come back?"

"Now's fine. How are things?"

"The pier framework is built, and my first story framed. I'll drive you by," she said. "And you'll be happy to hear that I've been getting more and more female clients. They keep me so enjoyably busy, I've done very little tailoring for men during your absence."

"I'm glad to hear you're happy. I can see it on your face. You look beautiful, Fayth." Was it his imagination, or did she frown slightly?

"Thank you." She held out her arms to him. "Let me help you with those packages."

"No, certainly not. A gentleman never lets a lady carry things for him."

"Are you a gentleman?" Her question sounded almost barbed. Had he done something wrong? He gave himself a mental shake. Her smile was still sweet, and her expression pleasant. What could he have done in such a short time? An image of Lou's latest whore came to mind. Had Fayth seen her come off the ship? He couldn't force himself to ask.

"I'm the well-mannered man my mother taught me to be. How long have you been waiting?"

"I haven't." She started walking, evidently expecting him to fall into pace with her. "I just arrived. You were docked with your gangplank down when I came up. Your men were so efficient they were already unloading."

She couldn't have seen anything. He must be imagining.

"What's in the packages?" She negotiated through the crowd and headed up the street.

"Presents for you."

She gave him a startled look. "You shouldn't have. Your coming home safely is present enough."

Did she toy with him? As if she read his mind, she winked. "I need your business expertise, and your clout with the city council. They're up to their usual shenanigans."

At home later, Fayth sat across from the Captain as he unloaded many packages with her name on them. Somehow she had managed to remain calm, to quell her jealousy, throughout the afternoon as he examined the new buildings. Now, her mouth ached from smiling, her heart from other causes. Here, in her own home, she felt more normal, less threatened. But her thoughts kept returning to the woman. Little thoughts niggled at her, making no sense. The Captain had seemed so happy to see Fayth.

He unwrapped a new parasol, and a hat, and handed them to her.

"Oh, Captain. They're lovely." She forced the smile again, perched the hat on her head, and shook it saucily with an air of happiness she did not feel.

"Beautiful!"

"Thank you. It'll look lovely with my blue gown." She rose and went to the hall mirror to preen. What did he mean by these gifts? What could he mean after carrying on with that woman? Were these meant to appease, or divert her attention?

"You carry our deception too far, Captain. I'm not sentimental. There's no need to treat me like a real wife. Next thing I know, you'll be expecting me to reciprocate by darning your socks and fetching your newspaper, cooking your meals. And I'm no good at any of that." She studied his reaction, but his expression was veiled.

He laughed. "You've lost everything, Fayth. Let me restore what I can." His expression became solemn and searching. Her heart caught under his returning scrutiny. Surely he spoke of something deeper, more meaningful than material things. She forced her gaze away, back to the mirror.

"What did your family think of your quick marriage? Were they were shocked?"

"Pleasantly surprised. They thought me long past finding someone."

She smiled at him in the mirror. "Your family must be very easy-mannered. If my parents were alive, they would disown me for marrying without their consent."

"They're an understanding crew, all right. But they're not likely to let me back in San Francisco without at least a photograph of you, though they'd prefer you in person."

The tenderness in his voice confused her. Of course he hadn't told them the truth about their marriage. Without meeting them, she liked the family he described, and had no desire to deceive them. "Maybe someday," she said tentatively.

He looked away from her. "When you're ready."

Con spent the bulk of the summer at sea. Busy trying to keep O'Neill Shipping afloat, his visits home were infrequent one-night stays. He and Fayth fell into a polite routine. Con couldn't overcome the feeling it was a kind of truce. If only he could figure out what the battle had been.

During the nights he spent in the cottage, he tossed in his bed, aroused, unable to sleep, knowing that two doors and a hall were all that separated him from her. That, and Fayth's reticence. How to change her mind? How to break through? She worked too hard, kept him at bay as she designed gowns for society types to wear when they entertained the territorial governor and other dignitaries. At last he convinced Fayth to go on a picnic with him.

A light breeze blew at the corners of the blanket and rattled the wrappings covering the remains of the picnic the Captain had brought. Fayth turned her face to the sun. The Captain sat next to her.

"My compliments, Captain. That was the most sumptuous picnic I have ever had." Her tone was light, buoyed by relief at having delivered her latest gown just that morning. Mrs. Wells had looked stunning in it. There was no denying it. And the lady had been pleased.

"Thank you. But the compliments must all go to the bakery and the butcher. I merely did the purchasing." His eyes twinkled.

Fayth enjoyed seeing him happy. "Yes, but only a man with impeccable taste would choose such fare."

His answering laughter rang deep and rich with good humor. "If only it were always so easy to please you," the Captain said. "Tell me, isn't it refreshing to be outdoors, rather than cramped in a chair, bent over volumes of fabric?"

"The way you phrase things, Captain, makes one look foolish denying them." She smiled.

He laughed again as he reached across the blanket for her sketchpad and held it out to her. "So I've been told before. It's a gift."

She laughed. "A gift? I wouldn't describe it that way."

"Could I use it to persuade you to draw?"

"How would you phrase it? How could you possibly make lounging on a blanket in such fine weather pale by comparison with hunching over a sketchpad?"

"You have a bit of the gift yourself," he said. "How will I persuade you now?"

"You have a beautiful smile, Captain." The sunshine made her feel light, and flirtatious. She took the pad from him. "It has convinced me. If it will make you happy, I will draw. But you are too eager for me to work."

"Wasn't that the reason for our outing?" He knew how to add just the right teasing inflexion to his tone. She felt, at that moment, that he could persuade her of anything.

"I thought it was for relaxation."

He shook his head. "No, it was for inspiration. Remember, suggesting that it would aid your work was the only way I could entice you."

Was it? Many things about the Captain enticed her—his looks, his humor. If only he knew. "What will you do while I'm busy?"

"Nap." He stretched out on the blanket with arms behind head, ankles crossed.

"No, you won't! If I'm going to work, so will you." She tugged at his arm, enjoying the confusion that flitted across his face.

"Doing what?" He propped up on an elbow.

"Modeling. I'm going to draw you." She tugged at him again. "Now stand up and walk over to that little bluff."

"No, Fayth. I brought you out here to draw nature."

"I will. I'll draw the mountains behind you, and the foliage around you."

"That's not what I meant. I meant for you to draw the pattern and variety of nature. Examine a leaf. Capture the symmetric design of its veins. Scan the horizon. Imagine a dress done in fabric the color of the purplish blue of the distant mountains—"

She laughed and shook her head in amusement. "Captain, I'm not an amateur. I did those very things as a girl. Now, I prefer more complex subjects. You want me to draw, I will. But only you."

He rose slowly.

"There, that way." She pointed. "To the top of the rise." He walked uncertainly to where she directed. "Stop. Now pose."

"Pose?" He stood straight, arms down at his side, feet slightly apart. "How? Like this?"

He looked distinctly wooden and uncomfortable. She couldn't help laughing. "No! You're too stiff. You look like an old stick."

"Why, thank you," he said.

"Relax," she directed as she smoothed out her paper. "Put one foot on that big rock. That's it. Now, lean in and brace one elbow against your knee. There." She cocked her head and paused to consider. Something about it wasn't right.

"How long will I have to stand like this?"

"As long as it takes me to draw you." He still didn't look right. The pose was too contrived.

"This won't do." He plunked down on the rock before she could protest. He sat with arms and ankles crossed, a smile spread across his face. "You'll have to draw me sitting."

"Perfect! You look dashing."

They sat in companionable silence while she sketched. Capturing his physique and his clothes, the foliage around him, the sky, and background was easy, even enjoyable. What other opportunity did she have to study him so minutely, so thoroughly? And he was fine to look at. But when she got to his face, she paused. She penciled something in, and frowned. She erased.

"Is something wrong?" Deep in thought, it took her a minute to realize he had spoken to her.

"Your face."

He cocked an eyebrow. "Don't tell my mother!"

"No!" She laughed. "I'm not insulting you. I just can't capture it."

He stroked his beard. "Shouldn't be too hard. A thick beard. Two eyes. A rather long, plain nose. A couple of dimples." He shrugged. She laughed again.

"It's not the features. It's you, the inner you. The face I've drawn isn't yours. It's flat, lifeless. What animates yours? What fires your dimples? What do you look like beneath the beard?"

"Want me to shave?"

"Such a gallant offer, but no." She laughed. How could she convey her meaning? "That's not it. I meant—who is Con O'Neill? What emotion lights your eyes? What drives it?" She laughed self-consciously. "I'm sounding like Coral."

"What do you think it is, Fayth?" His voice was gentle.

"I see intelligence, and wit, and good humor. But I don't know the man." She set the pad aside. "I wish I did." Her words were barely audible.

He looked serious. "And I wish I knew you."

"No, you don't." She looked down into her lap.

"Why not, Fayth?"

She drew her gaze back up and looked steadfastly into his eyes, intent on testing him. "Does anyone really want to see inside another person? Does anyone really want to reveal herself? We all carry an inner darkness."

He rose from the rock and seated himself next to her. "True enough." His admission of such fact surprised her, but he made no further confession.

"Tell me a secret about yourself, and I'll tell you one about me," he said.

She bit her lip, wondering what to admit, how vulnerable to be, how best to find out what she wanted to know.

When she didn't answer immediately, he spoke. "I don't communicate what I feel."

Only what you feel? How about what you do? She couldn't give voice to such thoughts. Instead, she played it safe. "How many people do? None of us want to be vulnerable."

"Few hold back as I do."

She saw nothing but honesty in his face. Was he confessing his feelings, or did he speak generally? Her heart pounded. Should she ask him? Did she dare?

He spoke before she had summoned enough courage to ask. "Your turn."

"Distrust."

He didn't seem shocked by her revelation. "Why don't you trust people?"

"So few people tell the truth, the whole truth," she said, watching him closely. His expression gave nothing away. Once again she felt as if they danced a fine intellectual dance, each reaching for something the other seemed determined not to provide.

"But is that any reason for such trepidation? Isn't it possible for a person to withhold opinions, even information, to avoid hurting another person? What about the proverbial white lie?"

"You spar too well, Captain."

He shook his head. "Something darker, more painful bred your overall distrust of people. Someone has hurt you deeply, Fayth."

He seemed to know her so very well, almost to read her thoughts.

"Who? I don't need detail, only some clue. I want you to trust me."

The depth of emotion in his eyes mesmerized her, carrying her away. How easy it would be to fall into his arms and become his. How easy, but nothing could be more foolish. He kept something from her. Something for her own good, or his? She answered his question. "I was jilted in love." She didn't speak necessarily of just Drew. Perhaps he sensed that, but he didn't seem surprised by her answer.

She smiled at him. "I see you are determined not to press me further. Have I given you clue enough?" She laughed. "But as business partners should keep no secrets, I will settle your curiosity.

"In Baltimore, I was engaged to be married. He was all I thought I ever wanted, and I expected him to make me happy and comfortable. To protect me, care for me. And I imagined he would, that he would never desert me. But he did. Just after my parents died. Just when I needed him most." She paused, took a deep breath before continuing, weighing how much to divulge.

"I didn't know a thing about business. Without the help of Father's lawyer, Mr. Benchley, I would have lost everything."

The Captain covered her hand with his. His expression was at once hard and sympathetic. He clenched his jaw, anger danced in his eyes. Anger? He gave her hand a quick, reassuring squeeze. He didn't direct his fury at her, but at whom? Drew?

"After my fiancé abandoned me, I sold the shop, took what little money the sale of the business provided, and came to Seattle." She looked down at her sketch and sighed. If only she could fill the face in, honest and handsome.

"It's a beautiful drawing, Fayth."

She pulled her hand from his and stood, thankful he didn't press her further, make an inane comment, or offer sympathy. Thankful there was no condemnation in his look or voice. "You're a shameless flatterer. It's not finished, but I promise you—I'll finish it another day."

Yes, another day. When she knew the man.

CHAPTER TEN

That evening, Fayth and Con sat at opposite ends of the kitchen table going over the books for their respective businesses. The Captain hummed happily. Fayth smiled, caught by his tune and the way the sound of his happiness lifted her spirits. Her account ledgers were only slightly less than depressing. Seeing the numbers, so many costs and such slender profits, should have given her nervous palpitations. Everything she held dear hung by the thread of her needle and her ability to bring in clients. But sitting next to the Captain, with his confidence and strength, she felt optimistic.

"Do you know anything popular?" She looked up from her books and smiled at him.

When he lifted his head, his eyes twinkled with amusement. "What?"

"I don't recognize the song you're humming."

He set his pen down. "You don't recognize a good Irish tune when you hear one?"

"No. Sorry. But I like your voice. Hum something I know." Yes, she liked the sound of his voice very much. Too much, perhaps, given their arrangement. But then, it wasn't a crime to enjoy the company of one's partner. Though perhaps it wasn't wise to sound so flirtatious.

"What do you know?"

"Nothing Irish." Fayth rolled her shoulders and stretched her stiff fingers. "My ancestors were all very British. My parents wouldn't have approved of me marrying an Irishman." She didn't know why she blurted that out. She was at a loss to understand her emotions lately and her motivations had taken on a life of their own. Was she trying to goad him? Or show him how independent and freethinking she was? That she chose him despite the values and prejudices that had been instilled in her?

"Wouldn't they?" He clucked his tongue. "Seems they didn't approve of much. Would their disapproval have stopped you?" He was still smiling, but he sat up straighter and watched her closely, as if her answer was vitally important.

How could she answer in a way that wouldn't disappoint him, or tip the hand of her delicate heart? She could love him. She was falling in love with him. She was honest enough with herself to admit it. But protective and savvy enough about their business arrangement to deny it to everyone else, including him. A simple, straightforward answer seemed best. "No."

He relaxed and his smile deepened. "You have a trace of the headstrong Irish in you."

She laughed, glad she'd answered correctly, happy that he was happy. "Now that would really upset my parents!"

She glanced down at her ledgers and frowned automatically. "Then again, they'd be disappointed in me for everything I'm doing. Father would scold me for carrying so much debt. Frankly, it makes me nervous, too. One small crisis will send the whole thing toppling. And Mother," she rolled her eyes. "If she'd ever found out I was sewing for a notorious madam like Lou Gramm, she'd have disowned me." She watched him closely for his reaction to Lou's name, for anything that gave away him and his suspected connection to Lou. But he seemed completely at ease.

"Then quit." He looked hopeful she would.

Which seemed natural enough in a protective husband. But equally so in someone who didn't want her too near his source of pleasure and wished to remain undiscovered.

She cocked her head, studying him. If only she could be sure of his motives. "One more dress and I will. Lou keeps threatening to bring in a new seamstress from back East, anyway. Let her and good riddance. I don't ever intend to sew for that flesh peddler again. Not if I go bankrupt! To be indebted to that woman is to sell your soul to the devil."

A look crossed his face, a creasing of his brow as fleeting as quicksilver. And then he masked it, becoming inscrutable. What had she just seen? Worry? Or worse, guilt?

Neither were a good sign. Her heart and spirits sank. There was a connection between him and the madam. Or more specifically, him and her girls. "Is something wrong?"

He smiled, but it didn't reach his eyes. "No. I'm sorry. My thoughts drifted back to my books. I should get back to work. Mathematics is puzzling enough when I've got my full wits, but when I'm tired, it makes no sense at all."

He was lying. She'd seen him work figures in his head. He was very good with numbers. But not so good at deception.

Con lay in bed, staring at the ceiling. When had he become such a liar? Not good at mathematics! That was the best lie he could think up? Man alive, he needed more practice. No, he needed to tell the truth, as soon as possible. Before he ruined any chance he had of making a real marriage out this sham with Fayth.

She suspected he was up to something; he'd read it on her face and known he'd slipped up. He should have told her about the loan from Lou from the start, but had feared her disapproval, and his own vulnerability. Still did. Would she see how much he loved her, if she found out the truth about why he'd taken a loan from Lou? Or would she throw it in his face?

He hated himself for his dishonesty. There was no honor among liars, and no trust. He wanted her trust. Hell, he wanted every part of her—her body, her mind, her heart. Would telling the truth win her affections, or lose them?

He squirmed uncomfortably as he adjusted himself. Thoughts of Fayth always aroused him. Couldn't she see how much he loved her? Here he was lying to her because he loved her. Damn the son of a bitch who had hurt her!

A cat mewled outside. Olive. Better get up, throw on a pair of pants, and let her in.

Olive, screeching and clawing at the kitchen door, woke Fayth. Immediately alert, like a mother in tune to her infant's cry, she swung out of bed, and swept across the room and down the hall to the kitchen without pausing to grab her robe. When she opened the door, Olive rushed in, tailed by a cold draft.

"Olive, you naughty girl. What gives you the right to go catting about town this late?"

Olive didn't look the slightest bit contrite. She arched her back and stretched lazily.

"You gave me a scare. I'm beginning to think that's all you're good for, you little deserter."

Olive mewed contentedly before scooting past Fayth across the kitchen. Fayth closed the door and spun around to chase her. No doubt the tiny traitor was headed for the Captain's room.

Con stood in the kitchen doorway, admiring Fayth, smiling at her rebuking the cat. Suddenly, Fayth spun around to face him. Her loose nightgown swirled around her, wrapping itself against her, revealing slender curves, and breasts pointed by cold. Wearing the thin, white cotton gown, she looked like a delicate moth floating in the dark. But even the dark did not hide the round circles of her nipples or the delicate curve of her hips. He clenched his fist, imagining the feel of that fine, sheer cotton in his hand as he slipped it away from her, revealing the full beauty of her form.

She had spun with arms outstretched like a young girl in full skirts, smiling as if she enjoyed it. Olive ran past him to the bedroom. When Fayth spotted him, her mouth fell open. His gaze lingered a moment too long on her breasts. Her arms flew up, crisscrossing to cover them. Pity.

"Fayth." He leaned against the doorframe as he felt himself grow hard, felt a tug at his crotch where he tented his pants in arousal. Maybe she wouldn't notice, or maybe she would. A man could hope. "I came to let the cat in."

"She's in."

"I see that."

Did he intimidate her, or was she afraid of her own desire? Fayth remained rooted in the center of the kitchen. He had no intention of moving. If she wanted to get back to bed, preferably his, she'd have to brush past him.

"Well." She took a tiny step. "We'd better get some sleep."

"Uh-huh." Did he see desire in her eyes?

She studied him. Her gaze traced his chest. She clenched herself tighter. "I'll just be going now."

"Fine." He didn't move.

Fayth straightened her shoulders and came toward him. He didn't give an inch. She'd have to squeeze past him. He'd at least get a feel. When she was directly in front of him, she cleared her throat. He motioned with his head to go on past. She looked like she was calculating her chance of successfully negotiating the tiny passage he'd left her. She turned sideways and tried to duck under the arm that held him in place. Nipples, firm and erect, brushed him. He turned, and trapped her. "Fayth."

"Captain."

Her eyes begged a kiss. Her mouth was open and moist. What was a man to do? He turned and pulled her into his arms, bringing his mouth down on hers. She smelled of rose water, and soap, soft cotton. Everything feminine and sweet. She opened her mouth and pressed against him as he bent at the knees to level their heights. His boy searched for home. When he pressed himself between her legs, he felt her tremble, heard a tiny sigh.

He ran his hands along her body, exploring her hips, hiking up her gown. Man alive, he wanted to feel, to see. With one hand, he cupped her breast. Perfect, a perfect handful. Round and firm. His own pulse raced wildly. The other hand continued sliding the cotton gown up, pulling it over her hips. He was a visual man.

He wanted to see. Naked in the kitchen would be fine, naked in his bed, better.

When his left hand slid to bare skin and tugged to pull the chemise up over her arm, she suddenly pulled back. She wrenched her mouth free and braced her hand between them, against his chest. "No."

"Fayth."

"No, I can't."

"What is it, darling? What's wrong? We're man and wife; this is what they do."

"No, you promised. Just partners." Her voice was soft and raspy. She didn't sound insistent.

"I lied. You're beautiful." He nuzzled her neck. She tried to pry his hands away. He paused to look at her. "Give me a good reason we shouldn't."

"I . . . I don't love you."

Her words slammed into him like a punch in the gut. Even his boy started to wilt. But he couldn't stop himself. He couldn't let her go. He could make her love him, if she gave him the chance. "So don't love me. Let me love you."

She shook her head. "No."

"Fayth, what's wrong with lust?"

"Everything." Tears welled in her eyes.

He let her go. She turned and ran down the hall to her room. What had he done?

Fayth's heart pounded as she slid into bed. Pressed against the Captain, she could forget everything. But then the woman came back, the whore from the ship. Fear pulsed through her. She curled into a ball, pulling her knees tight against herself. As she closed her eyes, she pictured him again. Biceps bulged nicely without being flexed. Stomach flat and rippled. His freckles ended at his forearms leaving the bulk of him pale and unblemished. His face, so perfect and handsome.

She squeezed her legs together, trying to push away the tingles, frustrated and without relief. Don't cry, oh, don't cry. Blast that whore, and blast him! What was his connection to Lou? Oh blast! She clenched herself tighter, trying to sleep.

Fayth was up early the next morning, pounding away at her sewing machine. Pumping the treadle. In and out. She would finish this dress for Lou and be done with her. And if Lou so much as hinted at her sewing a dress for her new girl, Fayth would . . .

Well, she felt like slapping Lou at the thought. What a horrendous night it had been.

"Fayth." The Captain called her name from the door, a newspaper tucked under his arm. He looked contrite.

She felt like guilt itself. What did she do now? What could she say?

He walked over to her. She stopped pumping. The noisy clacking ceased.

"Fayth, about last night—"

"Let's not talk about it. It's forgotten."

"Fayth, I'm sorry." Why did he have to apologize, sound contrite, look genuine?

"It's all right." She smiled.

"Peace offering." He handed her the paper folded open to an article. "Something to distract you from my sins." He possessed an uncanny knack for touching her with his thoughtfulness. No man had apologized to her before. Not Father, and certainly not Drew.

Fayth scanned the article. "The city's doing what!" Fayth's heart pounded with both anger and fear.

The Captain seated himself on the sofa. Olive jumped into his lap. "They're regrading Washington, Main, and Jackson. Raising them by anywhere from eight to twenty feet higher than their pre-fire levels, extending the impact of the ordinance passed in July to all streets south of Yesler." The Captain scratched Olive behind the ears.

"My building is nearly complete. How can they do this to us?"

"The Council is under Henry Yesler's thumb; you know that. They bowed to pressure by him not to raise the streets. People have been making a fuss at City Hall since July. They want the streets raised to fix the sewers. I guess our esteemed councilmen decided their political future was more important than Yesler's opinions. In retrospect, we should have waited until the fray was over before we started building."

"Waited how long, an interminable amount of time? The decision could have gone the other way just as well." She rose and stood in front of the window, pausing to stare out over the Sound.

"At least you see the folly of hindsight and regret," Con said. "We did what any good businessman does. We made a decision and proceeded according to the regulations of the minute.

"Look at it this way, now you've got a basement. You build your top floor over again, and nothing's lost. We're more fortunate than many. Several businesses have already completed their ornate first floor entrances. We've been warned in time to make ours simple and save the more elaborate decoration for the new street level entrance. The Council claims they'll maintain a series of underground walks to service businesses that have already built up. And they're promising openings and ladders at the new sidewalk level for access."

She tapped her foot, angry with the Council. The Captain's diversion proved effective. She now felt too distracted to suffer any embarrassment over last night, and too frightened. Everything shook the security of her business. Why was life so difficult?

"I'll be out hundreds of dollars! This means the addition of another complete story. I can't even guess at an estimate."

"You don't have to. I heard rumors a few days ago. I've already got my man working one up."

"And if I can't afford it?"

"We either afford it, or find a way to."

Why were men always so matter-of-fact? She wanted so much to trust him, to let him take care of her. But she didn't dare. "My business is my security."

"Oh, darling, I'm sorry to hear that—I thought I was." His tone was light, but he studied her carefully. And though her heart pounded, she tried to give no emotion away.

"Will you be serious a minute? The shop is the only thing I have any control over. Money is its lifeline and something I have none too much of since that blasted fire. I'm certain Mr. Finn won't lend me another cent." Why did this have to happen now? She was so tired of struggling.

"I have sources. I'll get you the money."

Could he really do that? She wanted to trust him. If only she hadn't seen him with that woman. "How does it affect the wharf?"

"Doesn't. We'll be open for business in a little over a week. The warehouse will be roofed a few days after." He laughed in his warm, rich manner and stood up. She was forgiven. "The sun's out today. I'd say it's a fine day for a stroll."

She shot him a look that told him what she thought—that he was crazy. "Yesterday's rains were near record. The streets will be muddy."

"Yes, the rain!"

"You're the only one that's happy about it. The rain came too late for the rest of us."

"Me, too. But given the fire, it helped me out. I'm not up and running again yet, but some of my fine competitors are. Unfortunately for them, their warehouses weren't roofed yesterday when the rain hit. They're out a pile of money in lost goods, while I . . ."

He shrugged good-humoredly, then set Olive down and stood.

"I thought you were a humanitarian."

"I am, but as they say, business is business."

She followed him into the entry. "Do things always go your way, Captain?"

He handed her the parasol he had bought for her. "Not always." His voice was soft and his look searching.

He spoke of last night. She knew he did. She didn't know what to say.

Then he smiled "Now let's go. There are sights you'll want to see." He held the door open and waved her out.

Fayth walked along with quick strides, trying to stay abreast of the Captain with his long gait, trying not to perspire in the humid heat. Her irritation at the Council drained away as they walked along, replaced by other thoughts. She realized that had been his intent. She did appreciate him. He bore her ill-temper well. If only . . .

"You're unflappable, you know that?" She stepped over a puddle. "I suppose that's why you're the captain."

"I'm the captain because I own the boat."

"Does anything get under your skin?"

His pause was evident. "Not much."

They rounded the corner. Fayth's new construction became visible down the block. She gently tugged her narrow skirt up so she could walk faster.

"The rain slowed construction. They haven't accomplished as much as they did earlier in the week." She reached the easement in front of her property. Construction workers crawled over the property, sloshing through mud and puddles to accomplish their tasks. Similar workmen occupied properties all down the street. Until Seattle was rebuilt they would have little rest. Sunday meant nothing but another day for labor.

Fayth scanned her property, taking in the tiny improvements made since her last visit. The sound of a carriage coming down the street, accompanied in its procession by lewd catcalls, diverted Fayth's attention.

Lou Gramm's new carriage glinted in the sun as it made its way slowly down the street. Each of her girls sat regally, exhibiting the established manners of a finishing school. At first glance they might have been a family out for a ride.

They waved politely at the men, but Fayth knew these men were not the kind of high-paying clientele Lou was out to catch today. She saw the woman, her nemesis. Oh, how she hated her! *Stay calm.* The brazen thing blew kisses to the Captain and waved familiarly. Fayth clenched her fists and watched him closely, but he gave no returning gesture, just frowned almost imperceptibly. He was the class of man the girls trolled for, and it angered her that they should encourage him with her standing right beside him. Their boldness revealed their true nature.

"You did too good of a job on those, darling," the Captain said.

Fayth felt all too aware of the physical distance between them. She stepped in closer to him, protecting her territory.

"You ought to take a clue from the ladies and advertise. People should know that you made those delectable gowns. "

Fayth frowned at him. "I'd be ruined if they did."

He laughed suddenly. "You need a sign. One with something like, *fashionable dressmaker,* printed in large letters."

Fayth didn't understand the humor in his voice.

"If the looks of the men up and down the street are any indication, Miss Gramm's establishment is going to be very busy tonight," he said.

"Wonderful." Fayth turned back to look at her building. The sooner she removed herself from Lou's control, the better.

"You need more money so soon, Con?" Lou Gramm sat regally straight, perched at the front of her chair in her office in her beautifully rebuilt parlor house, imitating a lady of quality. Her girls never saw her shoulders so much as brush a chair back. But then, they hadn't seen her in her own whoring days, when she'd seldom been off her back. These days she preferred the quiet role of madam. She'd always been an astute businesswoman, and now, in her early thirties, she was well past yearning for the wildness of youth. Exterior dignity suited her.

She looked Con straight in the eye, guessing they were nearly the same age. He was tall. Successful. Appealing. His exquisite hazel eyes leapt with great passion, especially when he spoke of business. Pity that he didn't patronize her house. Though she lamented the loss of business, he had her grudging respect.

Con sat back in his chair. "You know about the latest city ordinance requiring a regrade of the streets. We're no different from anyone else. It's costing us."

In the background, glasses tinkled and men's conversations joined together to form the comforting noise of a busy establishment.

"Oh, the boys! They allowed Mr. Yesler to block the regrading project for far too long. I'm glad they got up the balls to tell him to go to hell." Lou smiled sweetly.

Many of the *boys* to whom she referred, city councilmen and men of power, occupied tables surrounding their own. The bar owners had raised such a fuss that the ban on liquor sales had recently been lifted. A begrudging city council finally admitted that the immediate danger to the city posed by alcohol-induced rowdiness was past.

Lou had been smart enough to be one of the first to apply for the newly issued licenses. Now she served alcohol to many of the city's elite and powerful throughout the day, often free of charge. If they were tempted into sampling some of her girls' lucrative nighttime wares, that was not a bad thing either. Her establishment had become so popular, in just the last few days, that it had been nicknamed the second city hall. "Has Jacob sent you with another note of reference?"

Con didn't waver under her inquiry. He took a sip of beer before answering. The man was a wonder with a poker face. "I didn't bother with it this time, but I can get one if it would ease your mind."

"Oh, Con, how polite you are! I know I can trust you. What are you offering as collateral?"

"A greater share of the *Aurnia*." He set his beer down.

"No, I want a share of Fayth's little shop."

"This doesn't concern her."

"But this loan is for *her* business, isn't it? I can't in good conscience allow you to take the risk for her. The city ordinances don't affect the wharf. You wouldn't lie to me, would you, Con?"

"Her business is not mine to offer. I'm willing to assume the risk."

"You're her husband. Of course, it's yours. But Con, you're too fine a man to risk all you have for a woman. We aren't worth it in the long run." Lou paused in thought. "If the payments on Fayth's part of the debt fall behind, I can get payment in dressmaking services. What use do I have for a boat?" She held out her hand. He realized he was beaten. She saw it in his face. Maybe he wasn't so good with a poker face, after all.

He reached across the table and shook her hand. "Deal."

As Con arrived home, a red-faced man scurried down the walk, nearly bowling Con over as he stopped to read the new, neatly painted sign freshly installed at the end of the walk to his house, Fashionable Dressmaking.

"Shit," he mumbled to himself, "Fayth, what have you done?"

His musings were interrupted by Fayth, who yelled after the man from the front door. A pair of scissors glinted dangerously over her head.

"And don't ever come back!" Fayth screamed.

Con jogged the length of the walk in several quick strides and disarmed his angry wife. "I hope you don't mean me?"

"That man had the audacity to come to my home and solicit . . ." She blushed deep scarlet as her voice trailed off. "How dare he!"

"What can you expect with a sign like that out front? Whatever possessed you?"

She gave him a quizzical look. "You suggested it the other day."

"I was joking, couldn't you tell?"

"How should I guess? A sign is good advertising."

"Yes, but not a sign with that wording. It's likely to get you arrested. Bigfoot Matt has posted signs with that wording in front of all her temporary brothels since she was burned out of the Tenderloin. The police continue chasing her from neighborhood to neighborhood. You know the prostitutes in this town call themselves seamstresses?"

"Of course I know! But why should I suffer such indignity because of a lowlife woman named Bigfoot Matt? In the prostitutes' caste system, she's at the bottom of the pile! Is there no honor in being a legitimate seamstress in this town? What am I, the last honest seamstress in Seattle?"

He shouldn't have smirked just then, but with ire firing her cheeks to deep pink and lighting her eyes with indignant passion she was too appealing.

"Sailors! Leave it to them to know what every whore in the city is up to!" She turned on her heel.

He grabbed her by the arm. "That's not fair, Fayth. You should be a little nicer to this sailor, especially since he just got you your money."

"No!" Her eyes lit up.

Because of the money, no doubt. Just once why couldn't it be for him?

"Where'd you get it?" She sounded suspicious.

He shrugged. "I have connections. You're back in business, dear lady."

A smile spread across her face. She gave him a quick hug, pulled back abruptly, and cleared her throat. "Thank you."

A pathetic hug was all he was going to get for his trouble?

"Now, do me a favor?" She nodded toward the end of the walk. "Get rid of that hideous sign before I have another caller."

"My pleasure." Con sighed as he headed down the walk where he kicked the offending sign down with one swing. He had meant to tell her the truth about the loans from Lou, but he'd never be able to now. Look how happy she'd been. He couldn't risk upsetting her. He'd just have to pay them off before Fayth found out about them. He picked up the offending sign and carried it out back to burn.

Several days after the incident with the sign, the Captain sailed off on another short run. When Fayth found a bill for the shipping company among the household mail, she unhappily went to the office to confront Mr. Tetch.

"Mr. Tetch, this bill was in the household mail. It's the shipping line's and it's overdue." The Captain's new office smelled of fresh construction, and debt, Fayth thought ruefully as she faced Silas Tetch at his desk, wishing the Captain weren't at sea. "My husband pays you a generous salary to run his business. It is your duty to see that all bills are paid on time, isn't it?"

He reached for the bill. She pulled it back out of his grasp. "Mrs. O'Neill, I assure you, it was no oversight on my part, and nothing for you to be concerned about. If you will entrust it to me, I will log it and pay it at the first opportunity funds are available."

"Aren't funds available now?"

Tetch cleared his throat self-consciously and squirmed. "They will be shortly."

She cocked one eyebrow. How she'd like to intimidate the sallow man. "Shortly? The Captain took out a generous loan. Enough to cover his building expenses. Where did that money go?"

"Mrs. O'Neill, the Captain's business dealings are vast, and complicated. He has the shipping part of the business as well as the pier, which generates income from moorage fees, and the warehouse. The smooth operation of all aspects were disrupted by the fire—"

"I'm well aware of the scope of his business, but that does not explain this." She shook the bill in front of him, wanting to shake him instead. What a condescending man! Why did the Captain keep him?

"Shipping is our primary source of income, Mrs. O'Neill, and also the one most affected by the fire. The Captain took his time resuming operations. Let me assure you, ma'am, that things will soon be righted now that Captain O'Neill is back at sea."

Tetch cleared his throat again. "Also let me assure you this is by no means an extraordinary, or foreboding, event. The cyclical nature of our business does not allow for regular, scheduled payments by our customers. We juggle bills from month to month, but we never keep our creditors waiting for payment more than two months. What with the fire, and the extra, unforeseen expenses we've incurred, it puts us into such a situation again."

"What unforeseen expenses? The Captain received an honest estimate of rebuilding costs and he was not affected by the change in the city ordinances."

Mr. Tetch stared past her. "Ah, but you were."

"What is that supposed to mean, Mr. Tetch? My expenses are my own, separate from Captain O'Neill's."

Mr. Tetch looked down at the desk. When he spoke, it was with a quiet, sympathetic tone. "The Captain is a fine sailor and an excellent captain, Mrs. O'Neill. What he is not is an expert businessman. Unfortunately, he does not understand that the business's money is the business's, not his personal funds."

"What are you saying? That he took money from his operations to cover my increased expenses?"

Tetch squirmed again. "I'm saying he has taken funds for personal use in the past. He doesn't seem to understand the concept of stealing from himself."

She shook her head in disbelief. The Captain would not behave so. Tetch lied. She saw it in his face. But why? To protect his boss? From what?

Mr. Tetch shrugged and opened the ledger in front of him. "The books are open, ma'am. Would you like to authenticate my claim?"

"No." Her stomach knotted with worry, but blast! She wasn't about to let Mr. Tetch see her fear.

"Shall I log the bill then?"

"No, I'll take it to the mill and pay it myself. There's no reason to make them wait for money that I apparently owe." She stuffed the bill back into her purse. "Mr. Tetch, I would appreciate it if you don't mention this incident to my husband."

He smiled sympathetically. "Of course not, Mrs. O'Neill."

She turned to leave. He rose to get the door for her.

"Thank you. Are there any more overdue accounts?"

"Not at this time, ma'am."

She nodded "All right then. Good day, Mr. Tetch."

She stepped out on the street, discouraged and unsettled. Could the Captain, as astute as he seemed, be inept at business? She frowned. Something about the situation did not feel right. A man of the Captain's integrity could not let his creditors hang, not when everyone needed money so badly. Was the Captain's business in trouble?

Her heart thudded in her ears. Were things worse than she knew? As strong as a memory brought back by a whiff of a familiar scent, a nameless emotion gripped her, so hopeless and consuming it deserved a hideous name. Shaded by memories of Drew, the business failing, and insecurities best forgotten, she shivered. The security of everything she had left rested with the Captain, but she couldn't let her imagination get the best of her. There was no proof of anything other than his struggle to get his business up and running again. Just like every other business in the city.

Had he, as Mr. Tetch implied, taken money from his own business to fund her second story? She'd been so happy when he'd gotten her the money that she hadn't pursued the source with much tenacity. Now, she wondered. She could hardly imagine he had robbed his own business. There hadn't been time enough for him to build up such profits, not even by juggling his bills.

Where had the money come from? Another loan from Mr. Finn would explain the shortfall in his business, if the Captain were paying the bank instead of other creditors. By that assumption, Mr. Tetch spoke the truth. But there was something about his mannerisms that made Fayth believe he did not. Nothing made sense.

"Coral's not up yet?" Lou scanned the group of young women eating their breakfast at the oversized table. "I'd better go wake her. The bar will be opening soon and I want all of you up and looking your best. If Coral doesn't get something to eat she'll be no good tonight."

What does the girl mean by sleeping so late? Lou shuffled up the stairs. *Probably sick.* With the crowd she expected, the last thing Lou needed was to be short-handed. Lou reached Coral's door and knocked. No reply. *Come on, girl, wake up.* She knocked again, harder. "Coral, it's Lou. Open up."

"Go away, Lou. I'm not coming out today." The reply was half sob.

Lou's heart pounded. She cursed to herself.

"Coral." Lou barely kept the worried edge from her voice. "Open the door. I'm here to help." She heard slow shuffling and watched as the door handle turned. The door cracked open. Coral hid on the other side. Something was wrong. A bad client? Lou slid inside. Coral closed the door behind her.

The room was dark, the curtains drawn. Lou looked straight ahead, waiting for her eyes to adjust to the dimness, staring at the rumpled, blood-splattered bed in front of her. Coral breathed raggedly behind her, cowering against the door like a frightened child. Lou slowly turned toward her. In one sweeping gesture she scooped Coral into her arms and rocked her as maternally as she knew how.

"What did he do to you, baby? What did he do?"

Coral broke into full-scale sobs. Lou cradled and rocked her, giving her time to speak.

"He beat me up!" Coral's voice broke with despair.

"I can see that, honey, I can see. Why didn't you call for help? Use what I taught you about self-defense?"

"It happened too fast. I lost consciousness before I could react. When I woke up, I was too stunned and embarrassed to face the other girls. I knew you would come looking for me."

Lou slid her hand under Coral's chin and guided her face up to survey the damage. "Did he abuse you sexually?" It seemed an odd question, given their line of work, but Coral understood what she meant and shook her head. Lou let out an audible breath.

"The bastard! Damn him! Nobody beats up my girls! I shouldn't have trusted my youngest girl with a newcomer!" She looked again into the girl's face. "Can you breathe through your nose, or is it broken?"

"I don't know. I look terrible, don't I?"

"You do." Lou never held back the truth of a situation. Coral's left eye was swollen shut, her nose a bruised, bloody mess. "But it can be fixed. How about your ribs? The rest of you? Did he kick you?"

Lou thought the girl would break into tears again, but she held up long enough to answer. "No, just my face. My face! Mean drunk, took his anger out on me." The girl shuddered in her arms.

"Try to forget; don't let it haunt you. We'll take care of him later." Lou thought a moment. "You need a doctor. I don't think you're seriously hurt, but we want to be sure, and we need to see to your injuries. We'll have to get you out of the house until you pretty up again. We don't want the customers or the other girls upset. This stays under our hats, do you understand?"

Coral nodded. "But what will you tell the girls?"

"As convenient a partial truth as I can muster. They'll have to be warned about the danger, told something of what went on." She paused in thought. "Do you think Fayth can take you in for a few weeks? She owes us both a favor."

Coral nodded.

"Good. Get yourself dressed. I'll send for the carriage. You better be off to Fayth's at once. I'll arrange for Dr. Wall to meet you there." She gave Coral one final hug meant to encourage and left the room, closing the door gently behind her. She headed for the steps, fierce with anger.

"I hope you're long gone, mister," she said aloud, "because as soon as word gets out on the street that Lou's got herself a bad john, your comeuppance has been determined. And it won't be pretty; no, it won't."

Fayth sat in a chair facing Coral, hemming a skirt, still shocked by Coral's arrival. Coral watched from her inclined position in Fayth's bed. Dr. Wall had left, having pronounced Coral's injuries superficial and prescribing a few days of bed rest to calm the patient. Fortunately, the Captain was at sea. Fayth would have time to set up a room for Coral before he returned. She could not let Coral return to Lou's house. Coral would have to live with them until Fayth could establish her in some other profession and location. Where else was there for her to go?

Yet, even as Fayth made her plans, she felt trepidation about having a prostitute live with them. What would the Captain say? What would Elizabeth and her friends think? Her clients, what of their opinions? Fayth walked a delicate balance. She pushed her worries aside.

For now, as Fayth sorted through her feelings, Coral provided a convenient barrier between Fayth and the Captain. And heaven knew, she needed one. The Captain was never out of her thoughts long.

"I was thinking I might teach you to sew while you recover." Fayth set the skirt down.

"I'd rather learn to draw. Remember the fun we had before the fire? The beautiful sketches of gowns you drew, and the suggestions I made?"

"I do. And I'll teach you to draw, but I think we should make learning to sew a priority. It's a more practical skill."

"Yeah. Now that I look like this I won't be any good at Lou's and I'll never catch a husband. So much better to have a skill to fall back on." Her sarcasm and despair ate at Fayth.

"You'll be pretty as you please again long before the summer's gone. But you can't be a designer without having a knowledge of fabric and construction. Until the drape and feel of every cloth is part of your being, you can't design effectively. Sewing is the best way to acquire it. What good are drawings if they can't be turned into reality?"

"I suppose you're right. But what I really want is a rich husband. Why do you think I stay at Lou's? If I marry rich, I can draw all day long."

Fayth studied her closely, biting back what she wanted to say. Coral stood a much better chance of landing a decent husband, a husband at all, if she were out of the business. But she couldn't tell her that. "What you want is independence."

"So easy to say when you've found your man."

A knock at the front door interrupted them. When Fayth returned from answering it, she carried a stack of mail. Coral stood aside, watching as Fayth sorted through it. "What's so funny?"

Fayth hadn't realized she'd laughed aloud as she read her postcard from the Captain.

"A hand-drawn postcard from the Captain. A rather clumsy one." She held it up for Coral to see. "Look, just a cartoon. There, does that shatter your romantic notions about the Captain and me? No pictures of roses or declarations of love, just silliness." But she knew her face gave her away. She couldn't hold her smile down. "Some people shouldn't draw," she said softly, looking at the crude picture, imagining him drawing it.

"It's very romantic. A man only sends a card like that to a woman he's very intimate with, emotionally or otherwise. He loves you madly."

"You're a surprisingly hopeless romantic, given the kind of men you deal with."

"And you are hopelessly jaded and unromantic, considering the kind of men you know."

"Touché! Now, shall I show you how to hem?"

During the Captain's absence, the city council voted to keep the boardwalks at the original level. Only the actual streets were raised. Now a full story higher than the boardwalk, people who walked or rode along the street looked directly into second-story windows. To get from the boardwalk to the street required climbing a ladder. To get from the street to the entrance of any building, one had to climb down a ladder. Neither were easy feats while wearing a skirt.

The uncouth men of Seattle spit over the edge of the raised street down to the uncovered boardwalk below, and thought it great sport. Women had to carry umbrellas for protection. The horses hitched at street level didn't behave any better, backing over the edge to relieve themselves. But they at least held legitimate claim to being animals. Fortunately, Fayth successfully navigated the streets without incident as she made her way to the docks to meet the Captain's ship.

Now, standing in front of the office of O'Neill's Shipping, hands clasped demurely in front of her, knuckles white, watching the *Aurnia* glide through the sparkling waters into her moorage space, Fayth fought the urge to flee. She half expected another woman to emerge from the Captain's cabin. And how was she going to explain Coral's presence in their home?

The Captain held the helm, navigating the vessel into her tight berth. Moments later the *Aurnia* docked. He appeared on deck and shouted the command to tie up. Her heart flip-flopped at the sight of him; she wondered whether from her growing feelings for him or from the news she'd come to share with him.

She had pestered Tetch for information for days. She didn't want the Captain walking in and finding Coral before she had a chance to explain. Mr. Tetch finally sent word that morning that the Captain had wired that the *Aurnia* should arrive within the day.

Fayth waited for the Captain to spot her. When his gaze finally found her, his face lit with pleasure. He made his way toward her as soon as the gangplank was secured.

"Fayth!" He caught her in a hug of unexpected magnitude as his men watched from the deck above. She gave him a breezy peck on the cheek. If he was disappointed, he didn't show it.

"It's good to see you."

His eyes danced as he cocked his head and peered into her face. "We weren't due in until tomorrow. Spend all day with a spyglass to your eye? I don't see a ring around your eye."

She laughed—somewhat too nervously, she thought. "More like pestered Mr. Tetch for any word of your arrival."

He looked hopeful. "How long have you been waiting?"

"Forever."

He seemed to like her answer. He swung her around, his arm looped around her waist, and walked her toward shore.

"What about the ship?"

"The men know what to do. I'm happy to see you, Fayth." The warmth in his voice sounded genuine.

They reached dry ground before she worked up to mentioning Coral. "I need to talk to you about something." She was sure she looked guilty.

"Oh?" He was suddenly on his guard.

"We have a houseguest." Her voice pitched a little too high to sound completely innocent.

He cocked a brow.

"A long-term one."

"Who? Family of yours?"

"Not exactly." She took a deep breath. What would she do if he got angry and insisted that Coral leave?

"A girl from Lou Gramm's parlor house." She hurriedly continued, her words strung together to prevent interruption. "The girl I've been trying to get out of the business. A client beat Coral up about a week ago. She had to get out of the house and there was no place else for her to go. Lou sent her to me. What could I do, Con? I couldn't send her away."

He didn't say anything. Didn't even register that she had called him Con. She realized it too late herself.

"Lou wants her back when she's healed, but I'm trying to convince her to be my apprentice. With business picking up I could use one." She stopped, self-conscious.

"If you had seen her, you couldn't have turned her away either." She shuddered at the memory. It was involuntary, but effective. "You haven't said anything. If it makes you uncomfortable, I'll send her back to Lou." She hoped he wouldn't take up the offer.

He dropped his arm from her waist and turned to face her. "A girl from Lou's?"

He sounded stunned, but why shouldn't he? Blast her wicked thoughts that cast aspersions on him at every opportunity.

"I know what you're thinking, but—"

"I don't think you do, Fayth." It was almost as if he spoke to himself. He teetered on the brink of denying her. She saw it in his face.

"She's not as hard and jaded as the other girls, Captain. She's . . . salvageable."

"Salvageable?" He laughed softly. "Like a ship?"

"Redeemable, then. Please, give her a chance. She wants one. She needs one. She's led a tragic life." Fayth scanned his face for some kind of hope. "Her father abused her. She ran away to escape and ended up with Lou. Please, we can't disappoint her."

He stood there, silent, stoic. When he spoke, his words were wooden. "I'm not a hard-hearted man. I wouldn't ask you to send her back to that life, but neither can I permit a prostitute to live with us without voicing my disapproval." He sighed, his expression distant.

"As much as I admire your determination to save her, your good intentions on her behalf, I have to warn you—there is no escape from that life, Fayth. It drags down all who touch it; taints them. I would hate to see your reputation suffer because of it."

At his warning, a shiver slid down Fayth's back. Somehow she felt he spoke of more than her situation. Most likely, it was only her suspicious mind, but she felt he warned himself as well as her.

"But our house is your home as well as mine," he continued, "and so you have every right to have a guest. As for your business, if you want to hire her, I can't stop you. It is your business, and I agreed long ago not to meddle in it." His gaze rested on her. "I leave the choice to you."

"I can't turn her out," Fayth said.

The Captain looked resigned, as if he expected her answer. "As soon as she has recovered, she has to leave. If we have to help her find somewhere to go, we will."

As strongly as pride at his honor and kindness overwhelmed her, she felt his disappointment. It was almost as if he thought she had manufactured a house-guest to keep a distance between them. She hadn't, of course, but guilt crept over her. Coral did provide a barrier, and Fayth was glad for it. "We'll find her a place of her own once she gets established."

He nodded and the unspoken question hung in the air—was this the only reason she had met him?

She took his arm. "I wanted you to know before you got home. But of course, that's not the only reason I'm here." Her flattery went past him. Her nerves rendered her inept at flirtation. He remained distant. She forced a smile. "You should see the shop. The progress they've made the last week is astounding!"

The momentary flicker of hope in his eyes died as quickly as it had come and long before Fayth had time to be certain that it had been there at all.

CHAPTER ELEVEN

The girl waited for them, held the door wide open, smiled tentatively at Con when they arrived at the house. Con was relieved that at first glance she didn't look familiar. If he didn't remember her, maybe she didn't him. Con was about to set down the duffel he carried when she spoke.

"Welcome home, sir."

He straightened, recognizing her voice, and examined her closely. She was the youngest of Lou's girls. In that awkward moment, her return look warned him not to mention it. An ally?

Without aid of the harsh makeup Lou's girls usually applied, she was nearly unrecognizable. Except for the healing green-yellow bruises around her eye, she looked like any passably pretty sixteen-year-old. When she stood aside for them to pass, she moved gingerly, as if her side were tender. Probably had a few bruised ribs. Con suddenly had the urge to beat the man who had beaten her. What kind of coward abused women?

Aware that Fayth watched him closely, he allowed his indignation to show, smiled and greeted the girl, introduced himself. She responded politely in a voice devoid of recognition. Now that he looked closer, he was truly astounded at the difference in her from when he had last seen her at Lou's. She wore a new dress, obviously one of Fayth's, and her hair was done in a simple, unpretentious bun. She looked wholesome.

He smiled at his wife. Thankfully, she seemed unaware the two knew each other. His thoughts were momentarily diverted. Man alive, Fayth was beautiful. She was all he had thought about since leaving. Her feminine curves, her radiant smile, the soft slope of her shoulders . . .

And then there she'd been, waiting for him, but not for the reason he hoped. Had Fayth missed him at all? He felt Fayth watching him. Her gaze stalked him the way Olive hunted mice. Had Coral said something to her? Coral's presence made things damned awkward. He had to talk to her.

Fayth took his arm and led him to the kitchen. "Welcome home!"

A three-layer cake sat in the middle of the table surrounded by plates and forks, and freshly cut flowers.

"Let's have refreshments," Fayth said. "I'll cut." Fayth hurried to the counter for a knife.

"If you ladies don't mind, I'll unload the carriage while you set up. Where do I—"

"You still have your room." Fayth answered a little too quickly.

Hell, he had hoped he had a chance at sharing her bed. "You ladies share?"

"No, Coral is in the guestroom."

"What guestroom? You mean your sewing room? Where is your machine?"

Fayth smiled. "In the dining room. We never eat there."

"We certainly won't now." Coral laughed in a girlish, tinkling way.

"I guess we won't. Why miss what we never used?" He laughed in ironic response. Yes, why miss it. His thoughts were not on the dining room, but Fayth. He looked to the girl, with her infectious good humor. "Cut me a big slice of cake. I'll be back in a minute."

Fayth caught him in the hall, her expression a question.

"Until she's healed," he said.

She smiled and turned, leaving him in the hall.

That evening, Con sat in the kitchen with Olive tucked in his lap, watching as Coral busied herself preparing the evening meal. Fayth hadn't returned from town. He needed to speak with Coral, get things settled.

"You can hear Olive purring clear over here," Coral said. "How'd you get her to warm up to you? She hates men."

Con smiled. "Cats have a sixth sense. They know a warm heart when they meet one."

"Do they?"

Her manner was stiff, almost accusing. "When am I going to get you to warm up to me?" His voice held no innuendo.

"What do you mean, Captain?"

"Everyone, my crew excepted, calls me Con."

"Fayth doesn't."

"No, but you don't operate by her set of rules. I realize she calls me by my title to keep distance between us. It won't prevent the inevitable."

Coral stopped peeling carrots long enough to turn and look at him. "The inevitable?"

He winked at her. "I think you know what I mean."

"Fayth has a kind and susceptible heart. Unfortunately, it's bruised." Coral turned back and began slicing the carrots.

"Don't I know it. She's told me about her former fiancé. He left it to me to build her trust in men back up; at least that's the way I see it. And I intend to succeed."

Coral dropped the knife in the pan and turned to face him again. "Do you? Then what the hell were you doing at Lou's?"

The venom in her voice surprised him.

"Brave girl. Bring the issue right to a head, no mincing around. Now that it's out, think we can resolve it?"

She acted as if she wasn't listening. "Damn carrots! I hate cooking! What does it matter, anyway? You'll be sending me back to the house, and I'll be damned glad of it—at least Lou has a cook!" She strode toward the door.

"Where do you think you're going?" His commanding voice stopped her halfway. "I'm not sending you anywhere. Didn't I just ask if we could resolve this?"

When she looked at him her eyes were thin and narrow.

"I knew you recognized me. Why'd you warn me off?" If she wouldn't speak, he would.

"I won't see Fayth hurt."

The girl knew how to glare. He turned a serious look back on her. "What makes you think I'll hurt her?"

"Men *usually* go to Lou's for one reason. Having a husband who gets his pleasures at Lou's would kill Fayth. She believes in being faithful. Why should I believe you're the exception?"

"Not that I need to explain myself to you, but I've never patronized the girls. As for my reasons, I feel no need to divulge them to a young thing like you."

Her chin shot out straight.

"Did you ever see me go to a room with one of the girls?"

Her jaw relaxed. Uncertainty crept into her expression.

"The inner dealings of the city are conducted at Lou's, and Lou is often privy to them. The astute man knows where to make contacts. I was there on business."

She watched him closely, measuring him for the truth.

"I feel responsible. If Fayth gets hurt again . . . she isn't strong that way." She stepped back into the kitchen.

"Why are you responsible?" He gave her the look he reserved for disciplining the crew. She crumbled.

"I'm the one who told her you never went to Lou's. And you didn't, not until you were already married."

"So you're her source. You knew about her crazy marriage of convenience scheme?"

The girl nodded.

Olive scooted up Con's chest until she was tucked under his chin. "Coral, why do you think I married Fayth?"

The girl just stood there, staring at him.

He tried again. "Think about what she had to offer me. What would I want from her? Her money? Her business? I had everything but her."

A smile crept over her face.

He'd almost convinced her. "Why would I throw away my chance with Fayth for a moment of pleasure at Lou's, for an evening at most?"

"Captain, you are a romantic!"

He didn't answer, just smiled. "Have you told Fayth about my visits?"

"No."

He exhaled a long breath, both relieved and puzzled. What did Fayth suspect him of?

"Good. I'll tell her in my own time. For now, you and I need to come to an agreement. I don't like secrets, but I have my reasons for this one. Promise me you won't mention that you've seen me at Lou's? Won't mention what I said about marrying Fayth?"

"And I stay?"

"Until you recover."

"What if I don't agree, tell her everything?"

"I deny it just as adamantly. It's my word against yours."

She edged another step back into the room. "It doesn't bother you to have a whore living with you?"

He sighed. "It hasn't bothered me having a gutter child for a cabin boy. Or any assortment of crewmen that brawl, drink, and gamble. Or a business manager with sticky fingers. Why should a whore bother me, as long as she isn't practicing?"

Her girlish laughter filled the room. "You have yourself a deal, Con."

The back door swung open and Fayth steamed in. She held her sleeve away from her arm with two fingers, her nose wrinkled in disgust.

"Hello, both of you. Don't say anything to me until I've changed. I was spat on as I came out of the shop and I'm warning you, I'm in no mood for snickering." She marched past them toward her bedroom, emerging minutes later wearing a clean shirtwaist, carrying the soiled one.

"I'll be lucky if this tobacco juice comes out. This is the third incident this week alone. I was even carrying my umbrella and it got me!" She walked to the sink and submerged the shirtwaist. "I'm one spitting away from walking into Lou Gramm's in broad daylight, wrenching our esteemed councilmen's free drinks out of their inept hands, and pouring them over their heads!" She scrubbed at the stain with renewed vigor. "Or at the very least demanding recompense for my damages. If they don't figure out a way to cover the sidewalks; well, I tell you, I'm tempted."

Con still lounged at the table with Olive in his lap. Coral had joined him and was sipping a glass of water.

"Figuring out how to light them seems to be holding up the operation," Con said. Olive jumped off his lap and ambled away. "Why don't you organize the ladies and get some action, Fayth? The destitute from the fire have about all been helped. The women need another cause to keep them busy. Why not suggest one that benefits you?"

She narrowed her eyes at him. He held his hands out in mock defense. "I'm not insulting them. They're a powerful force in this town and when they get riled about something—"

"The last time they *got riled about something* the men didn't like it and got the Territorial Governor to repeal their power to vote."

Con ignored her. "You get them organized and when the issue comes to a vote I'll do my duty as your husband and vote for covered sidewalks. But now's the time to use your clout. Your colorful gowns are all the rage, and your resilience well-known. The downtown merchants will back you."

"I don't have time."

"You would take the time if you thought you'd lose customers to shops whose clients don't suffer the same indignities."

"Wonderful, another adversity to overcome."

"Yes," Con said. "But this time you're not alone."

Coral didn't get many visits from her colleagues at Lou's parlor house. Lou Gramm herself visited on relatively few occasions. Therefore, Fayth was naturally surprised, and dismayed, when Mabel came calling two days after the Captain's return. If Coral hadn't answered the door and invited her into the parlor, Fayth would have turned her away. Instead, Fayth poured tea for Coral and her guest.

"Coral, look at you. Living the life of a respectable woman, who would have thought?" Mabel said.

"Sugar?" Fayth poised, ready to intervene at any intimation by Mabel of Coral going back to Lou's.

"You must come back to work soon, Coral," Mabel said. "I'm earning five dollars a day now."

"Five dollars! Liar!" Coral said.

"Cream or milk?" Fayth hovered with the cream pitcher, studying Coral's reaction to Mabel's suggestion.

"No, thank you," the two girls said in unison, then laughed.

"We still think alike, Coral. I miss you at the house. The other girls all give themselves airs because they're older and more experienced."

"It's just jealousy, Mabel, you know that. Experience doesn't compensate for their youth and beauty fading away. They all know they're one step closer to the cribs."

Mabel smiled again. "It doesn't make it any easier. As for me, with the money I'm making, I don't plan on falling that low. Mrs. O'Neill will still be slaving over her machine when I've long since retired."

"If you live that long," Fayth mumbled.

"Pardon?" Mabel asked.

"Tea too hot? Shall I add a little cool water?"

"No, thank you." Mabel eyed her suspiciously, but Fayth only smiled sweetly.

"You can't be making that much money." Coral sounded suspicious. "Don't try to fool me. I know what an average girl's take is."

"But we are! You should come back."

Fayth watched Coral pale at the suggestion. She hadn't been the same since she'd been beaten up. Fear was the last thread keeping her at Fayth's, stopping her from backsliding into prostitution.

Mabel sipped her tea. "Since we've moved into the new house business is booming. You should see our new quarters. We've got brand new brass beds and gold gilded mirrors overhead."

Fayth did not like the turn of the conversation and cleared her throat loudly to dissuade Mabel from detailing the immoral decor. Mabel smiled back. "The genteel atmosphere appeals to many of our leading male citizens."

"Really?" Fayth's tone was at best deprecating.

"Really. I would name names, but Mrs. O'Neill would be shocked. Too bad keeping our clients' confidentiality is part of the business." She turned to Coral. "It isn't just the older generation that comes to us.

Many of the gentlemen send their sons in—for an education in the sexual arts. A young man should know how to please his future wife. I don't think their mamas know, or would approve, but the gentlemen are much more open-minded."

Fayth glared at Mabel. "Probably because they're the ones benefiting from an establishment like Lou's. They're the ones being unfaithful to their wives and sweethearts. Maybe their mothers would be more open-minded if they had an equivalent to Lou's. How do you suppose their husbands would feel about that? It's so easy for the sinner to plead liberality. As for the men, why not lead one's own son down the path to immorality? It ensures that his progeny will feel no superiority to him."

"Fayth!" Coral said.

Mabel ignored their exchange. "So you see, Coral, we've got many handsome young men coming. Come back and catch one."

"She will not. Coral will make the honorable choice and be my assistant. Women should be able to support themselves in an honest manner. It saves having to marry poorly simply because one needs a man to survive.

"Coral stands a better chance of meeting a suitable gentleman in her current occupation."

"I'm surprised at your narrow attitude, Mrs. O'Neill. Considering how frequently your own husband is seen at Lou's, one would think that you don't object to men seeking entertainment at our house."

Fayth froze, anger and fear making her stomach churn. "That's a blatant lie, Mabel. Tell another that slanders my husband's character and I'll show you out."

Mabel shrugged. "Go ahead and throw me out for telling the truth. I know what I see and I've seen him at Lou's with my own eyes."

"There's no reason you aren't both right. There are lots of reasons to visit Lou's these days." Coral eyed Fayth warily. "Everyone conducts business at the house. While I was there, I never saw him with any girls."

Fayth was grateful for her loyalty, but what did Coral know that Fayth didn't?

"Captain O'Neill does not visit the girls," Fayth said flatly.

Mabel smiled. "You seem to know your husband, Mrs. O'Neill. He does not visit the girls. He visits Lou. High honor indeed to visit the madam herself, though most of the boys like them younger."

"If the Captain goes for an occasional drink there with his manager Mr. Tetch, it's not for this wife to censure." Fayth hoped her bluff didn't show. Her stomach clenched with the new knowledge that the Captain went to Lou's. After the whore on the ship, what else could she expect? He and Lou were somehow connected.

"Oh, he comes for drinks, but he always has a private meeting with Miss Gramm. I don't know many other men who do, but maybe you're privy to your husband's private affairs and know more of what goes on than I do." Mabel laughed.

"Well, of course she does." Coral quickly took up Fayth's defense. "Mabel, surely you didn't come here to insult our hostess?"

"Indeed not. I apologize for my conduct, and the insinuations I made about your husband, Mrs. O'Neill. Please disregard my gossipy remarks."

It was like asking a jury to disregard testimony, but the maneuver was effective in preventing Fayth from throwing her out. Instead, she passed around a plate of shortbread biscuits, and presented a calm exterior while seething with insecurity inside.

Mabel had barely departed when Fayth began interrogating Coral. "Why didn't you tell me the Captain has been to Lou's since we married?"

Coral hesitated. "I knew it would hurt you. After all that was a criteria of yours for a man—that he not frequent places like Lou's. Since I was the one who investigated him for you, I felt like I'd failed. But I swear Fayth, he never came near the place, or any of the girls before the fire. In fact, not until after—" She cut herself off.

"After what, Coral?"

Coral bit her lower lip. "I would have warned you if he'd come in before the wedding."

Fayth was stunned. She knew it showed.

"See, now you're upset, and for what? I can attest to Mabel's observation. I never saw him with any of the girls. He did visit Lou in private, but we can't go making assumptions about people's character or motives without all the facts. Don't judge him, Fayth. At least give him a chance to defend himself." Coral sighed.

"Many of the important businessmen in Seattle frequent Lou's. And most only to conduct business. Half the Council agenda is voted on at Lou's. You know that. The savvy man who wants to succeed would have to go to Lou's."

Fayth had stopped listening. Her head spun. Who was the man she had married? One she thought she could trust? Or another?

The rest of the afternoon passed slowly as Fayth waited for the Captain to come home from the wharf. Her emotions danced awkwardly to an angry tune, faltering between hope and abject fear. She had to confront him. Finally, she heard the front door open, followed by his happy humming. She heard Coral greet him, then scurry away, presumably to her room. Wise girl. If only Fayth could hide.

Fayth rose and met the Captain as he came around in front of the parlor.

"Fayth." He wore his usual smile, and looked blissfully unconcerned.

"Where have you been?" Not the best way to greet a husband, she realized. Her tone came out harsh and unnecessarily accusing. If only he didn't fluster her so.

"The wharf, darling. And then Lou's." His smile deepened in concert with his dimples. Oh, wretched man. He watched her reaction with an intense, amused look. How could he have known what was on her mind? Could he read her so easily? But who could have warned him of her distress? Certainly not Coral.

Her mouth fell open at his easy admission, more from feeling intellectually naked in front of him than anything else. When she spoke, her voice rasped. "Lou's?"

He laughed. "Close your mouth, Fayth darling. It does not become you to look so surprised. You wound me with your obvious train of thought." He reached out to her and took her chin in his hand. Mesmerized by his touch and the humor in his eyes, she could not pull away. "If I had been there for that reason, would I admit it so readily?"

"I didn't—"

"Ah, but I think you did." He took a step closer to her. "So you know, I've been there for the reason any wise businessman in town goes—to get business. Unfortunately, Lou's has been adopted as the place where deals are made." He dropped his hand from her chin and shrugged. Only inches separated them. She half wished he would touch her again. Intelligent eyes and wry smiles had always intrigued her.

"It's not the first time I've been," he said. "Knowing how you feel about Lou's, I kept it from you. I may have been wrong. I apologize. It wasn't my intention to deceive you."

What could she do? She stammered an acceptance, accompanied by her own apology. By her own rules of the relationship, she had no right to interfere in his business practices. None at all.

He looked suddenly sheepish. "I don't owe you forgiveness, Fayth." He laughed again. "And though I hate to admit it, I'm not as honorable as I seem. One of my business associates caught hell—" He grinned again. "Pardon me. Had trouble with his wife when she found out where he'd been. His troubles gave me the idea to confess. I didn't want you looking foolish around the other women."

His words, his manner, were completely believable. His concern for her, touching. Guilt over her own thoughts crept over her.

"One further admission." He paused.

Her heart palpitated wildly.

"I'm in a unique position in that I'm frequently away from town. That leaves me out of touch with what is happening here." He paused again. "I don't know how to say it, other than straight out. Lou Gramm knows everything that goes on. On occasion, I've met privately with her and she's been gracious enough to fill me in."

Gracious was not the word that came to Fayth's mind. Exacting. Fayth was certain that Lou had extracted a price for her help—passage for one of her girls on the *Aurnia,* perhaps?

Though Fayth didn't like it, the Captain had done nothing more than she had herself. Bare inches separated them. A slight lean forward and she would be in his arms. Did she dare? Where would it lead? If only she didn't need time to digest this new information, to be certain—

Olive bounded into the room. Inserting herself between them, Olive cuddled the Captain's legs, meowing and flirting in a manner unbecoming to a man-hating cat.

Fayth looked down and stepped back. "You have an admirer."

"Do I?" He didn't sound like he meant Olive. He reached down and scooped up the cat, returning the animal's affection.

"Fayth, I want you to trust me." His gaze held hers, dark and penetrating.

"I will. I mean . . ." Fayth couldn't finish. Her own answer had given her away. He was stroking Olive tenderly. Suddenly, she wished for him to lavish such attention on her, knowing he would, if only she'd let him. When she knew she could trust him . . .

To divert herself, she told him about Mabel's visit, carefully omitting Mabel's accusations.

The next day, forced by Mabel's visit, Fayth went to see Lou. She sat in Lou's office reviewing her arguments to convince Lou to release Coral. The door swung open and in walked Lou, . seating herself behind her desk.

"What brings you here, Fayth? There aren't any fittings today."

"I've come about Coral. I'm here to ask a favor and enlist your aid."

"I take it Coral is ready to return." Lou gave no indication as to whether she was inclined to grant a favor.

"Physically, yes. Emotionally, I don't know. She still seems fearful."

"Understandable, but irrational. The culprit has been punished, and I assure you, he will not enter this establishment again."

"I understand, but the fear remains. That it happened once, means it can again, worse. The house is no place for Coral. I've offered her an apprenticeship in my shop."

Lou didn't give away any emotion. "Ever the crusader. Has she accepted your offer of righteous employment?"

"She will if you release her. Coral's fond of you. She respects you. She's told me many times how you saved her from her abusive father."

"And you'd like me to what? Recommend to one of my best girls that she quit the business?"

"Exactly that, Miss Gramm. I know you care for her. Give her a chance at another life. Coral doesn't have the strength and business savvy required to become a madam. As soon as her beauty begins to fade she'll start the downward spiral toward the cribs. She'll end up dying young of some dreadful, occupational disease. That's if she doesn't commit suicide first.

"She's a young romantic girl who dreams of her prince charming. She won't find him working for you. The best she might hope for is to become mistress to an established, and lonely, older gentleman, and even that could be only temporary."

Lou arched a brow. "You paint a bleak picture."

Fayth nodded. "It is a bleak picture. Miss Gramm, I'm appealing to your sense of compassion."

Fayth watched Lou consider her request. At last Lou spoke, "I will speak to Coral, urge her to consider your offer carefully, but the decision will be hers. But she's welcome back anytime. I'll tell her that as well.

"One other small matter. Coral owes me money." Lou grabbed a sheet of writing paper, dipped her pen and scribbled something, turning it toward Fayth when she finished. "I expect this amount to be repaid. Installments are fine." She tapped at another figure on the page. "This amount, the first of each month. Or Coral's back here on her back."

The sum was ludicrous. How could Coral have run up such debt? Lou's face was set, her eyes hard. Arguing with her would be futile.

"You'll speak with her soon?" Fayth tucked the paper into her purse.

"I have some time tomorrow. Send her to me in the afternoon."

"Thank you." Fayth rose to leave.

"Mrs. O'Neill, I am a cynic. I applaud your efforts to save Coral, but I don't believe for a minute you'll succeed. Coral will in all probability be back in my fold before a year has passed. But you have my word not to meddle. Good day."

When Fayth got home, Con sat at the kitchen table poring over a contract.

"What are you up to?" She unpinned her hat and set it on the table.

"Looking over my new government mail contract. They pay well, but the only runs available are local, little short things. Think you'll mind having me around more?" He seemed to watch her carefully.

She smiled absently, lost in her own thoughts. She was beginning to think not. "No, of course not."

"Something bothering you, Fayth?" He read her too well.

"I just came from Lou Gramm's. Tomorrow she's going to talk to Coral about staying with us, working in the shop."

"You don't look happy."

"Miss Gramm never gives anything away. Look at this." She handed him the paper Lou had given her. "Coral owes Lou a great deal of money. That's how Lou keeps her girls. They're always in debt to her. Never take a cent from that woman; you'll be in debt the rest of your life."

She shook her head. "I would never have imagined. Just the monthly installments Lou wants are more than the salary I expected to pay Coral. Fortunately, not much more." Fayth took a deep breath. "But how will Coral ever become self-sufficient? It'll take her years to pay Lou off."

Fayth slumped into a chair. "I'm sorry. When I took Coral in, I just didn't realize. I thought, a month, two? She'd be on her own." She didn't miss the hopeful look in his eyes.

"How did she amass this great debt?"

She shook her head gently. "Oh, don't get me started. I confronted Coral. Accused her of frivolous spending. Her response nearly made me cry.

"Lou uses those girls. She requires them to pay for room and board and charges them outrageous prices. And most of those poor girls are scared, insecure. They've no place else to go. What can they do but pay?

"On top of that, they're required to buy new clothes each month. Wouldn't want the men to get bored with their wardrobes. In my stupid ignorance, I thought they all were frivolous girls who simply loved getting new clothes and spent their paychecks for vanity's sake. I had no idea they were *forced* to buy new dresses from me every month." She clenched her fists. "I've been vain in my own way, thinking they so loved my creations they simply had to have more of them." She shook her head again. Why hadn't she seen through it before? "Lou does all the buying, floats them loans, as she calls it. Then she charges the girls for their individual purchases.

"I should have been suspicious of her business practices from the beginning. The only payments I ever receive are from Lou. I just thought she was making it easier for me by collecting the money and passing it along in one sum."

She pushed a tendril of hair out of her face. "Do you know, she charges them two, sometimes three times the price I bill her for the gowns I make? In addition, she charges them interest tantamount to usury! If I'd known how she worked, I'd have contracted with the girls directly. I'd have insisted on it. I'm sure the girls hate me for the prices I supposedly charge them." She let out a long breath. "Lou's been using me as well. I call myself a businesswoman, but I've been such a fool."

"Fayth—"

"No. Don't try to make me feel better." She shook her head. "I deserve to feel badly. I've been trying to help, but only harming. The girls are caught in an inescapable cycle and I inadvertently contributed to it." Her tone pitched high with fury by the time she finished speaking. She stood and paced. "I won't sew for

that woman again! Not if I go bankrupt. Thank goodness my business is growing and I have a loan from a
legitimate bank."

The look he gave her confused her. What did she
read there? Worry? For whom? Why? Hadn't he confessed all?

"Show Miss Gramm. Make your business the most
successful dress shop in Seattle. Save Coral. Sew only
for whom you want." His words were calm and reassuring, the fleeting look of worry gone. She smiled at him.

"Thank you, Captain. I believe I will."

The Captain left the next day, on the last of his long
runs before he began the mail route contract he'd won.
To distract herself during his absence, Fayth, along
with the other merchants on Washington Street,
waged a battle against the city council, demanding covered sidewalks. The Council capitulated and authorized
construction, touting the new sidewalks as a feat of
modern engineering. Sturdy concrete arches were con-
structed to support the weight of the sidewalk and pedestrians above, with steps and spiral staircases
installed. Had the lobbying of the honest, taxpaying
merchants gotten results, or had Lou Gramm's free
drinks and easy ear to local powers-that-be prevailed?
Lou and her lower-class sisters in prostitution benefit-
ed most by the new sidewalks.

The city ingeniously solved the problem of lighting
by installing skylights made of clear glass blocks in the
upper walks. A quick view of a woman's petticoats as
she scrambled up a ladder became passé. Standing un-

der a skylight, a man got all the sight of a woman's anatomy he desired.

All classes of prostitutes, from the lady boarders at Lou's genteel parlor house, to the girls in the cribs of the Tenderloin, played this to full advantage—free advertising! Ambitious working girls wrote their names and work addresses, often along with their fees, on the bottom of their shoes. Strolling along the walks and pausing over the skylights became the daily routine. Any woman who walked across the skylights was assumed to be a whore.

Fayth was furious. Her attempts to improve the business district had instead emphasized her dubious location. Faithful customers were no longer spat upon—they were forced to step out into muddy streets to avoid the skylights, laughed at by prostitutes who strolled boldly over the glass. And as for prostitution, Fayth had inadvertently aided the very profession she wanted to eliminate.

On Con's first day back in town, Con, Fayth and Coral strolled side by side through the business district on their way to Fayth's shop. Con talked on about his new mail contract. Fayth listened and smiled, happy to have him home, eager to have him. Eager to believe the whore on the ship had been some kind of favor to Lou for the gossip she imparted to him.

She made up her mind during his absence, that consequences be hanged, she wanted him. Fayth kept remembering his words when he had proposed—a wild and reckless time. A wild and reckless time indeed. But wasn't love always?

Though once it had seemed that they worked at cross-purposes where Lou was concerned, Fayth no longer had reason to suspect him. The coming statehood celebration, when Washington State would be welcomed into the Union, would be the perfect time to celebrate. How to hold him off until then became the question. Fayth smiled to herself. Between Coral and Con, they seemed to be making a romantic of her.

She walked on the outside of the threesome, in the street to avoid the skylights. Con walked in the middle. A man didn't need to avoid the things. Coral walked on the inside. She strutted boldly over. Half the men in town had seen her goods anyway. She laughed at Fayth's modesty.

"What are they going to see, Fayth?" Coral asked. "The soles of your shoes and yards and yards of frilly white petticoats? That's hardly titillating to a man, is it, Con?"

Coral's familiarity with the Captain annoyed Fayth and swept her up in the dust of jealousy. Coral shouldn't be making sexual references. How was she going to train the coarseness out of that girl?

"It's impolite to put the Captain in a position of revealing his personal tastes, and he can hardly speak for all men," Fayth answered for him.

"Fayth equates walking over the skylights with walking through fire," Coral said.

"No, I don't. I've done that, not so very long ago. And while it was frightening, it wasn't humiliating."

Con didn't speak.

With a rebellious look, Coral stomped on a skylight she passed over. "You rode through the fire under the secure cover of a wet blanket. It was our courageous Captain who faced the fire head on."

Fayth smiled sadly at her. Who could tame Coral?

They reached Fayth's new building, which stood two stories high, and thanks to council regulations, now had a basement. She unlocked the door and let them in with a look of satisfied triumph. "Complete, finished. Come see the second story. They installed the last of the fixtures yesterday." She led the way and stood back to watch as Coral and the Captain exclaimed over the latest details.

"Very nice, Fayth," Con said from the window where he looked out over the street. "Looks like our luck is turning. You've got a building, and I have my mail run."

He looked handsome silhouetted against the window. "These rooms or part of them could be nicely done up for Coral."

"Coral?"

"Yes, she should have a place of her own," the Captain said.

Fayth looked between the two. They looked like guilty conspirators. "No. I'm sorry, Coral, but I'm going to rent the space out. I need the money."

The Captain shrugged. "Coral doesn't need more than a single room. That still leaves plenty of space to rent."

"We'll discuss this later." How had she married such a conniving man?

Later that afternoon Fayth stood at the living-room window of their home, looking out past evergreens and nearly leafless alders toward Puget Sound. Coral had gone out. The Captain sat on a sofa behind her.

"When you're home, do you miss the sea?" She let the lace curtain fall into place over the window and stepped back, turning to look at him.

"Yes, and no."

"I heard Billy and some of the men grumbling about the mail runs. Billy told me you never wanted to be a mailman. What changed your mind?"

His laugh was almost a snort. "The fire, darling."

"Didn't it change us all? I hate to think of you giving up something you love."

"So do I." His gaze pierced.

As was so often the case, she suspected his words had double meaning.

"The government mail subsidies pay well. They're steady, reliable income."

"Yes, steady, reliable."

"I'm proud of you, Fayth. Look what you accomplished while I was gone. The building's finished, the sidewalks covered, and the streets of Seattle are graced with women in colorful new gowns."

"You flatter me. But let's not talk about those sidewalks. I still might storm into Lou's someday and give those councilmen a piece of my mind." She sat in a chair opposite him. "We need to talk about the building and Coral."

"I was afraid it would come around to that. It's time Coral was on her own."

What could she say? She had promised him. Still, she wasn't quite ready to let her go. "I'm worried about Coral. How does she look to you?"

"A little plumper, nice and healthy."

"A little plumper! She eats like she did at Lou's, drinks a quart of milk at a sitting, but she doesn't get half the exercise. She's filled out so much, she's out-grown the dresses I made for her just months ago." Fayth sighed. "She hasn't been happy here since you left."

She tried not to sound jealous, but she resented how the Captain could always keep Coral in good spirits.

"She complains that the house is too quiet. There are no parties, no professor to play the piano. No serv-ants, no cook. No men to pay her pretty compliments. She flirts mercilessly with any man who comes to the shop. Fortunately, most of the business these days is sewing for women.

"I don't know how to please her. She hasn't been paying Lou. You should see all the new baubles and trinkets she's purchased. I paid Lou myself last month. What if she falls back into the business?" She crossed her arms, and caught herself rubbing them as if to ward off cold thoughts.

"I wouldn't worry about her. She's been on her own before. Let her move to the shop."

"I don't know. She's irresponsible. And still girlish. She plays foolish little tricks." Fayth shook her head, remembering her confrontation with Coral earlier in the week.

Fayth had just closed the shop and retired to her desk. Coral was in the storeroom straightening up. Fayth felt something stuck in the sole of her boot. She took it off to examine it. When she turned it over, she found the words, *Con, I desire you tragically*, penned on the bottom. She pulled off the other to find a companion message. *For a good time, meet me at home. Anytime. Fayth.* Blast! On her best pair of boots.

"Coral!"

Coral had come running.

Fayth pointed to her shoes in disgust. "What is the meaning of this?"

"You only just noticed?" Coral struggled for control of her giggles.

"How long has this message been here?"

"Two days, but what do you have to worry about? You never walk over the skylights. Oh, Fayth, you should see your face."

Coral broke into a full laugh, little tears crowding the corners of her eyes. "I was only trying to help."

"Help?"

"Anyone can see how much you miss him. Why don't you just admit it? Seduce him when he gets back."

"What makes you think I want to?"

Coral dabbed the tears away with the back of her hand. "I've seen you study him, Fayth, and I've watched you hang on his every word. You love that man."

"He's a handsome man. Too handsome." Fayth laughed "What have I told you about attractive men?"

"Never trust them. So don't trust him, love him."

Fayth laughed again. "I see I'm going to have a hard time turning you away from your romantic notions. Will this ink come off?"

"Might wear off. Keep your feet on the ground, Fayth, and no one will ever see the message. That shouldn't be hard for a realist like you."

Later that night Fayth pitched the shoes into the back of her closet, wondering whether she could paint over the words. But she couldn't help smiling just a little. Coral did have a sense of humor, and a disturbingly clear insight into Fayth's preoccupation with the Captain. That night she had decided, why fight it? She would welcome him into her bed.

Fayth's thoughts returned to the present. "Captain, can we wait until after the statehood celebration to decide about Coral?"

"If that's what you want, Fayth. But let's not delay long."

"The celebration's only a few days away." She paused. "I hate to lose her. It's so quiet when you're at sea. I'll be lonely."

"You won't, darling. Now that I'm going to be running local mail, I'll be gone only days at a time. I'll be here to keep you company."

A last shaft of late November sunlight cut through Fayth's curtained window, fueling her spirits with its brilliance as she dressed for dinner. She smoothed her hand over the skirt of her newest creation, an evening gown of white India silk with three-quarter length sleeves trimmed with yellow velvet roses. The V-neck scooped low in front and back. Ribbons and bows of yellow velvet drooped from the upper and lower edges of the bodice. Three rows of ribbon outlined the train.

Just as the last of the light faded, she fluffed her crimped bangs and arranged the loose tendrils that curled at the back of her neck under an elaborate bun. Tonight he was taking her to dinner at a large party at the Occidental. Tomorrow they'd take the train to Olympia for the official celebration.

She would let Coral move to the shop. She'd tell him tonight. Would he see it for what it was, a desire to remove the barriers she had put up between them? She hoped so. Fayth grabbed her wrap.

She heard voices in the kitchen, and prepared to meet them with a fluttery heart. His voice. Fayth smiled to herself. He always came back, and unlike Drew, the Captain always took care of her. Hadn't he gotten her the money for the second story? Didn't he help her get the original loan? She smoothed her skirt and took a deep breath before breaking from the hall into the kitchen.

"Fayth, you look stunning." The Captain's voice was deep, warm, and barely perceptibly tentative. He studied her with the same hopeful manner that in the past had always confused her. Today, she hoped she read it correctly. Could it be? Was his calm unflappability cracking ever so slightly? Did she read desire there? "Seeing you looking so fine makes me glad President Harrison proclaimed Washington a state."

"Thank you."

"The carriage is parked just outside the door." He held her wrap, before offering her his arm. "You just missed Coral. She left with her escort, a respectable looking young fellow. Told me not to worry about her, or wait up."

"Aren't they all? The little scamp." Coral had never had a dinner engagement before. Had Coral and the Captain schemed behind Fayth's back? Fayth hoped so. "That means we're alone?"

"All alone."

CHAPTER TWELVE

A t the Occidental, Fayth and the Captain sat in the new dining room with the elite, in plain view of all. Fayth enjoyed the attention, especially that paid her by the Captain. Later, she would show him how much.

Green and yellow satin ribbons and flags festooned the heavily decorated room, hanging from every corner and table and nook. Rhododendrons in shades Fayth had never seen before adorned each table in lush bunches of lavender, pink, magenta, and green. The podium up front spilled over with them. Fayth wondered where the hotel staff had procured so many of the out of season flowers.

"Well, it's not Wong's," the Captain said, "but the food here will have to do."

She hesitated, but she had to ask. "Memories of the time we dined there together before don't . . . embarrass you?"

"Never."

What was he telling her? Had he been flattered by her marriage proposal? A girl could hope.

The Captain ordered for them both. As the waiter served their meal, Seattle's mayor stepped up to the podium and began the evening with one of many long speeches. At first intermission, the waiter came to clear the dishes. The Captain reached across the table and took Fayth's hand.

"Do you want to stay for the dancing?" The Captain didn't look enthusiastic about the prospect.

"Something tells me you don't."

"It's not the dancing, Fayth. It's the long prelude of speeches that we'll be forced to endure first. A man can only take so much of politicians jabbering. I've had my fill. I'm stiff from sitting, smiling, nodding, and feigning interest in what they have to say."

She smiled and reached for her purse. "Then by all means, let's leave before they get started again."

He stood and pulled her chair out for her. As Fayth glanced around the room, she noticed they weren't the only people eager to retreat. The Captain evidently noticed, too.

"There'll be a crush at the coatroom." He took her elbow.

"Are we going home then?"

He guided her into line to wait for their coats. "Not if you don't want to."

There was something suggestive in his voice. She hoped she didn't just imagine it. "Did you have something in mind?"

"I thought we might stroll up the beach toward the wharf. Maybe have a little dessert aboard the ship." He sounded too nonchalant, leaving her wondering what he meant by dessert.

Without thinking, she glanced down at her celebration gown.

"Oh, you're not dressed for a stroll. I'm sorry."

"No, please." She took his arm. "The carriage is parked at the wharf. We need to walk there by some route. The beach sounds more," she paused, "pleasant."

He noticed her pause. There was a suddenly hopeful look in his eyes. "Your gown?"

"It'll wash." She laughed.

They reached the coatroom. He handed their tickets to the harried girl on the other side of the counter.

Minutes later they walked along the deserted beach. Gray dominated the evening sky. The earlier rain had subsided, but more threatened.

"If this weather persists, tomorrow will be an abysmal day for an inauguration. Can you picture the crowd in Olympia with umbrellas and raincoats?" The Captain spoke as they strolled arm in arm under his umbrella.

"Easily. I don't think our politicians deserve less after their blatant campaign against suffrage." She snuggled close against him. Oh, he felt good. Her heart pounded at the turn of her thoughts and what she contemplated.

"You'll get the vote soon," he said.

"I hope so, but it should have been part of Washington's state charter."

Elliott Bay stretched dark and forbidding beside them as they walked along the waterfront. Waves broke into whitecaps, stirred by a damp, cold breeze. Fayth shivered.

The Captain tucked her hand under his warm arm. "Cold?"

"I was thinking of the water. On a night like this it terrifies me. Wild, beyond control, bottomless. I'm glad you stand on the shore here with me, safe."

He looked touched, and hopeful again, as his gaze followed hers to the water. Surely she didn't misread him.

"As they go, that isn't a rough sea," he said. "A good sail, a capable crew and this weather will take you for a ride worth braving. There's nothing like feeling the thrill of speed as you sail with the wind at your back, heightening the illusion you're flying. Traveling at the speed of the wind, not a hair on your head is disturbed. Almost, you are the wind." He stood looking out across the water.

Fayth watched him. Tall and proud in profile, he looked very much as he did when he captained the *Aurnia*. Very much like the man she had always imagined she wanted.

"Of course, these days we don't rely on the wind. Our steam engine is more reliable. A finely tuned engine gives nearly the same thrill."

"The ocean is your first love. I was never wrong about that."

His fleeting expression confused her. What did she see written in it? Denial? Hope? How could that be?

"She's a good love. At night the waters rock you to sleep like a lover's arms and in the day the spray refreshes your sense of being. Still, it's not quite the same as warm, feminine arms, a real embrace."

Lover's arms? Real embrace? Was he asking what she thought?

Broken shells and kelp littered the shore around them. Fayth picked her way through, heart thudding wildly. Feminine arms. He wanted her embrace, but did he want her love?

He pulled her toward the pier where the *Aurnia* was docked. "It's cold at water's edge. What do you say I make you some tea and we warm up onboard?"

Was this the invitation she had hoped for? She looked into his eyes, trying to discern his true intentions. But blast him! He'd always been good with a poker face, too calm and controlled for his own good, or hers. His eyes were masked, giving nothing away. She wanted to rattle him, for him to be as vulnerable and hopeful as she. She could play his game of innuendoes. "I would *love* that."

His expression didn't alter as he guided her toward the vessel and up the gangplank. Fayth paused at the top, allowing Con to skirt around her. He jumped to the deck and held out his arms for her, sweeping her down from the plank. The smell of bay rum filled her senses as he lowered her to the deck.

The *Aurnia* was deserted. The crew celebrated statehood in town, no doubt with whatever they could put in their glasses to raise in toast to the new state. Con guided her past the instruments in the wheelhouse back to the shipmaster's quarters, his hand planted firmly in the small of her back. She liked the intimacy of his touch, the warmth of it. Who was she kidding? She loved his touch.

In his quarters, she took a seat and watched as he lit the stove and lamps, admiring what she saw. Lean, hard lines. Muscles. Strength. Did she possess the nerve to go through with becoming his wife? Really becoming his wife and all that entailed. The possibility of children, having to give up the shop to raise them. Life always gave choices, but never simple answers, especially for women. A price must be paid for everything, even passion. Did it make good sense to risk the security she had for passion? What good was good sense in and of itself?

For far too long, she had locked her emotions away, lived life according to logic and sense. When was the last time she had felt passion stirring, and yielded, even in the slightest, to its calling?

Memories of the night of the Great Fire flooded back with startling clarity. The deck of the *Aurnia*, a stiff breeze, flames and smoke in the distance, and Con. Heat, passion. She would be his, make him hers. As for the consequences, come what may.

A soft glow reflected in the polished surfaces. Fayth shifted in her seat as Con put water on to boil. Soon a pleasant warmth filled the room. Con removed his coat.

After the damp coldness outdoors, the warmth made Fayth peacefully drowsy and serene.

"Your cabin is beautiful." She watched him get cups and jars of loose tea from the cupboard. "I've often wondered why you leave it to stay at the house. We have nothing to compare."

"Maybe you do."

Hope as dancing as the lamplight flickered within her. The water boiled. He made tea and set a cup in front of her before joining her at the table. As she let hers cool, she rose and wandered around the cabin, admiring his pictures, his books, pointing at things and waiting for his explanations, enjoying his gaze as it followed her about. Was he leering? He'd better be.

"I'm disappointed." Fayth held a framed photograph in her hand. "There isn't a single picture of you without a beard. You'd be most devastatingly handsome without one. This?"

"Grandam. I think you'd be devastatingly disappointed, probably accuse me of having a weak chin."

"I hope I get a chance to make that judgment myself." She inspected the picture. "She looks very stately, maybe even imposing."

"She's nothing but kind. Would you like to meet her, Fayth?"

Could he want her to meet his family? He'd mentioned something about them before, so long ago she'd nearly forgotten. Walking about the room had roused her from her previous drowsiness, awakening her nerves, fears, and hopes. The frame trembled in her hand. She set it down, hoping he hadn't noticed. Could he mean?

"I would. Will you bring them to Seattle?"

"If you like, but Grandam doesn't travel well. Claims not to have any sea legs, says I didn't get mine from her. Doesn't like the train much better. Besides, it doesn't run all the way here."

"I might consider going to San Francisco." She smiled at him. "Would you take me?"

"I'll take you anywhere you want to go." His words were laced with innuendo.

Her mouth went dry with anticipation. "Anywhere?"

"To heaven and back, Fayth. Anywhere." His eyes looked dark, but he didn't move from his chair. He didn't move a muscle. Why couldn't she ever read him? If he wanted her, why didn't he come get her? She looked to the galley, unable to resist goading him.

"I thought you mentioned dessert. I don't see a cake, a pie, anything."

"Don't you?" His voice became very deep.

"No, and I'm hungry." She matched her tone to his. He lost control. Desire danced in his eyes. If there was a deeper emotion behind it, he kept that masked.

"There's a cake in the cupboard."

What a strange and intimate game they played. Neither spoke of cake. She held his gaze. "Then by all means, serve it."

He stood suddenly, pushing the chair back with such force that it toppled over. He didn't pause to look back at it. The next instant he swooped her up and carried her down the hall back to the bedroom, never letting her gaze escape his. Her heart beat an uneven rhythm so loud he must have heard it.

Con's neatly made bed filled the room. She looked toward it and couldn't resist teasing him. "What does it say about a man when his bed fills the whole room?"

"In general, I couldn't say. Specifically, I'd say it's too damned lonely sleeping alone in such a monstrosity."

His answer surprised her as much as his sudden action. He set her on her feet in front of the bed and stood behind her. She felt his hot breath on her neck and the stillness of him. It took her a minute to realize he was giving her a chance to retreat. A chance she didn't need.

She turned around to face him, leaned into him, encouraging a kiss. His lips came down on hers, warm and wonderful. She circled his waist with her arms, pressing against him, marveling at how much more substantial he was to hug than her girlfriends. So manly, so perfect.

He bent at the knees to level their heights, pressing her close. He pulled away for a moment to peer seriously into her eyes. Did he fear another backing away? She had to show him she meant business. Trembling, she unbuttoned the first buttons of his shirt, and traced the outline of his collarbone lightly with her fingers.

He kissed the top of her head and ran his hands over her back, caressing her, pulling her against him until she felt his hard arousal through her skirt. She pressed willingly into him. Oh, he was wonderful, and if this was only lust for him, she didn't care. He caught her under the knees. She let him take her and carry her to the bed, kissing his bearded chin as they went. He laid her down and positioned himself beside her.

"Fayth, you aren't teasing me, are you?"

What did she see in the serious depths of his eyes? If only she knew. Did he ask for love, or only compliance? A night, or a lifetime?

"I'd never tease." She ran her fingers over his cheek, stroking the corners of his mouth. He turned to suckle her fingers like a baby at the breast, licking between them with his warm, wet tongue until she shuddered with pleasure and pulled them away.

"You know where this is leading?"

"I'm not a complete innocent." She pulled his head to the cleavage exposed by the V-neck of her dress.

"Fayth, don't tempt me if you're not serious."

Heated lips met her cool skin and she sighed. Oh, why was she unable to resist this handsome man? So much so, that she willingly risked everything for a night with him. She moved his hand to her breast, unbuttoned his shirt and pulled it from him. What a fine naked chest he had. Strong, firm. She slid her hands over it, pinched his nipples lightly as he pulled the dress from her shoulders, and with warm fingers between her breasts, untied her chemise. They fell back onto the bed, both topless, him braced above her, joined at the waist.

"Man alive, Fayth. You are beautiful."

Draw him in, Fayth. Draw him in.

He lay warm and hard against her, but too many clothes encumbered them. Needing to feel his skin against hers, she shimmied beneath him, scooting the dress past her hips, arching toward him. He bent, sucked her breast. She heard her own gasp. Such a small sound. She hoped he didn't think it described her pleasure at his touch. That was too large, too universal to be described by an utterance.

He sucked. She gasped. Exquisite pleasure. Tight nipples. A tightening deep within her.

Draw him in.

She fumbled with his pants. He rolled next to her, slid his hand up underneath the length of her chemise to the opening in her pantaloons. A gentle moan. She flattened her legs open against the bed. He stroked her gently.

"There?"

"There." Was that her own high-pitched, breathy voice that answered? She arched against his gently massaging fingers, trembling, more vulnerable than she'd ever been.

A cough came from the door. She snapped her legs together. Con froze, released her, fell over her, shielding her with his body.

An adolescent, cracking male voice came from the door. "Captain?"

"Billy! Don't you know how to knock?"

"I'm sorry, Captain. Didn't know you weren't alone. You've got to come. There's been a break-in at the warehouse. Police are waiting for you. Looks like we lost a lot."

Con cursed under his breath. "Meet me in the wheelhouse, Billy. I'll be out in a minute."

Billy backed out and closed the bedroom door. Con sat up. "Fayth?"

"Go."

He hesitated.

"Go. They're waiting for you; what else can you do? I'll be here when you get back."

"Fayth, I'm sorry." He grabbed his shirt. He was still tucking it in as he walked out the door.

Well, what had she expected? That fate would make things easy for her? She dressed and sat on the edge of the bed, trembling. They had almost made love. And he had not said he loved her, had not hinted that he did. Did it matter? If only it didn't.

In the days when she and Drew had been engaged, in the private moments Mother and Father never had known about, when he had petted and fondled her, Drew had whispered his love over and over again. Yet he hadn't loved her, not the way she had wanted, not faithfully. The Captain? Well, at least he didn't make promises he didn't keep. She went to the stateroom to wait for him.

It was hours before he returned, looking shaken and defeated. She was frightened by his expression; she'd never seen him anything but calm. "Captain?"

"They took everything small enough to cart away. Cleaned me out, Fayth."

Her heart pounded. What was he saying? "I'm sorry." Fear immobilized her. She couldn't make herself go to him, but she couldn't cry either. Were they ruined? She couldn't find a voice to ask.

He slumped into a chair at the table and ran his fingers through his hair until it stuck up at odd angles. "I didn't mention it before because I was going to turn it down, but I was offered a contract to haul from Southern California to Mexico. Old acquaintance. I did some shipping for him before. I didn't want it before, but now . . .

"He needs me for four, five months. Pays well. I'm going to take it. I have to. I'll leave in the morning. Bailey will be making my mail runs."

"The goods stolen from the warehouse," Fayth said. "They aren't yours. Won't their owners be responsible for their replacement?"

He shook his head. "My customers trust me with their belongings. As long as their goods are in my care, they are my responsibility. I have to replace them or reimburse their owners, Fayth. Otherwise, I will be ruined. No one will trust me to ship for them again. No matter that someone else is responsible." He sighed. "Another couple of weeks and the warehouse would have been cleared."

Blast his honor! Blast the thieves!

"Of course." She blinked back tears. "I'm sorry."

He wasn't looking at her, didn't seem to hear. She knew better than to say anything else.

He rose suddenly. "I'll take you home now, Fayth. I'll have to come right back. I've got a lot to do if we're sailing in the morning."

"I understand." She picked up her wrap and her purse. He met her at the door where she touched his arm. "I'll be here when you get back."

CHAPTER THIRTEEN

January 1890

Con sat in his cabin bent over a ledger, ostensibly studying columns of numbers, but his mind drifted elsewhere. The *Aurnia* rocked gently, which usually calmed his nerves. Today, nothing took the edge off. He had sent Billy away only moments before, claiming he needed to go over the books. Tetch was becoming increasingly greedy at a time when Con couldn't afford it.

He should confront Tetch, warn him off his current course of not-so-petty thievery. Con's respect and love for Tetch's deceased father, Captain William Tetch, made Tetch arrogant, and gave him a feeling of invincibility. Captain Will had taken a chance on the gawky fourteen-year-old Con and had made a sailor out of him. He had encouraged Con, even lent him part of the money to buy the *Aurnia*. In return, Con had promised the dying Captain Will to look after his wayward son, Silas.

Con had kept his promise, made sure Silas went to school, saw him apprenticed as a bookkeeper, hired him when no one else would. Unfortunately, Silas had quickly developed a reputation for having one hand in the till. Now, debt of honor or not, if Tetch continued, Con would have to fire his ass.

Con's gaze swept up toward the window. The memory of Captain Will unsettled him, reminding him of the careful mask he wore to hide his vulnerabilities, his deep emotions. He sighed, remembering his greatest failure, his last night with Fayth, months in the past now.

Not a day had gone by when he didn't torture himself for not revealing his feelings, for not telling her that he loved her. But he couldn't be sure she loved him, even as she had offered herself to him. If only he'd seen something in her eyes besides reckless abandon. He loved her so much and had been so desperate that he'd been willing to take that, if that was all she offered. But he couldn't allow his heart to be crushed, and he couldn't risk chasing her away with his professions of love. So he had remained mute, letting her imagine what she would.

Even now, he couldn't express his feelings in the letters he sent her. He knew his writing sounded aloof, businesslike, but he couldn't bring himself to bare his heart using words on a page. No, when he made his confession, it would be face to face so that he could see her response, so that she couldn't run. He had to know how she felt. The sooner, the better.

Nights brought no relief. His dreams picked up where his conscious thoughts left off. Different each night and frustratingly the same. He tried to steer the *Aurnia* into her berth, but the tide kept him out. He tried stoppering a bottle, but the cork didn't fit. He and Fayth had been so close . . .

Desire shackled him every time he thought about her arching beneath him, topless, her breasts tight and budded, bouncing, entrancing him. The feel of them in his hand, in his mouth. The arch of her slender neck, the part of moist lips. Creamy white smooth skin. He almost felt the softness of her skirts as he remembered shoving them up. How had he controlled himself? Billy's intrusion had sprinkled mere droplets on the fire of his mood and desire.

Damn thieves! Damn this business that kept him from her!

A late January rain pelted the window as Fayth sat in the Captain's office flipping through the stack of letters that had come for him. Mr. Tetch cast her furtive glances from his desk in the outer office. Weasel. She had never liked him. She should speak to the Captain about him when he came home.

Blast the break-in! She needed the Captain here, needed his reassurance, his touch. Since he had left, she had spent long hours at the shop, at her sewing machine. To her dismay, sewing no longer provided the calming effect it once had. Now she felt only a wild frustration when she pounded at the treadle. Sewing allowed too much time for introspection, for what-ifs. She wanted him home, wanted to know if he loved her. The way she did him.

She flipped to another letter, scanning it, barely seeing the text. Fearing another lapse in payment to the Captain's creditors, she had begun coming to his office to check on Mr. Tetch and make certain he left no payments outstanding. She would have taken over paying the bills herself, but the account books made no sense. She didn't have the time or the energy to straighten them out. In honesty, she didn't know if she could. And despite her hounding, Mr. Tetch seemed unable to decipher them for her. She set the letter aside and stared blankly out at the rain.

Please let O'Neill Shipping stay solvent.

The past week had taken a horrendous toll on her shop. Tuesday the newspaper printed an article about Fayth, condemning her for hiring a former prostitute, hinting that Coral might not be so *former.* Who had told the paper about Coral, and why were they malicious?

Fayth's intent had always been honorable. The same article, printed with another slant, might have made Fayth a heroine for rescuing Coral. Ah, well, what did it matter? Despite her reassurances, she lost customers. Others she kept only by slashing prices and condescending to meet them at their homes for fittings. But she couldn't keep it up much longer. Coral couldn't manage the shop alone while Fayth went out. Consequently, Fayth had to close up and lost even more business.

Fayth needed an assistant, a person to manage the place in her absence. But if the women of the city weren't willing to be waited on by Coral, who would work with her? A man could do it. But where in Seattle would she find a man with a knowledge of women's clothing, one willing to work for a woman serving women?

Thank goodness the Captain sent her money to run the household. She didn't know how she would manage without. In fact, she needed to stop by the bank and check on his latest deposit on her way home.

First she had to finish the mail. If the newspaper left it alone, maybe the whole matter would be forgotten and her customers would return. She continued sorting through the Captain's mail, picking up a letter with Con's name scrawled in a masculine hand across the top of plain white stationery.

Con,

You son of a bitch, you're late. Pay up before it's over.

Bailey

Fayth's stomach tightened involuntarily. The letter trembled in her hand. Not pay Captain Bailey? How could the Captain abuse his friendship by not paying Captain Bailey for making his mail runs? Who could blame Captain Bailey for his terse anger? But it didn't seem like something the Captain would do. Were things worse than she knew?

Fayth took a deep breath, but her hand continued to shake so hard it was difficult to read the letter. She set it on the desk. The note gave no sum owed. She couldn't confront the Captain, but the fact remained, Captain Bailey must be paid.

In a burst of frustrated anger, she called to Mr. Tetch.

Tetch poked his head in the door. "Yes, ma'am?" His tone like always was grating and polite, almost smug.

She pushed the note toward him. "Take care of this. You're more familiar with my husband's debts than I am."

"Certainly. Anything else?"

Tetch stared at her with an arrogant disdain she didn't understand, but hated all the same. "For the moment, no."

Tetch nodded. She watched him return to his desk. Enough of dealing with her husband's problems. Let Mr. Tetch earn his pay. She stuffed the rest of the letters into her bag and rose to leave, having suffered enough disillusionment for one day.

Later, at the bank, Fayth watched the teller count out her daily receipts and enter her deposit in his ledger.

"While I'm here I'd like to draw a draft on my personal account, and also make a cash withdrawal."

The teller nodded to a stack of paper and a pen, and kept counting. Fayth wrote out the necessary information and slipped it through the window. The teller replaced the ledger and drew another one out, flipping efficiently to her account before reading her completed withdrawal note. From the look on his face, she knew immediately that something was wrong. Her hands began to tremble.

"The Captain's deposit hasn't reached the bank yet?"

"I believe it has. There was a sizable deposit posted two days ago." The teller paused delicately. "But I'm afraid it's just enough to cover the draft you've requested. I can give you the balance of the account, but it isn't as much cash as you requested. And it will close the account."

Her mouth went dry. Her mind raced, goaded by horrible thoughts. She forced herself to speak calmly. "My mistake. Just the draft will be fine today."

"Yes, ma'am."

Jacob Finn walked by as the teller busied himself with her business. "Mrs. O'Neill! How pleasant to see you!"

"Mr. Finn."

"I was by your shop yesterday. It's a splendid looking structure."

"Thank you."

He paused. For a moment she thought he was going to ask about business or mention the article about Coral. "You picked a good husband. There isn't another man in town who could've rounded up a construction crew so quickly. Without Con O'Neill you'd still have nothing but a vacant lot."

Her mind still reeled with the weight of the teller's revelation. She fingered her purse and forced herself to smile. "I'm glad you approve of my choice, Mr. Finn."

"He's a good man on all accounts."

"Have you seen his new wharves? You loaned well on that account, too." For an instant she thought a look of confusion passed across his face. He opened his mouth to speak, then closed it and smiled. The teller pushed her draft back through the window to her.

"Take good care of this customer, Wilson." Jacob nodded to Fayth. "Good day, Mrs. O'Neill."

What had he been about to say? She scooped up her draft and stared at it. What was going on? Why had the Captain sent so little? She shuddered, imagining a shipwreck. Silly, he had to be all right. A dead man wouldn't have sent anything. She stuffed the draft into her purse with a trembling hand. She wouldn't think of it now. Worry would only distract her. She needed to get home, check on Coral, and finish Mrs. Terry's order.

When Fayth pulled up at the cottage, a strange carriage blocked the drive. She tethered her horse to a tree on the street, complaining beneath her breath. Her humor had not improved by the time she reached the house. Voices buzzed from the parlor. Coral must be home. Since the Captain had gone on an extended trip, Fayth had decided to keep Coral living with her until he came back. Who was Coral entertaining? It sounded like a man. *Coral, when will you learn proper decorum?* No wonder people talked. Fayth went to the parlor.

As she came down the hall, Fayth saw Coral, but not her guest. Coral faced the parlor door, seated on the red settee, transfixed by her companion. All innocence: a blushing, embarrassed schoolgirl, Coral was trying hard to impress someone. Fayth frowned, puzzled and worried.

The voice of Coral's male companion drifted to her, becoming distinct. *Drew.*

Fayth put a hand on the wall to steady herself. Stunned, she stopped just short of the parlor. *It can't be.* She spun on her heel, intent on retreat. After what he'd done, she wouldn't face him, wouldn't give him the satisfaction of her anger.

Coral called out. "Fayth's home! Come on in, Fayth. You have a visitor."

"Fayth." How could her spoken name sound so ominous?

She stopped and spoke without facing him. "Get out, Drew. I have no business with you."

He sprang from his chair and had her by the elbow before she could move. "Is that any way to greet me?"

"It's kinder than you deserve. I didn't invite you." Wrath was more emotion than he deserved.

Drew pulled her around to face him. "Look at me, Fayth."

His voice was the same as always—deep and seductive. Lying. He laughed and she knew what it meant. He expected forgiveness. Blast him! He'd ruined her life. All the trials of the last few years, starting with losing her reputation and then Father's store, could be attributed to him. What right did he have to forgiveness?

"Ah, Fayth, you always could hold a grudge, but you never fail to forgive in the end."

"I forgave you. That doesn't mean I want to see you."

Her rebuttal didn't appear to affect him. He laughed again. Did he think she teased? He pulled her into a hug without warning. "Thank God, I found you! Oh, Fayth!"

She wrenched away. "How?" It took an effort not to stutter, even on so small a word.

"Mr. Hanbrough just arrived minutes ago. We've barely made introductions." Fayth had forgotten Coral's presence until she spoke. Was that jealousy she saw in Coral's face? What had Drew done to Coral while she was out, the wretched charmer?

He swept both of Fayth's hands into his. "Fayth, you look lovelier than ever." He lowered his voice. "I've missed you."

"Liar." Fayth shook her hands free. She had to get rid of Coral before she lost her composure completely.

Drew laughed again. Was he so ignorant of the hurt he'd caused? Or did he hope that by acting as if he'd never betrayed her he could make everything well?

"Thank you for entertaining Mr. Hanbrough, Coral. Now that I'm home, you can go ahead to town and do the shopping."

Coral opened her mouth to protest.

"Hurry, or we'll have nothing for dinner."

"It was a pleasure meeting you, Mr. Hanbrough." Fayth recognized Coral's pout, but the girl left. Neither she nor Drew spoke until Coral was gone.

"That's a very cultured and elegant young woman you have living with you, Fayth. She said she's your apprentice."

"She is, and I'm glad you think so. Coral was very recently a prostitute."

He looked only mildly shocked.

"You always were an astute study of people, Drew."

He laughed again. Apparently, nothing she said could wound him. "That's my Fayth, always trying to save the world."

His glance flitted around the room. Fayth wondered whether he looked for evidence of a man in residence.

"Sheridans have always taken in strays. You ought to know, Drew."

"Touché! I deserve that, Fayth, and much more."

"You're lucky I wasn't home a few minutes earlier. I wouldn't have been as cordial as Coral." Anger wavered in her voice, and rage shook her until even her hands trembled with it. "Get out of my house and go straight to hell, Drew."

"Fayth—"

"I'll show you the door." She turned toward the hall.

"If it will appease your demons, tell me to go wherever you want, but don't throw me out without hearing me. I've come all the way from Baltimore because of concern for you." His voice cracked.

Could he be such a good actor? He wasn't moving. Maybe a sharp pair of sewing scissors would convince him she meant business.

"Tell me a lie I'll believe. Surely you can do better."

"I speak the truth." He looked properly sober and genuine. But then he always did when he lied.

"Really? What does your wife think of such concern?"

He dropped his gaze and hung his head. "I have no wife. It didn't work out with Florence."

She stiffened. "Didn't work out? She was pregnant with your child!"

When he looked at her, he wore a beaten expression. "Don't look at me like that—I didn't desert her. You must think more of me than that. Tell me you do."

"Less. Far less, Drew. Why should I believe better?"

"I'm not a total cad." He took a step toward her.

She stepped back. "You could have fooled me. Now get out of my house."

"Don't you want to know what happened?"

Fayth glared at him. "Why should I care?"

"Florence's parents sent her away while they arranged a proper wedding." He bent his head. His voice went soft. "While she was away, Florence miscarried. She lost my baby." His voice broke.

Fayth bit her lip to keep from screaming at him. What did he expect, sympathy? She felt sorry that an innocent's life was lost. But for Drew and his whore, she felt nothing.

"Her parents sent me packing." He snorted derisively. "Oh, Fayth! I never loved her, but I was willing to do my duty by her. When it was over, I almost ran right back to you, but I was afraid you wouldn't have me again. And I wouldn't have blamed you, but I hoped that if some time passed . . ."

He wanted absolution?

"How much time is enough to heal the wounds you caused, Drew?" She almost gave him the answer. The wounds he'd inflicted had already healed. Because of the Captain.

He held her gaze. He'd never been a man who backed down. "I finally came to my senses and went back to Baltimore. When I couldn't find you, I panicked. I was haunted by guilt and regret, and determined to find you. I worried about you, imagined the worst."

"Such a vote of confidence. You thought I couldn't live without you? That didn't bother you before."

"I knew you'd survive, Fayth. That's not what I meant."

"How did you find me?"

"I remembered old Benchley."

Oh, blast old Benchley! How could he have betrayed her confidence and told Drew where she was? And blast herself for thinking the old man could keep a secret.

"He told me about your letter. He feared you were going to make an unsuitable match. I took the first train to Seattle, promising Benchley I'd take care of you. If only that fool had not sat on the information so long."

Drew clutched her hands again, holding them too tightly for escape. "Fayth, I've always loved you. Since you were a girl."

"Don't lie, Drew."

He spoke over her objection. "I've asked myself a million times how I could have betrayed you. My sin is unforgivable. I'm a weak man where carnal needs are concerned. Please believe me that when I made love to her it was you I imagined."

Her anger burst out. Rage fueled her, giving her strength beyond her normal measure. She wrenched her right hand free. The sound of her hand slapping his face sliced through the room like the crack of a whip.

Drew staggered back. Her handprint blazed red across his cheek, and she was not sorry.

"Don't you ever speak to me of such vulgarities again."

"Fayth, if only you had given yourself to me."

Now he blamed her? Oh, pathetic man. The slap robbed her anger of its heat. It ebbed away. He deserved nothing from her, no emotion at all. Hatred and anger required a passion of their own to pursue. Drew deserved none of it.

"I'm not responsible for your lust, Drew. A year was all I asked."

For the first time, he looked almost contrite. "But you were lost in your grief, and I in mine. We dealt with it in different ways. I wanted the consummation of our love. You withdrew. I lost my head. I'll never forgive myself." He paused, studying her. "Fayth, you still care; I see it in your face."

For the first time since she'd known him, he misread her. He looked suddenly hopeful. If Drew possessed nothing else of meritorious size, his ego compensated amply for any other deficiency.

"Show me the ultimate example of mercy and forgiveness. Marry me. Marry me and let fate be as it was intended."

His words hung in the air for a precarious moment. Fayth could hear her own heart thudding dully. His words left no mark. "You're too late—I'm already married."

He fell back from her as if beaten away by her words. "No! I'm too late?" He looked genuinely stunned. "When?"

"Last summer, shortly after I contacted Mr. Benchley."

His face contorted, but she couldn't believe his pain was genuine. "I've been justly punished. How do I recover?" He held her gaze. "Surely you didn't marry for love?"

She hesitated, wondering whether Drew deserved any explanation. Drew jumped in with his own conclusions.

"You married out of desperation. Oh, Fayth! What have I brought on us?"

Why couldn't she just lie? Tell him she'd been wildly in love when she married?

"Spare me the theatrics, Drew."

"Tell me about him."

"The Captain is a good man."

"The Captain? A military man?"

What explanation did she owe him? "No. Captain and owner of his own vessel, a converted schooner."

"Ahh."

She recognized the look on Drew's face. Ironically, he was probably half proud of her. He thought her mercenary; that she had married for money. She was stunned. He'd managed to pierce her because in a way, she had.

"Is he handsome?" Drew mocked her now, a clear indication that she had hurt him. Could he really care, or was it only that she had wounded his vanity?

"Incredibly." She stared him down. "I'm sure you'll be returning to Baltimore soon. Seattle is no place for you, Drew. The men out here are tough and strong-willed." She sounded surprisingly calm considering what had just passed, even managing to lace her tone with pleasantness.

"I'm not going back." He hesitated.

She was finally on the verge of discovering his real motive for coming.

"Why should I lie to you?" he said. "I'm ruined in Baltimore. Florence's father wields great influence there. He ruined my good name. I can't set up shop or hope for employment." He looked beaten, defeated.

She hated herself for the tiny speck of pity she felt well up for him. But the events of the last year left her empathetic to anyone who'd lost everything and was forced to start over. "What will you do?"

"I don't know. I hadn't thought beyond starting a life with you."

"But you must have some plan?"

"Yes, go back to the hotel and drink myself sick."

She ignored his self-pity. It had always been a plea for attention. Drew used emotional weapons too effectively. "Where are you staying?" She almost hated herself for asking.

"The Occidental. Where is your captain? I'd like to meet him."

"I'm sure you would, but the Captain is at sea."

"Does the captain have a name, Fayth?"

"His name is O'Neill, but he is called Con."

He laughed, but it was a defeated sound. "Con as in convict or con artist?"

"A con is a navigator of a ship, Drew."

"Certainly, a man of such esteem must have an honest name." He looked uncertainly toward the door, as if contemplating retreat. "I must be going. My wounds need the nursing effects of solitude. But I don't intend to leave Seattle until I meet the Captain. Good day." He let himself out.

What was she to think? She watched him go, wondering how to get rid of him before the Captain returned.

Later, as they sat in the kitchen sipping tea, Coral was full of nothing but Drew. "Fayth! Drew Hanbrough is beautiful!"

"Is he?" Fayth responded dryly. "I'll give you he has a handsome exterior, but his heart?"

"Who cares!"

"Coral!" Coral's fascination with Drew frightened Fayth.

"What brought him to Seattle?" Coral's tone was casual, but Fayth knew she fished for information.

"Concern for my welfare."

"Oh, Fayth! How romantic! He comes to look out for you even though he has married another."

Fayth stared hard at Coral over the steaming teacup she held up to sip. "He hasn't. She lost the baby and the marriage plans fell through."

"What? He's available? Why did he come, Fayth? Confess." Oh, Coral's eyes were too eager.

"He proposed."

Coral stared and her mouth popped open. "What?" She hesitated. "Any regrets?" When Fayth didn't answer immediately she continued, "Con is a good man."

"Don't, Coral. I don't need cheering or reassurance."

"He still has your heart, then?"

"Emphatically not." Coral misread her, too. She didn't love Drew. She loved the Captain. Drew's arrival only verified it. But loving the Captain meant trusting him, and she just didn't know if she could, if she should. Before the Captain left she thought it didn't matter, but now with Captain Bailey's letter, and the Captain not sending her the money she needed, she worried. Was he leaving her? Could she give up the security of her business to be his wife in every sense, bear his children?

"Will Mr. Hanbrough be leaving Seattle soon?"

"I don't know, Coral. I don't think he knows."

CHAPTER FOURTEEN

hore. Whore-lover. Decent women beware.

W The ugly, white, painted words looked like gaping wounds in a surreal world against the bright red of the new brick exterior, like the building bled around them.

Fayth stepped to the sidewalk and ran her fingers over the fresh paint. She couldn't let Coral see this. It would destroy her. The newspaper articles had been one thing. But this, this show of cowardice and hate . . .

"They'll wash off. It'll take a good bit of elbow grease, but it can be done."

Fayth jumped, startled by Drew's voice coming from behind her, by the sympathy it held. He stepped next to her and pulled her by the elbow away from the hideous accusations. "Let's step inside, Fayth."

She obeyed him without thought. Inside, she spoke. "Why would anyone do this?"

"Why?" he replied. "Probably just a good bit of fun being had by adolescent boys, I expect."

"No," she argued. "I don't think so." She turned to look at Drew. Dark circles, evidence of a hard night of drinking and little sleep, rimmed his eyes. "Enjoy your evening?"

"You know too well I didn't, Fayth. I hardly slept."

"The alcohol didn't lull you to sleep?" Why couldn't she resist barbing him? But, as in old times, it seemed her duty to keep him in line. "What brings you here today?"

He didn't answer immediately. A dress on a display mannequin held his attention.

"Silk and velvet, decorated with silk cord." He ran his hand over the dress shoulder almost reverently. "Four-gored skirt nearly concealed by draperies. Look at the elegant hang over the long, slender bustle." He whistled under his breath. "Bodice with double bust darts, side-back gores, decorated with a *gilet*. What a beautiful creation, Fayth. I see your signature style in it." Drew moved toward where Fayth stood.

"You're coming into your own. That dress flows and hangs better than any of the sketches I last saw. I wouldn't be surprised if you become famous one day."

"Designing in Seattle? I don't think so." His flattery came easily today. What did he want?

Drew walked around the shop nonchalantly, looking at everything, picking things up and setting them down again. "So you earn your living here. Exclusively women's clothing?"

"As much of it as I can. I still do some men's tailoring."

"Seattle seems an unlikely city to prosper in the ladies' clothing business."

"I originally thought so, too. Until the fire last summer, I only sewed for men. But right after, I acquired a patroness who insisted I sew for women."

Lou Gramm did me some good, after all.

"I see. So this is what you've done with your father's business, turned it to ladies' fashions."

"This is *my* business." Did he realize he ventured toward dangerous topics? "I had to sell Father's, and got precious little from it."

Largely because of you, she thought.

Drew smiled, unaware of, or unwilling to follow, the turn of her mind. "I stopped by this morning hoping for an invitation to dinner. I'm eager to meet your captain."

"As I told you yesterday, the Captain is at sea, Drew. You're best off not waiting for his return. I don't know when he'll be back." She hated making the admission to Drew.

"I apologize. You did tell me, but I forgot. I was distraught." He leaned toward her and whispered. "Still am."

When she didn't respond, he paused and cleared his throat in an uncharacteristic, nervous manner. "A few minutes ago you asked what I'm doing here. I'll get straight to the point, Fayth." He cleared his throat a second time. "I'm not too proud to admit I'm a little down on my luck just now. The unfortunate event with Florence wiped me out financially. I'd intended to come to Seattle, marry you, and establish a business."

She snorted. "With what, my money?"

"Fayth, please give me some credit. I figured we'd get a loan. A man can always borrow for his start." He spoke a certain truth. "Truth is, I used the last of the money I had to get here."

She sighed. "What is it you want, Drew?" He'd always had a way of making her feel responsible for his misfortunes.

"A job." Her hesitation must have been evident. "Just temporarily, until I get back on my feet." He took a step toward her. "You need a man around to keep the riffraff away."

Fayth shuddered, remembering the words engraved across her building front.

"And Coral may be a sweet girl," he continued. "But how much does she know about fashion and sewing? She can't help you with the business. I heard about the newspaper article, and how it's costing you customers. I admire your principles, and your tenacity keeping Coral, but you need help."

Fayth frowned. "What a nasty spy you are. I'll thank you to stop prying into my business."

Drew laughed. "Not nasty, astute. Just from a quick look around, I see things that need improving. I'm probably the only man in Seattle with the skills you need. How many lumberjacks out there even know what a bodice is? Or a seam? Or an account ledger?"

"No, Drew."

"Don't be so quick to turn me away. Have you no compassion? I won't even be able to afford the hotel much longer."

"Drew—"

"I'll make you a deal, Fayth. I'll stay only until your Captain comes back, and I'll never let him know I worked here."

"I don't conduct business behind my husband's back."

"Would you turn me out on the street? I'm asking for mercy." He gave her his crooked little grin.

Despite what she felt, and how he had behaved in the past, she had to admit he had guessed correctly about the shop. She needed help. His help. The words scrawled on her outside wall frightened her. Without the Captain in town, she needed a man around. She made a quick decision she would probably regret.

"You have always been an astute observer. I can't trust Coral alone in the store. Since the article, I've been making house calls to keep my clients.

"I'll make you a deal. I'll give you a job as my assistant, my shop manager. The pay won't be much, but you'll earn a commission on each order you bring in. And I will try to forgive you, Drew. But forgiving doesn't mean condoning what you did. What you did was wrong. It doesn't mean reconciliation, either.

"In exchange for the job, you promise not to bring up our past and not to mention marriage again. And I promise to try to be cordial. Deal?" She extended her hand to him.

"Deal. And your husband?"

He had her there. What did she do when the Captain returned?

"That's not your concern. You promised you'd leave. You may have to. For now, let's plan to tell him the minimal truth. You apprenticed under Father, fell on hard times, and came to me for help."

"Thank you, Fayth."

"And Drew, there's a men's hotel down the street. The Captain's manager lives there. I've heard it's quite reasonable. You might see if they have a room."

"I will. When do I start?"

"Today. Your first order of business is to get rid of the graffiti out front before Coral shows up this afternoon."

"Done." He stepped up to her and took her hand. "One last time, before our agreement starts. I love you, Fayth, always will. If you ever need me—"

"Drew."

"Remember." He bent and kissed her cheek.

It took Drew less than a week to establish himself as a fixture in the business.

"Really, Drew." Fayth arrived at the shop and found him seated at the worktable, chatting with Coral as they ate their noon meal. The one Coral had packed and Fayth had paid for. "I'm going to have to start charging you board. I'm not my parents, you know. I have no obligation to feed you. You aren't my apprentice."

"You ladies always serve up more than you need. If I wasn't here, you'd throw it out."

"Does it occur to you the reason Coral brings so much is because she knows you'll be joining us?"

"I'll make you a deal, Fayth. I'll treat you ladies to a night out as soon as I get back on my feet."

Fayth set the mail she'd been carrying down on the counter and leafed through it. A letter addressed in the Captain's bold handwriting caught her eye and her pulse. She set it aside, shoved the rest of the mail to the back of the counter, and reached for the letter opener. Too often disappointed with the Captain's letters, she didn't trust herself to open it in the privacy of her office. The letters were well written, but the content was too predictable, too disheartening, too impersonal. They were almost newspaper accounts. A few tidbits about his business. A line about how he missed her. Insincere? What else could she think when he shorted her with the rent money for the cottage? Either the business was in trouble, or he'd forgotten his responsibilities toward her. Neither option was appealing.

Or maybe the small amount of, no, the near pleasure she'd given him wasn't worth the price. Lately, every time she thought of him, she worried about the businesses, his and hers. Would O'Neill Shipping sink and take her shop down with it? Dark images, fears she'd rather not face flooded her mind.

Well, at least she wouldn't fall prey to Drew again. And for all the evil she used to wish on him, Drew was keeping his end of the bargain nicely, starting with scrubbing that awful message off the building. He ran the shop with smooth efficiency, charmed the ladies, and brought in new customers by the dozens. And he hadn't made one untoward advance. She just might meet expenses this month. As much as she hated to admit it, Drew had already paid for himself, even figuring in that she was feeding him now, too.

She eyed the envelope again. Reading the letter in front of Coral and Drew would force her to maintain her composure. She slit viciously through the envelope.

Dear Fayth,

I have wired another deposit to the business account in Seattle. Mr. Tetch will subtract out the money for the business and deposit the rest in your household account. I hope the money will be sufficient to meet your needs.

Sufficient? Hardly. Had he no idea what it cost to run a household? Maybe he did, and had no intention of continuing to support her. She grimaced, hating herself for the thought.

Extreme weather and rough seas have delayed many runs. It looks like I will have to stay several more months to fulfill my contract. I miss you.

Yours faithfully, Con

She folded the letter and returned it to its envelope. No words of love, no echoes of regret over what almost had been, just business.

"Bad news?" Coral asked.

"He won't be home for several more months."

Drew frowned. "So long? I was looking forward to meeting him soon." His expression said anything but.

Clouds hung over the city, thick and gray, heavy with their frigid loads. Snowflakes had begun falling as Fayth left the shop. Now, standing on her own front step, she stamped her feet and shook herself off, feeling as burdened as the clouds laden with snow overhead. If only she could shed her problems, let them drift away, delicate flakes on the wind. Ah, to be a cloud and simply float off. At least she'd made it up the hill home before the roads grew slick.

Blast that Drew. Claiming he had errands to run, he'd left just after noon and had not returned. Maybe the snow had frightened him into hiding, as it had half the city. The coward. She dusted her sleeves off and sighed. Without Drew to run the shop, she'd been forced to close early. And though it seemed unlikely anyone would stop by, she hated the thought of turning away any customer, even one only a phantom of thought. As poor as business had been, she'd serve a ghost and gladly if he carried cash.

At the moment though, her main concern centered around Coral, who had left for home at noon, feeling sick to her stomach and suffering from an unbearable headache. Poor girl. Lately, her nerves had bothered her, and with the recent string of newspaper articles, who could blame Coral? Fayth felt raw herself.

Fayth peeled off her gloves and left them on the hall tree, not bothering to remove her coat before heading down the hall to Coral's room. Coral had been acting strangely these past days. Secretive, nervous, giddy? Fayth couldn't find the word to best describe her. Distracted with her worries, Fayth didn't hear the noises until halfway to Coral's room.

Thump. Thump. Thump. *Rhythmic, steady thumping? What?*

Fayth froze, trying to place the sound. An intruder? Her own pulse thudded in her ears, echoing in time to the pounding as realization dawned on her. Her hands began to tremble. Coral moaned.

No, Coral. No.

Thump, thump, thump, thump. The banging came faster and harder. The rhythmic squeal of bedsprings. The thumping of a headboard hitting the wall.

Please, please don't be conducting business in my house. Fayth wasn't sure whether she was praying or begging and to whom.

Coral's sigh of delight and ecstasy floated out under the door in direct contrast to the depth of disappointment washing over Fayth.

The thumping slowed, followed by laughter and giggles as if this was all some fabulous joke. Fayth turned and rested her head against the wall, heartsick. Finally, she forced herself to move and headed for the door, grabbing her gloves on the way out.

In the cold, numb with shock, she wandered aimlessly toward the street. Could no one be trusted? She snorted, watching the steam of her breath curl upward, and chided herself. Fool! Innocent, naive fool! To believe people could change, that redemption was possible.

Fayth squinted with anger, and turned to survey the house. "Who?"

As if the tenderly falling snow would answer. No sign of a gentleman's carriage or horse graced the yard or stable, but there was no doubt a man in the house. She gathered her skirts and ran for the street, slowing to a brisk walk when she reached the road. Several blocks later, she paused to lean against a tree in a vacant lot. Light flakes of snow fell around her.

For profit, or pleasure? Fayth shuddered. From revulsion, or anger, or cold, she scarcely knew. She wished she'd heard the man's voice. If only she'd maintained her composure long enough to eavesdrop.

How long had this affair had been going on? Fayth laughed at her own foolishness again. A good guess would be at least as long ago as Coral's secretive behavior began. She took a cold, deep breath. What to do now? Confronting Coral would push her back into Lou's. Fayth felt certain of that. To remain silent implied tacit approval and allowed the behavior to continue.

She leaned back against a fir tree, wishing fervently that the Captain were home. She leaned against the solid old fir until her body was as numb as her mind. Coral hadn't heard her, that much was certain. Which bought Fayth some time to consider her next move. For now, she had to get home.

Drew's rented carriage was pulled up in front when she arrived.

"Fayth! Thank goodness." He looked at her with a mixture of concern and relief. "I came by to check on you. Coral said you were out. I was just about to go out looking for you. A nasty storm's coming."

"Yes," Fayth replied, "A nasty storm indeed."

During the rest of the week, Coral gave Fayth no cause for worry. But Fayth found herself surveying Coral's every move, waiting for a confession, or bad news, all the same. When Fayth found Coral sitting behind the desk in her office, staring mindlessly out the window, her heart pounded with fear. Piled next to her were the supplies Fayth had sent her out for. A gentle rain pattered against the pane. In the gray lighting, Coral's fair-skinned profile looked indecently pale.

"Coral? Is something wrong?" Even as she voiced the words, Fayth prayed not.

Coral swiveled the chair to face her. "I ran into Lila while I was out."

Fayth walked over and sat against the desk next to her, her relief tangible. "And how is she, feisty and crude as always?"

Coral turned wide eyes on her. "Terrible, quiet, defeated."

Fayth frowned. "Really? Has she been ill?"

"Yes, and no." Coral paused. "Lou kicked her out two weeks ago. She's not going to last long. She's lost herself. She's too humiliated, doesn't want to live."

"No! But why? Where did you see her?"

Coral sighed. "On Pike Street, soliciting."

"Working for whom?"

"A crib. Oh, Fayth, a crib!" Coral held back a sob.

Fayth gasped. "What did she do that made Lou mad enough to kick her out?"

"She got old and sick. Lou's brought in a bunch of new girls. Young, fresh, healthy ones." Coral lowered her eyes and twisted her hands in her lap. Fayth remembered the girl from the *Aurnia*.

"Lila's age was showing before," Coral said. "But lately her illness has become more and more evident. She has the French pox, has for a while. Lila's clients fell away, chose other girls until she couldn't meet her monthly expenses anymore. Lou only has room for so many girls. You can't carry your share, you're out. Everyone knows the rules.

"Bigots and hypocrites!" Coral's outburst echoed through the quiet room, her vehemence at odds with her reflective posture. "Lila got her disease from a client. She's given the gentlemen pleasure and fun since we came to Seattle and now they've all deserted her."

Fayth silently agreed. "What about Lou's culpability? Why did she desert Lila?"

Coral shrugged. "What else could she do? It's business for Lou. She can't keep girls on forever."

Fayth was brimming with anger at the whole system and fear for Coral. "That doesn't mean she has to turn them out with nothing. She could give them something to live on, give back some of the outlandish money she's charged them—"

Coral shook her head. "From their very first trick everyone knows the rules." She paused and her voice was very quiet. "You should have seen Lila—so gaunt and thin. She had bags under her eyes and wrinkles I'd never noticed before. Her eyes were dead." Coral rose and walked to the window. "She's already showing signs of paralysis."

"You can't blame the men for not wanting to," Fayth paused delicately, "fraternize with a syphilitic."

"Maybe not gentlemen, but there's many men that will, the men she services now." Coral clapped her hands over her ears as if trying to squeeze out ugly thoughts. "She services dozens of men a night. Dirty, filthy, disgusting men so desperate for a woman they don't care how sick she is." Coral dropped her hands and leaned her head against the window.

Fayth rose from the desk and came to her, putting her arms around her.

"I gave her all the money I had left from making the purchases you asked me to. I know it was your money, not mine, but I had to do something." Her voice grew almost inaudibly soft. "She's only twenty-seven. I'll pay you back."

"No, you won't. You did the right thing. She needs the money more than I do." Fayth gave Coral a squeeze around the shoulders. "Don't worry. You're safe now." When Coral didn't answer Fayth pressed her further. "You aren't infected, are you?"

"No. It's just . . . I see what could be."

"Could *have* been. Not now. You're on a different path now."

Coral shuddered and rubbed her hands up her arms, trying vainly to warm cold thoughts. "I'd always known what happens to a sick or aging girl, but I'd never seen it happen before. I'm sorry. It's shaken me up more than I imagined."

"You have a sympathetic, merciful heart. I'd worry if you didn't feel something for Lila. Just remember, you mustn't worry. You're safe."

"Is anyone really safe?" A tear slid down Coral's cheek.

The lone lamp cast long uneven shadows on the wall behind Fayth as she leaned over the heavy ledger in front of her. She straightened and threw back her shoulders to cast off the stiffness from hours of sitting, studying the blasted thing. She couldn't make any sense of it. Numbers bounced between columns and accounts until large sums of money just seemed to disappear.

The accounts of O'Neill Shipping and Wharfinger were a frightening tangle of numbers. She should have stuck to her resolve and let Mr. Tetch handle it, but she'd felt the need to check up on the accounts, at least once in a while. She would have hired an auditor to shore it up, if she'd had the money. A second article had appeared in the newspaper, more vicious than the first. Those who'd been able to ignore the first, now had the second thrown in their faces. She'd lost three steady female customers just this week.

Women who could forgive her dubious location and cross The Line to patronize her store, wouldn't cross it now. As Mrs. Bates had said, "Your gowns are fabulous. I would do almost anything for fashion, but I will not sacrifice my dignity and honor. I will not stoop so low as to be waited on, or touched, or condescended to by that creature!" Even Drew's smooth talk and charm couldn't calm her.

Others, like Mrs. Fairhaven, were denied permission to shop at Fayth's by their husbands. "Mr. Fairhaven said he will deny payment on any purchases I make from your shop until you fire that . . ." Her voice dropped to a hush. "Woman. I'm sorry, Mrs. O'Neill. I really am."

Mr. Fairhaven and his ilk—unfaithful hypocrites! Stop by Lou's. Have a drink, conduct some business. Flirt with Lou's female boarders. Take a tumble with one upstairs before going home to the little wife, but protect her from contact with such creatures at all costs! Or were they merely protecting themselves?

Fayth had her back up, as Father used to say, but she had made up her mind. She would not fire Coral. She would fight for decency and compassion, and a second chance. Sooner or later people would come around and forgive. In the meantime she walked around with jaw set, chin extended, and fire in her eyes.

Drew commented on it one day. "Fayth, are you aware your chin is leading your face? You're scaring people away with that primed-for-battle expression."

"What else can I do?" she replied. "I'm making headway."

"Headway? Is that what you call having to make house calls to keep customers?"

She pushed Drew's cynicism aside. If visiting her customers at home was the only way to keep them, she would do it. As long as they did business with her, she had an opportunity to persuade them to change from intolerance, to argue for compassion.

The women were a problem, but men flocked in. Fayth's heart was not in tailoring. She let Drew handle them. He had always been excellent with customers, and he was no less so now. He cajoled, flattered, charmed. And, she suspected, used Coral as bait to draw more men in. But Fayth felt too discouraged to object or intervene.

She left the shop in Drew's care more and more often. What choice did she have? Coral couldn't be left alone. She needed protection from all the male propositions she received, and from the hurtful gossip and sniping remarks that drifted in. Drew was efficient, capable, and talented.

Her head throbbed. She forced herself to look at the ledger again.

She couldn't understand. Receipts were up at the wharves, expenses steady. She well understood the extra debt pressure put on since the fire. That explained why profits were down. But she was still bothered. Every month large, consistent cash withdrawals were listed, but no recipient was stated. Someone was making monthly payments and didn't want anyone to know to whom. Was the Captain pilfering the money for personal use as Tetch hinted? What would he use it for, and why didn't he tell her about it? And there were no payments listed to Jacob Finn's bank. Was the Captain defaulting on his loan? Or was it hidden in the mire of the account book?

Renewed suspicions about the Captain's association with Lou pounded through Fayth's temples, encouraging a headache. Could he be investing in Lou's?

She tried to add it in her head again, gave up, and reached for a separate piece of paper to list things out. With the mail subsidy, even though Captain Bailey was currently being paid to make it, and the receipts listed, O'Neill Shipping and Wharfinger should have been in the black. Why, then, did it look like red ink spilled all over the pages? Con was in serious danger of losing his business. Was that what Captain Bailey had hinted at when she saw him on the street yesterday?

She tried to remember his exact words. What were they? Something to the effect of "Heard from Con lately? Looks as if I may be taking over his mail run permanently. Rumor has it that he's entertaining an offer."

When she looked confused, he wished her a pleasant day. An offer? Was he going to sell the business before it went bankrupt? Was he running out on her and his debts?

She didn't know; she just didn't know. A week ago she had wished the Captain would come home. She needed his help. But now so much doubt, so much suspicion surrounded him she barely believed anything honest of him. Was he the kind, honest man that she believed she had married? Or was he a dishonest businessman, or merely inept? Did he frequent the whorehouses or abhor them? What was his relationship with Lou Gramm? Had she married a true man or was her husband what his name proclaimed—a con?

She stretched her neck back then collapsed forward onto her forearms over the book, so confused she wasn't sure his business was as troubled as she imagined. Maybe she was mistaken. Drew walked in.

"Fayth? I saw the light on and came to investigate. What are you doing here so late?"

"Looking over the business ledgers of O'Neill Shipping. What a mess, Drew. My husband's business is in trouble. How much, I can't discern. Unfortunately, I'm not an accountant." Without thinking, she had let her guard down and spoken to him familiarly about a business that was not his concern, just as she used to about her parents'. When had he wormed his way into her confidence?

"Not what you bargained for when you married for convenience?"

She looked at him sharply and closed the ledger.

Drew came up behind her. "How bad do you suspect it is? Could he lose the business? Could his loss force the loss of yours?"

She stiffened at the thought. She and the Captain kept matters separate, but were they one to the law?

Drew spun her chair around and knelt before her so that their heads were even. "You don't have to let him drag you down. You don't have to wait for fate to deal you another blow."

"Don't say it, Drew. You're getting dangerously close to breaking our agreement."

"Damn the agreement. I love you, Fayth. Run away with me."

"Drew, stop."

"You've been married for less than a year and he's already about to take you down. It isn't fair, and you don't have to be a part of it. Whatever problems he has are his; you owe him nothing. Together, we'll build a fashion empire. No more stodgy men's clothing for us, just sumptuous dresses and—"

"No, Drew." She tried to pull her hand from his. "I won't discuss this subject again."

"I don't accept that. Think about it, Fayth. I'll be here waiting for you as long as it takes." He drew her hand to his lips and kissed it.

CHAPTER FIFTEEN

May 1890

Seattle rose spring green and lovely on the shore before Con.

Home! Restored, refined, rebuilt.

Con scanned the wharf with a sharp gaze. The glare off the water made it difficult to spot detail onshore. Was Fayth there, waiting for him? He tried not to get his hopes up. He smiled, picturing her waiting for him, her spyglass in hand, scanning the waters. She couldn't know how much he had missed her, longed for her. Why hadn't he been able to tell her in his letters? As soon as he found her, his wife would be in no doubt of his feelings.

The smell of fresh timber and sawdust from the mills drifted out onto the water. Con inhaled deeply.

All would be well now that he was home. He couldn't wait to see Fayth. How had he let business keep him away so long?

His gaze swept the shore again. Where was she? She must be waiting in the office until the *Aurnia* docked. He had wired news of his arrival ahead. He wanted her to know, wanted her to be waiting for him. She had to be as eager as he was. He intended to have his wife, fully this time. He ran his glass along the length of the wharf. She wouldn't have to wait long—he'd already given Sweeney orders to take the helm when they docked.

Fayth sat at the drawing table in her office with Drew bent over her shoulder, watching her work.

"The neckline should be lower." Drew spoke solemnly.

She laughed, and it felt good. "Typical man. Always wanting to see more cleavage." She didn't alter the drawing.

Drew stepped back. "No, always wanting to see a perfect design. But you're too headstrong to listen. Always have been."

"Headstrong? I've always attributed that quality to you."

He leaned in, placing his cheek next to hers, so close that her hair brushed against his. He smelled of fresh soap and laundered shirts. Cultured, clean, impeccably groomed, he still didn't entice her. Drew gave a low whistle as he admired the drawing. "You should be in New York, Fayth."

"Always the flatterer." Fayth picked up a brush and swept her erasures away. "What do you think, more pouf to the sleeve?"

"I think you should run away with me to New York and live the good life."

"I thought you agreed not to mention that again." Fayth set her pencil down. "It's time for me to be heading home. I've a fitting appointment there with Miss Reilly. She's one of those who refuses to come to the shop."

"A word from you is all it will take to leave these troubles behind. A *For Sale* sign, a train ticket, and we're on our way to fortune and happiness."

She gave him an arch look. "Watch the shop for me while I keep my appointment? Coral should be back any minute now."

"Certainly." He helped her on with her shawl.

"Take good care of things in my absence."

The smiled died on Con's face. She wasn't at the wharf. She wasn't in the office. He barked at Sweeney, growled at Tetch who looked surprised to see him.

"Mrs. O'Neill hasn't been by?" Con asked him.

Tetch frowned. "Not in nearly a week, sir. You might find her at her shop, though in all likelihood, she'll be out."

Con frowned. "Why would she be out?"

"You haven't heard? Her business has been struggling. Women refuse to patronize it as long as a former whore works there. Mrs. O'Neill has had to resort to making house calls to keep the few loyal clients she has."

"Man alive," Con muttered. At least that partly explained Fayth's absence. Tetch watched him curiously. "Why does everyone seem so surprised by my arrival? Didn't you get my telegrams?"

Tetch shook his head. "Telegrams? I'm sorry, Captain, no. Mrs. O'Neill didn't mention a word last time she was in."

Con headed for the door. Why hadn't he come back sooner? "Oversee the unloading."

At the shop, Con smiled at the dainty tinkle of the bell as he walked in. The main room was empty. He made his way to the office, picturing her bent over her drawing table, her surprise when she looked up to see him. He wondered vaguely whether she hadn't heard the bell. He walked into her office without knocking, calling out her name. "Fayth!"

A tall, dark man was seated at Fayth's desk, bent over a ledger. He started and looked up. "May I help you?"

He recognized the man immediately. Damn! Her former fiancé. A little older maybe, but no doubt the man from the picture Fayth had kept. Con's stomach knotted, burning with the indigestion of rage and jealousy. When had that bastard come to town? How had he connived his way back into Fayth's life? Con fought to maintain his composure as he stared him down.

There was an awkward moment of silence as Con assessed the situation. The man seated in Fayth's place was handsome and arrogant, confidently assuming a role no longer his. Con watched Drew's gaze flick over him, no doubt taking in the cut of his suit, determining how best to make him over in fine cloth. Or did he know who Con was? Was he sizing up the competition? Con couldn't tell.

"I'm Mrs. O'Neill's assistant, Drew Hanbrough."

Con sensed Drew's immediate dislike. Funny how rivals could pick each other out.

"If you're looking for a tailor, I assure you I am quite capable of helping you."

"I imagine you are," Con said dryly. "My business is with Fayth. Do you know where I can find her?"

"She ran home to pick something up. May I schedule an appointment with her for you?"

"No, I'm quite capable of finding her at home." Con stormed out the door. He should have returned to the ship. He needed to calm down before he faced Fayth, but he was compelled to see her. Needed to hear her explanation of what the hell Drew was doing in Seattle, working for her. What did he expect her to say? What possible reason could she give?

He took a deep breath, trying to calm himself as he strode across the skylights and down the street. He smiled ruefully. Fayth hated those blasted things. Reason returned as he walked. He would calm down and go home. Bring her the gifts he brought for her. Act as if nothing had happened. Wait for her to confide in him. What did he have to gain by starting a fight with her? By accusing her? Drew might already have the upper hand. Putting Fayth on the defensive against him would only lessen Con's odds of winning her back. If he hadn't lost her already.

No. He wouldn't lose her.

Fayth was getting ready to head back to the shop when she heard the screen door in the kitchen creak open. "Coral?" She hurried to the kitchen. "How are things at the—"

She froze midsentence. Con stood near the door. At least, she thought he was Con, this cleanly shaved man who had Con's eyes and hair and a strong jaw firmly set that sent her heart tripping over itself. He held in front of him a potted rose bush in full bloom, so tightly his knuckles were white. He didn't smile.

"Captain?" Her gaze flicked to the rosebush.

"They're blooming in California now. I couldn't bring home fresh roses, so I dug up the whole bush. Billy had a trial keeping it alive." The sentiment was tender, but his words were hard.

She hesitated a second too long, reaching for it just as he set it beside him. She pulled back and forced a smile. "It's lovely. And so is the surprise of having you home. Why didn't you let me know you were coming? I would have met you at the pier."

He frowned. "You didn't get my telegrams?"

"No." She watched him study her carefully, gauging her response. Something was definitely wrong, so wrong there was ice in the air between them. She smiled again and tried not to act like an awkward stranger. "You shaved."

"Yeah, I feel naked." He rubbed his cheek.

On impulse, she took a step toward him and ran her fingers over his smoothly shaved jaw. "Well, you look handsome."

He stiffened.

She dropped her hand and kept smiling brightly, even though it was so forced her cheeks hurt with the effort. "You do have a chin," she said softly.

He nodded. "That I do."

This wasn't the reunion she'd pictured, not this stiff, cold stranger act. She didn't know this man in front of her, except from her nightmares. This is what she'd feared all along. But if he'd become so indifferent, then why had he come back at all?

She froze as an awful thought occurred to her. Why had he looked for her at home? Logically, he would have stopped by the shop first—

Drew! What had he done and said? How would she explain? She needed time to think. She spoke automatically. "How was your trip?" She took the Captain by the arm and led him to the sitting room as if nothing were wrong. "Are you hungry?"

"I ate onboard."

He obviously wasn't going to make this easy on her.

"Of course." Like two strangers, they took seats opposite each other. "You've been by the shop?" She smiled at him even though her cheeks felt stretched and tight.

He nodded. "I have."

"Then you've met my assistant, Drew Hanbrough?"

"Yes." His voice was serious, calm. "He's a handsome man, a real charmer. That must come in handy with the ladies."

She clasped her hands in her lap, trying not to let any emotion about Drew slip and frantically trying to remember if there was any reason for the Captain to connect Drew as her former fiancé. She'd been so careful not to mention him. And the Captain claimed never to have seen that picture she'd sworn she left behind in his cabin after the fire. "Drew Hanbrough, handsome? I suppose. I've known him forever so I guess I don't really notice anymore. But he can be charming. When he chooses. And the clients like him."

She knew she must look guilty and tried not to act it. She had to put him at ease about Drew, not set him immediately more on edge than he was. "He worked for Father as his assistant. It was really a piece of luck he came west and ended up in Seattle just as I needed him."

"As you needed him?" His gaze was unwavering and icy, his face masked.

She shifted uncomfortably. "I didn't want to worry you, but I've been under attack since you left." She launched into a description of her woes—the newspaper articles, the words painted on her building, the loss of business. "I was in a bind, having to make house calls and close the shop while I was out. I needed an assistant, but worried over where I would find one. There isn't a woman in town who will work with a former prostitute. Then Drew arrived."

"How very convenient. Drew?"

She'd slipped up and sounded too familiar. "Well, yes. We are on first name terms. As I said, I've known him forever." She told the truth, but her conscience pricked her. She lied by omission by not confessing that Drew was her former fiancé. But the Captain seemed so distant, and she was so uncertain. It just didn't seem like the right time for the revelation.

"Drew has done wonderful things for the business. I don't know how I would have managed without him." She tried to sound light. "But he'll be moving on soon."

"Will he?"

Her heart pounded. He'd always been able to read her so well. Did he suspect she wasn't telling him the whole truth about Drew? She stared at him again, unable to get over the impression that he was a stranger. He looked different and acted stiff. His manner frightened her. Had he come to tell her it was over? "You haven't said why you're back?"

"Briggs didn't need me anymore."

She looked away from him, hurt that he hadn't said something more romantic and reassuring. The words *all business* described him too well. What had she done to him? Nothing made sense anymore. Not Coral's morose mood, or Drew wanting her to run away, or the Captain's cool manner, not even her own emotions. She wanted Con, yet she feared he would be her ruin. She changed the subject rather than confront the situation. "How is O'Neill's Shipping?"

"It's fine."

"Is it?" She stared at him, wondering whether he was lying to her, too.

He studied her. "You sound worried."

If he wasn't going to confide in her, there was little point in discussing it. But she couldn't let it rest. "I'd check with Mr. Tetch. I handed things over to him after having trouble with some of your bills. I've tried a few times since, but I couldn't make sense of your ledgers."

He looked suddenly alert. "Nor should you have to. I'll talk to Tetch immediately." He rose to leave.

She softened. "You'll be back for dinner? We'll have a celebration. I can't wait to see Coral's expression when she sees your naked chin."

He gave her a halfhearted smile. "I can't wait myself. I'll be back." He nodded and rose to leave.

That night Con sat on his bed and stripped off his boots, dumping them onto the floor unceremoniously. Invited by Coral, Drew had come to dinner. How Con had suffered through it he didn't know. Confident, comfortable, jovial, Drew had acted as if he belonged with Fayth. Did he? Con ran his fingers back through his hair.

He hated that bastard Drew. Con leaned back against his pillows. Neither Fayth nor Drew mentioned that they were formerly engaged, which meant they schemed to keep it from him. Why? Was it innocence? Did Fayth fear his wrath, or his hurt? Or was there a more sinister reason? He hated even to think it, but what if Fayth still loved Drew?

He grabbed the glass from his night table and rummaged through his seabag for the Scotch he'd brought back for Bailey. Repressing anger always made him thirsty. He opened it and tossed back a drink, haunted by memories of his last evening with Fayth. If Billy had arrived just ten minutes later, she would be his. Just ten minutes. He took another gulp of whiskey. The brink of paradise, every remembrance of it brought a hard arousal.

Olive meowed at the door begging to be let in. He ignored her. He needed solitude. He needed to think. How long had Drew been in Seattle?

Long enough to establish himself with Fayth again. Long enough to restore her trust in him and elicit her sympathy—the charming snake. How had he done it?

"Damn!" He hated being put in the position of playing catch up.

This homecoming wasn't what he'd pictured. He hadn't planned to sleep in this bedroom again—not alone. Ugly, jealous thoughts crept through his mind, tormenting thoughts of Drew and Fayth together. He didn't believe she had been unfaithful with her body. He observed her closely throughout the evening, and saw no evidence of that kind of guilt in her actions. Drew looked clearly frustrated, like a man in need. She hadn't been unfaithful in body, but in spirit and mind? An ugly chill shivered through him. Lust was one thing. It could be overcome. But a heart engaged elsewhere?

He preferred not to think about it.

And what went on with Coral? The girl looked peaked, and queasy. She had barely touched her meal, looked green at the thought. Was she ill? Was he the only one who had noticed? He'd check on her tomorrow. And the infatuated looks she gave Drew? Trouble. But the man had barely noticed her. He had focused on Fayth.

A door opened in the hall. Someone scooped up Olive and carried her away as she mewed. He leaned back again and set the glass on the table by his bed. The alcohol settled over his senses bringing with it a temporary calm. He should have confessed his love for Fayth long ago. He sneered derisively at himself. He disliked dishonesty in others, hated it in himself.

He took a deep breath and pushed the bottle of Scotch away. He needed a clear head. He had fights on two fronts with stakes too high to lose. What had gone on during his absence? Fayth was worried about the business, almost resentful of his absence, and the money he made. During dinner she mentioned how hard it had been to pay rent and meet expenses, eyeing him as if he were to blame.

He had sent plenty of money, more than he should have. For all his faults, he wasn't a stingy man. Were her standards different from his? Or was Tetch getting bolder with his pinching from the till? Tetch no doubt pilfered money in Con's absence, but would he be so bold? Tetch would have to be more clever than Con gave him credit for to hide such avarice. The only alternative was that Fayth had a different standard of generosity than he did. He shook his head. Nothing made sense, not even the business. The bills were paid, the books looked normal, but he couldn't help feeling imminent disaster coming.

On the other front, he'd been forced to watch Drew's gaze rake over Fayth all evening, to swallow his words as Drew goaded. Drew wanted his wife. Con had no intention of letting her go, but what should he do now?

He took another breath to calm himself. Fayth was the only woman Con had ever loved. He wouldn't let Drew have her. He had to find a way to get rid of Drew. Would shanghai be a bad thing?

Fayth leaned against the closed door. She heard Con turn in the hall and walk toward his room, then his door banged shut. She hung her head, guilt engulfing her. The evening had been a long, personal game of charades. She walked toward her bed, unbuttoning her bodice with trembling fingers.

She hadn't counted on the pull she felt toward Con, or his returning coldness. Without his beard, with his hair so stylishly trimmed, he was more handsome than Drew. If only she could decide, could know Con was true, know he loved her. If only she could feel secure again. But she felt herself flailing and grasping wildly for security, as desperate as if it were air itself. She threw her dress over the chair and pulled her nightgown on.

Con had the power to drag her down with him. If his business failed, if he was somehow involved with Lou—

She shivered at the thought. If he loved her, if he didn't . . .

Which was worse? Which did she fear most?

Coral paced the floor wildly. Dr. Wall had been kindly, but definite, confirming her suspicions. She would have a baby, Drew's baby. She'd been careless. When she worked for Lou, she'd been careful to use the small doses of opium always discreetly available for the girls. Never enough to become addicted. She'd seen the sad effects of that, but enough to stop her monthlies. Used in proper doses, opium was effective in preventing pregnancies. But she had given up the habit when she had come to stay with Fayth.

She had to think. She had to leave. She couldn't keep living with Fayth. She felt traitorous enough as it was. If she stayed, Fayth would certainly realize the truth soon enough. She already acted suspicious.

Coral smiled. She would have to see Drew. He loved her. He would marry her. She didn't want Fayth hurt, but there was no alternative now. What was, was. Now that Con was home, he'd take care of Fayth. What good timing that he had come home unexpectedly yesterday. Coral was tempted to tell him her news, but, of course, she couldn't. She noticed Con watching her last night at dinner, a worried look on his face. He suspected something, maybe thought she was ill. Oh, well, he'd find out soon enough, too.

She bit her lip and smiled again, slowing her pacing long enough to glance out the bedroom window. It would all be for the best. Without her to worry about and intrude on their privacy, Fayth would have to see Con's devotion. Maybe then Fayth would finally admit that she loved the Captain. When Fayth recovered from the shock and realized her own happiness, she'd forgive Coral. With that glorious, happy thought in mind, Coral grabbed her shawl and headed for the door, a bounce in her step. She would tell Drew immediately. She hurried to his hotel.

"Well, I seem to be quite the virile buck," Drew said when she gave him her news. They were not the words she expected, but he didn't sound unhappy. "You're certain I'm the father?"

She nodded. He didn't speak, just sat a moment in silent contemplation. Her heart pounded.

"At present, I don't have any money. Fayth has been my means of support. Maybe I can put it to her for a loan. But I'll have to think of a lie. She can't know of this. You haven't told her?" He spoke sharply. He seemed too worried over Fayth's knowledge of the event.

"Certainly not. She knows nothing of it, or us."

He smiled. "And indeed she shouldn't. I don't want Fayth hurt. I'll get you the money, I promise, as soon as possible. We can't let this go on long. It's too dangerous."

"Drew? What are you saying?"

"Surely a woman of your occupation knows what I'm saying—rid yourself of the baby. See an abortionist."

"No!" She couldn't help herself, she started crying. She'd beg if she had to. "I'm not a whore anymore. Drew, I love you. This is not like when I worked at the house. You must marry me!"

He looked at her with an odd mixture of indifference and sympathy. "Poor, naive girl. You misunderstood my motives from the beginning. You're beautiful and spirited, and a very good lay, but that's it.

"If you were an innocent, or the first girl I'd gotten in this condition, I might be tempted to oblige you, but having been here before, I can assure you it's not worth the trouble. Unfortunately for you, I've been burned once and that's all it took to cure me of all honorable intentions."

His words made no sense. He loved her. He'd made love to her, whispered tender things. And she loved him. "I'm afraid of having an abortion. Girls die. You've got to marry me!"

Drew seemed to lose his patience. He snorted. "You can't believe I would marry a whore?"

His words stung.

"Bastard!" She lunged at him, fingers curled into a claw. He intercepted her swipe and restrained her as she struggled. "I thought I meant something to you!"

"You did, dear. As I said, you were a very good lay—the best."

She struggled futilely against him. "I'll tell Fayth—"

"You won't. You don't have the strength to lose her friendship. Without her, you're nothing."

She stopped struggling. Drew was just like all the other underhanded men she knew. Blackmail was the best way to defeat him. "I'll tell the Captain."

"Tell him, by all means. What do you think his reaction will be? He'd be a weak fool if he didn't throw you out of his house. You're an immoral influence on his wife. Then what would he do? Come after me? I would deny it, you know that."

Coral tried to hide her fear, but knew he sensed it, because he released her and smiled patronizingly. "Come around and see me day after tomorrow. I'll have the money by then."

Fayth came into the house through the kitchen. She shouldn't have closed the shop early, but with her feelings about the Captain and the animosity between him and Drew, and her worry about Coral going home sick, she couldn't concentrate on business. Earlier in the morning before she left for work, Con had insisted she give Drew the day off. They had fought. He had no right to dictate what she did with her business, but she capitulated to gain an uneasy truce. Con acted jealous, but that made no sense. He couldn't know who Drew was, and she hadn't flirted with him in the slightest. The Captain acted cold and distant to her in every other way. It broke her heart, but what could she do?

She sighed. Without Drew, there wasn't much she could do but close. What was she going to do about Drew and the Captain? Fayth unpinned her hat and went to hang it on the hat rack, too tired to think. Coral sat on her packed bags in the entry. At the sight of her, Fayth's spirits plummeted to a new low.

"Coral? Are you going somewhere?"

A tear slid down Coral's cheek. She dabbed at it with a handkerchief. "I can't stay and ruin your business any longer." Her defiant tone was at direct odds with her sentimental expression.

Fayth frowned. "What?"

Coral silently handed her the day's newspaper fold-ed open to a story.

It is rumored that a young woman, well-known for her easy virtue, is still under the employ of one of our town's favorite young seamstresses, Mrs. O'Neill. Mrs. O'Neill's defenders, the Ladies' Christian Committee members and other sympathizers, applaud Mrs. O'Neill for her attempts to rescue one so young from the evil clutches of such a sinful life. Her detractors, however, deny that such a thing can be accomplished. Moreover, since the young woman resides with Mrs. O'Neill, and since the lady's husband, Captain O'Neill, is frequently at sea, they fear the evil influence her presence will have over the young businesswoman.

A source, who asked not to be identified, acknowl-edged seeing unescorted men come and go from Mrs. O'Neill's home. This is no reflection on Mrs. O'Neill, who was not at home during any of the visits. Moreo-ver, the source fears that Mrs. O'Neill, despite her good intentions, is being played the fool. . . .

Fayth snapped the paper shut without reading fur-ther and handed it back to Coral. "Garbage! Utter and total garbage! Nothing much different from what they've printed before. Don't let it upset you."

"Your good name has been tarnished because of me. The paper won't stop reminding people who and what I am until I'm back where I belong."

"Where you belong! You belong here. You're not the girl you were. Those who know us know the truth. My reputation speaks for itself, as does yours. If I ever find out who the source is—"

"Fayth, I've lost the fight. That's the third article they've printed in two weeks. If I leave, they'll leave you alone."

"I'm begging you to stay. If you leave, they've won and you've lost everything." Fayth walked over to her and took one of her hands. "Coral, please reconsider."

Coral shook her head. The sound of a carriage coming up the drive caught their attention. Fayth went to the window in time to see Lou descend from her carriage, aided by her driver. Coral didn't wait for a knock, but opened the door and called her greeting.

Lou swept in and took Coral in her arms, leading her toward the door. "I must thank you for taking such good care of our girl, Fayth. You gave it a good try."

Lou ordered the driver to load Coral's things. She wished Fayth good day and ushered Coral out the door. Coral looked back as she descended the doorstep. "Come visit me. Don't desert me. Forgive me." The last words were a mere whisper.

Fayth watched them from the window until the carriage was loaded and they drove out of sight.

Later that afternoon, Fayth's mind was heavy with worry as she went up the walk to Lou Gramm's parlor house. Fayth had been to the newspaper office and confronted them, demanding to know their source for the damaging articles. The reporter she talked to had given nothing away, except to say that a man had submitted the information, demanding they publish it for the public good. Dead ends, always dead ends.

Several men waited on the porch to be let in. They gave Fayth odd looks, and coughed self-consciously. Well blast them anyway! She didn't care two hoots what they, or anyone else, thought. She meant to drag Coral back.

Maddie opened the door. The men tumbled in and disappeared. "Mrs. O'Neill?"

"I'm here to see Coral."

"No disrespect to you, Mrs. O'Neill, but she's under Lou's care now. I must ask you to leave."

Lou's bouncer, Rusty, hovered nearby.

"I'm not here to cause a scene. I'm worried about Coral. I've helped Lou out when she needed me. Now she owes me the favor of letting me talk to Coral."

Maddie sighed, and motioned for Rusty to get Coral. "Follow me. I'll show you where you may wait for her." At the door of a small room, Maddie extended her arm, indicating Fayth should enter. "I wouldn't worry about Coral, Mrs. O'Neill. Lou will take good care of her. I'm thinking her problem is a gentleman. Miss Coral was always romantic."

Maddie surprised Fayth with her sympathy. "I'm inclined to agree with you." She thought back to the thumping and moaning she had nearly walked in on months ago.

"Some man jilted her, poor thing, or I miss my guess. I've seen it happen before, seen girls come running back. Lou is like a mama to them, nurses their wounds."

"But who is he, Maddie?"

"Doesn't matter who. Any gentleman will do. Those that come to the House like their pleasure, but they aren't about to upset their society and standing by marrying one of our lady boarders. I've seen my share of girls fall in love, but in all my days working for Miss Gramm, in San Francisco and now here, I've never seen one of the gentlemen marry one. It isn't done."

"Such a cruel fact of fate."

"A fact all the same. The girls are well aware of the rarity of such doings when they enter the business."

"Yes, but who can hold back where the heart is concerned? Who couldn't help but hope?" Fayth was as much a fool as any of Lou's girls, at least where the Captain was concerned, and Drew, when she'd be younger.

"You sound like Miss Coral. Make yourself comfortable." Maddie left her.

Coral appeared minutes later, a telltale puffiness surrounded her eyes, hinting of tears.

"Fayth." Coral's voice was as dull as her eyes. She hugged Fayth without enthusiasm. "Why did you come?"

"I'm not happy with the explanation you gave."

"The newspaper." Coral stared at the floor. "Your customers will be returning by the dozens now that I've gone."

"Profit has never been the motive for my life." It was hard not to sound fierce because Fayth certainly felt it, railing inside at the injustice in the world.

"Maybe it should be." Coral's laugh was wretched and eerily hollow. Heavens, was she using opium again already?

"Lou says I can raise my fees. Isn't infamy wonderful? I'll be making more money than I ever thought possible."

"Stop it!" Fayth wanted to shake her. "I don't need the business of sanctimonious biddies, and you don't need the patronage of those, those—men!" She softened her tone and pleaded. "I do need you to be all right. You were my first friend in town. Don't give up on yourself."

"I need some fresh air. Let's take a walk." Coral turned on her heel and strode to the door, leaving Fayth no option but to follow her.

They walked to the waterfront without speaking and stared in silence out across the water. Coral rocked herself in silence with arms folded protectively across her chest. Fayth stood calmly, waiting.

"I'm pregnant." The confession stole Coral's agitation. She stopped rocking.

Fayth went numb. She should have suspected. She kept her tone sympathetic and soft. The last thing Coral needed was judgment. "How far along?" The pregnancy explained so much.

Coral turned to face her with tears brimming. "You don't seem surprised?"

"No." Fayth paused. "I should have suspected. It's a wonder I didn't. I came home early one day. I may be naive, but I know what you were doing. I didn't want to confront you. I tried to warn you against such behavior." Fayth paused delicately. "Who is the father, Coral?"

"Think about the business I'm in Fayth. How would I know?"

Without thinking, Fayth gasped.

"I'm sorry, that was thoughtless." Fayth's words tumbled out. "I just . . . I thought that maybe . . . maybe the man at the house was someone special—"

"You didn't think I would ply the trade in your house? Sorry to disillusion you, Fayth. Once a whore, always a whore." The words exploded into the gentle sounds of lapping of water and soft breeze.

Coral looked suddenly contrite. "I'm sorry. My nerves are jangled."

"Mine, too."

Coral trembled, and her eyes were glassy and dazed. Opium, certainly. Fayth had to get her out of Lou's. "Do the rest of the girls know? Does Lou?"

"Lou, no one else. If the other girls knew they'd think I was silly, a baby." Coral lost her bravado. Suddenly, she looked like the scared sixteen-year-old girl she was.

"Why is that?" Fayth's kept her tone gentle.

"Because to them the solution is simple—abort."

"And what do you think?" Fayth feared the answer, but the question had to be asked.

"I can't." She clutched Fayth's arm, her eyes wild. Fayth exhaled too loudly. "I'm afraid. If it's not done right, it could kill me. Besides I . . ."

Fayth waited for her to continue her thought, but she didn't. "What did Lou say?"

"The decision is mine. If I want to keep it, I can work until my condition's evident, then I have to leave. I can come back when I've delivered and gotten my figure back. But not with the child. If I want to abort, she knows a competent doctor." Coral's shoulders shook, tears flowed down her cheeks. Fayth pulled her into a hug. "I can't raise a child. I'm not ready. I have no way to support it, other than . . .

"A baby shouldn't be raised in a brothel."

Elizabeth came to mind. "What if I could arrange an adoption?"

Coral shook her head. "It's no good, who wants a whore's baby?"

"Coral—"

"And I can't afford the time off. I have to buy new clothes, not to mention perfume and rouge. And I still owe Lou money from before. I'm in too much debt to quit."

"I can help you with the clothes. I can sew for you at cost. As for the rest—how much more do you owe?" Fayth should have known, but she was too tired to calculate it.

Coral pulled out of her embrace and stepped back. "I know what you're thinking Fayth, but it's more than you can afford."

Fayth rested her hand on Coral's arm. Coral was right. It would take months just to recoup from the business she lost because of the scandal surrounding Coral, and she had her own debts. "You didn't answer my question before—how far along are you?"

Coral took a minute answering. Fayth assumed she was counting the weeks. "Less than three months."

Fayth sighed. "We still have some time before you start showing. Maybe we can find a solution."

"Maybe." Coral started rocking again and turned her gaze to the water.

"Come home with me, Coral. Come home and let me take care of you."

"No!"

"Please. The Captain is home now. Between the two of us we'll manage. We both love you so much."

"Nothing you can say will convince me. You're better off without me, both of you. I need to be where I am. It's the only safe place." Coral's face was set, her words puzzling. Lou's safe? But what could Fayth do? She couldn't force her.

"Any time you want to come home, just come."

Coral nodded, but her expression said she wouldn't.

"In the meantime, give me time. I know someone who's always wanted a baby. Maybe I can arrange something. Just promise me you'll take care of yourself. Start eating. The baby needs food. Give me your word you won't do anything until I've had time to work things out."

"What would I do?"

Lou sat opposite Con in her burgundy leather chair, her back straight, her deportment that of a refined woman. She wore a lavender gown, low cut in front to display ample cleavage, a bow at bust's peak. Lace covered the upper dress from the shoulders to just below the bottom of her hips where a ribbon of deep purple bisected the dress to the floor. It was unbustled, loosely short-sleeved to cover large upper arms and there was no indentation where a waist should have been. Lou was past her prime, but the dress was becoming. Its designer knew how to flatter a woman's shape. Con recognized it as one of Fayth's. Saw in it the passion of the woman who created it.

Con often wondered what sort of woman lay beneath Fayth's proper exterior. Did she, in her dressmaking for these women of easy virtue, release her own fantasies? Reveal her truly expressive self? He longed to see her curves draped in a dress as revealing as Lou's— loose, free flowing.

"Well Con, just a few more payments and you're done with me. I can hardly bear the thought. You're one of the few men who interests me. I always look forward to hearing your opinion on matters of the day. Most men are too caught up by the demands of the bulge in their pants to pay attention to the world."

"Isn't that how you make your money?" He smiled.

Lou laughed. "Even so, it can be damned tiresome. But perhaps you'll find another venture to pursue and borrow my money again?"

"I hope not, Lou. Your rates are too high. The banks have more appeal."

"Ah, but for those the bank has refused . . ." Lou shrugged her shoulders delicately. "What can they do? And what can I do when I take on such extra risk?"

"Even still, I don't foresee any new ventures in the near future."

"You're content with your lot? Surely a bigger boat, or a new warehouse will catch your eye one day soon?"

Con shook his head. "Afraid not. In fact, I'm considering leaving the business."

"Getting out? You can't mean leaving the sea? What would you be—a land-locked farmer?" Lou laughed.

Con was solemn. "I'm considering selling." It was a relief to confide in someone. "There's an outfit based out of San Francisco that's had their eye on the *Aurnia*, and me, for some time. They've offered to buy her and my wharf interests here in Seattle if I'll take on the job of captaining their new ocean liner. She'll be a brand new beauty, state of the art. She's under construction now.

"The pay they're offering isn't pennies. I'd have no headaches of ownership and I'd be out on the open waters again."

"But what of your Seattle interests?"

Con exhaled deeply. There was no use holding anything back from Lou. She was not judgmental and her discretion was well-known. "Business has not rebounded as it should have since the fire. I've never been interested in the actual business dealings of my company before, it's the sea that I love, but even such a meager business mind as mine can't ignore the signs. If I don't find the source of the problem, or a way to turn things around soon, I'll go under."

"Selling is the easy way out."

"It may be the only way out."

Lou adjusted herself in her chair. "I was speaking of your other Seattle interest—Fayth. Will she want to relocate?"

Con put his guard up. It was one thing to reveal one's faults in business matters. It was another to reveal faults of the heart. "Could be she wouldn't. Sometimes it takes a man to own up to his defeat, his mistakes. I shouldn't have married Fayth believing I could make her love me. There are some games good sportsmanship can't win."

"Then play dirty." Lou's eyes twinkled, but she wasn't joking.

Con shook his head. "I played dirty to get her in the first place, and look where it's gotten me."

CHAPTER SIXTEEN

Shortly after Fayth arrived home, the Captain came in. He called to her from the kitchen. When she met him, he presented her with a bunch of delicate red roses. Oh, blast! In her confused, worried, upset state of mind, the last thing she needed was the Captain playing suitor. First he was jealous and cool toward her, now flowers? What was she to think? And yet, she wanted to send him away and run to him for comfort, at the same time.

"Fayth?" The Captain looked uncertain, boyish and charming in his confusion.

Frustration won Fayth over. She reacted defensively. Fayth snatched the flowers and smashed them on the table. "What right do you have to court me?"

He stared at the flowers a moment, looking stunned by her outburst. Fayth followed his gaze. The bruised roses lay on the table, tragic testimony to her confusion, to their failing relationship. One rose fell away from the rest, its petals separated from the body of the flower, damaged, like she felt.

"What right?" His words exploded into the kitchen. He ran a hand through his hair and took a deep breath as if trying to regain control. "I'm your husband."

She glared at him. "Yes, what right, Con O'Neill? We had an agreement. This is a marriage of convenience. *We* exist for business purposes only. Husband or not, you have no right."

He laughed then, and for the first time there was no humor in it, only derision. "What am I supposed to do, Fayth? Sit idly by while you make time with that dandy from your past?"

He grabbed her arm and pulled her around into him. "You promised me your fidelity." His tone was low and solemn. It frightened her.

She tried to wrench free of his grip. "And I've been completely faithful."

"Am I supposed to believe you? When you spend hours alone with Drew after hours at the shop?" He took a deep breath and lowered his voice. "You've been unfaithful, darling, with your business talents if nothing else. The businesses belong to you and me. Yet more and more it appears that Drew is your partner. Your attention to our common interests is all I have claim on. By our own agreement that belongs to me."

"Nothing *belongs* to you!"

His expression narrowed and he gave a snorting laugh. "I'm at least owed your discretion. It's all over town how you've been trailing after him. Tetch told me."

"Why should you believe him?" Fayth's heart thudded in her ears. She didn't know the jealous, angry man before her—had no idea how to handle him, or the situation.

"He has no reason to lie."

"Jealousy doesn't become you. I suggest you keep your wild accusations to yourself." Her breath came in quick angry gasps. She couldn't stop herself from lashing out at him. "How can you speak to me of discretion? All I ever asked of you was the same. Yet you flaunt your relationship with Lou, going to her house whenever it suits you, undermining the very things that I stand for. What is your relationship with her? Is she your partner, like I am?"

He released the grip on her arm and stepped back. She'd hit a weak spot.

Fayth didn't understand her own angry torrent of emotions. She needed to escape before she broke into wild, jealous sobs, but he caught her arm again as if he'd read her thoughts.

"Fayth—"

"I saw that whore come off your ship."

He paled.

"No defenses? I thought not. She was one of Lou's girls. Was she for your own use, or were you merely helping Lou grow her business?" Her own laugh floated eerily through the room, seemingly disembodied.

"Damn it, Fayth. How can you even accuse me? You want explanations, I'll give them to you, but I doubt you'll like them, or understand my motives." He sounded suddenly defeated.

She didn't want to hear them, didn't want the last of her illusions to crumble. "No, you're probably right. But I do want to know what you have done to Coral. At least give me that truth."

"To Coral?"

"She moved out today, back to Lou's. You come home and she leaves, what am I to think?"

"Fayth—"

"She's pregnant."

"Man alive!" He looked shaken. "You can't think—"

"No, the timing isn't right." Her words sliced the air viciously. She saw him reel with the shock of them, as stunned as if she'd slapped him. She hurt so badly, she couldn't stop herself from hurting him.

"Fayth, how can you think these things about me? I haven't done anything to Coral." He looked directly into her eyes.

She had to give him credit for courage, facing her like that. For herself, she could barely look at him.

His tone was soft. "What have I done to you to make you doubt me like this?"

She didn't answer. She couldn't.

"Listen to me." Defeat edged his voice. "I should have told you the truth a long time ago. But I thought . . ."

He continued staring at her. "Our relationship was so new. I thought I'd lose any chance I had at winning your affections." He sighed. "I thought you'd never have to know. And except for the break-in, you wouldn't have."

Fear pulsed through her, setting her stomach rolling, her hands trembling, even blotting out his admission of feelings for her.

"I went to Lou's to borrow money. And later to make payments. And as for the girl you saw on the *Aurnia,* transporting her was part of the payment, a favor called in."

She stopped still. "What?"

"For the second story of your building."

"Loan? My building?" Understanding would not come.

He laughed, but it was more at himself than anything. "Lou has nearly as much money to lend as the banks. When a man can't get a bank loan, Lou is his best bet. With the interest she charges, a man has to be desperate, as I was."

At first, she was too stunned to reply. Understanding came slowly. Her words were slow and deliberate, filled with malice. "You mean I'm in debt to Lou?" Since Coral's defection, Lou was lower than silverfish on her list of despicable creatures.

"We both are." He shook his head slowly and looked far away. "Blasted thieves!" he mumbled. "I tried to offer O'Neill's as collateral, but Lou wouldn't have it. I had to back the loan with your business."

Her breath surged from her, as if she had just fallen flat on her stomach. Her stifled cry was almost a parody of speech, barely audible. "No!"

"I'm sorry. It was the only way to get the money." He tried to lift her chin to look at him. "I took the loan because I loved you, because I believed in you. It was either you failed then and there, or I took out the loan. I knew you'd make it, Fayth. I thought I would. I've been making the payments."

Stunned by his admissions, of both love and betrayal, she could only utter the most rudimentary question. "How much?"

He named a figure. It only explained part of the money that disappeared each month.

"You, you . . . I can't even think of a name vile enough. I'm ruined! Tetch is right—you're nothing but a thief. O'Neill's Shipping is going to fail, and me with it. There's no way I can make payments to both Lou and Mr. Finn."

She shook free of him and strode to the door, pausing to look over her shoulder and throw out a final insult. "By the way, I saw you at Lou's before we needed money for the second story—the day after our marriage. You still lie. I wish you'd just leave!"

He wore a masked expression. She could no longer read anything in his face. "I'll be happy enough to oblige you in the morning. I'm sailing for San Francisco."

She didn't turn to look at him before she stormed down the hall into her room, slamming the door shut behind her. But she couldn't push the hurt, defeated tone of his voice from her mind. Nor her fear, tantamount to panic.

Oh, blast! She didn't know what to do.

She sat on her bed, trying to calm herself. An array of emotions washed over her in such quick succession that they blended together and were nearly impossible to separate by name. Anger. Fear. Betrayal. She had loved only two men in her life, one openly, and one despite herself, and neither one turned out to be who she thought he was. She could ascribe her misreading of Drew to immaturity. But she had no excuse for Con. She had researched his background carefully, well before feeling any emotional attachment to him. But she had been fooled by everyone, and everything, including her own pride. What vanity caused her to believe she could discern the true nature of a person through observation?

As she sat there, she didn't know what hurt worse, that Con had gone to Lou for the money, or that he did it behind her back. Where were honesty and trust? Oh, what a hypocrite she was! She hadn't told him who Drew really was. Why had she been afraid of the truth? Had Con felt the same, been as fearful?

She hated being suddenly in debt to the madam. She morosely pictured herself working for Lou for the rest of her life. She snorted. *Yes, that's exactly what I've always wanted to be—seamstress to the whores.*

To succeed, she had to overcome so much, from her location and the blasted skylights, to Coral's reputation. She could explain Coral on the grounds of rescuing her from the clutches of sin. But how could she ever explain a business loan from Seattle's most infamous madam?

She rubbed her temple. It was quiet in the hall. She grabbed her jacket and headed for the door. She'd go to the shop to calm down and think, to escape.

When Fayth arrived at the shop, a light was on. What was Drew doing working when she had given him the day off? She almost turned around, but he saw her and waved. Reluctantly, she went in.

"I thought I gave you the day off." She took her jacket off and hung it on the coat rack, trying to appear calm.

"You mean your Captain did. We're behind. There was sewing to be done. What are *you* doing here?"

He sounded sincere and concerned, just like old times. She needed a friend. She spilled out details of the fight without thinking of the consequences.

"What did you expect from a man of so little moral fiber, Fayth?" Drew said when she finished.

"But how could he? It's my business. He had no right."

"He had no right, but he did it. You can't change that. You've told me time and again how much you admire his ability to take charge and make decisions. Well, darling, you've just discovered the disadvantage of such an admirable trait."

Fayth clenched her fists in front of her and leaned her nose into them in thought, aware that Drew carefully watched her from across the room. Finally, she straightened. "What should I do? I'm ruined. I can't pay both Lou and Jacob Finn. And I don't know which would be worse to default on. If I don't pay the bank, I lose the business. If I don't pay Lou, she takes my business, or I spend eternity sewing for her. I won't do it!"

"Of course not. You have too much talent to waste it on such women. Isn't that what I've been telling you all along?" Drew's voice was smooth, calm.

She stood to pace, too frustrated to sit long. Drew watched for a moment before standing and intercepting her. He took her in his arms in a familiar manner.

"My dear Fayth, you are too talented for Seattle in general. What keeps you here? Loyalty to a man who has betrayed you? What kind of a man are you shackling yourself to? A liar. A cheat. A fraud. And though I don't mean to be indelicate, a patron of whores. The man is so far beneath deserving you, that I can't . . . well, I can't bear it."

"What should I do?" She spoke into his chest.

He rested his chin on the top of her head and suddenly she felt as she did years ago, when Drew had been her untarnished hero. She needed an answer.

"I've been telling you what to do for some time. Run away with me to New York."

She was shaking her head before the words were fully out of his mouth. "No."

He grabbed her head between his hands to stop her disagreement. "It will work. We're so good together."

"You make it sound plausible."

"Because it is. Fayth, what's stopping you?"

The Captain, she thought, but she couldn't say it. It was the thought of never seeing Con again.

Fayth entered the kitchen through the back door with Drew's proposal on her mind. She had no intention of going with him, but during the trip home escape had come to sound good. She could start over; she could take what she could salvage before everything collapsed—the business and her heart.

It was late, but Con had neglected to draw the curtains. The house was quiet, as if no one were home. She pulled the curtains closed, and leaned on her elbows against the kitchen counter, lost in thought.

What kept her in Seattle? Her honor? Her business? Drew was right, as far as business went, she would be better off in New York. Why stay in Seattle where her talents were appreciated mostly by women of easy virtue who wore her gowns to entice men into sin? She sighed, imagining her creations on debutantes and society matrons.

What else? Her marriage? Con? It hurt too much to think about him. How could she stand it? He was leaving tomorrow. Would he come back? Long ago she congratulated herself on making a wise choice, one that would never affect her heart. She fought falling in love with him, but she had. She sniffed, fighting tears, pushed herself back off the counter and retrieved her gloves. She would leave, without Drew. How could she stand the hurt any other way?

She turned from the counter and noticed the table for the first time. The roses Con had given her were carefully arranged in a vase. She stepped closer to examine them. Con had carefully removed all the damaged petals, somehow making them new and whole again.

A note propped against the vase caught her attention. She picked it up and read it. *I'm sorry.*

She fought back tears and fled the room. As she turned into the hall, she noticed a lamp shining in the parlor. She stepped inside the room to extinguish it and found the Captain asleep on the sofa. The lamp washed him in a soft, almost heavenly, golden glow. His lanky form sprawled over the dainty sofa. His mouth fell open, but his face was not slack. She traced his silhouette from the billow of his hair, past thick curling lashes that should not decently belong to a man, to his feet hanging over the sofa arm.

Oh, heaven, he was beautiful. Seeing him lying there like that, she remembered how he seemed at first, honorable, upstanding, heroic. In his presence, she felt safe, even now.

Olive had curled herself into a ball on his chest, as sound asleep as her master, her little cat head snuggled into the hollow of his neck. Fayth's sewing box lay open at the base of the sofa, her needles and threads spilled out beside a badly mended pair of pants.

The wholly pure and unpretentious scene before her brought tears to her eyes. After all the hurtful things she had said to him, she hadn't expected him to stay. The *Aurnia* was certainly as comfortable, more so since he wouldn't have to confront her, and much more elegant than the cottage. Yet Con had chosen to stay, to wait up for her, to mend pants, however badly, to act like they would have a life together. While she busily concocted a plan to run, he pointedly remained.

In that moment, Fayth recognized her first epiphany for what it was and felt as contrite, humble and guilty as Paul on the road to Damascus. She, too, should have fallen to her knees. How had she been so blind? She loved the man that slept trustingly, waiting for her return, and knew that she could not make a life alone, or with another. Maybe it was time to stop running, emotionally as well as physically.

She colored guiltily. What had she done to merit his faith? Listen to and consider another man's adulterous proposal? She hung her head as the disgusting truth of her own actions overcame her. Drew had corrupted her. Hadn't he always?

The words of Con's simple note sang through her head and bubbled onto her lips. "I'm sorry." There was nothing else to say. Her softly spoken words danced through the still air, but to her disappointment did not wake Con.

Life seldom gave one a fair set of circumstances. Con might be all the terrible things she accused him of, but he was not afraid to take blame and responsibility.

She spun on her heel and ran down the hall to her room through a haze of tears. She closed her door and leaned her forehead against it, tears streaming down her face in earnest. Thoughts of a dozen thoughtful and romantic things Con had done came to her. The way he charged through the fire to rescue her, the look of concern on his face. His expression when she first proposed to him. The hurt when she said it was a matter of business only. Why hadn't she given them any credibility before?

Her life came into clarity before her. The picture of Con and Olive on the parlor sofa flooded her mind again. Con, his face firm and handsome even in sleep. The spray of freckles across his forearm as it fell over the sofa edge. She wanted that same man in her bed sleeping beside her. She would accept no substitute.

She pushed aside insecure thoughts of losing the business. The business was only a thing, nothing compared to losing Con. Somehow, together, things would work out.

She would send Drew away. And while Con was gone she would find a way to salvage the businesses. A small nasty thought niggled at her—what if she couldn't?

"The time for negative thinking is past," she said softly to herself. "What if I can?"

She turned from the door toward her bed and gasped. Her coverlet and pillows were covered with rose petals. "Oh, Con!" Tears spilled down her cheeks. She didn't bother to wipe them away as she shimmied out of her clothes and curled up on the bed in the midst of the petals, exhausted by the heavy emotions of the last hour. Tomorrow, she would make everything right. Her eyes felt heavy, but her was heart light as she drifted into a perfumed sleep.

Morning dawned too clearly, forcing Con to admit the truth. Fayth didn't love him. Never had, never would. Stiff from a night on the sofa, he rolled his shoulders and shoved clothes into his duffel. He'd made every conciliatory gesture he could think of, and she had ignored every one. This morning he found her door closed. He'd waited up for her and slept on the sofa intentionally, hoping she would see the rose petals and come to him. But she hadn't. It was time to concede defeat. He had been patient, but every man had his limit. If she wanted her freedom, she could have it.

Fayth woke to the sound of the Captain shuffling in the kitchen. He was leaving? He couldn't. Her heart pounded out of control. She had to catch him. By the time she pulled on a robe and raced to the kitchen, he was headed toward the door, his duffel in hand.

"Safe journey." Why couldn't she say what she felt?

He turned, as calm and composed as ever. But something about his stance and lack of expression colored her with a wash of fear. His eyes were blank, a hazel void. Oh, please, let him feel something!

"Godspeed." Where was her tongue?

He nodded and turned back toward the door. Why didn't he say something?

"Wait!" She rushed to his side and took his arm. "I'm sorry."

He grunted an unintelligible reply, started to say something else and stopped himself. "So am I."

She dropped his arm. His words were not a mate of her own, a request for forgiveness. They were an admission of defeat. But how could that be? Where was the romantic who had sprinkled her bed with flower petals? Did a romantic ever lose hope? Stunned, she dropped her hand from his arm.

He left without uttering another word.

Confused, she stood in the middle of the kitchen, looking at the floor until she heard the screen door bang shut. She hurried to the window in time to watch him walk down the drive with his shoulders set, back straight.

Fayth's heart beat double time as she sank into a chair by the table. With trembling fingers, she picked a fallen petal from where it rested in the shadow of the vase on the table. Tears filled her eyes. She had lost him. No. She couldn't allow herself to think such a thought. She would not lose him. She sniffed, and brushed a tear from her cheek, letting her thoughts wander. Adversity strengthened her will to succeed. What she must do to keep him ticked through her mind like a finely honed battle strategy.

She had to get their business life in order so they could concentrate on their marriage. She would start by repaying Lou, sewing for her if she had to. She grimaced. There was no other way. She must earn the faith Con had in her. Prove him right—that the loan had done her no damage. Besides, how could they ever overcome the hurt of last night's argument with a source of contention between them? The Captain, however misguided, had meant to help her. She saw the love in the act now as clearly as the rose petals in front of her. Fallen love, fallen hope. She picked another petal up. Tears stood in her eyes as her thoughts continued.

"And I must send Drew away." The room concurred, echoing her words back to her. Braver, more confident, she raised her arm and dropped a petal, watching it flutter as it fell. There was a time to sever with the past. The time for her was now. Drew would never be other than a thorn in her life, always pricking, never blooming.

The petal landed on the table. She smiled softly, tears of hope brimming in her eyes. It was impossible to undo the acts of the past, just like it was impossible to reconstruct a flower using wounded petals. But like the petals on her pillow, maybe it was possible for her to take her hurtful actions of the past, and use them, if only by way of contrast, to build a new future, and prove a mature love.

An overturned picture frame lying face down at the far end of the table caught her attention. She frowned as she slowly reached for it. When she turned it over, Drew's face met hers. The frame trembled in her hand before sliding from her fingers onto the table with a crash.

Her picture of Drew, the one she'd thought she'd lost on Con's ship!

She leaned forward, steadying herself against the table. Con had had it all this time. He knew! He'd known who Drew was all along. That explained his jealousy, but what did he mean now? Was he giving her a choice? Him or Drew?

She should have been despondent, but oddly, a tiny flame of hope flickered inside her. Just last night he had said he loved her. Maybe he still did. She could hope. She would hope. She loved him.

The hall clock struck the half hour. She would start redeeming herself by paying off Lou. A client was meeting Fayth at the shop at nine. But as soon as Fayth could get away, she would be off to call on the madam.

CHAPTER SEVENTEEN

C on caught Lou alone in the dining room just as
she finished her breakfast. He pulled up a chair
beside her and pushed an envelope toward her.
"What's this?"

"Payment in full for my wife's debt to you."

Lou cocked an elegantly sculpted eyebrow.

"It's all there."

"I don't doubt that, but why?"

He laughed, hoping he didn't sound as downcast as
he felt. His life was in shambles. He'd lost Fayth. Because of Drew, the business, or his own dishonesty, he
couldn't say.

Con had spent the evening praying for Fayth's return, futilely waiting for her. He should have gone to
the *Aurnia*, but somehow he'd kept thinking she'd

come back, make up. He wrote her an apology, rear-
ranged the flowers, and in a stupid romantic gesture,
covered her pillow with petals. Still, she didn't come.
Hope turned to a need for normalcy. So he tried mend-
ing his pants, reading the newspaper, common things.
Nothing helped. When strained normalcy turned to
desperation he took the picture of Drew and turned it
over on the table. Childish, he knew, but even this
morning he couldn't force himself to remove it.

Finally, exhausted, Con cuddled with Olive on the
sofa, taking comfort from her unfailing affection, and
mulled over his life. The business was failing. Con
needed cash, more than he'd be able to come up with in
time to save it. He had no choice now but to sell it and
salvage what he could.

Only his honor remained. In that late hour, with Olive purring on his chest, he'd made up his mind to salvage Fayth's business and leave her to her life. If she
wanted, he'd annul the marriage and sail away. Then
he fell asleep, still hoping she'd come to him.

This morning he'd been relieved to see that she had
come home, eventually.

"I'm sorry", she'd said, and stiffly wished him a safe
journey.

Sorry for what, their life together?

This morning, for the first time in Con's life, he
took money for personal use from O'Neill Shipping.
But what did it matter now? He would sell the business,
leave Fayth alone to live her life as she wanted.

"To appease my wife. Fayth found out about the
loan," he said to Lou.

"And she was mad as a hellcat, I don't doubt. You're making amends?"

"Something like that."

"She'll be relieved, I'm sure. She's considered me in the same light as the devil since Coral's come back. Though I had nothing to do with that. If only she knew." Lou swept the envelope up. "She knows she's free of obligation to me?"

"I'll let her know when I get back. For now, it sets my mind at ease. I know I've done the right thing by her. When the time comes it might soften the blow."

"What are you talking about, Con O'Neill? You're not going to take that offer you told me about? You'd be a fool to ignore my advice. And I tell you myself, as someone who has lived both places, Seattle is much the superior city to San Francisco."

He shook his head. "Many would agree with you. But I hear the open waters calling. Been landlocked too long." He stood to leave. "Appreciate it if you would keep what I've told you quiet until everything's official."

Lou smiled graciously. "Con, I am discretion itself. But I do hope you'll reconsider."

Con was gone, but life still went on. Fayth had business with Lou. At the parlor house, Maddie let Fayth in, and showed her to Lou's office. The evening crowd was already filing in.

"Miss Gramm's with the latest professor." Maddie wrinkled her nose. "She's reprimanding him. His skills at the piano aren't up to her standards, and he's been sniffing around a little too close to the ladies. Men!"

"You said it."

Maddie looked momentarily taken aback, but broke into a chuckle ready enough. "Seems we all got our problems with them, one way or another. Miss Gramm will be in as soon as she's finished."

"Thanks, Maddie." Fayth seated herself in the red velvet chair opposite Lou's desk, and settled in to wait. Lou bustled in a scant five minutes later. "Hello, Lou. You've put the latest professor in his place so quickly?"

Lou waved a dismissive hand in front of her. "Maddie talks too much. Unfortunately, I'm stuck with him for another week. The next man on the circuit won't be here until Friday."

"Have you considered hiring one of the women from the Christian Committee? I hear many play nicely."

Lou's throaty laugh filled the room. "What a dry wit you are! Trying to shut me down, Fayth? How very devious. What a picture that would be—pious ladies playing church hymns and preaching about the dire consequences of immorality and lust. Wouldn't that bring in the customers! And my girls—what would I do if they got religion?" Lou's laugh calmed to a chuckle.

"Hire more, I expect."

"You are so very right, but why borrow trouble?" She pointed at Fayth. "You must play?"

"Sorry, never learned. My hands were always busy with needle and thread. Besides, I've been banned from proselytizing, so what would be the point?"

"That's what makes you so very acceptable." Lou settled into her desk chair. "Well, we're both busy. I don't suppose you came to pay a social call, Fayth. What brings you here?"

"I came to make arrangements to repay my loan."

"Oh?"

Fayth could tell that she had caught Lou off guard.

"The Captain told me about it. You don't need to feign ignorance." Fayth straightened her skirt nervously. "Look, Lou, I know that he's been making the payments, but it's not his responsibility. It's time I took care of my own debts. I'm afraid there's only one problem—at the moment my cash flow is tight. I've come to ask for lenient terms. I was hoping that you would let me keep my interest current by allowing me to work off some of the debt."

Lou cocked an eyebrow in an exaggerated expression. "The Captain *is* a liberal man! He's consented to lend you to us?"

Fayth shook her head. She refused to let Lou's sense of humor rile her. "With my sewing skills."

Lou smiled. "You can't pay me back at all."

"What?" A dozen angry thoughts welled up inside Fayth, but she was astute enough to bite them back. "Whatever our personal differences, I never imagined you to be vicious."

Lou held up a hand to silence her. "I'm not being vicious at all, my dear. Con paid off your debt before he sailed."

Fayth had to fight to keep her surprise and fear from showing. Somehow she finished her business with

Lou. Minutes later, Fayth sat in Lou's parlor staring at the promissory note Lou had given her, waiting for Coral. Elizabeth wanted to adopt her baby.

Stunned surprise prevented Fayth from recalling with any accuracy the last minutes of her meeting with the madam. Her thoughts were consumed with Con. How had he managed it? Why? Part of her leaped with hope that he meant the gesture as a way of making amends. Another part feared that he was cutting his losses, and running. Paid in Full was stamped across the document just as if Lou were an institution as legitimate as a bank. Fayth cringed, remembering Lou's familiar use of Con's name, but her worry over it was trivial compared to larger issues.

From the construction bids, Fayth knew the cost of building her second story. Con could not have paid such an amount without robbing a bank, or cleaning his own business out of every dime of operating capital it had. His actions made no sense. Why should he rob his business to keep hers going? Did he have a plan? If he meant to sail out of her life, but had the decency to leave her solvent, had he succeeded? Couldn't her business be seized to pay his debts? Without consulting a lawyer, she couldn't answer the question. Instead, her head kept spinning around the inconsistencies and worries surrounding his actions. Indecision restrained her from action.

Coral walked into the room. Fayth told her about the adoption plans she'd made with her childless cousin Elizabeth, how much Elizabeth and Sterling wanted a child, how Coral would be sent away and her expenses paid for during her pregnancy and for several months after. Coral accepted the offer readily enough. As Fayth prepared to leave, Coral grabbed her harm.

"Your Mr. Tetch has been in here throwing away large sums of money, lately," she said. "Spending time with the most expensive ladies. Bringing them gifts. Buying the best liquor. He's spending as if he owns Con's business rather than works for Con. Watch him, Fayth. Something doesn't feel right about his new habits."

"What are you saying?" Fayth wanted to hear the accusation spoken.

"The Captain can't pay him half what he's spending. Just watch him."

Fayth spent the night on the edge of sleep. Morning came as a welcome relief. Restless thoughts plagued her. What did Con's actions mean? Mr. Tetch had to be embezzling from him. It all added up, but how to catch him? She brewed herself a cup of tea, made from dried mint she'd picked from the garden last summer and hung in the carriage house to dry. A knock on the front door shook her from the baffling puzzle of thoughts.

"Captain Bailey?" Fayth was momentarily taken aback by the presence of Con's friend on her doorstep so early in the morning. Worse still, he appeared worried and nervous, decidedly uncomfortable calling on her. "Won't you come in?" She stepped aside to let him pass. "If you've come to see the Captain, I'm afraid you've missed him. He sailed yesterday."

"Yes, ma'am. I know. Ran into him yesterday out on the water. Had a little race." As he smiled, the crow's feet at the corners of his eyes deepened. He swept off his hat and moved just inside the entry. "I'm sorry to bother you, Mrs. O'Neill, but I've come to see you. I hope I'm not inconveniencing you?"

"Me? No. I was just having a lonely cup of tea. Won't you join me?"

He followed her back to the kitchen, though she meant for him to wait for her in the parlor while she got the tea tray. But as he seemed more relaxed in the casual setting, she motioned him into a chair and set a cup of tea, the sugar bowl, and a spoon in front of him. He set his hat on the chair next to him before scooping two teaspoons of sugar into his tea and stirring vigorously. She wished she had a sweet to serve him, but he didn't seem to mind her lack of hospitality.

"You have my curiosity, Captain Bailey. What brings you out to see me?"

He blew across his cup and took a sip before speaking.

She smiled and matched his sip, liking his easygoing manner.

"I don't know exactly how to begin. I had my thoughts all organized, but now that I'm here...well, I'm a little nervous speaking to a lady. Especially about the matter that brings me."

Oh, heavens, what now? Fayth forced a smile. "Then speak to me as you would the Captain."

"I don't think so, ma'am." The teasing twinkle in his eye quickly disappeared as he continued. "Truth is, I'm worried about Con. I'm worried his business is in trouble."

Although she should have been steeled to such news, although she believed it herself, her stomach tightened. She set her cup on the table. "What makes you think so, Captain?"

"I'm sure you know Con subcontracts his mail runs to me when he can't make them."

She nodded. *Oh, no, here came the demand for payment.*

"When Con got the government contract last summer we entered into a gentleman's agreement, just shook hands. No paperwork, didn't need any. I've known Con since he was fourteen."

She nodded again, unsure where the conversation was leading.

"Are you familiar with the way government contracts work?"

"No, I can't say that I am."

Captain Bailey nodded. "Then I'd better explain. We bid on government mail subsidies. The powers-that-be select a contractor and specify an amount they will pay him to deliver the mail. It's up to the contractor to make sure the mail's delivered. Doesn't matter if he's sick, or his boat breaks down, the mail must be delivered. That's why we all have subcontractors. Men available to make our runs when we can't. Government lets us choose them and set the rates we pay them ourselves. Only stipulation is that subcontractors be certified."

"I see. You're my husband's subcontractor and you shook on the rate he would pay you for each run you make for him. What has aroused your concern?"

"I'm coming to that. Con agreed to pay me almost what the government pays him. It's a generous offer; most contractors keep more profit for themselves. Myself, I think he felt a little guilty for beating me out for the deal." He winked and set his own cup down. "Couldn't have a better friend than Con.

"Well, the point is, Con was as good as his word until yesterday. I went in to get my money from Tetch and he hands me a draft for a considerable amount less than I'm used to. Gives me a story along with it that Con has instructed him to reduce my payments. Business is slow and he's in trouble. Tetch tells me Con knew I'd understand." He paused. "So you can see why I'm concerned."

Fayth had a hard time concentrating on Captain Bailey's explanation. Too many thoughts jumbled and tumbled through her at once. What did Captain Bailey mean to imply?

"I can understand that you're upset about not getting what's owed you. I give you my word that we'll find a way to pay you what's due."

Bailey shook his head. "I don't want the money. You couldn't make me take it. Hell, I'd write the whole amount off for Con's sake. Pardon my language, ma'am." He watched her closely, as if looking for understanding.

When none came, he continued. "You must not realize the character of your husband. Con would never go back on his word. He'd let his whole business go to the devil rather than cheat a friend. His business is in trouble all right. Tetch is boldly skimming from the company coffers. This time at my expense. At who else's, I can't say."

Fayth went nearly lightheaded with excitement. Confirmation of Tetch's embezzling so quickly? But maybe Captain Bailey made a hasty assumption of guilt like Coral had yesterday. "How can you be so sure? Maybe the Captain did tell him—"

"Sorry to interrupt you, ma'am. But in the first place, Con would never back out of a deal. In the second, if he ever were to, he'd talk to me directly. We saw each other out on the water yesterday and he made no mention of it. And it's not like he'd forget it. Con's always been too blasted responsible."

Fayth remembered waking on the *Aurnia* the day after the fire, the *Eliza* snuggled next to it. Remembered the two friends shouting in friendly conversation from deck to deck, uninhibited. She believed Captain Bailey, but she had to pursue the truth.

"Why would Mr. Tetch steal from my husband now? He's employed him for years. I trust his opinion of people enough to believe he would have fired Mr. Tetch long ago if there had been any indication of this in the past." She held back her unfavorable opinion of Mr. Tetch, as well as Con's tolerance of him.

Captain Bailey chuckled and took another sip of tea. "I'm glad you have faith in my friend, but it's clear you don't know the half of the situation. Your trust is misplaced. Tetch has stolen from Con for years, with Con's tacit approval. But it's been petty stuff."

"No, I don't believe you." She stared at him, stunned.

Captain Bailey looked amused as he continued to drink his tea.

Fayth blushed. "I'm sorry. I didn't mean to call you a liar, but I don't understand."

"There's not much to understand. Tetch's father gave Con his start. Since then Con's felt he owed him, so he took Tetch on. Con has always been good-natured and generous. Money never meant much to him. Once he bought the boat, he had all he really wanted. As long as Tetch stayed within reasonable bounds and remained discreet, he let him take it. Saved Con having to give him a raise, so Con joked." Captain Bailey set his cup down.

His tone became serious. "Do you understand my concern now? The minute Con leaves town, Tetch starts his stealing. This time it's not just petty cash we're talking about. And he's stopped any pretense of discretion. In fact, it boils my blood to think of him lying in Con's name."

Captain Bailey flushed with anger. "I don't think Con suspects how greedy Tetch has apparently become." He shook his head in disillusionment. "And I don't think he believes Tetch would embezzle when the business is in such tough shape. Con's been worried about it for some time."

Fayth chewed her lip, trying to concentrate and understand. "What do you think this means?"

"I believe Tetch is planning to abandon the ship before it sinks, so to speak. And take all he can get in the process."

Fayth's mouth went dry, but she was too stunned to reach for her tea. Coral's suspicions, Tetch's behavior, Captain Bailey's evidence—pieced altogether Captain Bailey's theory fit. She had just one small doubt. "Why wait until now to mention this?"

Captain Bailey frowned in confusion. "What do you mean?"

"Surely you remember the nasty note you sent the Captain."

He looked blank. Either he was an excellent actor, or he really didn't recall.

"You know, the one that called him a foul name and asked him to pay up. It was back in January. I told Mr. Tetch to take care of paying the debt. Surely you must have suspected then?"

Bailey broke out laughing. "That explains why Con never placed his bet. Tetch pinched that too." Her confused look prompted him to explain. "I like to race the *Eliza*. She's a fast girl, faster than any other. However, I have to prove that to Captains Riggs, Fulbright, and Scott every year. We hold an annual race, always take bets. Con didn't place his wager this year. Guess with the break-in and all, he forgot. I sent him a friendly reminder is all."

"Oh." She felt foolish.

"What were you thinking? That Con cheated a friend?"

A hot, guilty flush crept over her. She looked at the table, reaching for her cold tea as a cover.

"Mrs. O'Neill, let me tell you something about your husband. He's a true friend, an honest man. In all the time I've known him, he's only done one dishonest thing, and that involved you." A devilish little glint lit his eye. He looked down into his teacup.

Fayth guessed he'd finally come to the second point of his visit.

"I probably shouldn't even mention it," he said.

"Me?" Her heart pounded. Would Captain Bailey confirm her suspicions about Con's connection with Lou? She didn't want to know, but morbid curiosity prompted her. "Captain?"

"You'll have to swear never to tell Con I told you."

Her mouth felt like batting, dry and thick. She forced a weak smile as she tried to lighten the atmosphere. "A lady never swears, but I give you my promise." She watched Captain Bailey, imagining his internal debate as they sat silent.

"Now that I've opened my mouth, I guess I better say, or I'll have you imagining the worst. I can see from your expression you already do."

"I'm that transparent?"

Captain Bailey gave a nervous chuckle. "Yes, ma'am." He took a deep breath, muttered something about Con forgiving him and plunged ahead. "Con has been in love with you for a long time. Long before you proposed to him. Ordered himself about half a dozen shirts he didn't need, just so he could see you."

She smiled, the first genuine one in days. He had? He loved her? What romantic notions he had.

"But Con had this odd plan about how he was going to go about courting you. He was thinking; well, I don't know exactly what he was thinking." Captain Bailey paused.

"That's the dishonesty?" It wasn't dishonesty. It was joy!

His next words stopped her mental dancing mid step.

"No, ma'am. I'm getting to that. He turned down your marriage proposal, felt real bad about it."

A scarlet blush flashed across Fayth. She felt the heat flame all the way down her neck

Captain Bailey was kind enough to look a bit embarrassed himself. "I guess he figured to win you over himself, given enough time. But the fire came and disrupted his plans. After the fire, he was certain you were going to go off and propose to someone else. He knew you wouldn't propose to him again, and he didn't think you'd accept his proposal without some help, so he forced your hand."

Fayth shook her head, uncomprehending. If only she could shake away the mental dust blocking her understanding.

"How could he do that? I accepted of my own will. You make it sound as if he held me hostage." Amusement crept into her voice as she spoke and the humor of Captain Bailey's assertion came to her.

"He did, in a way. He went to Jacob Finn, and made sure he didn't give you a loan. Oh, he wouldn't have

Finn compromise his ethics, just asked him to scrutinize your application carefully. Give a conditional refusal and allow time for Con to make his proposal to
you. I don't know what story Con used to convince you.
But you should know that his deception has eaten away
at Con all this time. And I wouldn't have brought it up
at all, except that—"

He cleared his throat nervously. "From Con's manner, I gathered there were problems between you. It
worries me, thinking of Con with trouble at home, and
trouble with the business." Captain Bailey sat in his
chair looking like he expected a lashing.

Fayth realized she was gaping, snapped her mouth
shut, and thumped back against her chair. Captain Bailey stared uncomfortably into his lap. A mixture of relief and joy filled her. She started to giggle. She tried
to restrain herself, but happiness bubbled to her lips in
laughter. The irony!

"I thought it was Lou Gramm who got to Mr. Finn!"
Her words came out garbled by laughter. Tiny tears
slid down her cheeks. "You mean it was the Captain all
along? I just gave Lou her power over me. No wonder
she was confused!"

Captain Bailey looked at her like a bird, head cocked
sideways, brow furrowed. "Are you all right, Mrs.
O'Neill?"

"I'm hysterical. You couldn't have made me happier!" She wiped her cheeks with the back of her hands,
and took deep breaths, interrupted by insidiously persistent giggles, as she tried to calm down.

Captain Bailey still looked confused, but he smiled now, seemingly pleased with himself.

She picked up her napkin and dabbed at her eyes. "The only thing you could tell me that would add to my elation is that I'm the only woman Con has ever loved. And even to mention it is egotistical of me, and irrelevant, as long as he loves me now."

Captain Bailey smiled ear to ear. "I believe you are the only woman."

"Captain Bailey, bless you and your candor." Her tone sobered. "Speaking of the traitorous Mr. Tetch, what should I do about him? Does Mr. Tetch know the Captain knows that he has been stealing from him?"

"Probably not. The man has a gigantic, arrogant ego. Believes he's brilliant enough to get away with anything. If Con ever confronted him, he would have to stop, or Con would be forced to fire him. Tetch knows of Con's fondness for his late father. Tetch has to feel Con would forgive him almost anything, especially petty thievery, at least once. I'm sure Tetch feels confident Con would give him a second chance. He has before."

"What do you recommend I do, Captain Bailey?"

"Keep an eye on Tetch from a discreet distance. I'll do what I can, but I'm out of town most of the time. I'll ask a few friends to be my eyes while I'm out. Secondly, get the books for the business. Without arousing his suspicion, if possible. We don't want him taking the midnight train out of town before we find out what he's up to.

"If you get the books, I'll have my accountant take a look at them. See if we can find out if Tetch has been taking larger amounts than we suspect."

Fayth nodded. "Thank you."

Captain Bailey rose. "Let me know if he makes any suspicious moves. I'll be in and out. If it looks like Tetch is about to leave town, contact the sheriff."

CHAPTER EIGHTEEN

F ayth's heart danced. Bailey's words washed away doubts that had been months in the making. Doubts that stood between her and the man she loved. She allowed herself the indulgence of dwelling solely on Con for some minutes. She stood in the garden and hugged herself in rapturous delight, sighing like a girl infatuated. Moments later, when she could no longer ward off thoughts of Tetch, she broke into a frown.

Cold, hard fury filled her. What if Mr. Tetch had been pilfering large sums of money all along? Wouldn't that explain why Con's business was in trouble? Further, what if Mr. Tetch had hidden the money somewhere? He certainly couldn't bank it. What if he planned to retrieve it and sneak away soon? Then again, what about all that spending Coral had mentioned? Had Mr. Tetch already blown through it all?

As Fayth wondered about things, she developed a new and startling suspicion of Mr. Tetch. A pattern of behavior became suddenly apparent. Every time Fayth set about righting Con's books, Mr. Tetch planted some new fear in her, or she met some new adversity that diverted her attention away from O'Neill Shipping, almost always while Con was away.

It was Tetch who told her that Con pilfered from the business, and all the while it was him. Had Tetch left Captain Bailey's letter where she'd find it and misconstrue it? In retrospect, Tetch had seemed totally unconcerned about it. Suddenly, though she'd probably never be able to prove it, Fayth felt quite certain that Tetch had been behind the newspaper articles and the threats. Who else had anything to gain by them, or knew so much about her business? Blast him! She wouldn't let Tetch get away.

If Tetch still had the money, Fayth would find it and return it to Con. If Mr. Tetch had taken enough to weaken the business, returning it should provide a large enough cash infusion to make the business solvent again. She would have to find out whether it existed, and if so, where it was. And she would have to do so soon.

A thorough search of the offices after Tetch left for the evening turned up nothing to incriminate him, or point to a hidden stash of cash. Fayth scanned the account ledgers, but they were suddenly fastidiously maintained and legitimate looking. Either Mr. Tetch suddenly had mastered good accounting techniques, or the books had been doctored or replaced since Fayth last had checked them. Several cabinets were locked, but Fayth was pessimistic that they held anything important to her search. Tetch would be most likely to keep anything of importance at his room at the Sealth Men's Hotel. She'd have to search his room, but she needed his keys. She went to see the only person she thought would be of any help—Coral.

As Lou's serious business hours were just beginning, Coral met Fayth on the walk outside the parlor house. She wore a low cut gown with a lacy shawl over it. Coral's actions were jumpy and agitated as Fayth explained her plan.

"In answer to your question, Tetch comes in on Wednesdays, Fridays, and Saturdays, always around seven."

"He'll be in tomorrow then. How long does he usually stay?"

In reply to a cool gust of wind, Coral pulled her shawl closer over her thin shoulders. "He seldom pays for a full night with a girl, but he usually stays for a few drinks after his call. Visits with friends, that sort of thing. If you assumed he'd be out two or three hours, I think you'd be safe."

"You can get his keys?"

"Easily. It'll be just like the days when my old man was alive. I used to pick my old man's pockets for money to feed us all the time." Coral's expression warned Fayth away from any show of sympathy. "I owe you at least this favor before I go. When do you want to do it?"

"Tomorrow evening."

Coral nodded. "Wait for me in front of the shop. I'll bring the keys to you. It would be no good for Tetch or anybody else to see you loitering around the house. I've got to get back now." She left.

When Fayth got home, she found a note from Drew tucked in with her mail. She opened it without enthusiasm, scanning it quickly. He wanted to see her. He begged her to make up her mind quickly. She crumpled the paper up. She'd been so distracted with other matters, she'd forgotten about Drew. Fortunately, he'd had the good sense to stay away from the shop. He probably believed Con was still in town. If he didn't know, she wasn't going to tell him. As soon as she took care of Tetch, she would send Drew away. For now, she couldn't be bothered.

The next evening, Fayth paced in front of the shop for nearly twenty minutes, heart pounding in her ears before Coral showed up with the keys at seven thirty.

"Tetch was late," Coral said between breaths. She looked winded and fragile as she held the keys out to Fayth.

"Thank you," Fayth said. "How long before he misses these?"

Coral frowned. "Not long enough tonight. He seemed agitated and anxious. He didn't bother to wait for his usual girl, just took the first one available." Coral rested her hand on Fayth's arm. "Don't go to the hotel tonight. He mentioned something about having to get home early."

"Blast, I'll have to wait until tomorrow," Fayth said as she looked at Coral. "You don't think he'll suspect you stole these?"

"No. His wallet is still there. Why would someone steal keys and not his wallet? He'll think he misplaced them. I have to get back." Coral slid out the door.

Fayth patted the keys in her pocket and turned from the window, mulling over her next step. She would let Tetch stew over losing his keys for at least one night.

Every morning, especially now with Con gone, Fayth realized how much she missed Coral's company and help. Dressing alone was tedious and time consuming. She never got her waist as small as Coral tugged it down to. It was a barely adequate blessing that she cinched herself tight enough to fit into her dresses at all. Coral was right. She needed a servant. Someday, when the businesses flourished again . . .

Fayth wrapped her corset strings around her waist and tied them in front. She felt nervous, fluttery with excitement over the hope of recovering what Mr. Tetch was supposed to have stolen. Humming one of Con's silly Irish tunes, Fayth pulled her deep mirage blue watered silk gown over her head and began buttoning the bodice. Fayth hummed a little louder, filling in the melody with the few unintelligible words she remembered, dreaming of Con's homecoming and how she planned to make everything up to him. After Captain

Bailey's confession, how could she doubt Con would come home? Please, let him still love her.

She finished dressing, pinned on her hat, and tucked the keys into her dress pocket, intending to spend the day at the offices of O'Neill Shipping, imagining Mr. Tetch's distress at losing his keys. Could she keep a straight face? The moment Mr. Tetch left the office, on even the briefest of tasks, she would search the locked cabinets.

She went to the kitchen. A raucous jay chattered outside the window as she wrapped a cold biscuit in a napkin and grabbed her bag. She opened the window and tossed a biscuit to her noisy blue friend, and heard the crunch of carriage wheels on the drive.

She shut the window and turned in time to see Lou Gramm's unmistakable, gilded carriage rock to a stop. Rusty hopped down, opened the door, and helped Maddie out. Maddie, her gray-laced hair pulled severely into a tight bun, a tiny hat askew on her head, stepped out of the carriage. The sight of the conservatively dressed Maddie always reminded Fayth of a headmistress at some exclusive girl's school. Fayth's heart stopped for a moment as she wondered whether Lou had somehow discovered her theft of Mr. Tetch's keys and had sent Maddie to dish out retribution. Fayth's heart pounded.

She plastered on a smile and opened the door. "Hello, Maddie. What brings you . . . here?" She stammered, confused by Maddie's expressionless face. Her smile felt heavy and awkward, until finally her own mouth fell into a straight line to mimic Maddie's.

"Miss Gramm sent me to fetch you." Her toneless words matched her expression.

Fayth caught a flutter of blue from the corner of her eye. The jay landed on a tree and scolded them happily, his animation at odds with the stillness of their meeting. Anxious, fearful beyond the expectation of a simple reprimand, she forced herself to speak. "Why has Lou sent for me?"

"It's Miss Coral. She's—" Maddie's voice cracked.

Fayth saw for the first time a sparkle of a tear at the corner of her eye and noted the deep circles beneath her eyes that spoke of a sleepless night. Memories of Coral, beaten and bruised, flashed through her mind.

Maddie found her voice and continued. "She's lost the baby. She's dying and she's asking for you." Maddie's shoulders shook with a silent cry.

"No!" Fayth's tone was rebuking. "Why did Lou send you here with such a cruel joke? Coral's fine. I saw her last night, laughing, running." Her heart refused to process what her mind told her to be true.

"Please hurry. She . . . won't last . . . can't hold on much longer." Maddie broke up, her chest heaved with genuine sobs.

Rusty put his arms around her and led her to the carriage. Fayth pulled the door shut and followed them, mute, stunned.

When they were secured in the carriage, bouncing their way over rutted streets to the heart of town, Fayth summoned the courage to face her thoughts and ask a question. "Who beat her up this time?"

Maddie's eyes were large with confusion, like a dazed owl's in sunlight. "No one. Women lose babies for other reasons." She looked into her lap.

Another more ominous possibility came to Fayth. "Who? Who did this?"

"No one. No one. It just came." Maddie sobbed again.

Fayth didn't believe her. Coral was too healthy to lose a baby without help. Had she gone to an abortionist after all?

Dr. Wall met Fayth in the hall outside Coral's room. He addressed her without preface, his face grim. "She's weak, but begging to see you. You may go in." Fayth brushed past him. He grabbed her arm. "Have you seen anyone die before?" His tone was gentle.

"I have."

He nodded, seemingly satisfied that she could handle the situation. "So you know, I gave her something for her pain. She looks drugged up. Call me if—"

She shook off his sympathetic hand before he could say more, not up to hearing more solemn, disparaging words. "Of course." She stepped into Coral's room.

Light filtered through the yellow shade covering the window, casting a pall across Coral's bedroom. Shadows from the barred window striped the wall, giving Fayth the impression of life held prisoner by shadow. Heavy odors of cigar smoke, perfume, and stale perspiration filled the stagnant room, symbols of gaiety and life from the night before counterpointing the solemn mood of impending death.

Lou stood at the end of the bed. She looked up. "Thank goodness you're here. Poor thing, she couldn't rest without speaking to you." Lou sounded like a grieving mother. She wiped away a tear. Fayth was at once aware of how petite Lou actually was. The madam looked somehow smaller, more human in her grief. She moved back from the bed and toward the door, motioning Fayth over. "She wants to see you alone. I'll be right outside."

As Lou gently closed the door, Fayth seated herself in a chair pulled close to Coral's bed. Coral lay on her back, a sheet tucked around her. Her long hair fanned out around her head, almost floating on the pillow. Fayth was oddly disquieted by the lack of evidence of violence, by the calm of the room, the apparent wholeness of Coral's body outlined by the sheet. There seemed to be no reason for tragedy and no one to blame.

With sickening realization, Fayth took in the hollow, pale complexion that had replaced Coral's youthful radiance of the night before. Saw her sunken eyes, the pinched look about her nose. Heard her rattled breathing and recognized the sound of death coming. An image of Father lying in the hospital, broken and bruised filled her. She could no longer deny the truth, but realization made it no easier to face.

Fayth caught the odor of stale, heavy blood and turned to see the bedside table cluttered with blood soaked rags, evidence of the doctor's ministrations and an empty womb. Gently she picked up Coral's cold hand and rested it between her own, trying in vain to warm the life back into her. Coral opened her eyes and focused on her.

"Tell Elizabeth I'm sorry."

"Shh. It's not your fault." Fayth swept the hair back off Coral's damp forehead. "Women lose babies."

"I killed this one." Coral shuddered, and turned her head toward the illuminated window as if trying to draw absolution from its light. "He wanted me to see an abortionist, but I was too afraid. Wanted this baby. Did. Couldn't give it away. Couldn't keep it knowing . . . end up like me."

She took a rattling breath. Her words came individually; each took tremendous effort. "I took an overdose. Thought I would sleep, then fade painlessly away. Didn't know it would be so bloody, hurt so bad.

"My baby! My poor, dead baby. Not possible . . . me to go . . . leave baby behind." Coral choked on a dry sob.

Fayth looked around wildly for a glass of water.

Coral gripped her hand, bringing Fayth's attention back to her face. "Forgive me."

Fayth fought tears. Her voice grew faint, a choked whisper. "For what?"

"It's Drew's baby."

Coral's gentle whisper rocked the room, leaving Fayth suddenly breathless; she struggled not to gasp when it felt as if the air had been kicked from her, tried not to frighten Coral with her shock. The stays of her corset crushed in on her. Her ears rang. She bowed her head in a fight for control.

A faraway voice brought her attention back. "Forgive me."

So plaintive, so desperate. How could she not?

Fayth returned the pressure of Coral's grip and spoke with the grief-stricken voice of a stranger. "I forgive you."

Coral's body gave a giant spasm and jerked the sheet off, exposing a hiked up gown and bare thighs with rags clamped between them. She curled up like a baby, hugging her knees, crying over Drew, whispering his name.

Bastard! The word echoed through Fayth's mind with such screaming, furious force she felt as if someone had shouted it in her ear. She bit her lip, holding her accusations against Drew inside for Coral's sake. She reached to cover Coral again.

Coral pushed her attempts away, but grabbed her face and pulled Fayth close. "Con. Tell him . . ." Her words sounded drowsy, almost relaxed. "He loves you. He told me. He married you because he did. Don't let him go. Promise."

"Promise." Fayth's voice cracked.

Coral closed her eyes and lay flat. Fayth took her hand again, watching her rattling chest labor to breathe. Coral convulsed. A gush of fresh blood spilled from her body, soaking the rags between her legs, staining the sheets, taking with it the remaining faint pink hue from Coral's skin. With the last of Drew's child, life left Coral. Her chest stilled. The room went silent.

Fayth put a hand to her mouth and just sat. Empty. Blank. A person with no emotions attached. When thoughts came, they were clear and condemning, like crisp black words on a page. Guilt overwhelmed her.

She had killed Coral, maybe not as directly as Drew had, but it didn't matter. The result was the same. She had killed Coral by omission, by failing to protect the little girl she failed to see. Somehow, because of Coral's lost physical innocence, Fayth had assumed Coral was impenetrable, savvy, strong. How could someone so worldly be naive? But Coral the romantic had been naive enough to believe a betrayer. To be seduced by charm and good looks. To believe in a dream, a promise, where no possibility of fulfillment existed. Fayth took this child from a world where she knew the rules, and left her unguarded in one more cruel.

She should have thrown Drew out the moment she walked into the parlor and found him there all charm and no substance. She saw that as clearly now as she saw her own weakness. She let one man's actions, one man's character be her definition of human character. For too long she had used a faulty, artificial standard to judge all actions. Why hadn't it made sense before? Each individual must be judged by his or her own actions. Each person given an opportunity to prove him or herself. Her trust and distrust in all the wrong places had cost Coral her life, and quite possibly, Fayth the love of hers.

"I'm sorry, Coral. Forgive me."

The thought of Drew made her livid with rage. He had assured Fayth of his faithfulness, all the while taking advantage of Coral.

The click of the door handle caught her attention. She turned to find a semicircle of Lou's girls surrounding the doorway; Lou anchored like a compass point at their center.

"She's gone."

Tears, wails, sounds of mourning filled the hall as the girls collapsed on Lou. Fayth looked without seeing. Heard Lou's gentle reassurances. Dr. Wall appeared and pushed his way through into the room. A bubbling, turbulent fury welled up in Fayth, pounding in her with the force of a tumbling waterfall. She rose and strode to the door. "The snake who did this to her won't be in town much longer. I promise."

Fayth unlocked the door to the shop. Empty, quiet, impeccably neat, there were signs of Drew everywhere. His thimble on the counter. A receipt done in his hand. A hat perched on the coat rack. She grabbed his hat and slammed the thimble inside before setting it down again, tearing up the receipt and tossing it in the air.

"Fayth? What's going on?"

She hadn't heard Drew enter. She started and turned to face him.

Without thinking, she strode over to him and thrust the hat into his hands. "Congratulations, the second child you fathered just died." She stood inches away from him, her stance mimicking Con's when he took command. "Maybe I should amend that—the second child I know about."

The color vanished from his face as quickly as water through an open drain. He didn't question or defend, just stared, evidently stunned. Epithets whirled through her mind, but died on her lips. He wasn't worthy of lowering herself to their use.

"Aren't you even going to ask how Coral is?"

"Fayth." He reached out for her. She stepped back. "She never meant anything to me. She was just—"

"Convenient," Fayth finished. Fresh fury burned in her. She angrily wiped a tear from her eye, hating him for his disdain of Coral and the sympathetic, apologetic look he gave her. "How could you use her like that? She was so innocent—"

"Innocent? Come, Fayth."

"Yes, in spirit, in maturity. She loved you." Her voice grew softer with recollection. "She died whispering your name."

"Died?" Fear trembled in his voice.

"Just. Hemorrhaging with your child."

His Adam's apple bobbed. They stood inches apart, staring each other down.

He grabbed her arm. "Get your things. It's time we left this city."

She shrugged him off. "You egotistic bastard!" She spat the words at him. He appeared stunned. Fayth couldn't tell if it was caused by the shock of Coral's death, or if he was merely calculating his tactical error. "It's time *you* left the city. My life is here."

"Fayth, I love you. Somehow I keep hurting you, but I don't mean—"

"Spare me your lies and excuses, Drew. Save some small thread of dignity for yourself."

Fayth turned and marched toward the door, holding it open for him. "You've got an hour to get packed. Lou's bouncer Rusty will be meeting you at your room to make sure you catch your train."

"First you'll allow me to take my things from the office?"

She strode back and flung the office door open. "Certainly. Help yourself. But pardon me for leaving. I can't stand being in the same room with you. I'll watch you leave from across the street."

"Fayth—"

"Forget it, Drew. It's over. Don't come back."

CHAPTER NINETEEN

C on sat on an overturned crate in the cargo hold of the *Aurnia. The belly of the whale,* he thought, wondering darkly if things could be worse. He heard the scuffling feet of his crew overhead as they scoured the *Aurnia,* readying her for the sale. Preston pressed him for an answer, and there seemed no advantage in delaying the inevitable. Preston would be out this afternoon to look her over, a formality only. The deal was good as done.

He bent over and rubbed his temple. He ought to thank the Almighty for James Preston and his offer, but . . .

Damn! He didn't want to lose his girls. Not Fayth. Not the *Aurnia.*

When he'd left Seattle he'd thought he could leave Fayth, forget her. But in the days since, he had discovered the impossibility of it. He still meant to do the honorable thing and give her freedom if that's what she wanted. But if there were any way to avoid it, any chance of making her happy . . .

All he needed to stay afloat was one small ebb in his tide of bad fortune. He kicked at the floor, sending a loose metal nut rolling. The sun shining through the open hatch above illuminated it. Con's gaze followed it.

The nut clinked against the side of an overturned metal box wedged against the wall, and bounced back, spinning several seconds before landing at rest. Con sat upright before jumping to his feet. Why hadn't anyone claimed this box? Reported it missing? He'd ordered the crew to empty all cargo, but they had overlooked it, as he almost had. Small, painted the same color as the hold, it was easy to miss. And the way it was situated, it was as if it had fallen from a hiding place.

He picked the box up, turning it over, looking for an ownership tag and finding none. The blasted thing was surprisingly heavy and rattled like it was full of coins— some child's pennies no doubt. He tried jimmying the inexpensive lock. When it wouldn't give, he grabbed a crowbar and wrenched the thing open. The force of the crowbar sent the box toppling as it popped open, spilling gold coins that glinted in the sunlight as they rolled in every direction.

Con stood back, amazed, before reaching for the box. A ledger slid from the strongbox, resting on its

bent pages, cover up. Halfway to reaching for it, he recognized the neatly lettered label. *O'Neill's Shipping.*
How the hell?

A dim memory came. Tetch on the night of the fire. A dolly stacked with boxes, the cash box on top. Tetch awkwardly angling it down the plank to the hold. Later, Tetch's account of its theft.

"Damn him!" Con squatted and picked the ledger up by its spine. A wave of fury directed at Tetch crashed over him. The bastard nearly had cost him the *Aurnia*!

Con stooped to scoop up a fistful of twenty-dollar gold pieces in hands trembling with rage. There was easily several thousand dollars scattered on the floor. A month's receipts and more. Evidence of more than petty pilfering. Tetch must have hidden the box in the rafters, expecting to recover it later. Con smiled grimly, imagining Tetch's consternation when Con had arrived in Seattle, announcing he'd sold the *Aurnia*. What would Tetch do? Hire on with Preston?

A calm amusement settled over Con. Tetch had inadvertently saved O'Neill Shipping. Con stood and scanned the rafters, wondering what had dislodged the box. The corners of his mouth curled up in a full-face smile as a plausible explanation came to him. Bailey and his races! He remembered the lean and yaw of the *Aurnia* when they had raced the *Eliza* as they had left Puget Sound.

A heavy thump near the engine room had aroused Con's concern. He'd backed off the throttle, giving Bailey the race and costing him his wager. The cash box had fallen—he hadn't lost a race, he'd won back his business. Laughter welled up from deep within him, purging him of his anger. The *Aurnia* was no longer for sale. He'd be taking at least one of his girls home. He laughed until his sides hurt and he had to sit on the step. Billy called to him from the hatch.

"Everything all right, sir?"

"Billy! Get down here and help me. We've got a mess to clean up!"

Con wasn't a vindictive man, but during the long hours of the voyage home it gave him great pleasure and amusement imagining Tetch stewing and brooding, scheming a way to get his hoard off the *Aurnia* before Con sold her. Tetch didn't know Con had planned to finalize the sale on this latest trip south. Con had grown wary of Tetch months ago and had since kept him deliberately uninformed. Now, as he sat in his office facing Tetch, he thought he detected Tetch's glance flitting out the window to the *Aurnia* more often than necessary.

"You had a pleasant trip, Con?"

"Yes, I would say so, all told. Amusing and interesting, at least. Very nearly sold the *Aurnia*. Almost had to take the train to Tacoma to get back to settle my business."

Tetch fidgeted in his chair.

"What stopped you?"

Tetch was a cool-headed bastard. Con pulled a gold coin from his pocket and flipped it with his thumb, catching it with open palm as it descended. "Preston extended his offer. The completion of *The Princess* has been delayed." Con thought Tetch relaxed a little.

"When does he expect your final decision?"

Con took his time answering, continuing to flip the coin and catch it. "Recognize this, Tetch?" He held the coin up for a confused Tetch to examine.

"It's a double eagle."

"Very astute. But then, I should wonder if you weren't familiar with this particular issue of coin. I found it stowed aboard the *Aurnia* in a cash box with several hundred others, my ledger piled neatly on top."

Tetch went white. "Listen. Con—"

"You're fired, Tetch."

"Con, I didn't mean to—"

"Spare me excuses. I've known for years you pilfered from the business, but because of your father, I overlooked it. You've moved from petty theft to out and out thievery and nearly bankrupted me. Consider whatever debt I owed your father paid.

"You have five minutes to pack up whatever's yours. Then we're going to your hotel room where I'm going to watch you pack the rest of your miserable possessions and you're going to hand over whatever else is mine." Con smiled at the affront on Tetch's face.

"And while you're at it," Con said. "You're going to tell me how much you shorted my wife from the funds I sent her, and tell me exactly what lies you told her about me."

"Pack?"

"You have two options, Tetch. Stay in Seattle and have me deliver you to the sheriff. Or take the coach out of town. And you'd better get way the hell out. I get word that you're anywhere near me or my concerns and I'll have you shanghaied so far East you'll never be able to dig your way back. Shall we be going?"

Two hours later Lou's maid Maddie, accompanied by Rusty, escorted Con into the parlor. Maddie said that Lou was out. As long as he was here he might as well check up on Coral. "How is Miss Coral doing? Could I speak to her a moment before I leave?"

Maddie paled, and tears welled in her eyes.

"Maddie?"

"I'm sorry, sir. I thought you knew. Miss Coral passed away a week ago." Her last words were barely audible.

"I'm sorry." He spoke automatically, too stunned to think. "H-how?"

"She miscarried and hemorrhaged. There was nothing Dr. Wall could do."

"Man alive!" He raked his fingers through his hair, overcome with sadness and loss. He had to get home. "I *am* sorry." He didn't know what else to say. "How is Mrs. O'Neill taking it?"

Maddie dabbed at her eyes. "She's only been by a couple of times. To sort through Coral's things. And, of course, she was at the funeral. But from what I have seen, I would say she's torn up. Blames herself in some way."

Con frowned. "Why?"

"I can't say. I do know, though I wasn't supposed to, that she and Coral were up to something the night before Coral died. Coral hinted at an adventure. Heard her say something to one of the other girls about getting revenge and recovering money. It didn't make any sense to me, but I didn't pay much attention. Coral was a fanciful, romantic girl."

Maddie's eyes sparkled with fresh tears. "And she hadn't been herself lately." Maddie leaned close to him, her face upturned, as if she was about to part with a secret. She hesitated, then spoke in a soft voice. "I think I can tell you, Captain, because I know you cared for Coral. She was using opium in large doses since she came back. It was affecting her mind."

He rested a hand on her shoulder, feeling great empathy for the grieving Maddie. "Thank you for confiding in me, Maddie. Poor Coral. We'll all miss her."

She nodded.

He dropped his hand. They stood in silence a moment. Uncomfortable in the situation, Con cleared his throat and spoke, "I have to get home now, but it's urgent I leave this for Lou." He pulled an envelope from his pocket.

Maddie sniffed and resumed a professional demeanor. "I'll just let you into Miss Gramm's office, Captain. You can leave it there."

"Ordinarily that'd be just fine, but this is a bank draft for a rather large sum—"

"Oh, well then, we'll just take it to the gentlemen's drinking room and have Joe store it in the till until Miss Gramm gets back."

"Thank you. Would it be possible to leave a note for her in her office?" Con felt more comfortable and less impotent with the conversation turning to business.

"Certainly."

"And if you'd be so kind as to inform her of my visit?"

"Of course. This way, Captain."

Twenty minutes later, Con reined his horse in just short of the driveway to his home. The house looked surprisingly quiet. Where was Fayth? The shop was closed. Out making a delivery? Where was Drew, and why wasn't he running the shop? A cold wave of fear lapped over him—had they run off together?

He tethered the horse and strode nervously up the drive. He let himself in, called for Fayth, and got no response. His heart pounded in his ears like the surf, his worst fears drowning all common sense and rational thought. A quick scan of the entry and parlor revealed everything in its place. The surf in his head crashed louder. Her personal things—that's what she'd take if she left.

He dashed down the hall into her bedroom and threw open the doors to her armoire. A bundle of dried lavender hanging on a nail inside the armoire door thumped against it, dropping flowers onto the floor and filling the silent room with fragrance. Dresses hung neatly on the bar. Clothes were folded and stacked on the shelves. He took a deep breath as his heart beat wildly.

Slowly, he turned to examine the room. Her spyglass rested on the nightstand with her brush and mirror beside it. She hadn't left, and there were no packed suitcases or valises to indicate she intended to. Still, his fear and jealousy didn't subside. His questions remained unanswered. Where was Fayth and with whom? He needed to get back to the *Aurnia* and sort things out, make a plan.

He let himself out of the house and walked back up the drive. He had just mounted his horse and ridden out of sight of the house when he heard a carriage coming down the street from the opposite direction. He paused and turned.

Fayth drove in from the north, turning the carriage into the drive without seeing him. He should have ridden right back and confronted her. Confessed his feelings for her. Apologized for his abrupt departure, explained everything to her. Told her about Tetch. About his loan from Lou. About the money. And hope to hell she'd take him back. But jealousy and fear of rejection stopped him. Instead, he sat, stuck to the saddle like a barnacle, and watched her.

Fayth tore into the house feeling harried and rushed, peeling off her gloves and shedding baubles as she went, leaving them where they fell. Much as she wanted to, she didn't have time to change out of the gown she had worn to call on Elizabeth. She reached to unpin the mourning brooch she wore, pausing to tilt it up and stare at it. She blinked a tear back, her throat closed, and she sniffed. A miniature strawberry blond braid of Coral's hair hung from the jet fixture. Her hand fell back. She left the pin on—she would take this much of Coral with her tonight.

Elizabeth had engaged her longer than she intended. But how could she leave when poor Elizabeth was wrought with such grief? It was almost as if Elizabeth had miscarried herself. Elizabeth had loved Coral, too. Odd that Fayth should be the one to offer her comfort, when Fayth felt so lacking. If not for the thought that Con would be coming back soon, if not for the hope that she could win him back, she would have given up and blown away like empty chaff.

She wished she could confide in Elizabeth about Coral's suicide, but she realized Elizabeth was comforted by the thought that all that had happened was simply a tragic twist of fate. To reveal otherwise would be to lay on Elizabeth a new grief, and tarnish Coral's memory. No, sometimes secrets must be kept for the benefit of others. But the isolation was almost unbearable. She yearned to unburden herself.

Elizabeth was so stunned and beside herself with grief, she barely had seemed to listen when Fayth told her Drew had left. She didn't question, merely murmured something about it being for the best. But she was too distraught to even look relieved.

Fayth pushed her thoughts back to the immediate task as she flew into her bedroom. *Inconspicuous.* She must be as inconspicuous as possible if she hoped to avoid being caught sneaking into Mr. Tetch's room. Why couldn't she be more adept at spying?

The tick of the clock filled the room, hurrying her on. Mr. Tetch would have already left for Lou's house.

It was Wednesday night. A week ago Coral had been her accomplice. She pushed the thought away. She had just two hours to locate the cash Mr. Tetch had to have stolen. Tetch had certainly hidden the real books and receipts somewhere. He was much too organized and arrogant a man to have destroyed them.

She stepped out of her slippers and into her boots, mentally going over the plan again. She knelt down, reached under her mattress, and pulled out Tetch's keys. They rattled in her trembling hand. She'd never make a good spy, but tonight she must try. She grabbed her shawl and headed for the coach house.

Con looked at his watch. Fayth had been in the house less than ten minutes before emerging again, wearing the same dress, but stripped of her accessories. Her actions spoke of hurry. She glanced around as if she suspected someone of following her, or at least taking note of her movements. She dropped something and stooped to retrieve it..

Con's heart pounded wildly, thumping inside his chest like a caged animal. If Fayth didn't look like a woman on a clandestine rendezvous, he didn't know who would. Damn! He mounted his horse and prepared to follow her, half fearful of discovering her destination. What if she met Drew? What did he do then? He wanted to beat that dandy unconscious, take Fayth away. Make her his, physically, intimately.

He frowned, confused by her appearance. Why would a woman going to meet her lover take off her finery?

Fayth untethered their horse and carriage. The wind gave her skirt a flip. She was wearing her work boots, with so fine a dress? It didn't make sense. She climbed into the carriage and pulled out of the drive. Con cooed to his horse and moved out after her.

Fayth left the carriage in a stall at the wharf and walked the three blocks to the Sealth Men's Hotel, pausing to summon her courage before opening the door and plunging into the lobby. She quickly found Tetch's room. Alone in the hall, she rapped confidently on his door.

"Mr. Tetch? Are you at home? It's Mrs. O'Neill."

When no one answered, she tried the door. To her surprise, it swung open. So much for the wasted effort of stealing the hotel key. She slipped cautiously inside, closing it behind her. She leaned against the backside of the door, head back, eyes closed, heart pounding, organizing her thoughts and imagining the task before her. She didn't dare turn on a light, which meant she must work quickly, before the receding light of dusk disappeared completely. First, she must inventory the room to ensure she left it as she found it. She opened her eyes and began. Tetch's bed was neatly made, his nightstand clear.

Her eyes widened as she took in the dresser and the armoire that stood in the corner. Drawers were open, wardrobe doors askew. Goosebumps sprung up on her arms. Her first wild thought was that the room had been ransacked and Mr. Tetch robbed. But when she had forced a calming breath and looked around the room again, a more sickening thought twisted her stomach—Mr. Tetch had fled Seattle.

The drawers were clearly empty and even in the fading light it was obvious there were no personal effects left. No thief would bother stealing clothes and shaving mugs. Tetch had run and most likely taken Con's fortune with him. Impulsively, she turned toward the door, intent on heading to Con's office. Just as suddenly, she stopped.

Surely Tetch was smart enough to clear his things from the office first. Wouldn't his personal effects be the last thing he'd stop for on his way out of town? She walked back to the middle of the room and plunked onto the bed, stunned. She reached her own conclusion— Tetch was guilty. What else explained the circumstances? What or who had tipped him off? She sat for a moment, her mind blank.

When the initial shock wore off and rational thought had returned, she realized there was nothing to do but look for clues as to where he was headed. If she didn't search his room now, she wouldn't get the chance again, certainly not before any clues were erased. She turned on the light. There was no need for secrecy now. Mr. Tetch would not be returning. With wooden steps, she moved to the dresser and began pulling open drawers.

Con took a seat near the window at the tavern across the street from the Sealth Men's Hotel, seating himself where he could watch the hotel door. He'd just give them time to settle in and get cozy. Maybe he should say intimate. His heart raced. His stomach turned at the thought of Drew touching his Fayth. He ordered a beer to calm his nerves. He had to know for certain the nature of their relationship. His tortured thoughts haunted him, and there was only one way to exorcise them—catch Drew and Fayth in the act, or discover Fayth's innocence. Hell, a man had a right to know. If they were guilty, if she preferred Drew, he'd bow out. But not before he beat the shit out of Drew.

He tipped his beer up and swigged it down in a single raise of his elbow, banging the glass on the table when he was finished. Time to find out what was going on. He pushed his chair back and walked across the street to the lobby of the Sealth Men's Hotel.

The lobby was empty, no sign of Fayth. What did he expect? That she and Drew would be having a pleasant conversation in the lobby? The desk clerk looked bored as Con strode over and greeted him with a smile. "Slow night?"

The clerk looked him in the eye. "About normal. Never gets busy this shift. May I help you?"

"Yeah. Friend of mine's staying here. Thought I'd stop by and call on him, but I don't know his room number."

"Name?" The clerk reached for his guest register, ready to search the pages.

"Drew Hanbrough."

"Hanbrough?"

Con nodded. The clerk looked up, setting the register aside. "Sorry, mister, but you missed him. He checked out close to a week ago." The clerk nodded for emphasis, maybe sensing Con's disbelief.

Con frowned, confused. What the hell was going on? What was Fayth doing at the Sealth Men's Hotel?

"Thanks for the help." Con left the hotel and returned to his seat in the bar across the street. There was nothing to do now but wait for Fayth to come out. He'd just settled in and ordered another beer when a light came on in a room in the hotel across the street. Wasn't that Tetch's room? Had they rented it again so soon? A slender figure of a woman was silhouetted against the shade. Fayth?

Frustrated, Fayth plunked onto the bed. Half an hour of searching turned up nothing. Silas Tetch was gone, seemingly without leaving a clue behind as to his destination. Quietly, she left the room and made her way to the lobby. The clerk at the desk had no record of Tetch checking out. Seems he had skipped out on them, too.

Sick at heart, she made her way to the exit. All her dreams of saving Con's business ebbed away like the waning tide. What was she going to do now? How would she explain to Con what had happened? She couldn't let herself picture the look in his eyes when he found out all that had gone on in his absence. Maybe he would forgive her behavior. Maybe sending Drew away would be enough proof of her love. But would Con believe that she meant to send Drew away before she found out what he'd done with Coral? Would he believe that she loved him before that? Would he forgive?

Tomorrow, she would check the coach station and the shipping lines for news of Mr. Tetch, but she wasn't optimistic she'd find anything out. She opened the hotel door and descended the steps, more fearful than she had ever been. Afraid that she was losing the only thing that mattered—Con's love.

Con spotted Fayth as she descended the steps of the Sealth Men's Hotel. After half an hour alone with his thoughts while he nursed a beer, certain things became clear. Coral going back to work at Lou's. The timing of Drew's departure and Coral's death. The girl's obvious admiration of the bastard. Drew had fathered Coral's child and fled town when things went awry. Did Fayth realize what had happened? Did she throw Drew out, or did he leave on his own? Con didn't know, but he hated the man for what he'd done to Coral, and to Fayth.

Damn him! What had this betrayal done to Fayth? Would she return to her distant, removed self? Close Con out again? It was too early for relief. For all Con knew, Fayth might still believe Drew innocent. And even Drew's departure didn't guarantee she'd throw her affections his way. In the meantime, what was she doing in Tetch's room?

Fayth reached the sidewalk. Con threw some coins on the table and prepared to follow her.

It was dark outside when Fayth left the hotel. Familiar goosebumps dotted her arms again. Late spring evenings extended into what could decently be considered night, but daylight still disappeared shortly after nine. Too bad Mr. Tetch hadn't liked to take his pleasures earlier in the evening. She laughed grimly to herself—tonight he hadn't taken them at all. She started toward the wharf. Outside in the dark unaccompanied, the walk to the wharf suddenly seemed daunting and fraught with danger. She straightened her spine and tried to walk bravely down the sidewalk. It wouldn't do to look like a victim.

Abruptly, she lost her nerve and did an about-face. The shop was less than a block away. She would spend the night there rather than risk the walk to the wharf, and pick up the carriage in the safety of morning light. The horses were boarded safely enough for the night.

Con walked nearly half a block behind her on the opposite side of the street. She turned around suddenly, catching him off guard. He had to duck into a doorway to avoid being seen. What the—?

It took him a minute to realize that she was heading for the shop.

Fayth inhaled deeply as the shop came into sight down the block, picking up her pace in anticipation of safety. Intent on not spending one additional minute on the street, she reached into her pocket for her own set of keys. Bawdy music spilled into the street from the many taverns along the row. She was crossing back in front of the Sealth Men's Hotel when two rowdy young men emerged through the door into the street in front of her. She took a step back, waiting for them to clear the sidewalk. One of them caught sight of her immediately. His face beamed in apparent recognition.

"Joe!" he said to his companion. "Look what we got—one of Lou's girls walking the street."

It took Fayth a minute to realize they were talking about her. She laced her keys through her fist in anticipation of trouble. The two men came toward her.

"You boys are mistaken. I'm not one of Miss Gramm's girls."

"Sure, that's what they all say to men they don't consider gentlemen, isn't that right buddy?"

"It is. The willing arms of Lou's boarders aren't so open to those of us without means, but it doesn't mean we don't dream about them just the same."

Fayth stood her ground boldly. "I am not a prostitute."

"Lou's bouncer ain't never let us past the front door, but I've always had a hankering for one of her refined ladies."

"I'm not one of them. Now, step aside so that I may pass or I will have to yell for an officer."

"The lady does protest, but she wears one of them fancy dresses that Lou's girls wear out on their Saturday carriage rides." He had a drunken gleam in his eyes. He took a step toward her. "You see, little lady, we may not be able to touch, but we always look."

"Looks like tonight we're gonna do better."

The man lunged for her. Fayth screamed and stabbed at him with her keys. Her attacker wasn't expecting her to defend herself and fell back surprised. Fayth saw her opportunity and took off running past them before they could react. She heard them cursing behind her and then footsteps pounded after her. From their tenor she knew they were some distance behind her. The entrance to the underground lay just ahead. If she could make it down, she could lose them long enough to get into the basement entrance of the store. She had the advantage of knowing her way, even in the darkness.

She swung into the stairwell, her feet pounding down the steps. She wished for the quiet whisper of her slippers. Her boots clattered noisily. She tripped on her skirts several times before reaching the bottom of the stairs. Footsteps rang out behind her. She picked up her skirts and started running. Laced much too tight for running, she panted and gasped for breath. Despite her trouble drawing a breath, she hiked her skirts up and lengthened her gait. Her basement door was no more than fifty feet away. The footsteps gained on her. Her pulse raced in her ears. She couldn't get a breath, her corset confined her. She felt ill. Intent on reaching the door, she didn't bother to watch her feet. She stumbled in a hole in the uneven walk and went tumbling, screaming as she fell. She hit the ground with enough force to knock the remaining wind out of her. Her ears rang and her eyes filled with static as she slumped into a faint.

CHAPTER TWENTY

"Fayth! Fayth!" Con's voice called her name through the fog that enveloped her senses, but how could that be? He was at sea. She forced her eyes open. His concerned face hovered over her, clearly defined amid the blur of her vision.

"Captain? The men!" Her voice pitched higher.

"It's all right, darling. They're gone."

Her head rested on his arm. Despite her confusion, she felt safe with him and happy for his return. Oh, Con. She sat dizzily and tried to push up to stand. "How did you get here?"

"I came back early. Take it slowly." He helped her to her feet and folded her into his arms. "There. How do you feel?"

She leaned into his chest, resting her head against it. "The men will come back. They were chasing me. They think I'm one of Lou's girls."

"They won't be back. I scared them off."

She shook her groggy head, still confused—how did he get here? How did he know where she was? How long had she been out? "They were chasing me—"

"I was chasing you, Fayth. Didn't you hear me call?"

She closed her eyes and shivered. A cool draft blew across her back. Her breath came too easily. She reached for the back of her dress.

Con looked sheepish. Holding her steady with one arm at a time, he shrugged out of his jacket. "I had to cut your stay laces."

He averted his eyes as she pulled his jacket on and gathered it up against her chin as a child does a security blanket.

"Let's get out of the underground." He scooped her up into his arms. They were at the shop's basement door before she protested. "No! I want to go home, please!"

"We'll just stay long enough to let you recover your equilibrium." He started to set her down so he could unlock the door.

"No, please, I want to go home—now. The carriage is in the stall at the wharf."

He carried her to the wharf and into the carriage, and from the carriage into the house where he settled her, still dressed, into bed. Her nerves were still jangled, but the cool night air cleared the static away from her mind. Con left the room, returning a minute later with a glass of water. She raised it shakily to her lips while Con sat on the edge of the bed, watching her with an intent, burning expression. She couldn't tell if it was anger or jealousy she saw. One thought sprung to mind—she had to tell him about Mr. Tetch and her theory that he had stolen large sums of money from Con. Maybe Con would be able to find him.

"Mr. Tetch has been stealing from you." She clutched at Con's sleeve. "I believe he's embezzled a large sum of money from you. Tonight, I went to his room at the hotel to try and find it. The room was empty. He's left town."

Con's expression was blank.

She tightened her grip on his arm. "You have to find him. Get the money back."

"You went to Tetch's room tonight?"

"Yes, at the Sealth Men's Hotel. I knew he'd be out. He always is on Wednesdays."

"Yes, he's out," Con muttered, seemingly lost in thought.

She grabbed his arms, tried to pull him to her. "You have to fire him. You must make him tell you where the money is. I'm sure he's spent some of it, but he couldn't have spent all of it, not here. It would have aroused too much suspicion. It can't all be gone." She started to cry.

He wrapped her in his arms, warm, strong, secure arms. For the first time in weeks she felt safe. But it might all be an illusion. If he knew all that she'd done, all that had come to pass. She had to tell him. Her tears fell freely. She clutched at his shirt.

"Fayth, please don't cry. It's all right. I've taken care of things."

She shook her head, bunching and wrinkling wads of his shirt in tightfisted hands, afraid to let go. Afraid he would leave as her. "No," she said between sobs. "Nothing's all right. If only you knew—everything's wrong. And it's my fault."

His arms tightened around her, his chin rested reassuringly on her head. Neither spoke while she sobbed outright. She must tell him everything. When she composed herself enough to speak, her voice was a bare, hoarse whisper punctuated with sniffs and hiccups. "Coral's dead." She let the words hang in the air.

He said nothing. When she chanced a fleeting glimpse into his eyes he looked solemn and sad, but not surprised. She laughed, a pathetic, ironic snort.

"You knew." She bobbed her head and bit her lip. "I don't know how you do it, but you're somehow omniscient."

"Just observant."

He handed her a hankie.

She dabbed it at her eyes. "I sent Drew away a week ago. Coral died . . . Coral died miscarrying his baby."

It took every effort of will she possessed to continue. She stole another glance at Con. He looked strong and composed, and his eyes reflected sympathy. She could tell him. He wouldn't judge Coral. "It wasn't . . . an accident, or even simply nature. She killed herself, Con. Killed herself. Over *him*."

There was no recrimination in his eyes.

"We're the only two who know. Not even Lou . . . don't tell." She fought back tears again. "My fault. I didn't see it." She stopped and took another breath. "I only found out just before she died." Her voice cracked. "Elizabeth's heartbroken. She was going to adopt the baby. Everything is a mess."

His silence was somehow reassuring. The last things she wanted to hear were platitudes and false promises, glib hopeful commentary that most of her women friends were likely to give. He was the man he'd always been—the man who understood. She looked into his eyes through her own, bleared with tears.

"Oh, Con! You'll never believe me now, but I only hired Drew because the business was such a mess. I was going to send him away before, before I found out about Coral's baby, when I realized how much his presence upset you." She lowered her voice. "I didn't know you knew who he was." She wiped at her eyes. "Forgive my deception. I didn't think you would understand. I thought you would never know."

Con spoke softly. "It seems we've both suffered our share of dishonesty."

Fayth nodded and continued. "Drew's a snake. Tempting, ruining lives. So many lives." Tears rolled down her cheeks. She let them fall; she watched him swallow, watched his Adam's apple bob, but he didn't speak. She didn't understand; he seemed almost to smile. "After we fought I went to see Drew."

Con's arms tensed around her.

"He wanted me to go away with him." Sobs broke into her speech. "I didn't want to go with him, but I did want to escape. I was afraid. I came home and saw the flowers, saw you sleeping—I couldn't do it. Couldn't leave. I was going to send him away, but everything happened so fast. Then Coral died."

She dropped her gaze and let go of his shirt, falling into him, circling him with her arms, resting her head in the hollow of his neck. She pressed her cheek against his chest and pleaded into his shirt. "Forgive me. Please, forgive me."

"Fayth."

Soft kisses caressed the top of her head. Strong, callused fingers brushed the tears from her exposed cheek. She pulled back and looked up into eyes that glowed almost brown. With lips trembling, she lifted her face to his and gently found his mouth. His lips came down over hers and she was swept away. Away from crisis, away from pain, consumed by her love for this man.

She leaned into his kiss, opened her mouth to his. A complex stirring of love, lust, intimacy, and raw passion overcame her. She waited for the shame, for the pain, but none came. His kiss was like heady wine spreading its pleasant warmth out to her body. Without taking his mouth from her, he pulled his jacket off her shoulders and over her arms.

"Fayth." Her name on his lips sounded like a sonnet. She pulled the torn bodice off, one shoulder at a time. Her corset, its laces cut, fell away on its own. She dropped it over the side of the bed, feeling suddenly light and free and unashamed.

He smiled. His gaze dropped to her transparent cotton camisole, to the tightly pointed nipples she felt poking through. He pulled her close, bent to kiss the hollow of her neck. No questions. No hesitation. No doubts. This time he asked no permission.

His face, with its lightly bearded shadow, scrubbed against her skin. She leaned her head back, thrusting her chest toward him, urging his kiss lower as she squirmed to pull the camisole loose. He clasped his hand over hers; together they freed the garment. She pulled her arms out of the straps, his hand assisting, and then arched away from him to pull it over her head and drop it off the side of the bed. She sat topless before him and smiled, not only invitation, but pleasure.

"Beautiful," he said.

"Wondrous," she answered, standing, dropping her skirt and undergarments away until they sat empty on the floor, testaments to a former inhibition. She watched his breathing quicken.

"Wonderful."

She climbed into his lap, wrapped her legs on either side of him, straddling him. There was a reverent moment when they just stared, neither one moving. His eyes reflected her, and in them, she saw herself engulfed in hazel brown, flushed and beautiful. He told no lies—the way his soul saw her, there was no guilt, only promise. The distrust and fear that held her emotional flywheel immobile fell away. She dug bare heels into the fluffy pouf of her goose down featherbed behind him and pumped. Pumped like she worked the treadle

on a dozen sleepless nights eons ago when she tried not
to love him.

The buttons on his shirt came undone, one by one,
until his shirt fell open and away. Still, she pumped. He
stood, holding her like a bobbin around a spindle and
she pumped. She rocked until his boots, and his pants,
and his undergarments disappeared.

"Fayth."

She pumped and rubbed, and thrust her tongue into
his ear.

"Fayth." His voice went deep.

She sucked his neck, traced his shoulder with her
mouth, and pumped, encircling him with her legs,
holding him too tight for him to ever slide away.

"Man alive!" He spun them both around, like thread
twirling a bobbin, until he faced the bed. Then, they
fell into it and she became the cloth. One with the soft
cotton linens beneath her. Surrounded, encased by it,
and Con braced on his elbows over her, as he began to
pump.

"Fayth," he spoke her name with each rocking,
pumping movement, long, hard, and warm against her
stomach until her name became no more than an urgent grunt. The headboard thumped against the wall
imitating a pounding treadle. She loosed her leg grip,
allowed him to pull back, position himself. And then he
became the needle, and she, the virgin cloth. She
gasped. A piercing pain. In. Out again. Wild pumping—their bodies, her heart, her pulse, the bed, her
soul. Pleasure. He pumped, weaving into her intricate
interlocking sensations and emotions—pain of the first

time, overwhelming pleasure, joy and love, all sewn together as they coupled and bonded. Her own breath came in gasps. He collapsed closer to her, his breath hot against her neck.

Pumping, pumping. Faster, faster. He rocked her. In. Out again. The needle, the cloth. Two becoming one. Forgiveness asked and given. Pleasure needing relief. Her feet moving to the rhythm, her body tensed. She laced her fingers through his thick, wavy hair.

He gave a single staccato grunt.

Release. "Con!" His name filled the room. "Con." She uttered a gentle whisper, spent.

He lay on top of her, sparkling with perspiration, muscled chest firm, until his breathing slowed. Then he rolled from her onto his back, pulled her into the crook of his arm, and rested his chin on her head as she gently traced his chest with her fingertips. His eyes closed. She became incredibly drowsy, content.

"At last," he said. "An honest seamstress." With eyes closed, he hummed, soft and deep. "I love you, Fayth." It was the last thing she remembered before drifting off to sleep.

She sits in a small sailboat, surrounded by sparkling water. A breeze stirs the sails overhead. Con smiles as he navigates and steers. The boat heels, thrusting her toward the water until her back is only inches above it. He sits on the high side. She laughs, dips her fingers into the cool water. He pulls on the rudder and brings the boat about.

Thump.

The anchor—why is Con dropping the anchor?

Thump. Thump.

Knocking? Who could be at the door at this hour? Fayth smiled. Let Con get it. "Darling, get the door." She rolled over to cuddle against him, and found only Olive curled in his spot. He was up already? She sat up straighter. His pillow was still hollowed where his head had rested. His clothes were no longer piled on the floor where he'd tossed them the night before. Where had he gone?

"Con?" The only answer was an insistent knocking at the door.

"Just a minute!" She slid out of bed and put on her robe, sweeping the hair out of her face with a quick movement. "I'm coming!" She opened the door a bare crack, not wanting anyone to see her in her night-clothes, hoping it was only a delivery boy she could quickly dispatch.

"Fayth." Lou Gramm greeted her from the other side of the door. As always, her expression was one of perverse amusement. "I see that I have disturbed your sleep. I do apologize, but I was under the impression that you were an early riser. Is the Captain at home?"

Fayth opened the door, not caring how she appeared to the madam. She was more concerned over how Lou knew so quickly that Con was in town. "I'm afraid he's out."

Lou swept past her into the entry. "Ah, so it is the Captain who's the early riser, my mistake. I'm sorry to find him out. I was hoping to catch him before he left for his offices. I can hardly meet him down there;

though, I think that people would be more likely to understand my making a visit to a shipping office than a seamstress's shop. Silly, isn't it? As if I have no need for clothing! Still, I would not have gossip started."

"What business do you have with him?"

Lou smiled in her affected way. "I came at his request, making as much haste as possible. I only got to his note late yesterday. Unfortunately, I was out when he stopped by."

"What are you talking about?"

Lou held an envelope out to her. "Fayth, do calm down. I came in person, out of respect for the Captain. He has been an interesting and most amusing business venture. By far the most honest of any man I've dealt with."

Lou rattled the envelope. "I've brought Con his promissory note stamped paid in full, as requested. As I said, I was out when he stopped by with his final payment yesterday."

Fayth took the envelope slowly as understanding dawned. "You mean his loan was with you, too?" Fayth suddenly remembered Con's words—we're both in debt to Lou. He'd told Fayth himself. She just hadn't been paying attention.

"Yes, darling. Jacob Finn sent him to me."

"But why?"

"Because after Finn lent you the money for your rebuilding, he was not at liberty to loan Con the sum that he required, while I. . ." Lou smiled lightly. "I've made plenty of good investments in my time. I always seem to

have a little extra cash on hand to lend to those worthy."

Con had never married her as a business arrangement. She knew that now, had recognized the fullness
of it last night, but still such proof, and on the lips of a
madam, was overwhelming. Their marrying cost him,
sent him to Lou. According to Captain Bailey, caused
him to lie. How she loved that man! But what a terrible
influence she had been. No more! She meant to rectify
that, at least. But Lou's deception still angered her.

"That's why he visited the parlor house? To make
payments? Not that it matters now, but why didn't you
set me straight before?"

Lou smiled, unperturbed by the accusation. "Because, Fayth, a man's business should be his own. Con
made me promise not to, and I always keep my promises." She handed the note to Fayth. "I only confess now
because of my regard for you on Coral's behalf. She
was particularly fond of you and you treated her well,
right up to the end. That you didn't reproach her. . ."

Fayth watched Lou swallow a lump, and her anger
vanished. If she could forgive Coral, she could forgive
Lou.

"Well, I must get back to the girls. Wish Con well in
his new venture."

Fayth froze, her mouth went suddenly dry. "What
new venture?"

Lou looked surprised.

"Lou?"

Lou stared at her a minute as if weighing her
thoughts. "I thought you knew. He's selling the *Aurnia*

and his interest in the wharf. He's been losing too much money to salvage it. I assumed that's why he paid me off, so he could sell free and clear, though frankly, I was surprised that he came up with the money."

Fayth felt the color drain away from her face. "What?"

"Fayth, you really have no clue, do you?" Lou looked surprised. "Con told me awhile back that the owner of a large line offered him the position of captain on a long voyage, international vessel based out of San Francisco. I can only assume that he has a wish to return to the sea."

"He's leaving?"

Lou smiled tiredly, almost sympathetically. "You think you can stop him with a single tumble around the sheets?"

Fayth gasped.

Lou laughed. "Fayth! Don't deny it, I know my business well enough to recognize afterglow. You haven't wanted him around, not since your old beau came back. Con has enough pride not to want to stick around and watch his wife make a fool of him. He's giving you a respectable out, not that you particularly deserve it. You're throwing out a good man."

Fayth's mind clicked away too quickly to be slowed by Lou's insults and insinuations. "Did he say when he has to respond to the offer?"

Lou must have noticed Fayth's genuine expression of concern. Her expression was momentarily sympathetic. "I assumed as soon as possible. I guessed that's why Con was in such a hurry to get this note. The same

line that wishes to hire him has made him an offer on
the *Aurnia*. It's all part of the package."

"No!" Fayth made no attempt to stifle her cry or
hide her agony. "That must be where he's gone—to the
telegraph office." She looked down at her nightclothes.
"I have to get dressed. I've got to stop him."

She knew he loved her. Even Lou could not dispel
the confirmation of last night. But with Tetch running
off with the money, and the business floundering, what
choice did he have but to sell? She wouldn't let him do
it. She'd sell the shop, go to work for someone else,
whatever it took to make sure he hung onto something
so important to him. She ran to the bedroom to change,
leaving Lou standing in the doorway.

"Good-bye, Fayth," she heard Lou call, followed by
the closing of the door.

Fayth hurried around her room, throwing on
clothes. As usual, haste made her clumsy. Little things
went wrong. She couldn't find her boots, tossed who
knows where in the passion of the night before. She
tossed shoes out from the closet searching. She could-
n't be hampered with dainty slippers or heels, she
needed boots for running if she was to have a chance of
catching him.

Her furious mind worked over the details. How long
had he been gone? She simply had no idea. She dug her
way to a pair of boots at the back of the closet and
slipped them on. Minutes later she was out the door
and riding off toward town in the carriage.

Fayth parked the carriage at the wharf, checked for
Con in his office and, not finding him, headed immedi-

ately for the telegraph offices. She ran down the street, oblivious to the stares of pedestrians she passed. Fortunately, she'd dressed in too much haste to lace her corset tightly, leaving her with enough breath to run. Her dress gapped in the back, but was covered by the small waist length, matching jacket. She ran uphill into the city, panting, her skirts held above her ankles, ruing that the wharf should be downhill from everything. She ran up the sidewalk, veering into the street only to avoid those traveling too slowly for her immediate haste. Up ahead she spotted the back of an auburn head and square shoulders. "Con!"

He didn't hear her. She ran faster, debating whether she'd gain any time by heading into the underground. Con went into the entrance. She had another half block to go before she could duck in to follow him. She shot little arrow prayers heavenward, praying that God would slow Con's progress, that she wouldn't lose him.

She ran over the sidewalk skylights, peering through them as she ran, hoping for a glimpse of him below. Fayth was halfway across the second one when she spotted Con beneath her. She stopped and backed off the skylight, screaming his name into the glass. He didn't look up. She walked onto the skylight and stomped with all her might. She couldn't see past her skirts to tell whether he looked up. If he did, he'd recognize her.

Seconds later Con emerged from the staircase to the underground. He came at her in a full run, sweeping her off onto solid sidewalk before releasing her.

"Fayth! What in heaven's name are you doing?"

"Walking across skylights for you."

"Advertising for me on the bottom of your shoe?" His eyes danced, his voice teased.

"You alone. God bless Coral." Tears welled in her eyes. It seemed like yesterday, and eons ago, that Coral had inscribed those boots. If not for them, Con surely would have continued on with his errand, wondering about the boldness of whores these days.

"You missed me so quickly?"

"Yes." She let her love for him shine in her eyes.

"I can remedy that. Let's go home."

She grabbed his arm, wondering at his glib tone. "Con, you left without a word, I was afraid."

"I'm not leaving you, darling."

"Con, listen to me, you can't sell her. I'd rather we sold the shop. We'll make it work somehow."

He frowned. "What are you talking about, Fayth?"

"I'm trying to tell you that I love you, Con O'Neill. I don't want you to go. I can't imagine life without you. And I won't, under any circumstance, allow you to sell the wharf and the *Aurnia*."

The nearest she could describe the look that came over him was an idiot grin, much like the one he wore on their wedding day, only finer. "You mean that, Fayth O'Neill?"

"Tell me I'm not too late."

"Tell me you love me again."

"I love you, Con."

He swept her into his arms. "You could never be too late, Mrs. O'Neill. I love you." His lips came down on hers.

EPILOGUE

Fayth sat on the grass of the hillside with her skirts tucked beneath her, a spyglass held to her eye as she scanned the sparkling waters of Puget Sound. Below, in the near distance, the city was emerald again. Strong spring rains following a mild winter had worked together to create lush foliage and a brilliant early summer flowering. Seattle was once again a colorful phoenix. On the far horizon the Olympic Mountains, still white-capped, reflected the sun with radiant white. She caught a glimpse of a small vessel on the waters. She leaned forward for some minutes until it was near enough to spot its flag. She broke into a smile and lowered the spyglass.

"Look, baby." She held the glass to the eye of the auburn-haired toddler who played beside her. "See Papa's ship coming? Your father is a very fine captain. Look at the way he guides her in."

The toddler pulled the glass down and mouthed it.

Fayth laughed and pulled it away. "We'll make a sailor of you yet." She stood and scooped the child up. "If we hurry we can make it to the dock before Papa does."

What would Con be without his ship and what would she be without him? The child cuddled against her neck and wound a stray lock of her hair around his chubby finger as he sucked his thumb. She paused at the road to catch her breath. In that moment she turned back around for a final glimpse of the water.

"Yes, if we hurry, we'll just make it."

Gina Robinson lives in the Pacific Northwest with her husband and children. She loves humor, romance, suspense, and spies. Not necessarily in that order. She writes contemporary romance, humorous thrillers, historical romance and women's fiction.

Most days she writes while wearing slippers, flip-flops, or tennis shoes, depending on the season. But she loves a great, sexy heel and has a closet full for special occasions.

She belongs to Romance Writers of America and International Thriller Writers. To find out more about Gina, visit her website at www.ginarobinson.com

www.ingramcontent.com/pod-product-compliance
Lightning Source LLC
Chambersburg PA
CBHW071218250626
47163CB00001B/36

* 9 7 8 0 6 1 5 8 2 3 5 3 9 *